HA
DREAMS

THREE-IN-ONE COLLECTION

CAROLE GIFT PAGE

ISBN 978-1-60260-331-8

Scripture quotations are taken from the King James Version of the Bible.

This book is a work of fiction. Names, characters, places, and incidents are either products of the author's imagination or used fictitiously. Any similarity to actual people, organizations, and/or events is purely coincidental.

Cover design: Kirk DouPonce, DogEared Design

Published by Barbour Publishing, Inc., P.O. Box 719, Uhrichsville, Ohio 44683, www.barbourbooks.com

Our mission is to publish and distribute inspirational products offering exceptional value and biblical encouragement to the masses.

Printed in the United States of America.

Dear Readers,

I have always been intrigued by Hawaii—its beauty, its history, its culture. As a young girl I enjoyed reading James Michener's massive novel, *Hawaii*. Over the years my husband, Bill, and I have taken several cruises to Hawaii and toured the various islands. But Hawaii didn't become personal to me until my daughter Heather moved to the Big Island to work at the mission-oriented University of the Nations in Kona. There she met her future husband, Adam, and there they made their home for over two years. She became my favorite reference source for these novels. She knew the people and the places of Hawaii with a familiarity I couldn't have achieved on my own. And the more we explored the many facets of Hawaii together, the deeper my love for that exotic state became. Of the 48 books I've written over thirty-plus years, Hawaii has been my favorite place to write about.

My prayer is that God would speak to you through the lives of the women in these stories. Like you and me, they struggle to find the path God has for them. But even when they stumble, God proves Himself faithful.

In *By the Beckoning Sea*, Ashley must look beyond the many distractions in her life—including two ardent suitors—to see that "every day is a new chance to show Jesus how much we love Him."

In *To Love a Gentle Stranger*, Marnie faces overwhelming trials, even losing her own identity. But she discovers that God never forgets who we are.

In *Sweet Joy of My Life*, Kayli must face her deepest fears. Only then does she realize that faith isn't a onetime thing; it's a full-time thing, and only in God's presence comes fullness of joy.

Thank you for reading *Hawaiian Dreams*. I hope you enjoy these stories as much as I enjoyed writing them. I'd love to hear from you. Please write me c/o Barbour Publishing. If you would like a personal reply, please include your e-mail address.

Celebrating His love,
Carole Gift Page

BY THE BECKONING SEA

Dedication

To my beautiful daughter, Heather Gift Lillengreen, who as a newlywed living in Hawaii shared with me her knowledge and love of the Big Island. And thanks to Heather and Adam for giving her dad and me the "grand tour" of that tropical paradise.

Prologue

Mr. & Mrs. Alexander Bancroft
cordially invite you to share their joy
at the marriage of their daughter
Miss Ashley Bancroft
to Mr. Bennett Radison
at 5:00 p.m.
on the third Saturday of June
at the Hilton Hawaiian Village on Waikiki Beach
Honolulu, Hawaii
Beach reception and luau following ceremony

Chapter 1

Ashley Bancroft would remember her wedding day for the rest of her life—the cluster of family and friends gathered on the white sandy beach near the jutting lava rock wall; the panoramic view of the deep blue Pacific Ocean at dusk; and the distant, majestic Diamond Head volcano framed by Hawaii's lush green, palm-fringed coastline.

The fragrance of blooming bougainvillea and plumeria trees mingled in the evening breeze with the pungent scents of orchids and lilies in Ashley's bridal bouquet. She could hear the ukulele player strumming the "Hawaiian Wedding Song." She could smell the smoked kalua pig and sweet potatoes roasting in the luau pit nearby.

And she could see her beloved Ben facing her in his black cutaway tuxedo with the customary green leafy lei draped around his neck. Those moments were like a dream now, full of possibility and romance—she in her strapless satin A-line gown with its beaded embroidery and lace, her hair wreathed in hibiscus, her rhinestone sandals sinking into the soft white sand as Pastor Kealoha led them in their vows. The images were etched indelibly on her mind's eye—vivid, surreal, and now utterly painful.

Diamond Head was the only thing that didn't erupt the day that her cherished dreams shattered into a nightmare.

And yet it had all started out so beautifully.

She could still hear Pastor Kealoha's voice rising and falling with a predictable, lyrical drone. He obviously loved weddings, for he was waxing eloquent, as if performing for some unseen theater critic. She could imagine some reality show judge pronouncing him a natural thespian, or an impossible ham, or just plain boring.

For some reason she couldn't focus on his words, couldn't make sense of them, although she knew they were important, something about God's plan and purpose for the home. She needed to comprehend their meaning—this was crucial—make the words her own, make them real to her, but they seemed just beyond her grasp.

It was all she could do to keep her ankles from wobbling, to keep her sandaled feet from sinking into the shifting sand. *Relax*, she told herself. *This is the best day of your life. Enjoy it.*

She wanted to enjoy it but felt too light-headed, her stomach unsettled. At dusk, the tropical air was heavy and warm, stealing her breath. She couldn't see her family and friends now—they were behind her—but she could feel their presence, sense them surrounding her, pressing in on her with all their hopes and expectations. Or maybe the problem was her lace bodice; the gown was cinched too tightly at the waist. Was it possible she had gained weight since her fitting?

She wondered, *What if I faint dead away at Ben's feet?* She had seen television videos of wedding disasters—grooms fainting, brides falling into their wedding cakes.

She stole a glance at Ben. He looked as discomfited as she. He was a lean, graceful man with short-cropped, straw-blond hair, a ruddy complexion, and a ready smile. Wire-rimmed spectacles framed merry, half-moon hazel eyes. But now perspiration beaded his high forehead and upper lip. His jaw was set, jutting forward, as if he were grinding his teeth.

It's not supposed to be this way. Everything should be perfect.

She closed her eyes. Her moist palms tightened around her bridal bouquet. *Lord, this is what You want for me, isn't it?*

Pastor Kealoha's voice caught her off guard. He was instructing the happy couple to face each other and recite their vows. She handed her bouquet to her maid of honor, her best friend, Dixie Salinger, then turned and faced Ben as he took her hands in his. With only a slight tremor in her voice, she repeated the words she had carefully written and memorized.

"Ben, when I first moved to New York City three years ago and started working for Haricott Publishing, I was just a timid, small-town girl striking out on her own. I never imagined I'd meet the man of my dreams. When you hired me as your editorial assistant, I was thrilled to be working for such a distinguished and renowned editor. Bennett Radison, the talk of the literary world. Every woman in the office was jealous of me working so closely with you. At first, I was in awe of you, afraid of doing something to displease you. But then, as we became friends, I realized what a remarkable man you are—considerate, creative, strong, stubborn, smart."

She drew in a quick breath, her heart pounding so hard she could hardly hear her own voice. "We—we have so much in common, Ben. We both love good literature. We love taking a walk in the park after a long day's work and splitting a mushroom pizza while we watch the late show. I don't even mind when you critique my feeble attempts at writing the Great American Novel. You are the man I want to be my husband and the father of my children someday—a loyal, loving, godly man who will be by my side for the rest of my life."

Her words hung in the air for a long minute. It was Ben's turn now. Pastor Kealoha nodded. The silence lengthened, becoming uncomfortable. Ben tightened his grip on her hands as her eyes searched his. There was something in his eyes she couldn't read, a dark intensity, as if he were struggling with something deep in his soul.

"Ben," she whispered, "if you've forgotten your vows, just say what's on your heart."

He nodded and cleared his throat, then spoke over rising emotion. "Ash—my beautiful Ashley. I love so much about you—your kindness, your wit, your passion for life, your devotion to your work, your deep faith, your generous spirit. I love the way the sun turns your hair golden and the moon puts little blue stars in your eyes.

"I remember the first time I saw you, I couldn't take my eyes off you. You weren't like other women in the office in their drab business suits and no-nonsense hairdos. You looked like a free spirit in your bright, trendy clothes and long, crimped curls. I pictured you running through a meadow with the wind in your hair. As if you weren't quite real. As if I'd imagined you—an illusion, a fantasy. I thought you were a lightweight. I didn't expect you to last long. But you blew me away with your first editing assignment. You were good. Amazing. You still are. I can always count on you to do your best, to be true to yourself, true to God, and true to everyone around you.

"I can't tell you how happy I've been to have you in my life. You've changed me, made me a better man. You've made me realize things about myself I never knew. You've taught me the importance of utter, absolute honesty, even when it hurts. That's why. . ."

He stopped, his expression darkening. His eyes broke away from hers. But not before she glimpsed something in them that knotted her stomach and sent her heart racing with panic and dread. She felt her smile freeze on her lips. Everything was slipping away, her future collapsing around her, the whole world suddenly off-kilter. Nothing had happened; yet everything was different. She knew it was over before Ben even said the words.

"I'm sorry. I can't do this, Ash."

"Don't," she implored.

"I love you. I'll always love you. But I'm not the man for you." He circled her waist with his arm and turned her toward their wedding guests, as if this were a natural part of the ceremony. She could hardly make out the sea of faces through her tears.

"It's my fault," Ben told everyone in his most sonorous voice. "I'm sorry. There won't be a wedding today. But please stay for the luau. The tables are brimming with island delicacies—lobster and mahimahi, pineapples, poi, seviche. Enjoy the food and fellowship." Had he actually said *fellowship*? That was her word, not his. He gazed down, his eyes entreating her. "Please don't hate me."

Before she could find her voice, he began walking her down the flower-strewn pathway just the way they were supposed to do, except without music, without a marriage, with only the stunned silence of their family and friends heavy in the air.

The rest of the evening was a blur—a cacophony of sounds, a crazy quilt of colors, a kaleidoscope of motion as the wedding guests milled around on the beach, sampled the sweet guava juice and virgin mai tais, then gathered around the roasting pit for the luau.

But Ashley wanted no part of the festivities.

"Let me go back to the hotel," she begged Ben.

"Not until we've talked. Let's take a walk down the beach. Somewhere private."

She removed her sandals and tossed them aside, then gathered her satin gown up around her knees. He pulled off his shoes and socks, rolled up his pant legs, then took her arm firmly in his. Surely they made a peculiar sight as they strolled barefoot along the water's edge. When they found an isolated cove, they sat down on a smooth outcropping of rock, where the waves washed in over their feet. She thought fleetingly of protecting her wedding dress, then dismissed the idea. It wasn't as if she needed it anymore. They sat side by side, close enough that their arms touched, yet worlds apart. The muggy night air was electric with unspoken words, unshed tears.

Minutes ago they were ready to pledge their undying love. Now they were like colliding strangers trying to extricate themselves from one another.

She forced out the words, "You don't want to marry me. What else is there to say?"

"Plenty."

She didn't want to hear it. For the first time she wished Ben was like other men who grunted single-syllable replies. But not her Ben. He loved words. He analyzed everything to death. Even their marriage. Or *near* marriage.

"We've had a good thing going, Ash." He massaged his knuckles, weighing his words. "I loved the idea that you were a pure Christian girl with high standards and values. From the beginning I've tried to measure up to what you expected of me."

"And you have, Ben. You've always been a perfect gentleman. We share the same values, the same faith. That's what I love about you."

"That's just it, Ash." He reached over and squeezed her hand hard. The sky was darkening, with strokes of violet and crimson slashing the horizon. Ben's voice broke, husky, uneven. "I've tried to be the person you wanted. I did the whole church bit. I thought I could make it work. But it's not me. I'm not into this whole Jesus thing like you are. The truth is, I don't get it. And today when I stood at the altar looking at you, I knew I couldn't sentence you to a life with a man pretending to be something he wasn't. You deserve the truth. You deserve a man who lives his faith the way you do. But I'm not that man."

Whatever else Ben said fell on deaf ears. Ashley wasn't there, was no longer conscious of her surroundings, or of Ben's presence, or of the sounds and voices drifting from the luau. She could think only that she was the victim of a terrible joke. Surely everyone was laughing, and nothing in her life would ever be right again.

Chapter 2

Bennett Radison flew home to New York early the next morning. Ashley spent her so-called wedding night alone in the bridal suite of her beach-front hotel. Not alone actually. Her parents stayed with her, alternately offering comfort and warm milk—her mother's solution to every distress—and decrying Bennett Radison for his cruelty and callousness. "You're better off without that heel," her mother said over and over as she fluffed Ashley's pillow or stroked her forehead.

Ashley didn't want to hear it. She wanted sleep—a deep, soothing slumber that would erase all the pain and memories of the past few hours. But sleep eluded her, taunted her with brief moments of dreamy repose—only to startle her awake with shards of bitter reality. *Ben doesn't want me. He's forsaken me. How could God let this happen?*

Her mother didn't help matters, the way she hovered over Ashley like an anxious nursemaid, reassuring her, "God will bring a wonderful man into your life, sweetheart. Just you wait and see."

Pulling the pillow over her head to block out her mother's voice, Ashley shrilled, "I don't want another man! I want Ben!"

But Ben was gone.

The next day Ashley convinced her parents to go home without her. "Don't worry, I won't be alone. Dixie promised to stay in Hawaii with me for a few days. We'll do some sightseeing and catch up on old times," she said with more bravado than she felt.

"Well, if anyone can cheer you up, it's Dixie. She's such a funny, eccentric girl. But after that, what will you do, honey?" Her mother's face looked pinched with worry and lined with wrinkles Ashley hadn't noticed before.

"I don't know, Mom. I can't go back to New York yet. How can I face people? I don't have a husband. I won't even have a job."

"Of course you have a job. Everyone at Haricott Publishing loves you."

"Not Ben. There's no way I'm going back to work as Ben's editorial assistant. I'll have to find another job."

Ashley told her friend Dixie the same thing that afternoon as the two sat in lounge chairs on the hotel lanai, sipping sodas and gazing out at the vast, cerulean-blue ocean. "I'm not going back to New York, Dix. I'm moving somewhere else."

"Where?" Dixie's dark brown eyes flashed with astonishment. "You love

New York. Your whole life is there."

"Not anymore. Ben was my world. Without him, everything else is meaningless."

Frown lines furrowed Dixie's pixie face. She set down her glass, her apple-red lips pursing in an exaggerated pout. "That's not my best bud talking. Who are you? What did you do with Ashley Bancroft, the gal who faces every trial with such amazing faith?"

Ashley flattened her straw between her teeth. She wasn't sure she could cope with Dixie today—bouncy, bubbly, exhausting Dixie. As much as Ashley adored her ditzy, freewheeling, heart-of-gold pal, sometimes Dixie was a downright pain. "You're questioning my faith just because I don't want to go back and work for the man who rejected me in front of the whole world?"

"Not quite the whole world, Ash. Just family and friends and a few hotel employees."

"You know what I mean."

"Oh, and Pastor Kealoha, of course, but he's cool. He wouldn't—"

"Stop it, Dix. I've made up my mind. I'm going somewhere where no one looks at me with pity."

Dixie reached over and squeezed Ashley's hand. "Just one request, girlfriend. Don't make any permanent decisions for a few months. Give yourself time to heal."

"You make it sound like I've got a disease."

"The scourge of the broken heart. But they say it's not fatal."

"Says who?"

"Wiser folks than me. Doesn't the Bible say something about God healing the brokenhearted?"

"I know all the verses. Jesus bore our sorrows. He loves me and will never leave me." Tears gathered behind Ashley's eyes, pressing so hard her head ached. She spoke over a rising sob. "Then why does it hurt so much, Dixie? Why do I feel so abandoned?"

"I don't know. But I'm not going anywhere, Ash. Just tell me how I can help."

Ashley pulled a tissue from the pocket of her terry-cloth robe. The robe was provided by the hotel, so at least she didn't have to wear her satin honeymoon lingerie. She blew her nose and swiped at her tears. "When I was a kid in Sunday school, it was so easy to sing all the songs. 'Jesus is all I need.' 'I surrender all.' 'You can have the whole world, but give me Jesus.' But how do I live those words, Dixie? The truth is, I don't know how to give up everything for Jesus. I don't even know how to give up Ben!"

"We'll start by doing stuff to take your mind off that big lug."

"What stuff?"

Dixie shrugged. "We're here in Hawaii. We'll go sightseeing. How long can you keep this hotel room?"

"Two weeks. It's already paid for. Ben told me to stay and enjoy it—as if I could."

"Why not? We could have a lot of fun in two weeks."

Ashley sighed. "And then there's the cruise."

"Cruise?"

"Ben signed us up for a ten-day cruise around the islands. It's not for two weeks yet, so we were going to do the tourist bit first, then take the cruise."

"I'm surprised your workaholic Ben was willing to take that much time away from the office."

"He had his bases covered with the rest of the staff. Besides, he had ulterior motives. Anthony Adler, one of Haricott's bestselling authors, is doing a lecture series on the ship. Ben figured we could combine business and pleasure. Go on our honeymoon and talk with Adler about his upcoming book."

"Anthony Adler? I've heard of him."

"He's been on the *New York Times* bestseller list. I love his novels, especially the ones set in Hawaii. He tells such a great story. So full of action and emotion. And they're never smutty. He manages to make 'wholesome' exciting."

"Hey, you're really impressed with this guy."

"I did some line editing on his latest books, and I've talked with him on the phone a few times. He's quite an extraordinary man."

"Come to think of it, I've seen his picture on his books. He's not bad on the eyes."

"He has a beautiful soul. When you read him, you feel like he really understands a woman's heart." Ashley gazed off into the distance, her voice softening. "I was really looking forward to meeting him and getting a few pointers about my own writing. Ben's helped me with my novel, of course, but I'd love a seasoned author's opinion. Now that'll never happen."

"Why not?"

"Because I'll have to cancel the cruise."

"No, you don't."

"Yes, I do. I can't go without Ben."

"Didn't he tell you to enjoy your honeymoon because everything's already paid for?"

"Yes, but. . ."

"Then let's go."

"Who? The two of us?"

"Sure. I've got the time. That's one advantage of having my own cosmetics business. I can ask myself, 'Dixie Salinger, may I take off work to go on a cruise?' And my alter ego replies, 'Absolutely, Dixie Salinger. Go and have a wonderful time.' "

Ashley shook her head. "It's a crazy idea. Totally insane."

"You want to meet Anthony Adler, don't you?"

"Yes." She felt herself weakening. Why did she always give in to Dixie's screwball schemes?

"Then call the cruise line and change one ticket from Ben's name to mine."

A sprig of hope blossomed in Ashley's heart. "We *could* do it, couldn't we?"

"We *will* do it! Or my name's not Dixie Salinger."

Ashley laughed, surprising herself. "There must be a fate worse than taking your honeymoon cruise with your best friend instead of the man of your dreams, but I don't know what it is!"

And that's how Ashley Bancroft found herself at the Honolulu harbor two weeks later, boarding the magnificent *Sea Queen*, with fun-loving, free-spirited Dixie Salinger. They stifled chuckles of amazement as the attendant showed them to their luxurious suite with its king-size beds, sprawling balcony, and panoramic windows.

If Ashley had qualms about taking the cruise with Dixie, her anxieties dissipated as the excitement and welcoming ambience of the ship enveloped them. They followed the crowd to the pool deck and had a delicious buffet lunch at the Oceanview Café, then went back to their stateroom and unpacked. When the alarm sounded just before sailing, they pulled on their bulky life jackets and joined the other passengers for the emergency lifeboat drill. They sipped frosty tropical fruit drinks at the sail-away party, then quickly changed for dinner and headed for the formal dining room.

"I'm still full from lunch," Ashley confided as they sat down at the posh, linen-draped table bedecked with gleaming silver, crystal, and china.

"They must think I'm going to eat a horse," said Dixie, sitting down. "They've given me enough silverware for three people."

Ashley scanned the menu and smiled. "Don't worry, horse isn't even on the menu."

Dixie opened her menu. "Wow! Seven courses. Looks like we won't go hungry."

"Everything sounds wonderful. Shrimp cocktail, lobster, filet mignon, baked Alaska."

"Whoa! I'm definitely avoiding the caviar and snails."

After a sumptuous meal, they went to the theater for the Welcome Aboard show, featuring a juggler, a comedienne, and an Irish tenor singing show tunes. Afterward, they walked around the ship, visiting the gift shops, photo gallery, library, cinema, and spa.

"I love this spa." Dixie's gaze swept over a sculpted King Neptune surrounded by colorfully painted porpoises and graceful sea creatures. "I'm coming back here for a sauna, a lomilomi massage, and one of those Japanese silk facials."

"You mean where they put mud all over your face and cucumbers on your eyes?"

"Why not? I'll start a whole new fashion trend."

Ashley laughed. "Count me out. You go do your extreme makeover and I'll curl up with a good book in the library."

But there was hardly time to pick up a book, let alone read it. The weekend flew by—a steady stream of shipboard activities—shuffleboard, table tennis, golf lessons—and shore excursions to the Haleakala Crater and Eden Botanical Garden, with lunch at a Maui tropical plantation and snorkeling off a sixty-five-foot catamaran.

Ashley tried not to think about Ben. But she couldn't help herself. *It should be Ben and me standing here gazing at the sea at sunset. It should be Ben and me eating dinner over candlelight or strolling the deck at midnight.* No matter how much she threw herself into cruise activities, the ache in her heart never went away. At night, after Dixie fell asleep, Ashley slipped out onto her balcony and wept and prayed, prayed and wept, but she found little solace. Had God forgotten her? She had always felt His comfort before. Why not now?

On Monday morning Anthony Adler's lecture series began. There was a full-page write-up about him in the ship's daily newspaper.

Dixie scanned the article. "It says, 'Come hear world-renowned, bestselling author Anthony Adler talk about Hawaii's history and read from his novels on Hawaii.' We'd better get there early, Ash. The place may be packed."

"I'm coming." Ashley knew she was spending too much time applying her makeup and styling her long, honey-blond hair. Why did she care how she looked or what this man thought of her? As she slipped into her white capri pants and a stylish sea green blouse, she vowed not to worry about any man's opinion ever again.

"You look great. You're sure to impress Mr. Adler," Dixie told her as they walked to the conference room.

"I'm not trying to impress anyone," she countered, a bit too defensively.

The room was indeed packed. As they found seats in the next-to-last row, Ashley kicked herself for not coming early. What was wrong with her? She was dying to meet this man, and yet scared to death.

Anthony Adler was right on time. You couldn't miss him—a tanned, ruggedly handsome man with broad shoulders and curly black hair. He strode to the podium with the self-assured stride of a man who knew how to captivate a crowd. He was taller and more imposing than Ashley expected, with a brooding, roguish mystique she couldn't quite define. Perhaps it was the way his unruly locks tumbled over his high forehead or the way his heavy brows crouched over piercing, ice-blue eyes. He shuffled his papers, then smiled out at the crowd with a wry, controlled half smile.

"It's good to have you all here today," he said in a husky baritone. "You could have been onshore seeing Hawaii for yourself, but instead you chose to be here listening to me talk about Hawaii. I'm both flattered and humbled." He cleared his throat and looked down at his notes. "Hawaii became our fiftieth state in August 1959. The Aloha State, as it's called, lies 2,400 miles from the US mainland—the most isolated group of islands in the world and yet everyone's idea of paradise on earth."

Ashley's heart sank. *Don't tell me this is going to be a history or geography lesson. The man is obviously a better writer than speaker.*

Adler talked on about the Polynesian immigrants who settled in Hawaii over a thousand years ago, about Captain James Cook arriving in 1778, and about King Kamehameha uniting the islands in 1796.

I'm sorry, Mr. Adler, I've already studied Hawaii's history, she protested silently. *I know native Hawaiians are descendants of the Polynesians and represent one-eighth of the population. I know sugarcane and pineapples are Hawaii's most important crops and the tourist industry the most significant source of imported income. I don't want to hear facts and figures.* She had come to hear Mr. Adler read from his marvelous books and talk about how he had been inspired to write them. She sensed the crowd felt the same as she did. There was an undercurrent of whispers and shuffling feet, which ceased the moment Adler reached for one of his novels and began to read.

"At last!" Ashley sighed under her breath.

For the next hour the crowd was mesmerized as Adler talked about his books and his life, about how he had moved to Hawaii from the mainland when a Hollywood movie studio had filmed one of his novels in the lush, tropical beauty of Kauai's Waimea Canyon, the "Grand Canyon of the Pacific."

As Adler shared several personal anecdotes, Ashley found herself drawn to the man and unnerved by him all at once. Adler had put aside his notes now and loosened his tie. "My first editor told me to quit writing and paint fences or sell encyclopedias," he said with a hint of amusement. "He said I'd never be published. I took his words as a challenge. I vowed I would not give up until I had sold something to that man. It took me three years. He bought my first book, which was later made into that movie on Kauai."

The audience broke into spontaneous applause.

"The point is, don't give up your dreams," he concluded with a lilt in his voice and a twinkle in his eyes. "My advice to writers, to anyone, in fact, is live a passionate life. An inspired life. Have a passion for your work, whatever it is. Have a passion for people and a passion for God. Don't let a day go by without doing something that challenges you and stirs your passions. Life is too short. Time is a gift. And I thank you for giving me the gift of your time and attention today. I hope to see you all again tomorrow."

More applause. A standing ovation from some, including Ashley. As the audience filed out, she made her way to the podium. Adler was already autographing copies of his books for eager fans. She picked up a copy of his latest novel, even though she'd already read it, and handed it to him to sign.

"To whom?" he said without looking up.

"Ashley."

He scribbled something on the title page, then handed her the book.

He was already looking at the next person in line when she said abruptly, "Excuse me, Mr. Adler."

He looked at her for the first time. "Yes, miss?"

Her voice came out breathy and uneven. "I'm Ashley Bancroft, Ben's editorial assistant at Haricott."

Adler's brows shot up. "Oh, you're *that* Ashley!"

She nodded, taken aback. What did he mean by *that Ashley*?

"We've corresponded quite often over the past few years, haven't we? Even talked on the phone now and then. You've sent me my galleys and lots of corrections from Ben."

"I suppose I have."

"Wait a minute." He leaned forward, his vivid blue eyes locked on hers. "You and Ben were getting married and coming on this very cruise. He invited me to the wedding, but I was lecturing on a cruise ship in the Mediterranean at the time. Then I heard the wedding was canceled. And yet here you are. Does that mean you are Mrs. Bennett Radison after all?"

"No, I'm not. I'm still Ashley Bancroft." She felt the impatient stares of those waiting for their autographs. "I came on my honeymoon—I mean, it's not my honeymoon. It's just a cruise. I came on the cruise with my friend Dixie." She looked around, growing more flustered, only to spot Dixie standing off to one side, taking everything in. She gave Dixie an entreating glance: *Come get me out of this!*

Dixie sashayed right over and clasped Ashley's elbow. "We'd better hurry if we want to keep that appointment with the, uh, captain."

"The captain, eh?" said Adler, bemused. "You have an appointment with the captain?"

"N–not exactly," said Ashley. Why had she thought Dixie could bail her out? She was only making this moment more embarrassing.

Adler extended his hand. "Before you go, Miss Bancroft, would you like to have lunch sometime? Chat a little? You can catch me up on what's happening at Haricott Publishing."

"I'd love to," she blurted, then turned on her heel and rushed off with Dixie before Anthony Adler could say another word.

Chapter 3

There was a phone message waiting for Ashley when she returned to her stateroom. It was Adler. "If you're still available for lunch, meet me at the Oceanview Café at noon. If you don't get this in time, perhaps we can talk tomorrow after my lecture. I trust you will be there."

"Well?" said Dixie. "You are going to meet him, aren't you?"

Ashley walked over to the sliding glass door, opened it, and stepped out onto the balcony.

Dixie followed her. "Did you hear me, girlfriend? This is your chance to get acquainted with the legendary Anthony Adler. Why would you even hesitate?"

"I'm not hesitating. I'm just feeling a little overwhelmed. He's so—so intimidating. And I feel so embarrassed about—you know—Ben leaving me at the altar. Mr. Adler must surely think I'm a loser with Ben walking out on me that way."

"Sure, and that's why he wants to have lunch with you."

"Don't make more of it than there is, Dixie. He just wants to find out what's happening at the publishing house."

"Whatever." They stood at the rail gazing out at the ocean—a sheer, sparkling span of cerulean blue. "Are you going to take your manuscript?"

"To lunch? Of course not."

"But you brought your novel all the way from New York because you wanted Adler's opinion of it."

"I do, but that would be rude of me to sit down and thrust my manuscript at him like a starry-eyed, unpublished novice."

"But isn't that what you are?"

"Yes, but I have my pride."

"Oh, well, that'll get you published for sure."

Ashley drummed her fingers on the polished cedar rail. "I already feel humiliated facing him, Dixie. I'm not going to dig myself in deeper."

"What's a little more humiliation if you get some expert help with your book? Imagine getting some direction from an author of his stature. That's to die for."

"I may do just that if he tells me I have no talent."

"Better to hear it from the best."

"Thanks. I thought you believed in me."

"I do, Ash. You're a terrific writer. But what do I know? I sell lipsticks and lotions. You need to hear it from someone who can encourage you and point you in the right direction."

"Well, Ben always said I have talent, but I was afraid he was prejudiced. I never had the courage to test the waters."

"We're sitting right here in the ocean. What better time to test the waters?"

By lunchtime, Dixie had convinced Ashley to take her manuscript with her to the Oceanview Café. She went with fear and trembling, her palms so moist, the thick manila envelope was damp. She held it behind her when she spotted Anthony Adler waiting by the café entrance. He strode over and greeted her with a beaming smile.

"I'm glad you could make it, Miss Bancroft. Or may I call you Ashley?"

"Please do, Mr. Adler." He looked as if he intended to shake her hand, but her hands were behind her, clutching her work.

"You may call me Tonio. All my friends do."

"Tonio?"

"It's a nickname that has stuck with me since childhood. My Italian grandmother called me Tonio."

"But Adler isn't Italian, is it?"

"No, I changed my name to Adler years ago. My birth name would be too long for most book covers. And no one could spell or remember it."

They made their way through the buffet line, then he carried both trays outside to a table near the pool. "Is this all right?"

"Perfect. The breeze feels great and the view is amazing." She set her manuscript at her feet. She shouldn't have brought it. No doubt Mr. Adler had noticed her balancing her tray on it in line.

He touched her hand. "May I ask a little blessing on the food?"

Surprise brightened her voice. "I'd love that."

He prayed a simple prayer, but it was enough to set her at ease and give her hope that Mr. Adler was a kind, approachable man after all. Perhaps he even shared her faith. "How are you enjoying the cruise?" she asked as they ate.

"Very nice. I've done several of these lecture cruises. The Mediterranean two weeks ago, as I mentioned. And Hawaii, naturally. Of course, I already live in Hawaii, but this gives me a chance to visit the other islands. I especially like the green, jagged mountains and soft white sand beaches in Oahu. You'll have to see—"

"Mr. Adler! Mr. Adler!"

A stout, middle-aged woman in shorts and a halter top bustled over to the table with one of Adler's novels clutched to her chest. "Excuse me, Mr. Adler. It really is you, isn't it? I was just lying there on the lounge chair reading your book." She paused to catch her breath, her gaze taking in Ashley. "I'm sorry, I don't mean to interrupt, but I just love your work. I'm your greatest fan. Would you mind signing my book—*your* book—oh, you know what I mean. Make it out to Greta. Greta Morrissey, m-o-r-r-i-s-s-e-y."

Adler autographed the book and handed it back with a patient smile. Ashley watched as the woman returned to a cluster of people beside the pool, waving her prize.

"You must get that a lot—people chasing you down, wanting your autograph."

He sipped his iced tea. "It comes with the territory. People love having the chance to meet their favorite author. I figure they're my bread and butter. If I can make their day, why not?"

"That's a very generous attitude."

"What I don't like," he said in a confidential tone, "are those people who tell me a story and are convinced I'll want to write it. Of course, they're willing to share the millions we'll make when their story becomes a bestseller and is made into a movie."

Ashley laughed in spite of herself. "I suppose everyone has a story."

"Yes. Everyone does. What's yours, Ashley?"

She gazed down at her plate. "Nothing special. I grew up in a little town in downstate New York and started working for Haricott right out of college three years ago."

"You enjoy editing?"

"Yes. But I prefer writing."

"Good for you. So do I. Writing is so much more fun than editing." His clear blue eyes crinkled with amusement. "That reminds me of another of my vexations—people who ask me to read their manuscripts and tell them whether they can write or not."

Ashley choked on her lemonade.

"Are you okay?"

"Yes, fine." She dabbed at her mouth with her napkin. "Does that happen often?"

"What?"

"People asking you to read their manuscripts."

"Oh, yes, all the time. Everywhere I go. They just assume I have all the time in the world. I'm afraid most of their so-called masterpieces belong in the recycle bin."

Ashley kicked her manuscript farther under her chair. "I can't imagine people being so brazen as to intrude on you that way."

"Nor can I. But it happens. Now, you're in the publishing business, so you know how exhausting editing can be. I would never presume to ask my dentist to stop by after work and clean my teeth, or ask my barber for a free shave."

"Of course not!"

Adler shrugged. "But people expect writers to always be on call. For example, if I were having lunch with some pleasant young lady I had just met—not you, of course—but some other attractive woman like yourself, I would hardly be finished with dessert before she would pull a sheaf of papers from her purse and ask me to have a look."

"You must be kidding."

"Not at all. Why, if I didn't know better, I would suppose that fat envelope you've been kicking around under the table was a novel or collection of stories you were hoping to show me."

Ashley's face flamed. "Oh, Tonio—Mr. Adler—I wouldn't!"

"Of course you would. I don't mind. You're not some rank amateur. You're in the business. Let me take a look." He reached down and grasped the envelope. "What is it—a novel?"

"Yes. Romantic suspense. It's only a first draft. Something I just threw together. Not very good, I'm afraid." She drew in a sharp breath and met his penetrating gaze. "Actually, it's my sixteenth draft." *And I poured my heart and soul into it. And if you say it's no good, I'll simply shrivel up and blow away!*

He pushed aside his tray, removed the hefty stack of bond paper, and began reading. Ashley shifted in her chair, crossed her legs and uncrossed them, sipped her lemonade, and stole a glance at Adler. His expression was inscrutable. She looked around at the sunbathers, the tanned bodies frolicking in the pool, the glittering, sun-washed ocean—her gaze roaming everywhere, except in Adler's direction. Her heart was pounding so loudly, surely he could hear the terrified thumping. How could she have put herself in such an appalling situation—allowing the great Anthony Adler to read and criticize her work? It was her precious baby, after all, the fragile child of her soul. How could it survive his critical, merciless scrutiny? How could *she*?

He read for nearly ten minutes without saying a word. His expression remained cryptic. Was he bored? Amused? Intrigued? The waiting was excruciating. Ashley inhaled sharply, desperate for more air. She couldn't decide where to rest her eyes. If she kept them focused on Adler, he might assume she was growing impatient. If she pretended to busy herself with her napkin or lemonade or a chipped fingernail, he might think she wasn't interested in his opinion. He had no idea that the world hinged this moment on the slightest arch of his brow or the curl of his lips.

After what seemed an eternity, he looked up at her. "May I take this back to my stateroom and finish reading it?"

"Of course." Her pride kept her from asking what he thought of it.

Surely he wouldn't make her coax him for a response.

He returned the pages to their envelope and stood up. "May I see you again, Ashley? Other than at my lectures?"

She stood up and gripped the table, her ankles weak. "Yes, I'd like that."

He tucked her manuscript under his arm. "Until tomorrow then."

She nodded, her mouth too dry to speak. As she watched him walk away, her spirits nosedived. *What did you think of my novel, Mr. Anthony Adler? Did you love it? Hate it? How could you be so cruel as to leave me hanging this way?*

Chapter 4

"Tell me everything." Dixie was beside herself with questions when Ashley returned to their stateroom. "Is he as wonderful as he seems? Did he read your novel? Does he love it?"

"He didn't say."

"But you showed it to him?"

"Yes. He took it back to his room."

"That's a good thing, right?"

"I don't know if it's good or bad. He sat there reading my manuscript at lunch and never said a word. Never even cracked a smile or nodded his head. What have I done, Dixie? What if he thinks it's garbage and he's just trying to figure out how to let me down easy?"

"It's not garbage. It's good. I know that much. Just wait. He'll think so, too."

Ashley sank down on the sofa and crossed her arms on her chest. "I don't think I can face him again."

"Of course you can. You're going to tomorrow's lecture."

"I suppose. And he did ask if he could see me again."

Dixie's brown eyes brightened. "See you? As in a date?"

Ashley waved her hand dismissively. "Not a date. How could I even think of a date after losing Ben? Tonio and I are colleagues. Sort of. I'm sure he just wants to talk about the writing business."

"Is he married?"

"Stop it, little Miss Matchmaker. I've had enough of romance for a good, long time."

"Then he's not married?"

"He's a widower. His wife died about five years ago."

Dixie's voice softened. "Oh, I'm sorry. Me and my big mouth."

"I don't know much about it. It happened before I started working at Haricott. I heard he didn't write for nearly two years after her death. He must have loved her very much."

Dixie sat down beside her. "I wonder what happened. Usually the tabloids flash all kinds of headlines about famous people. But I don't recall hearing anything about Anthony Adler. Of course, I don't pay much attention to that sort of thing anyway."

"Nor do I. Even Ben, who's his friend as well as his editor, has never said a word about Tonio's personal life." Ashley absently twisted a strand of her hair.

"But I do know one thing. Tonio's a very complex man. Compelling. Maybe even a bit eccentric."

"Maybe he's keeping a secret, something he doesn't want the world to know. Something tragic and unspeakable."

Ashley shook her head. "With your imagination, *you* should be the writer."

"Don't you see it, too, Ash? He's mysterious, mystifying. A man of secrets."

"He's a writer."

"So?"

"Let's face it, Dixie. By nature, writers are a little odd. We go around listening to voices in our heads. Sometimes our characters are more real than the people around us. We're a strange lot."

"You can say that again."

"And so are the people who befriend us."

Dixie made an exaggerated flourish. "*Moi?*"

"If the shoe fits. . ."

Dixie jumped up. "What time is it? I have an appointment at the spa for a hydrotherapy massage. Or is it an aromatherapy wrap and seaweed shower to detoxify and decongest my body systems? I forget which I signed up for."

"Are you sure you're not going to end up in some weird vegetable stew?"

"Are you kidding? I'm going to be gorgeous inside and out."

"Spare me the details."

Glancing in the mirror, Dixie fluffed her short auburn hair and checked her ruby red lipstick, then headed for the door. "I'll see you at dinner. Don't forget this is karaoke night. The Rendezvous Lounge at ten."

"I'm not singing."

"Then come cheer me on. It's my time to shine."

"Just don't sing those schmaltzy love songs that make me cry."

"I'm going to go with the eighties tonight. Don't worry, I'll stay away from the ballads."

Ashley smiled. "I'll bring my earplugs just in case."

That evening, against her better judgment, Ashley joined Dixie at the karaoke program. But her mind wasn't on the singing. She couldn't stop thinking about Ben. In her memory she replayed the events of their wedding; more accurately, the wedding that never was. She wondered what Ben was doing now, back in New York City without her. Did he pass by her empty desk at work and think of her? Did he miss her as much as she missed him? Did he regret calling off the wedding?

Halfway through the karaoke program, a strange thing happened. Instead of Ben's face, Ashley found herself picturing someone else's. She heard a different voice in her imagination. Not Ben's. Whose was it? Whose features was she tracing in her mind's eye?

The dreamlike image taking focus in her thoughts startled her.

Anthony Adler.

She pictured him giving his lecture, a bit stiff at first and then warming to the crowd. She traced his aquiline nose and the cut of his jaw as he sat reading her manuscript at lunch. She could hear his deep, resonant voice as he talked about a writer's passion.

Her face warmed with embarrassment. She had no business thinking of a man she had just met and hardly knew. Anthony Adler meant nothing to her. All right, he meant something. She had admired him from afar. Not him; his talent. She dreamed of being able to write as well and producing novels that people loved to read. But that was it. She wasn't the sort of empty-headed girl to be starstruck or beguiled by someone famous.

Give yourself a break, Ashley. You're at a vulnerable place in your life since Ben left you at the altar. It's only natural you'd want to find someone else to think about. Sure, that was it. Her broken heart was grasping at straws, seeking a distraction. What harm was there in getting acquainted with a handsome, charismatic man like Anthony Adler, who also happened to be her favorite author?

And don't forget, he may be in his stateroom reading your novel at this very moment.

That thought alone unnerved her. What would he say to her at his lecture tomorrow? She could imagine him holding up her manuscript and telling the audience, "There's someone in this room who actually believes she can write well enough to be published. Listen to what this poor, deluded girl wrote."

Ashley clasped her hands over her ears. "No, please, I don't want to hear it!"

Dixie slipped into the seat next to her. "Wow, Ash, I didn't think my singing was that bad."

Ashley broke into laughter. "Not you, silly. It's—oh, never mind. Just my crazy imagination running wild again."

The next morning, as Ashley entered the conference room, visions of Adler making fun of her novel lingered in her mind. She had almost decided not to come. But Dixie persuaded her, threatening to tell Adler why she was avoiding him. *She thinks you're going to read her book aloud and laugh at her.*

It was a silly, irrational fear; nothing to worry about. Ashley knew that. Something more was giving her misgivings about seeing Tonio again. *Tonio.* He had told her to call him that—the name his grandmother had given him. He said only his friends called him Tonio. Wasn't that a sign she was more to him than a face in the crowd?

But why would she want to be more?

Ashley mused over that idea—being more than a face in the crowd—as Adler greeted the audience and shuffled his notes. She tried to keep her mind on his lecture, but her thoughts meandered off to surprising places. She wanted to be sitting with Tonio at lunch again, chatting face-to-face, as if they were the only two people in the world. She wanted to hear him speaking in that caring, confidential tone, his gaze fixed only on her.

Maybe I'm just desperate to know what he thinks of my writing.

It can't be anything else.

After his lecture, Anthony broke away from the crush of autograph seekers and called her name. "Ashley, wait a moment, please."

She glanced at Dixie.

"Go ahead, girlfriend. I'm running off to an ice-carving demonstration. I'm dying to find out what they do with those ice sculptures after they melt." She winked. "Just kidding. You and Mr. Hemingway have fun."

Ashley gave Dixie's arm a squeeze. "I'll catch up with you later."

"Let's hope he's crazy about your novel."

"If only!"

Ashley lingered near the podium while Adler signed his books and sent his jubilant fans on their way. As he stuffed his notes into his briefcase, she watched for a glimpse of her novel. It wasn't there.

"Would you like to have lunch together again?" His voice was buoyant, his eyes expectant.

"Yes, I'd like that."

They fell into step together, their arms touching as they walked. "Well, Ashley, we can eat again on the pool deck, or we can enjoy the formal luncheon in the dining room."

"Formal is fine." She grinned. "I'm actually getting used to linen and fine china and a dozen pieces of silverware."

"The trick is to start from the outside and work your way in."

"But what about the silverware at the top of the plate?"

He shrugged. "You've got me."

"Maybe the extras are for when you drop your fork and don't want to tell anybody."

"There you go. You've solved one of life's greatest mysteries."

She smiled. "Just call me Sherlock."

Ashley's hopes of having Tonio to herself were dashed when the maître d' seated them at a table of ten. When the female guests realized a famous author was sitting at their table, they were abuzz with questions and lavish praise.

"I've been reading your books since I was a girl," said a woman who was obviously decades older than Adler.

"Thank you, ma'am." He kindly avoided pointing out that he was only in his midthirties.

"I loved your last book," said another. "But you never should have let Jasmine die. I cried for two days. I'll never forgive you for that."

"My apologies. I rather did like Jasmine myself."

"What are you writing now, Mr. Adler? Can you give us a little sneak preview?"

"I'm sorry, ladies," he said in his most benevolent voice. "I never discuss a work in progress."

"Oh, please, just a little hint?"

"Perhaps just a hint." Amusement played in his eyes. "But it must go no further than this table. It'll be our little secret. Agreed?"

With a flurry of excited exclamations, the women all agreed. In no time Tonio was on a roll, a showman at heart, thriving on the adulation of his fans. Ashley gave up any hope of having a private conversation about her novel.

After lunch, Tonio walked her to the grand foyer. "I'm sorry if the table conversation got a little carried away. I had hoped the two of us would have more time to talk."

"Me, too," she said, stifling her disappointment. "Maybe another time."

"Are you taking a tour of Kauai this afternoon?"

"Yes, Dixie and I are doing a tour of Kahili Falls."

"Are you going to play in Kauai's famous red mud?"

She laughed. "I don't know about the mud, but they say we'll be traveling along old sugarcane roads and through lots of buffalo grass."

"Well, in my opinion, the only way to see Kauai is by air." As he touched her arm, the sensation warmed her. "Would you like to join me after class tomorrow on a helicopter ride over Waimea Canyon? Your friend is welcome to join us, of course."

"Sounds like fun," she said, suppressing her eagerness. "I'll check with Dixie and let you know."

But Dixie begged off, explaining that she had made plans with several other passengers who also happened to be in the cosmetics business. Ashley didn't press the issue. She figured Dixie was giving her some alone time with Tonio in hopes of easing her heartache over Ben.

It turned out Dixie was right. Not that Ashley was about to forget Ben, but at least she was pleasantly distracted.

Over the next few days, she experienced some of the greatest adventures of her life. But as much as she enjoyed the tours, it was Anthony Adler who made the days special.

On their first sightseeing excursion, they rode the helicopter over the vast Waimea Canyon with its craggy, colorful peaks and lush green vegetation. "Mark Twain called this the 'Grand Canyon of the Pacific,' " Tonio told her as they gazed down nearly four thousand feet into the rugged canyon below.

She didn't have the courage to tell him she was afraid of heights. She gripped his hand so hard her knuckles turned white. But with him beside her she felt safe even as her stomach churned.

The next day the ship arrived at the Big Island and docked at Hilo, a rustic, picturesque town with Victorian houses overlooking a half-moon bay. After a picnic dinner under the massive banyan trees, she and Tonio toured the summit of the Mauna Kea volcano, one of the world's highest mountains. "The ancient Hawaiians considered this the meeting place of heaven and earth," he told her as they watched a glorious sunset give way to a deep blue, star-studded sky.

"It's breathtaking," she agreed, meeting his gaze in the moonlight. But it was more than the scenery that stole her breath away. Anthony Adler was stirring her emotions in ways she hadn't expected to feel again, certainly not so soon after her breakup with Ben. *What's wrong with me?* she wondered. *Am I so fickle that I'm already attracted to another man?*

That evening the ship sailed to the western side of the Big Island and dropped anchor at Kailua-Kona, where Tonio lived. He insisted on showing Ashley and Dixie around his city, so early the next morning they took a tender ashore. Ashley was relieved to have Dixie along; maybe now her silly infatuation over Tonio would go away.

"This was once a major fishing community, but now it's considered the tourist and commercial center of the Kona Coast," he told them as they walked along the seawall and browsed nearby souvenir shops. "There's a lot to see and do here. We can go swimming, deep-sea fishing, snorkeling, kayaking, scuba diving, or, if you like, we can take an aerial expedition over the Big Island."

"If you mean a helicopter ride, this time I'll pass," said Ashley.

"Okay, we can do something that doesn't involve heights. How about a submarine or glass-bottom boat ride, if you're into tropical fish and coral reefs. Or if you're interested in the history of the island, we can visit the Captain Cook Monument, or Hawaii's first church, the Mokuaikaua, or the Ahuena Heiau temple where King Kamehameha died."

"I'm not much into dead kings," said Dixie. "Personally I like to shop 'til I drop. But history's okay, too, as long as it's not too heavy."

"All right," said Tonio. "Maybe you'd like to visit the University of the Nations, where Christians from all over the world are trained for ministry."

"I'd love to," said Ashley.

"And you'll both probably want to see Pu'uhonua o Honaunau National Historical Park."

Dixie shook her head. "See it? I can't even say it!"

"It means 'Place of Refuge,' " said Tonio. "It's beautiful. I think you'd like it."

"Sounds good to me," said Ashley. "Let's start there."

The three of them packed the next two days with hiking, swimming, and sightseeing. They saw lava fields, volcanoes, black sand beaches, blowholes, sheer cliffs, and coffee farms. They visited historic churches, temples, and museums. And to placate Dixie, they stopped by every kiosk and souvenir shop on the island.

By the end of their second day in Kona, as they headed back to the ship, all three had to help carry Dixie's purchases—T-shirts that changed colors in the sun, floppy, wide-brimmed hats, enormous beach bags, flip-flops, sunglasses, plastic plumeria leis, and heavy cans of Kona coffee and macadamia nuts.

"You'll never get this all home on the plane," said Ashley, pulling a carved coconut monkey out of one sack.

"Sure I will," said Dixie. "I'll wear the shirts and hats and leis, and stuff everything else in the beach bags."

"I can see it now," said Ashley with a chuckle. "My best friend, the bag lady."

They all laughed, but the thought of flying home struck a wave of apprehension through Ashley's heart. *How will I face Ben again? What am I going to do with the rest of my life?*

Chapter 5

On the last day of the cruise, questions about Ben and her future were still playing in Ashley's mind. It had been twenty-four days since he left her at the altar. Her weeks in Hawaii and on the cruise had given her a sweet reprieve from reality. But now it was time to return to a world that was painful and complicated. How would she face Ben again? Would she have the courage to quit her job? What was God's plan for her life?

Leaving the ship also meant leaving Tonio, a man she had grown to care about in such a short time. The thought of never seeing him again left an emptiness inside her. As much as it surprised her, she wasn't ready to let their friendship go.

Besides, they still had unfinished business. He hadn't once mentioned her manuscript—a fact that she had pushed to the back of her mind. Maybe he had forgotten it. Or perhaps he wanted to let her down gently. She had been foolhardy and naive even to show it to him. He was no doubt saving both of them an embarrassing moment. Whatever the case, a perverse sort of pride kept her from inquiring about it.

On their last evening together, as the *Sea Queen* docked again in Honolulu, Tonio invited her to dine with him in one of the ship's exclusive, reservations-only restaurants. They were seated at a candlelit table for two by a gleaming wall of windows overlooking the back of the ship. Tonio looked amazing in his tuxedo; he told her she was breathtaking in her jade-green satin gown. The sunset was resplendent. Violinists strolled from table to table, serenading the guests. The ambience was magical, the night filled with romance.

They ordered baked stuffed shrimp, poke salad with tamarind honey dressing, mahimahi sautéed with macadamia nuts, and crème brûlée. As usual, Tonio declined any alcoholic beverage; she appreciated that, as a fellow believer, he shared her conviction.

And she loved the way he reached across the table and took her hands when he asked for God's blessing on the food. His simple gestures of faith warmed her heart in a way she had never felt with Ben.

"What are you thinking, Ashley?" The candlelight danced in his blue eyes and accented his tanned, chiseled features. "You look so far away. I hope I'm not boring you."

"Of course not." She touched the back of her neck. "I was just thinking that this is our last night together."

"Don't remind me."

She lowered her gaze, searching for words. "You–you've been so kind to me. I don't know how to thank you. You've lifted my spirits and made this cruise one of the most memorable events of my life."

"No, Ashley, I should be the one to thank you." He leaned toward her as if he was about to share a secret. "I came on this cruise expecting to give my lectures, enjoy a few tours, and go home the same man I was when I came. But you've brought something special into my life. Something I don't want to lose."

Her face warmed as she murmured, "Nor do I, Tonio."

The waiter brought their appetizers then, so they lapsed into silence as they ate. They made only small talk as each course was presented. It was as if they had so much to say, but now that time was running out, they didn't know how to say it. When the waiter served dessert, Ashley held up a spoon from the top of her plate and said, "Now that the cruise is almost over, I finally know which silverware to use."

"You're ahead of me," said Tonio. "I prefer a simple knife, fork, and spoon."

When they had finished dessert, Tonio reached for something beside his chair. A manila envelope. How had Ashley not noticed?

"I have something for you." He held out her manuscript.

She caught her breath. "I thought you had forgotten."

"No, I was waiting."

"Waiting for what?"

"Waiting to decide what I would say."

"Was it that bad?"

"No. That good."

"Really?" Her heart hammered in her chest. "You liked it?"

"Very much. You've created believable characters and placed them in some fascinating situations. You have a knack for dialogue and your plot is solid. I'm quite impressed."

Tears welled in her eyes. "When you didn't say anything, I thought you hated it."

"I loved it, Ashley. Naturally I made a few notations in the margins, just minor changes and suggestions."

"Of course. I appreciate any help you can give me."

He cleared his throat. "The truth is, I've been mulling something over for several days. I have a proposition for you."

"Proposition?"

"Wrong word. A proposal." He laughed. "For a writer, I'm having an awfully hard time expressing myself. What I'm trying to say is, I'd like to offer you a job."

"A job?" This conversation was getting more peculiar by the moment.

"I know you're reluctant to return to your position at Haricott Publishing."

She lowered her gaze. "I can't work alongside Ben anymore."

"That's why I think my proposition, uh, I mean, my job offer will solve both our problems."

"I don't understand. I know my problem is Ben. But what problem do you have?"

"I need an editorial assistant. Someone to do what you do at Haricott."

"You mean, edit manuscripts?"

"Yes. And someone to do research. A research assistant. Someone to help me prepare my next book for the publisher. I have a tight deadline and, as you know"—he smiled grimly—"my editor is a stern taskmaster."

She matched his smile. "Yes, Ben certainly is that, isn't he?"

"See? You know him so well—how he thinks, what he likes. You would be perfect for this job."

"I'm not so sure. You work at home, right? In Kona?"

"Yes. You would need to move to Hawaii. To my estate actually."

She felt suddenly shy. "You want me to live at your house?"

"Not exactly. I have a cottage behind the house. A very nice little place. It used to be the caretaker's cottage, but it's empty now. We could fix it up for you. Naturally, we want to avoid any impropriety."

"I appreciate that. The cottage sounds wonderful—that is, if I decide to take you up on your offer."

"Well, think about it, Ashley. Go back to New York and see how things are. If you feel comfortable staying at Haricott, I certainly understand. But if you find the situation intolerable and would like to test the waters, well, I would welcome you with. . ."

She sensed he was about to say "open arms."

"Uh, let's just say I would be very pleased to have you as my assistant. And there's no pressure. If you decide you don't like the job, or Hawaii, or me, or whatever, you're free to leave at any time—with a glowing job recommendation, of course."

"You say that before you even know my work?"

"I've read your work. And I know Ben would never have hired you if you weren't the best."

She turned the stem of her crystal water goblet between her fingers, her thoughts racing. *Lord, what do You want me to do? Is this Your answer for me? Help me to make the right decision.*

Tonio set his linen napkin on the table. "I can see I've overwhelmed you. Let's go out on the deck and get some fresh air. Don't give my offer another thought for now."

They both stood up. It surprised her how weak her knees felt. She gripped the table to steady herself. Tonio stepped over, put his hand at her waist, then led her out of the opulent restaurant to the open deck.

She welcomed the moist, salty breeze against her flushed cheeks. She and Tonio leaned against the mahogany railing, side by side, elbows touching. She inhaled deeply, wondering whether the past hour had been merely a dream. Had the great Anthony Adler actually asked her to be his assistant?

He looked down at her and smiled. She loved the way the moonlight played on his face. Softly he said, "Ashley, I hope I wasn't being presumptuous, asking you to quit your job and come work for me."

"No, Tonio. I'm flattered. And pleased. I want to say yes, I really do." She drew in a steadying breath. "I'm so tempted to say yes right now. But I need to pray about it. Everything in my life will change, and I need to know it's what God wants for me."

"I'll be praying, too. God willing, we'll be facing a fascinating future together. . .in the writing business."

She laughed lightly. "We'll show Ben Radison. We'll come up with a book that knocks his socks off."

Tonio clasped her hand. "That's the spirit! We'll knock him right off his feet."

They chatted for another hour or so, mostly small talk about the cruise and the quirky twists and turns of the publishing industry, with a few companionable silences tossed in. At last, he turned to face her. "I hate to see this evening end, but I do have some last-minute packing to do."

"So do I. They want our luggage outside our doors by midnight."

"That doesn't give us much time."

She sighed. "Not much at all."

They were silent as he walked her to her stateroom. He paused at the door while she searched her satin bag for her room key. "Will I see you in the morning for breakfast?" he asked.

She put her key in the lock but didn't open the door. "Sure, I'd like that."

"What time does your plane take off tomorrow?"

"Dixie and I fly back to New York at one."

"I fly to Kona at noon."

They weren't alone in the long, elegant hallway, but, for Ashley, it seemed they were the only two people on earth. Tonio studied her for a long moment, his gaze unnerving. She felt awkward, unstrung, like a girl on her first date, reluctant to let her beloved go.

"May I give you a good-bye hug now?" he asked as he drew her into his arms. "Things will be crowded and hectic tomorrow."

Before she could utter a sound, he wrapped his arms around her. She loved the delicious warmth of his embrace.

"This isn't good-bye, Ashley," he whispered. "I'm counting on us being together again." He lowered his face to hers and brushed a kiss against her cheek.

Surprised, she turned her head, only to find his lips touching hers. They lingered a moment too long for the kiss to be accidental. Even after they had said good night, she still felt the sweet sensation of his lips on hers.

Chapter 6

Hey, girlfriend," said Dixie, "do you have room in your suitcase for my coconut monkeys?"

Ashley stood in the doorway, gazing around her stateroom as if waking from a dream. Tonio's kiss had left her dazzled, distracted. She couldn't quite process the scene before her—Dixie surrounded by brimming suitcases and bulging beach bags. Their room looked like a souvenir shop with leis hanging on the closet door and hats and aloha shirts stacked on the desk.

Dixie plopped herself down on her suitcase and tried zipping it shut. "And I can't fit my conch shells in anywhere, Ash," she rushed on breathlessly. "Do you have an extra bag?"

"Maybe, maybe not."

Dixie stopped zipping and gave Ashley a long, hard look. "Are you okay? You sound weird. Like you're a million miles away."

"I am."

"You are what?"

"A million miles away."

"Now you're talking in riddles."

Ashley covered her cheeks with her hands. Her face felt warm, flushed. "You'll never believe what happened."

Dixie was listening intently now. "Tell me before you explode."

Ashley's words wafted on a sigh. "Tonio kissed me."

Dixie scrambled off the suitcase, took Ashley's hand, and led her over to the sofa. They sat down, facing each other. "He actually kissed you? Tell me everything."

"It was accidental."

"An accidental kiss? How does that work?"

"He didn't plan it. I didn't expect it. He kissed my cheek."

"Then it was just a friendly good-night kiss?"

"It started out that way. He surprised me and I turned my head. And then our lips were touching."

Dixie rubbed her hands together. "This is getting good. What happened next?"

"For a moment neither of us moved. We just stayed that way, our lips touching ever so lightly."

"And then?"

"And then he said good night and left." Ashley sat back and hugged her arms to her chest. "And now I don't know what to think or how to feel."

Dixie shrugged. "It doesn't really matter, does it? You live in New York, he lives in Hawaii. You'll be an ocean and a continent apart. You'll probably never see him again."

Ashley sat forward. "That's just it. I may see a lot more of him than I ever imagined. He asked me to come to Hawaii and be his editorial assistant."

Dixie's mouth dropped open. "Are you kidding me? Is this one of those reality shows where you try to shock your best friend with some wacky news flash? Come on, where are the hidden cameras?"

"I'm serious, Dixie." Ashley repeated the details of Tonio's offer, finishing with, "He really wants my help. He says, together we can come up with a novel that will totally amaze Ben."

"So that's it!"

"What?"

"This is about Ben. About making Ben jealous."

"No, it's not. I never even thought of that." Ashley stood up and strode over to her bed, away from Dixie's probing gaze. She took the chocolate mint from her pillow and tore off the wrapper. "It's a wonderful opportunity, Dixie. You know I can't go back to Haricott. I could never work with Ben again."

"Then you're going to accept Tonio's offer?"

She popped the mint into her mouth. "I told him I'd pray about it."

"But wouldn't you be, I don't know, jumping from the frying pan into the fire?"

"How so?"

"Ben just broke your heart. Are you going to risk that again with Tonio?"

"It's a business arrangement, Dixie. Not a romance."

"He kissed you. And you liked it."

Ashley closed her eyes and savored the melting chocolate on her tongue. There was no use trying to explain to Dixie what she herself didn't understand—her undeniable attraction to Tonio and the certainty that she had to pursue this wild-eyed adventure, no matter how crazy or irrational it seemed. Her heart had already decided. Unless God shut the door, she would be packing up her life and heading for Kailua-Kona and the beachfront estate of Anthony Adler.

Three weeks later Ashley boarded a plane for Hawaii. She had severed all ties with her former life—quit her job, moved out of her small, high-rise apartment, resigned from teaching her middle-school girls' Sunday school class, and said good-bye to family and friends.

As hard as it was leaving Dixie and her parents, she found it hardest of all to walk away from Ben. She kept reminding herself that he had left her at the altar, and yet a part of her kept saying, *If you stay in New York, maybe Ben will come to his senses and take you back. If you leave, you're ending all chances for a reconciliation.*

She had almost weakened when she stopped by the Haricott office to gather her belongings. Ben had wished her well and told her if she decided to come back, her job would be waiting for her.

Oh Ben, don't you see? It's more than my job I want from you. Tell me you want me back, and I'll stay here forever.

But, of course, he said no such thing. Smiling politely, they exchanged pleasantries and were still flashing their pasted-on smiles when they said good-bye.

Now, a new, uncertain future lay before her—a lush, tropical paradise and the suave, sophisticated Anthony Adler. Ashley had no idea what to expect from either of them.

Tonio was waiting for her at the Kona airport. He greeted her with a circumspect hug, then collected her luggage and walked her out to his SUV. "How was your trip?" he asked as he opened the door and offered his hand.

She accepted his gallant gesture and climbed inside. "The flight was long. Lots of turbulence. And a two-hour delay in Honolulu."

"Well, you'll have a Hawaiian feast waiting for you at home."

She stared at him. "You cook, too? Is there no end to your talents?"

He laughed. "No, I don't even boil water except when I'm desperate for my coffee. Mika does all the cooking."

"Who?"

"Mika Kimura. She and her husband, Harry, work for me. She's my housekeeper; he's my gardener."

"Servants, no less! Don't tell me they live in the little cottage you told me about."

"They did for several years, but now they have a place of their own nearby. Mika arrives before breakfast and leaves after she's prepared dinner. They know that when I'm writing I'm a hermit at heart. A veritable recluse, I'm afraid. Mika acts as my unofficial secretary, fielding phone calls and keeping visitors at bay. She and Harry both know when to keep out of my way."

Ashley made a soft whistling sound. "I guess that's something I'm going to have to learn, too."

Tonio reached over and squeezed her hand. "That won't be necessary. You and I have many long hours of work ahead. I'm already behind deadline, so I'll be grateful for every hour we spend together." His voice took on a reassuring tone. "Not that I intend to be a slave driver, mind you. We'll take time to do all the touristy things I'm sure you'd like to do. I won't let you work yourself to death."

She managed a smile. "I'm glad of that." Privately, she wondered, *What am I getting myself into? Who is this man I've come halfway around the world to work for?*

They drove for about ten miles through lava fields that offered little of the beauty she had seen on the other islands. But minutes later, as Tonio headed up a winding, palm-lined road toward the cliffs, a glowing sun turned the sky burnt orange and cast fiery streamers on the ocean. She had never seen anything more breathtaking.

"We have a panoramic view here, Ashley. A little touch of heaven. I hope you love it as much as I do."

"I'm sure I will." Did she sound a bit hesitant? Did Tonio sense how self-conscious she felt?

In the distance she spotted a sprawling, plantation-style house perched on a rugged cliff. Tonio followed the circular drive around an expansive, manicured lawn to the front entrance with its wraparound porch flanked by towering palms. Bright orange birds-of-paradise stood like sentries among a colorful profusion of exotic flowers and plants.

"I'll show you around the grounds tomorrow," Tonio said as he unloaded her luggage. "The light will be better and you'll be rested."

"I look forward to it," she said, gathering up her purse, laptop, and cosmetics bag.

As they climbed the porch steps, he nodded toward the north. "Over there is a coconut grove and to the south, an avocado orchard. And if you walk far enough, you'll see acres of citrus, mango, and jacaranda trees."

"It's more beautiful than I imagined."

He showed her into an elegant entry hall with marble flooring and a grand teak spiral staircase. "Harry will take your luggage out to the cottage. I think you'll like it there. It's cozy and closer to the ocean. The main house has plenty of guest rooms, but as I said. . ."

"You're right. As a Christian, I wouldn't want to give anyone the wrong idea."

"Agreed. And by now Mika should have dinner ready for us."

"It smells wonderful. What is it? Spareribs?"

"You'll see. One of her pork dishes. You'll get a taste of authentic Hawaiian food."

"I can't wait."

She followed Tonio down a long hallway to the great room with its vaulted ceiling and teak paneling. The room was accented with mosaic tiles, etched glass, hanging plants, and tropical flowers. Leather sofas were grouped around a coffee table made of a mahogany tree trunk. At one end was a massive stone fireplace; at the other end French doors led into the dining room. But most spectacular was an entire wall of pocket sliding glass doors opening onto a covered lanai, blending inside and outside in a stunning vision of raw nature and unbridled opulence.

Ashley crossed the room and looked out at the sweeping view. "Oh Tonio, it's amazing!" Tiki torches surrounded a huge swimming pool and spa. Beyond the pool lay a quaint cottage and Victorian gazebo framed against an orange and violet sky. Beyond the cottage, a rocky promontory led down to the turquoise splendor of the Pacific.

"I wish I were an artist," she told him. "I'd love to paint this scene."

"Paint it with words."

She smiled. "Maybe I will."

"Make yourself at home, Ashley. I'll check on dinner."

She pivoted, taking everything in. "Your home is gorgeous, Tonio. You have exquisite taste."

He raised his hand in protest. "Whoa. It's not me. None of this is me. I would have been happy in a little bungalow with inside plumbing and electricity."

"Then who designed and built all of this?"

He walked over by the French doors and gazed up at a framed portrait of a woman with remarkable beauty. "My wife," he said huskily.

Ashley's breath caught in her throat. This was the first time Tonio had mentioned his wife. And now, to see her in the vivid colors and swirling brush-strokes of this oil painting was more than Ashley had bargained for. Suddenly she felt like a trespasser, barging into the privacy of a stranger's life.

"Brianna created this estate," Tonio said with a hint of irony. "She was born into wealth and inherited a fortune from her parents. That and my income allowed her to have everything she wanted—all these luxuries and amenities. She was relentless in her decorating, acquiring the best from all over the world—Italian marble, African mahogany cabinets, ceilings trimmed with monkeypod wood, Brazilian oak floors, and of course, lots of Hawaiian artifacts. She planned every detail, down to the native hardwood sculptures and glasswork."

"She did a fantastic job."

"Yes, she was a very talented woman." A long pause, then, "But she never lived to enjoy it."

Before Ashley could summon a proper reply, Tonio opened the French doors and called out, "Mika, we're here, and we're as hungry as bears."

A short, squat woman with ebony hair, round cheeks, and twinkling eyes bustled out and flashed a smile that lit up the entire room. "Aloha, Mr. Adler. Dinner is served."

Tonio nudged Ashley forward. "Mika, this is Ashley Bancroft, my new assistant. Ashley, this is Mika Kimura. She keeps my life running like a Swiss watch."

Mika beamed. "*Mahalo*, Mr. Adler." She reached out and clasped Ashley's hands between her calloused palms. "*Pehea `oe*, Miss Bancroft? How are you?"

"Fine, thank you, Mika."

"*Maika `i, mahalo*."

Ashley looked at Tonio, as if to ask, *What did she say?*

He grinned. "She translated your words—'fine, thank you'—into Hawaiian. In no time she'll have you speaking the language like a native."

"I look forward to it, Mika."

They followed her into the dining room where the table was set for an island feast. Platters brimmed with barbecued pork ribs, sweet potatoes, fried rice, fresh pineapple, papayas, and passion fruit. Tonio pulled back Ashley's chair.

"Thank you. I mean, *mahalo*," she said, sitting down.

"You're welcome. You catch on quickly." He sat down across from her and held her hand as he asked the blessing. Then he passed her the ribs. "Mika wants to make a good impression on you."

Ashley speared several succulent ribs dripping with barbecue sauce. "Tell her she definitely did."

He passed her another dish that looked like purple paste. She eyed it skeptically. "What's this?"

"Poi. Made from the taro root. An acquired taste, I'm afraid."

"I'll try it." She scooped some onto her plate. "Why not? I have an adventurous spirit."

"You certainly do." He flashed a look she couldn't quite read, but it pleased her. "You've proved that, Ashley, by coming here."

She squared her shoulders and tasted the poi, then puckered her lips. "Maybe I'm not quite that adventurous yet."

"That's okay. You have lots of time to develop a taste for island cuisine."

She liked the sound of that. Lots of time for the two of them to get better acquainted. Lots of time to discover whether she had come here for more than a job.

They ate at a leisurely pace, and when they had had their fill, Mika brought out a tray of chocolate macadamia nut clusters, chocolate-covered ginger, and hot, black Kona coffee.

"You're spoiling me," Ashley protested. "If I keep eating like this, I'll rival the kalua pig in size."

Tonio laughed. "Never! You're perfect, Ashley. Graceful and lovely. Remarkable in every way."

Her face warmed with pleasure and embarrassment. She could think of nothing to say in return, so she focused her attention on her coffee cup. She sipped too quickly. The hot liquid made her face even warmer.

After dinner Tonio walked her out to the cottage—a rustic, charming little house with a thatched roof, covered lanai, and bay windows, nestled among plumeria trees, lush ferns, and tropical flowers.

They crossed the lanai, and Tonio unlocked the door, then handed her the key. "Your luggage should already be inside. With jet lag and the time change, I'm sure you'll want to sleep in."

She nodded. "No alarm clocks for me."

"Mika will fix you breakfast whenever you're hungry. Just come on over to the main house when you're ready."

"Thanks. I feel like I could sleep for days." She laughed. "I'm kidding. I'll be ready to work tomorrow whenever you say."

They entered the cottage, Tonio leading the way and flipping on a light switch. "We'll play it by ear, Ashley. I want my assistant bright-eyed and bushy-tailed."

"I can't promise bushy-tailed."

"Okay. Perky then."

"Sorry. I don't do perky, either." Her gaze took in the wicker furniture, open-beamed ceiling, stone fireplace, and polished bamboo floors. Simple, unadorned, comfortable. She liked it. "But I promise to be alert and ready to work hard tomorrow."

"Can't ask for more than that."

He showed her around the cottage—the roomy living room with fresh-cut flowers and plants, a cozy kitchen with a bowl of fruit on the counter, and a pleasant bedroom with native art on the walls and a homemade quilt on the bed.

After a minute they walked back out to the living room and he opened the door. "I'd better get out of here and let you settle in." He moved toward her ever so slightly, as if to offer a kiss or an embrace, then drew back suddenly and straightened his shoulders. "Sleep well, Ashley," he said. "I'll see you in the morning."

Then, without a backward glance, he was gone. Ashley was alone in her little cottage by the sea, a million miles away from everything and everyone familiar.

Chapter 7

Ashley woke to the sweet twitter of birds outside her window. She stretched leisurely, then rolled over and hugged her pillow. For a moment she couldn't remember where she was. New York? No. She opened her eyes and looked around.

Hawaii. Her little cottage by the sea. A little bit of heaven.

She climbed out of bed, padded barefoot to her tiny kitchen, and put on the teakettle. Surely there would be instant coffee in the cupboard. Or did Hawaiians drink only freshly brewed Kona coffee?

While she waited for the kettle to boil, she opened her wood slat blinds and gazed out the window at the shimmering ocean. *They say if you watch closely you can see whales and dolphins playing in the surf. Wouldn't it be sweet if I could phone Mom or Dixie and say I'm whale watching on my private lanai?*

She looked at the clock over the stove. Almost nine. She had overslept. No time for whale watching this morning. She'd better gulp down her coffee, throw on some clothes and a little makeup, and head over to the main house. Tonio had told her to sleep in, but she wanted to make a good impression her first day on the job.

A half hour later she was on her way, passing the gazebo and swimming pool. A lean, deeply tanned man in a straw hat and work clothes was trimming the hedge around the pool area. He looked up and grinned as she walked by. "Aloha, sistah."

"Excuse me?"

"You in da Aloha State, sistah. Everyone is family here."

"Oh, I see. Thank you."

"How you doin' dis fine mornin'?"

"Just fine. So you must be Mr. Kimura." She offered her hand. "I'm Ashley. Glad to meet you."

He rubbed his hand on his overalls, then gingerly accepted hers. "You gon call me Harry. Dat's what dey all call me."

"Harry then. I suppose Mr. Adler is already well into his day."

"Ah. You gon find him in da office. But I tink he gon wait fo you fo breakfast."

"Oh, that's sweet of him. I'm looking forward to your wife's cooking. She fixed us a delicious meal last night."

"Ah, dat's some *ono kine grinds*. You know, some good food."

"It certainly is. Well, you have a good day, Harry. Aloha."

Ashley gave a little good-bye wave and hurried on to the main house. Mika was already setting Ashley's place at the table. After exchanging pleasantries, Ashley sat down and spread her linen napkin on her lap. Mika poured her a cup of steaming coffee then spooned a cheese omelet and Canadian bacon onto her plate.

"You like sweet bread French toast, Miss Bancroft?" Without waiting for a reply, Mika placed a crusty wedge beside the omelet.

Ashley stifled the impulse to tell her she rarely ate more for breakfast than a protein bar. "Thank you. It looks delicious, Mika."

A rustling sound behind her drew her attention. Tonio came striding into the dining room with a coffee cup in his hand. "Good morning, Ashley." He sat down across from her. "How did you sleep?"

"Like a log. I didn't hear a thing until the birds started chirping."

Mika brought the coffeepot over and refilled his cup. "You ready for your omelet, Mr. Adler?"

"Yes, Mika. With a little salsa and sour cream."

"You didn't have to wait for me, Tonio. You must be used to eating at the crack of dawn."

"Not quite that early. I didn't want you eating alone your first morning here."

"I'm not used to eating such big breakfasts. At this rate, I could end up a blimp."

"A very nice blimp, I'm sure."

She chuckled. "You're no help, Tonio."

He winked. "Don't worry, I'll keep you so busy you'll burn every last calorie."

After breakfast, Tonio showed her to his office—a large, teak-paneled room with mahogany furniture, an entire wall of books, and floor-to-ceiling windows that faced the sea.

"Sweet!" she said. "I could get used to working in a place like this."

He pulled back a chair for her at the massive desk. "I'm counting on that."

She sat down, her gaze sweeping the dictionaries, research books, used coffee cups, and stacks of manuscript pages and unopened mail surrounding the computer. One thing for sure, Tonio was no neat freak.

"You can see I need some help," he said, sitting down beside her.

"It looks like you need a secretary." She picked up a handful of letters. "Is this fan mail?"

He nodded. "I have several stock reply letters on the computer, but it still takes time to read the letters and decide which reply to send."

"So that will be my job?"

"A small part. Mainly I need help with my current writing project."

"What do you want me to do? Research? I'm pretty good at that."

"Yes, research. And editing. I know you did a terrific job for Ben."

"Yes, but I wasn't editing *his* writing. Most authors are so protective of their 'literary babies,' they dread an editor red-penciling their work."

"I'm not like that, Ashley. I know I tell a good story, but I'm not into the details. Right now I need someone with a discerning eye, someone who can keep me focused and on track, someone who can keep me accountable and moving ahead."

She pursed her lips slightly, wondering, *What am I getting into?* "I hope I can live up to your expectations."

"You will. I feel it in my bones."

"So where do we start?"

He handed her a loose-leaf notebook. "Here's the synopsis of my current novel. You'll find the plot outline, plus detailed sketches of all the main characters. I'm well into the book, but the deadline was last month. Ben has given me an extension, but it's still going to require a rigorous writing schedule over the next few months."

"You're not the only writer who's had to ask for more time, Tonio. It happens all the time. Authors sign contracts with a certain deadline, but then life intrudes. Sometimes it can't be helped."

Tonio cracked his knuckles. "This was totally my fault. You probably already know my last novel didn't do as well as my previous ones. Haricott is putting the pressure on. Not Ben. It's not editorial; it's the marketing division. They said they won't be putting as much promotion and advertising into this one unless the advance sales are high."

She gave him a sympathetic smile. "It's a recipe for trouble when a writer starts focusing more on marketing and sales than exploring the lives of his characters."

"Well said. See? You're already helping me put things in perspective. Let's get into these characters and see what we can do with them."

Ashley flipped through the notebook, scanning the plot points and character sketches. "I'll read through this later. For now, just tell me in your own words what the book's about."

He sat back in his chair and tented his fingers. "It's the story of a man—Philip Holt—whose wife is murdered. Holt has been a roustabout, a jack-of-all-trades, doing undercover work for the FBI and CIA, but that's all behind him now. He messed up, and now he's out on his own, doing small-time detective work. But his life is consumed with finding out why his wife was killed. What did she know or what did she have that made someone want her dead? And will that someone want him dead, too? So his mission in life is to track down his wife's killer. His motives aren't merely rational; they're emotional. He wants justice for his wife and revenge for himself."

"I like it," said Ashley. "It's bursting with tension, conflict, and emotion. A story like that should practically write itself."

He smiled grimly. "You'd think so. But it's not happening. I'm dead in the water."

"Well, let me read what you've written. Everyone faces writer's block at one time or another. Maybe you just need a little push to get you over the next hurdle."

He handed her the stack of manuscript pages. "Be my guest."

They spent the rest of the day working, reading, dissecting the story line, and batting ideas back and forth about the characters' motivations. Mika slipped in sometime around noon to bring them ham sandwiches and iced tea, but they continued discussing the novel as they ate.

Later, as Tonio set their empty plates aside, he said, "We should have taken an actual lunch break, Ashley. I apologize."

"No, I don't mind. We're on a roll. I'm used to eating while working."

"I promise you a leisurely dinner and maybe a movie on the DVR tonight."

"That sounds pretty tempting. But I'd rather spend the evening reading what you've written so far, so I'll be up to speed tomorrow."

"All right. We'll save the movie for another night."

Ashley stayed up until after midnight reading Tonio's work. The next morning she gave him her opinions. The writing was solid, the story line complex and captivating, the characters well drawn. "But there's a problem with Philip, your main character."

"Not macho enough?" said Tonio playfully.

"No, he's plenty macho. But I never felt like I really got into his head. There's all this action, but it all seemed to be happening from a distance. I wasn't living it inside Philip's skin. You didn't make me care enough about him. He's just a guy with troubles. Big troubles, sure. But he could be any guy."

"Okay, that's a valid criticism. What do we do about it?"

She shrugged. "You tell me."

"I have an idea. Let's make a game of it. Why don't you try your hand at writing a few scenes? I'll do the same and we'll compare notes."

"Sounds interesting. And a little intimidating. I'm not sure I want to be comparing my writing to a pro's."

"Aw, come on. It'll be good experience for you. And it'll help me see my work with fresh eyes, another point of view."

"Okay, you're on." She held out her hand. He shook it and didn't let go until she withdrew it. "I guess we'll have to put off that movie for another night," she told him. "Looks like tonight we'll both be busy writing."

Tonio glanced at his watch. "Actually, I won't be home tonight. I have an appointment in town."

"Oh? Do you want company?" The question had slipped out before she realized how forward it sounded.

"Not tonight, Ashley." There was something troubling in his voice. "This is something I have to do alone."

His sudden sternness flustered her. "I'm sorry. I wasn't trying to impose on your plans. I'll spend the night curled up with my laptop."

His tone softened. "Any other time I'd love to take you into town and show you the sights. It's just not possible tonight."

"I understand. You don't owe me any explanation."

After dinner that evening, Tonio excused himself and left the house with only a brisk good-bye. *Maybe he has a date and was afraid of hurting my feelings,* Ashley mused as she walked back to the cottage alone. *I'm only his assistant. I have no right to be concerned about what he does or where he goes or who he's with.*

Ashley spent the night writing. She became so engrossed in the story line, she forgot about Tonio until she heard his SUV in the driveway. It was after ten o'clock. *He won't have any time to write tonight,* she mused.

Sure enough, the next morning, when she showed him the three scenes she had written, Tonio admitted he hadn't completed his part of the assignment. "I'll write twice as much tonight," he promised. After reading her work, he sat back and whistled through his teeth. "This is amazing, Ashley. This is even better than what I read of your novel on the cruise."

"Really?" Her stomach fluttered. Was the great Anthony Adler actually raving about her work?

"You've got to do more. These scenes are riveting. Let your imagination go. See what else you can do."

"Okay. I'll try a few more scenes."

The next day she delivered a dozen more freshly written pages. Tonio was effusive in his praise. "These are excellent. You *will* be published, Ashley. It's not a matter of *if*. It's *when*."

Like a schoolgirl receiving an award, Ashley basked in his approval. She had waited all of her life for moments like these. "I'm blown away, Tonio. I was so afraid you wouldn't like my work."

"Like it? I love it!"

"Now it's your turn," she ventured. "What did you write?"

He waved his hand. "Nothing like this. A few scribblings. They're rough. You'll see them after I've polished them."

The days took on a predictable routine. She showed him what she had written, and he lavished her with praise. But he somehow avoided showing her his work, saying it wasn't suitable yet for an editor's eye.

On Sunday morning, he took her to a quaint, open-air church where a worship band accompanied the congregation as they sang praise songs. Ashley loved the pastor's simple, heartfelt message and the friendliness of the people.

After church he drove her around town, showing her the sights. They spent hours browsing the art galleries of Holualoa, a quaint artists' community on the hill above town. They had dinner at a charming little restaurant on the boardwalk just past the seawall on Ali'i Drive. They ordered green salads with sesame-ginger dressing, bow tie pasta with scallops and shrimp, and finished with pineapple sorbet for dessert, all the while watching a ripe orange sun set over the cruise ships in the harbor.

On Monday they went back to work on Tonio's novel. She wrote more scenes and sketched out ideas for future chapters. And he gave more excuses for not showing her his writing.

The days slipped by in a seamless routine, one that was becoming more troubling to Ashley. It seemed that Tonio was going out almost every other night, with never a word about his destination. Whenever she inquired about his mysterious appointments, he changed the subject. Even Mika seemed close-mouthed on the subject. "Mr. Adler is a busy man. He has important things to do. Very busy."

But I'm his assistant, she protested silently. *Shouldn't he take me into his confidence?*

One night Ashley's frustration came to a head. Tonio had gone out for another of his mysterious meetings, leaving her at home alone to write. As much as she enjoyed sharing her creative efforts with Tonio and receiving his feedback, she had come here to edit *his* work. But how could she edit what he refused to let her read? And how could he write when he was gone so much?

It wasn't just Tonio's capricious behavior that bothered Ashley tonight. She was feeling lonely and homesick. She missed everyone back in New York. Her parents. Dixie. And Ben. From time to time Ben would phone for an update on Tonio's novel. She always tried to remain detached when she heard his voice, but all her resolve melted when he said her name.

Making things even more complicated were her growing feelings for Tonio. How could she be having romantic feelings for him when she still loved Ben? And why did she allow herself to care for Tonio when he was her employer, nothing more? Actually, he was more. He was her friend. *Just a friend,* she realized with a ripple of disappointment. There hadn't been a hint of romance since their last night on the cruise.

At about ten o'clock Ashley closed her laptop and reached for her Bible. She needed some alone time with God. She read for a while, but the air was too warm and muggy to concentrate. She went out to her screened lanai and stretched out on the lounge chair. She needed to pray, but she felt empty of words tonight. "Lord, my feelings are so jumbled, I don't even know what to say. So maybe I'll just sit here in the darkness and listen for Your voice in the breaking surf."

She closed her eyes, letting the rhythmic roar of the waves relax the taut muscles in her arms and legs.

Sometime later—was it minutes or hours?—Ashley woke with a start. Every nerve in her body bristled. Had she been asleep? What had wakened her? She held her breath, listening.

Then she heard it. The rustling sound of footsteps, someone walking near the gazebo. Was it a prowler? Until now it hadn't occurred to her how vulnerable she was—a young woman alone at night on a flimsily screened lanai.

She slipped off the lounge chair and looked out toward the pool. A shadow loomed near the hedge. She couldn't be sure, but it looked like Tonio. She started to call out to him, then thought better of the idea. He was a man who cherished his privacy. If he wanted to be alone, she wasn't about to intrude. But why was he out roaming around his property in the middle of the night?

Ashley's curiosity got the best of her. If Tonio was out walking around at this hour, she was going to find out why. She put on her sandals, quietly opened the lanai door, and walked through the pool area to the surrounding hedge. No sign of anyone. She looked beyond the hedge to the woods that led to the promontory above Tonio's estate. Was that someone moving through the citrus and jacaranda trees? She couldn't be sure. Maybe it was just a gentle wind coming off the ocean, rustling the trees.

No, it's Tonio. I know it is. Something's going on. I've got to find out what.

She crossed the lawn and made her way through the dark wilderness of trees. The air was heavy with the muggy scents of earth and tropical foliage. With the thick overhang of branches, she no longer had a bright full moon to show the way. She stumbled on a gnarled root and nearly fell, but her hands caught hold of the tree's rough bark. She steadied herself and caught her breath.

What if it's not Tonio? What am I doing wandering through a forest alone at this time of night? I must be insane.

Just as she considered turning around and going back, she came to a clearing at the edge of the cliff. The moon lit the way again, and what she saw took her breath away. Tonio stood on the rocky ledge gazing down into the wind-tossed sea. She stopped dead in her tracks, not moving a muscle, lest he hear her, turn, and lose his footing. She wanted to cry out, *Tonio! Get back before you fall!* But something in his stance kept her silent. Was he thinking of jumping? Surely not. And yet, why had he come here in secret in the dead of night?

After a minute he stepped back from the edge and knelt down beside something in a neatly manicured patch of grass. From her vantage point, Ashley couldn't see the object of his attention. *Please, Lord, don't let him discover me here. He would never forgive me for violating his privacy this way.*

He remained in a kneeling position for several minutes, so long that Ashley's legs went numb from standing so still in the shadows. She sighed with relief when he finally straightened his torso, flexed his shoulders, and strode off through the woods back toward his estate.

She waited until she was sure he had time to get back to the main house.

Then she stole out of the shadows and made her way over to the object in the grass that Tonio had found so riveting. Reeling with shock, she stared down at a sculpted angel glistening in the moonlight. The angel was holding an urn. The base of the sculpture bore the inscription:

In Memory of Brianna Adler
Beloved Wife
June 22, 1973 – September 17, 2003

Chapter 8

Tonio is still in love with his dead wife. He must be. He made a memorial to her on the cliff. Her ashes may even be in that urn. He's still totally devoted to her. He'll never have a place in his heart for another woman.

Those were Ashley's thoughts as she darted through the woods back to her cottage. How could she have been so foolish as to let herself become emotionally involved with a man she hardly knew, an eccentric, reclusive man with so many secrets?

It was nearly three a.m. when she finally climbed into bed. But she couldn't sleep. She was heartsick, imagining Tonio still carrying his grief around like an iron shield over his heart. There was no way a mere woman could penetrate that kind of pain. No wonder Tonio was having a difficult time writing. He was too bound by his sorrow to tap into his creativity. Why hadn't she seen that before? No wonder he made no romantic overtures. That kiss on the ship had been an accident, an aberration, a fluke. He had made sure it never happened again. If he ever suspected she had a crush on him, he would no doubt be mortified.

I've got to focus on the reason I came here. I'm his assistant. I'm here to help him get his book written. I'm going to edit his work, whether he feels the material is ready or not.

She fell asleep at last with a new resolve to accomplish the job she had been hired to do. Maybe her time on the island would be shorter than she had planned. Maybe in a month or two she would return home to New York and start a new life for herself.

The next morning, Tonio was late coming to the office, so Ashley lingered in the great room with a second cup of coffee. She was drawn to the portrait of Brianna Adler on the wall by the French doors. As she studied the exquisite face and striking green eyes, she felt as if Brianna were speaking to her from the grave. *You have no business in my home. You're an intruder. Get out, and let Tonio grieve in peace!*

She shivered. The words weren't audible, and yet they thundered in her mind like a death knell.

"Well, you look deep in thought."

She whirled around. "Tonio, I didn't hear you come in."

"I apologize for being so late. Would you believe, I forgot to set my alarm." He managed a grim smile. "The truth is, I didn't sleep very well last night."

"I know. Uh, that is, I know what you mean." She pushed back a stray wisp of hair. Had he guessed she was there at the cliff last night? "Neither did I. Sleep well, I mean."

"Then we'll have to make an early day of it and get our rest tonight."

"No argument from me."

He walked her to the office and they sat down at his desk. He reached for a stack of letters. "Let me go through some of this mail. Then we can buckle down and get some work done on the novel."

She turned on the computer. "You know, I think I forgot to back up yesterday's work." She scrolled down through several files, copying them to the flash drive, until she came to one she didn't recognize. "That's strange. This wasn't here yesterday."

Tonio set down his letters. "What wasn't there?"

"This file. 'Material for Ben.' "

"It's nothing. Just ignore it."

"But if it's for Ben, it must be important."

"I said ignore it, Ashley. I changed my mind. I'm not sending it."

"Why? Because you don't think it's good enough?"

"I didn't say that." His tone sharpened. "Just let it go, Ashley."

"I can't, Tonio. Ben has been wanting to see something for weeks." She clicked on the file. "Let me read it, and if I think it's good enough, I'm going to e-mail it to him."

"Don't!" Tonio reached over and seized her hand that held the mouse. "I don't want you reading that."

But her eyes were already scanning the words on the screen. "I don't understand." She scrolled down several pages, reading the all-to-familiar lines. Her stomach knotted. "These are the scenes I wrote. Why would you be sending them to Ben?"

Tonio's hand tightened on hers. He looked away. "I was feeling lousy last night. I knew Ben was getting impatient. I read over your scenes again. They could have been my words. They said exactly what I wanted to say."

"You were going to send my work to Ben?"

"I considered it, for all of a minute."

"You mean you were going to pass my scenes off as yours? That's plagiarism! How could you even think of such a thing?"

Tonio put his head in his hands. "I never would have done it, Ashley. But the fact that it even occurred to me scares me senseless. I was dead wrong. I was feeling so desperate that for a brief moment it seemed like a solution. I knew as soon as I copied the file that I was on a slippery slope. I wrote Ben a note at the end of the file. Scroll down and read it."

Ashley went to the end of the file and scanned the brief note.

Ben, I wish I could say I had written these scenes, but I didn't. Ashley wrote them. What would you think of letting her coauthor this book with me? Just a thought.

Tonio

She looked up at him. "I don't understand you, Tonio. First you consider plagiarizing my work. And now you want me to be your coauthor?"

"No. I realized that was a cop-out, too. That's why I didn't send the e-mail to Ben. I realized I have to do this myself, on my own, with God's help, of course, if He'll forgive me for almost yielding to a very serious temptation."

"He will, Tonio, if you're truly sorry."

"I am. I've always considered myself a man of honor. I pray God will help me to live up to those words. And I pray He'll help me work through this dry spell."

She touched his arm. "You're the real thing, a genuine novelist with his own voice and style and message. You don't need to hide behind anyone else's writing. Certainly not mine."

He sat forward and lowered his gaze, his jaw tightening. They fell into an uneasy silence. He massaged his knuckles, cracking one, then another.

He looked at her, his brows furrowing. "Have I lost your trust, Ashley?"

"Why would you say that?"

"I can see it in your eyes."

"I want to trust you. I need to trust you, Tonio. I could never work for someone I had doubts about."

"So you admit you have doubts?"

"No. You're twisting my words."

"Am I?"

"It's just that the truth is very important to me. If people aren't honest with each other, what do they have?" A thought came unbidden: *What about you, Ashley? Are you going to tell him you were on the cliff watching him last night at his wife's grave?* She pushed the thought away. "I do trust you, but the truth is, we still don't know each other very well. We both have a lot to learn."

He stood up and walked over to the windows, his back to her. "One thing you'll learn very quickly, Ashley. I'm a very private person. I don't share my feelings easily. Maybe that's why I write fiction. That's the only way I'm able to get my feelings out. I pour them into the lives of my characters and let them deal with the fallout."

She nodded. "I think all novelists do that to some extent. I know I do. I'm probably saying this badly, so forgive me, but. . ." She paused, searching for the right words. "The truth is, I don't see those emotions in your current book. Maybe that's why you're struggling with writer's block."

He pivoted and returned to his desk. "Okay, I've admitted I'm having a dry spell. But who says I'm struggling with writer's block?"

"Aren't you?"

He sat down and spread his elbows over the padded arms of his chair. "You've got me there. So you want the truth?" He handed her his notebook. "Look at the tripe I've produced over the past few weeks. It's all garbage, junk I would have thrown out if even a beginning student had turned it in to me."

She thumbed through the notebook for several minutes. "It's not bad, Tonio. A lot of research. Some well-developed plot points. But—okay, I'm being honest now—I don't see the heart of your story here. It's what I said before. You've got to let me into your main character's heart and head. Your reader has to feel he knows Philip Holt as well as he knows himself."

"What you're saying is, I've got to open an artery and let it bleed all over the page."

She nodded. "Something like that."

"Any suggestions?"

"Maybe. If you're willing to listen objectively and not argue with me until I'm finished."

A smile played at the corner of his mouth. "You're asking a lot, lady."

"There's a lot at stake."

"Agreed. So what are your ideas?"

She picked up a pencil and tapped it on the desk. "Give me a minute to gather my thoughts, okay?"

He stood up. "Take your time. I'll get us some fresh coffee."

When he returned with the coffee, she was already jotting down notes. She set down her pencil, accepted the cup, and sipped the hot liquid. *Lord, give me the right words,* she prayed silently.

She moved her chair closer to his and placed his notebook on the desk so they could both read it. "Look at your story line. You have Philip giving up his entire life to find and get revenge on his wife's murderer."

"Right. And I think it's a solid story."

"It is. We agree on that. But you're still holding Philip's feelings back from the reader. You've made Philip clever and strong, like an iron man, a Superman doing incredible feats of bravery."

"That's what my readers like."

"Of course they do. But I think they want more."

Tonio shrugged, as if to say, *What more do they want?*

She lifted her chin decisively. "They want to see Philip's soul."

He drummed his fingers on the desktop. "This isn't some melodramatic romance novel, with emotions dripping on every page."

She bristled. "There's nothing melodramatic about portraying a character's emotions, whether it's women's fiction or a mainstream novel like this."

"You're right. I'm sorry. I spoke out of turn."

"Apology accepted."

A hint of defiance edged Tonio's voice. "So tell me what Philip is missing, and I'll do my best to correct it."

Ashley hesitated. How could she separate Philip, the fictional character, from Tonio, the flesh-and-blood man? Neither was successful in expressing his grief. How could Tonio tap in to his character's pain when he was so desperately hiding his own?

Lord, I've got to say this carefully. I don't want to offend Tonio. I don't want him to feel I'm trespassing on his private life. Help me to keep this just about his book.

"Ashley, did you hear me? Tell me the problem as you see it."

She drew in a sharp breath. "Okay. Here goes. The problem is we don't feel Philip's anguish over losing his wife. Your readers have lost loved ones, too. They want to know what Philip is experiencing—the pain, the regrets, the struggles—and they want to know how he copes with his grief, and how his grief makes him stronger. You do a wonderful job of portraying the physical action of your story, but you ignore what Philip is going through on the inside. Do you see what I mean?"

Tonio rubbed his chin thoughtfully. "If you're suggesting I dump my private torments onto my readers, I must deny your request. They don't deserve that, and neither do I."

"That's not what I'm saying. I'm not suggesting you expose your personal life to your readers."

"Really? It sounds like that's exactly what you're saying."

Tears welled in her eyes. *Oh no, Lord, don't let me start crying like a silly schoolgirl!* "I'm just saying—I know you've been through a terrible loss—I know you don't want to talk about it. Maybe you think it's a sign of weakness to admit you're hurting—I don't know—I just know your novel will be stronger if you let yourself explore your feelings about your wife's death and if you bring those feelings to your characters. That's all I'm saying."

Tonio said nothing.

Before succumbing to a deluge of tears, she bolted out of the chair and hurried from Tonio's office, slamming the door behind her. She ran back to her cottage, threw herself on the bed, and let the tears flow. What was wrong with her, that her emotions were suddenly so ragged? Was she crying for Tonio, or for herself? Or both?

After a while, she got up and washed off the mascara from around her eyes. "Ashley Bancroft, you look like a raccoon," she muttered to her reflection. She went back to her room, sat down on the bed, and picked up her Bible. "Lord, I was so shaken that Tonio would even consider passing off my material as his. Thank You for delivering him from that evil. Help him to find the breakthrough he needs in his writing. I know he's hurting, and I don't know how to help him. In fact, I'm afraid I've really made a mess of things. He probably hates me now for poking my nose where it doesn't belong. I can't fight what he feels for his wife. I can't make his pain go away. Only You can do that."

After freshening her makeup, she went back to the main house. She dreaded facing Tonio after her unceremonious departure. But she had a job to do, no matter how embarrassed she felt.

It was lunchtime and Mika was serving coleslaw, fish sandwiches, and chips in the dining room. Ashley took her place at the table and placed her linen napkin on her lap. It was all she could do to meet Tonio's inquiring gaze. "I'm sorry," she mumbled. "I don't know why I ran out like that."

"No problem. The conversation was getting a little intense. We'll start fresh after lunch. I promise to keep things peaceful and pleasant."

"Me, too."

When they returned to the office, Tonio was carrying a plate of freshly baked macadamia nut cookies. "These will give us a much needed pick-me-up when the conversation gets too heavy," he said with a bemused wink. "No one can have a sour expression on their face when they're eating one of Mika's cookies."

Ashley sat down at the desk and folded her hands on her lap. "Well, just so you know, I plan to keep my opinions to myself from now on. I'm your employee. I have no right meddling in your personal life."

Tonio gave her shoulder a brief squeeze as he sat down beside her. "You had every right to speak up, Ashley. You're more than an employee. You're a friend. I've been alone for so long, I don't always say the right thing. When it comes to being sensitive to other people's feelings, I'm sometimes like a bull in a china shop. I feel like a jerk for making you run out of here in tears."

"You didn't. I don't know why I got so emotional. It's just that I care so much about, um, your book." She bit her lower lip. She had almost said, *You. I care so much about you!*

He grinned. "That's what I love about you, Ashley. You care about this cumbersome pile of manuscript pages almost as much as I do."

She met his gaze. "Yes, I do. So maybe it's time to get to work."

He put his hands on the keyboard. "I'm going to do what you suggested. I'm going to explore Philip's emotions about his wife."

"Wonderful! What can I do to help?"

"Continue your research on some of the topics I'll be covering. And remind me to come up for air every once in a while. This could get pretty deep."

She stifled a laugh. "Just let me know and I'll send out a rescue crew." She reached over and touched his wrist. "One more thing."

"Yes?" His blue eyes twinkled.

"When I write, I always pray first for God's guidance. He's the Author of all creativity and my partner in writing, so I want every word to be blessed by Him."

Tonio nodded. "Don't know why I didn't think of that. We ask God to bless our food. Why not our words?"

"Would you like to do the honors?" she asked.

"No, you go ahead. I have a feeling God really listens to your prayers."

"He hears yours, too."

Tonio turned his eyes to the keyboard. "I know He does. And I do pray. But the truth is, it's been a while since I felt really close to God."

Ashley swallowed hard. Tonio had just delivered a zinger with hardly the bat of an eye. She had considered him a devout man. Was he saying his faith was superficial? Was he just going through the motions? He was waiting for her to pray, so she bowed her head and said the appropriate words, but her mind was spinning with questions. *What is Tonio really like? Who is he in his heart of hearts? Every time I think I'm getting to know him, he does something to throw me off. Have I even begun to know the real man?*

Chapter 9

Tonio spent the next three days writing furiously. Ashley busied herself with research and answering fan mail, but the suspense was excruciating. What was Tonio writing? Had he really had a breakthrough? Was he digging deep into his own emotions to bring life to his characters? Whenever she hinted that she'd like to read his new material, Tonio simply smiled and said, "You'll see it when it's done."

On the afternoon of the third day, he handed her a sheaf of papers. "Here it is, Ashley. You can read the hard copy, or you can read it on the computer. If you're like me, you like real paper and ink."

She accepted the manuscript with a look of wonder. Would she find the real Tonio in these pages? Had he truly made himself vulnerable for the sake of his characters? "I'll read it, but you can't watch me."

He stood up. "Fine. I'll go pester Mika for some more of those macadamia nut cookies."

She chuckled. "We finished those two days ago."

"Don't worry. There are more where those came from." He strolled out of the office, leaving her alone to read.

She went over to the sofa and sat down, curling her legs up under her. She wanted to read leisurely and savor every word. Her eyes scanned the first page.

Philip Holt had always been a man in control—of his life, his emotions, his future. He prided himself in mastering his environment, in orchestrating his days, in manipulating the people around him. He never second-guessed himself. He knew what he wanted, and he knew what it took to achieve his goals. If a human being could be invincible, he was that man.

Until the day someone murdered the only woman he had ever loved. . . .

The night of her funeral he went to her closet and buried his face in her clothes. He breathed in the scent of her perfume. He fell asleep hugging her pillow, imagining that he still held her in his arms.

He discovered places within himself he had never known existed—pockets of pain so intense he was convinced he was having a heart attack. No one had ever told him a man could die of a broken heart, but now he knew it was so.

Ashley had to stop reading. Tears blurred her vision, and a lump had formed in her throat, so painful she couldn't swallow. She reached for a tissue, blew her nose, and blinked back the tears. Now, at last, she knew how Tonio felt about Brianna. He had finally confronted his grief. Now perhaps he could begin to heal.

She continued reading. Every page was as vivid and compelling as the one before. It was as if a dam had broken in Tonio's emotions. He was holding nothing back.

She didn't hear him return to the office until he set a plate of cookies on the end table beside the sofa. She jumped, startled, her hand flying to her chest. "Oh my goodness. You scared the life out of me!"

"I'm sorry. I didn't mean to disturb you."

"It's okay." She stood up and handed him the pages. "I was just so caught up in the story." She looked up at him, tears running down her cheeks. "It's incredible, Tonio. Your best writing ever. You made my heart ache for Philip. I love it—every word."

Tonio beamed. "You mean it? You're not just saying what I want to hear?"

"Would I do that?"

"Not for a minute."

"You've found your voice for this story," she went on, her excitement building. "It's no longer just a great suspense-adventure novel. It has the makings of a literary masterpiece. You'll win an award for this book, I'm sure of it."

He laughed. "You may be going a little overboard, but don't let me stop you."

"I'm serious. You've broken through that mental barrier. Your writing is so honest and vulnerable. So real."

"Thanks to you, my sweet little nag." Impulsively he gathered Ashley into his arms and swung her around, her feet flying in the air. "We did it, lady! You wouldn't let me get by with anything less."

When he set her down, her head was reeling and her knees weak. She realized he was still holding her in his arms, her head nestled against his chest. She could hear his heart pounding through his nylon shirt. After a moment, he tipped her chin up to his and kissed her soundly on the mouth. She returned the kiss, dazzled, the fragrance of his aftershave filling her nostrils. She had lived all her life for a moment like this. *Don't let me go, Tonio. Please. Never let me go!*

All too soon he released her and stumbled backward, bumping the desk. His face was flushed, his ebony hair cascading over his high forehead. "Wow! Talk about getting carried away." With the back of his hand he rubbed her lipstick from his mouth. "I'm sorry, Ashley. I didn't mean to do that. It was just such a wonderful relief to know you liked the writing."

"That's okay," she murmured, sinking down on the sofa. *Is that all it was to you? A kiss of gratitude? Don't you see that everything has changed between us?*

He sat down beside her and touched her face, tucking a strand of hair behind her ear. "I hope this won't change anything between us, Ashley." His clear blue eyes looked so earnest, so contrite. "I know I was out of line. It won't happen again. Please don't think less of me."

"I don't. I wouldn't." She blinked to keep back her tears.

"I can see you're upset. If it's any consolation, I'm as surprised as you are. I honestly didn't see that kiss coming." He raked his fingers through his tousled hair. "It was just one of those things. We've both been under a lot of pressure lately."

She nodded, afraid to speak lest she start to bawl. For a brilliant author, he sure could be a blockhead at times.

"Tell you what, Ashley." He gently stroked her cheek. "Let's quit work for today. What do you want to do? Go out to dinner? Or we could go over to the hotel in Keauhou and watch the manta rays. At night the locals watch them swim in the ocean under the bright lights beamed from the hotel."

She sniffed. "Why don't we save that for another time."

"Okay." His enthusiasm faded. "Do you just want to go back to your room and catch some shut-eye?"

She shook her head, still holding her tears in check.

"Then how about a swim in the pool? You do like to swim, don't you?"

She nodded, biting her lower lip.

"Great. Go change and meet me in the pool in ten minutes."

She nearly sprinted from the room. She couldn't wait to get back to her little cottage where she could release her pent-up emotions and let the dam break on her tears. She wept not only because the kiss had meant nothing to Tonio, but also because it had meant everything to her. She was falling in love with a man she could never have. How could this be happening to her so soon after her breakup with Ben? What was wrong with her that she could be in love with two men at once?

She vented to God as she washed her face. "Lord, I must be a terrible person to be so shallow, so fickle. No wonder You took Ben from me. You knew I didn't deserve him. Is this what it's like to be on the rebound? If so, I hate it. My emotions are all over the place. Do You want me to leave Hawaii and go home? But then I'll have to face Ben again. Lord, help me. I'm so confused."

She put her hair in a ponytail, then changed into her bathing suit.

By the time she got out to the pool, Tonio was already swimming. "Come on in," he called. "The water feels great."

She considered jumping off the diving board, then decided to slip in on the shallow end. The water was perfect—warm and refreshing, sparkling with diamonds of sunlight. Ignoring Tonio, she swam several laps. She would show him she wasn't fazed by his kiss. Finally, she stopped and treaded water, catching her breath.

Tonio swam over beside her. "You swim like a pro. I didn't know you could swim like that."

"You never asked. I was on the swim team in college."

"Care to race, say, ten laps?"

"Why not?"

He gave her a playful grin. "How about a movie on cable tonight? Winner picks the movie, loser makes popcorn."

"You're on!"

They swam to the deep end of the pool, Tonio gave the signal, and they both kicked off, swimming side by side. By the sixth lap she was ahead, but by the tenth, he had passed her by half a length. "I won," he declared, grabbing the edge of the pool. "You make the popcorn."

Catching up with him, she slammed her palm against the water, drenching him. He shook the water off and sent a shower back in her direction. She coughed as water went up her nose.

"This is war!" she rasped. She lunged forward, placed both hands on top of Tonio's head, and pushed him under the water. He came back up with a *whoosh*, grabbed her around the waist, and plunged back down, taking her with him. Holding her breath, she kicked and flailed until he released her. They both popped up out of the water, laughing and sputtering.

"You're a worthy opponent," he gasped.

"And don't—you—forget it." She choked out the words.

Tonio climbed out of the pool, then helped her out. They both collapsed on the grass, trying to catch their breath. He looked over at her. "I feel like a kid again."

She laughed. "I hope Mika and Harry weren't watching. They'll think we're crazy."

"So what? It was fun."

Her gaze lingered on his handsome, sun-bronzed face. "Yes, it was fun." She hadn't expected Tonio to be so playful and funny.

He scrambled to his feet and pulled her up. "We'll just have time to shower and change for dinner. I'll meet you in the dining room in half an hour."

"Make it an hour and I'll be there."

The evening turned out more pleasant than she had expected—a delicious dinner of salmon and sweet potatoes, then on to the great room for a movie of Tonio's choosing—a slapstick comedy—and brimming bowls of buttered popcorn. Tonio sat at one end of the sofa, she at the other. If any awkwardness remained over their afternoon kiss, neither of them admitted it.

When the movie was over Tonio walked her back to her cottage and playfully nudged her chin as he said good night. His mood was lighter than she had ever seen it. "Ashley, this has been one of the best days I can remember."

She couldn't quite muster up the same enthusiasm. "I'll never forget it either, Tonio."

"And you've forgiven me my faux pas?"

"There's nothing to forgive." *What I can't forgive is that the kiss meant nothing to you!*

"Good night then. Sleep tight. Don't let the bedbugs bite." He chuckled. "My mother used to say that to me every night. Not a very pleasant saying, now that I think of it."

She laughed in spite of herself. "My mom always had me recite the prayer asking God to take my soul if I died before I woke. You wouldn't believe how many times I lay awake worrying that I would die before morning."

"And then there are all the nursery rhymes with all the terrible hidden meanings that would scare kids out of their wits. But it's late, so I guess we'd better save them for another time."

She nodded. "Yes, another time. Good night, Tonio."

"Good night, Ashley. See you in the morning."

Tonio may have achieved a breakthrough in his writing, but if Ashley assumed they had made a breakthrough in their relationship, she quickly realized how wrong she was. If anything, Tonio seemed more remote than ever. He spent the next two days writing while she edited his material. It was all work and no play. On Saturday he drove her to Waimea, where they had lunch and visited the Kamuela Museum. On Sunday they went to church, walked along the seawall, and had dinner at a quaint little bistro on the beach.

But for all their time together, their conversations seemed flat, superficial. It was a letdown after the excitement they had shared the previous week over his writing. Was he deliberately pushing her away? If so, why? Did he no longer need her now that his writing was on track? Was he so much a loner that another person in his life threatened his well-being? The questions kept piling up, but the answers remained elusive.

On Monday night Tonio left the house for another mysterious meeting. He was gone again on Tuesday night without a word of explanation. *He must be seeing someone,* Ashley told herself as she sat alone in her little cottage. *Otherwise, he would tell me where he's going. There would be no reason to keep it secret.*

And yet, Tonio didn't act like a man in love with some mystery woman. His mood was often solemn, even morose, as if he were mulling over weighty issues or struggling with some private torment.

I thought his bad mood stemmed from his writing problems, Ashley mused as she climbed into bed late Tuesday night. *But his writing is going well now. Why is Tonio still so glum?*

A thought came to her: *It's Brianna, his dead wife. She haunts this place. She haunts his mind. She won't leave him alone.*

"That's crazy," Ashley said aloud as she rolled over and fluffed her pillow. "I don't believe in ghosts. At least, not the kind that come back from the dead to haunt people. But the *memories* of Brianna—that's what could be haunting

Tonio. What terrible thing happened in their relationship causing him such torment?"

Ashley fell asleep pondering those questions. Sometime in the night she awoke. Had she heard a gate creaking by the pool? She lay still, listening, her eyes scouring the darkness. A cool breeze wafted through the open windows. She climbed out of bed and looked out toward the pool.

A shadowed figure was walking past the gazebo, heading toward the woods. There was no question this time. It was Tonio!

Ashley pulled on a shirt, sandals, and cutoff jeans, grabbed a small flashlight, and slipped out of the cottage. She followed Tonio at a safe distance, padding cautiously through the thick underbrush. When she reached the clearing beside the cliff, she positioned herself near Brianna's memorial site, turned off her light, and hid behind a sturdy palm.

Tonio was already there, standing, head bowed, facing the sculpted angel. He knelt down on one knee on the manicured grass, put his head in his hands, and remained like that for several minutes. Ashley heard him speak in a low, agonized voice, hardly more than a whisper. Was he speaking to Brianna? Praying? Ashley listened intently, but the only words she heard were, "Forgive me, Brianna. God forgive me!"

Forgive you for what? Ashley wondered. *What did you do that you so desperately need her forgiveness? And God's!*

A twig snapped under Ashley's sandal.

Tonio jumped to his feet and looked around. "Who's there?"

Ashley pressed her spine against the tree trunk and held her breath.

"Someone's there," Tonio insisted. "Who is it?"

Ashley's heart thundered in her chest—surely Tonio could hear it—but she remained stone-still. She watched through the thicket as Tonio stepped back and looked around. Her heart lurched. He was too close to the edge of the cliff. Another backward step and he would tumble a thousand feet to his death.

An anguished cry erupted from her throat. "Tonio, watch out!"

He turned abruptly, his foot sliding on the uneven slate, sending a spray of loose stones ricocheting into the black ocean below. He caught himself at the very edge and regained his footing.

"Ashley? Is that you?"

She stepped out of the shadows into the faint wedge of moonlight. "Yes."

He strode over and seized her wrist. "What are you doing here?"

She was trembling. "I know I shouldn't have come. I—I was afraid for you."

"You had no business coming here."

"I'm sorry."

Pushing his way through the brambles, Tonio led her through the murky woods back to the cottage, pulling her along as if she were a child requiring discipline. Ashley had never seen him so filled with rage.

When they reached her door, he released her and stared her down. "How dare you intrude on my privacy that way? I trusted you. You could have got us both killed out there tonight."

She was sobbing now. "I—I just wanted to help."

"Then don't sneak around scaring me out of my wits."

"I won't, Tonio. Never again."

"I'll hold you to that promise." As his wrath dissipated, his voice softened. "It's late. Go back to bed. Get some sleep." He rubbed the back of his neck, then turned on his heel and stalked off toward the main house.

Chapter 10

First thing the next morning Ashley started packing. She had had enough of Anthony Adler, with his mood swings and mysterious ways. And his behavior last night had proved he was more than finished with her.

"So let it be," she told herself stoically as she stuffed shirts and jeans into her suitcase. She had accomplished what she came here to do. Now it was time to move on.

She wasn't sure where she would go, but God would show her the way. Maybe she would look for a job at another publishing house. Ben would give her a good recommendation. Maybe Tonio would, too, once he got over his anger. She still shuddered when she thought of how furious he was with her on the cliff last night. How could she have been so foolish as to follow him like that? And so reckless? It must have been all those old Nancy Drew mysteries she had devoured as a teenager.

But this was real life, not some storybook whodunit. Instead of solving a mystery, she had angered and disappointed a man she deeply admired. There was only one thing to do—leave!

When she had finished packing, she walked over to the main house for breakfast. She dreaded facing Tonio, but it had to be done. She wasn't going to be spineless and leave without a proper good-bye, although the thought had crossed her mind.

Tonio was already at the table, reading the paper and drinking his coffee. Seeing her, Mika flashed her usual smile. "Good morning, Miss Ashley."

"Good morning, Mika."

Ashley sat down across from Tonio. He put down his newspaper and gave her a look she couldn't quite read—a smile on the surface but conflicted emotions underneath. "Hello, Ashley."

"Tonio." She couldn't summon any other words.

Mika poured her a cup of coffee, then brought out two plates of steaming buckwheat pancakes drenched in maple syrup.

"I can't eat all of these, Mika."

"Yes, you can, Miss Ashley. You need meat on your bones."

"I'm really not that hungry."

In a slightly brittle voice, Tonio urged, "Humor her, Ashley."

"I'll eat what I can, Tonio." He was making her feel like a scolded child. "Thank you for a wonderful breakfast, Mika."

"Don't thank me. Thank the good Lord."

"I was just about to," said Tonio. He bowed his head and murmured a prayer. Ashley could tell his heart wasn't quite in it. Then he attacked his stack of hotcakes without a glance her way.

She took a few bites then set down her fork. She wasn't hungry. No use pretending she was. She cleared her throat. *Might as well get this over with now.* "Tonio, I—I have something to tell you."

He stopped sipping his coffee. "What is it?"

Her heart hammered. "I'll be leaving today."

"Leaving?" His cup clattered on its saucer. He stared at her as if he hadn't heard her clearly. "Going where?"

"Back to New York." Her words tumbled out in a rush. "I called the airlines. I might be able to get a standby flight out today. If not, I'll get a hotel room until a flight is available."

He shoved his plate away. She winced at the shock and outrage on his face. It wasn't supposed to go like this. She had expected him to be glad she was going.

"Why on earth are you leaving? Our work isn't done. You haven't given me any notice."

Her lower lip trembled. Why was he making this so hard for her? Why couldn't he just let her go in peace? "Tonio, you know why I'm going."

"Because of last night?"

She lowered her gaze. "Yes. You made it clear I'm no longer welcome here."

"I did no such thing." He slammed his fist on the table, shaking the china dishes. "Okay, so I got mad. I never dreamed you'd follow me out there to the cliff. I didn't even know you knew about that spot."

"I was wrong to follow you. I'm sorry."

He sat back and drew in a deep breath. "Fine. I accept your apology. Now let's just forget the whole thing."

"I can't."

"What do you mean, you can't?"

"I mean, I can't live like this, never knowing whether you're going to be in a good mood or a bad one. I just went through a painful breakup with Ben. I need some peace and stability in my life. I thought I could find it here, but I was wrong."

Tonio's expression softened. "No, Ashley, you weren't wrong. This is exactly where you should be. I was upset last night, but I shouldn't have taken it out on you."

"It's not just last night," she said, struggling for words. "I don't understand you—your mood swings, your aloofness. I never know whether you're going to be friendly or distant. You don't let anyone get close to you."

His brow furrowed. "I didn't realize I had made life so miserable for you."

"You haven't. I've loved working for you. It's just—"

"Just what?"

"I just think it's time for me to go."

"Think it over, and in a few days, if you still feel the same way. . ."

"I'm already packed," she mumbled, fighting back tears.

His voice thickened. "Then go unpack. You're not getting away that easily. You can't just walk out on me because I lost my temper."

"I think it would be best." She sounded so lame. She had rehearsed an entire speech in her mind, but it was gone now.

Tonio reached across the table for her hand. "Finish breakfast. Then we'll talk, okay?"

She withdrew her hand and picked without interest at her food.

When they had finished eating, he said, "Listen, Ashley, I'll make a deal with you. Promise you'll stay until I've finished writing my novel. Then if you still want to leave, I won't say a word."

She lifted her chin decisively. "Just the first draft."

"Final draft. Please."

"First draft. That's all I can promise for now."

Tonio's blue eyes blazed. "Then I guess there's nothing more to say." He pushed back his chair, stood up, crumpled his napkin, and tossed it on his plate. "Mika, I'm going to run some errands in town. Don't wait on me for lunch."

"Yes, Mr. Adler. You have a good day, sir."

He glanced down at Ashley. "I don't suppose you want to go with me."

"No, thank you. I—I have some research to do."

"And some unpacking?"

"That, too."

Even after Tonio strode out the door, a chill remained in the air. As Mika cleared the table, Ashley finished her coffee and nursed her hurt feelings. Would she ever feel close to Tonio again, or would there always be this feeling of unease between them?

"Miss Ashley, don't pay Mr. Adler no mind," said Mika as she refilled her coffee cup. "He don't mean to be so gruff. He's a broken man. You're the first to make him smile again."

Ashley nodded. "I know he's still mourning his wife's death. I wish I knew how to help him."

"He don't let nobody help him." Mika carried the sugar bowl and salt and pepper shakers to the kitchen.

"How did she die?" asked Ashley. It was the question she had never dared ask Tonio.

Mika returned to the table for the cups and saucers. "You talking about Mrs. Adler?"

"Yes. Did she have an illness? Cancer?"

Mika stopped and gave Ashley a curious glance. For a moment, Ashley thought Mika wasn't going to answer. Finally she solemnly replied, "Mrs. Adler was never sick a day in her life. She died in a car crash."

Ashley looked up, startled. "Oh? I hadn't realized it was an accident. I just assumed. . ." She let her voice trail off.

"Mr. Adler never forgave himself," said Mika in a hushed voice. "He never mentions her name."

"Was she alone, Mika? Alone in the car?"

"No. Mr. Adler was with her. He lived. She died."

"Where did it happen?"

"Not far away. A mile maybe. On the winding road near here."

"You mean the road that winds along the cliffs to this house?"

Mika nodded. "The car went over the cliff into the water. Mrs. Adler drowned."

An icy shiver shot through Ashley as she pictured Tonio standing at the edge of the precipice, near Brianna's memorial, staring down into the turbulent sea below. *No wonder he's so obsessed with the ocean surging a thousand feet below him. It claimed the love of his life!*

Ashley got up from the table. "Thanks for everything, Mika. I'm going to the office to do some research."

"Miss Ashley?"

"Yes, Mika?"

"Please don't leave Mr. Adler. He needs you. Don't go."

"I won't, Mika. At least, not right away."

On her way to the office, Ashley paused by Brianna's portrait. The face and eyes were more haunting now than ever, bespeaking a tragedy Ashley couldn't even imagine. What secrets were locked behind the unseeing eyes of that painting? Why had Tonio never mentioned how his wife died? What else was he hiding behind his handsome, mysterious, ironclad veneer?

It's time to do some sleuthing of my own. I've got to know more. I can't let this go until I know exactly what happened.

Ashley opened her laptop on Tonio's desk, logged on to the Internet, and began browsing several search engines. *I don't know why I never thought of this before. There should be dozens of articles about Tonio online. What was the date of death on Brianna's memorial angel? September something. Yes, that's it—September 17, 2003.*

Ashley found countless articles on Tonio and his books, but they covered little of his personal life. Clearly he was a private man who knew how to keep himself out of the limelight. Ashley tried another tactic. She typed in "Brianna Adler, wife of Anthony Adler," and several tabloid articles appeared. The headline of one screamed out at Ashley: FAMED AUTHOR'S WIFE DIES IN CAR CRASH.

Ashley quickly scanned the article. The details were horrifying. The couple was on their way home from a party given to celebrate the release of a movie based on one of Tonio's books. The car swerved off a mountain cliff near their home and plunged into the ocean. Tonio was able to get out of the car and swim free. By the time he returned to rescue his wife, she had perished.

Ashley's gaze lingered on the last paragraph.

> *Authorities refuse comment until they have finished investigating the accident. Questions remain as to who was driving the vehicle. Mr. Adler, who, according to test results, had been drinking heavily, could be held on a manslaughter charge if it is proved he was behind the wheel. Some who witnessed the couple arguing heatedly at the party speculate that the crash may not have been an accident after all.*

Ashley shuddered, her thoughts reeling. Everything she had ever known about Anthony Adler was suddenly suspect. Who was this man she had imagined she loved? A drunkard? She had never seen him drink a drop of alcohol. A murderer? Inconceivable! And yet the words blazed in black and white on her computer screen. A drunken Anthony Adler had apparently caused his wife's death!

Ashley desperately scanned other articles, praying they would exonerate him. But they all suggested the same thing—Tonio was likely driving the fated vehicle when it made its death-plunge into the churning Pacific. But because it couldn't be proved, charges were never filed.

Ashley sat back, stunned. She couldn't take it all in, couldn't wrap her mind around the malevolent portrait the articles painted. How had she not seen this dark side of him? Or had she been too blinded by love to see the truth? Was Tonio really the monster the tabloids presented?

Ashley closed her laptop with trembling fingers. *I've got to get out of here. I can't stay another night. I can't look Tonio in the eyes again. He'll see the horror in my face. He'll know I know what he did.*

She stood up. *What to do now? I'm already packed. I'll leave before Tonio gets home. I'll phone for a taxi. Yes, that's it, a taxi.*

She reached for the phone, but it rang before she could dial. She jumped, startled, then answered with a tentative, "Hello."

The voice that replied was both foreign and familiar. "Ashley? Is that you? This is Ben."

Her mind was moving in slow motion. "Ben?"

"Yes, I'm calling for Tonio. Is he there?"

"No. He—he went into town. He'll be back after lunch."

"Okay, fine. Will you give him a message for me?"

She sat back down and reached for a pad of paper. "Yes, Ben, what is it?"

"Tell him I loved the last chapters. They're the best he's ever done."

"I'll tell him." Her mind was spinning away somewhere in space. She couldn't focus on Ben's words. When he said, "I'll see you tomorrow," she was sure she had misunderstood.

"Did you hear me, Ashley?"

"No, I'm sorry, Ben. It sounded like you said you would see me."

"Yes. Tomorrow. I'm flying to Kona in the morning."

"You're coming here? Why?"

"I have some business to discuss with Tonio, and I think it's time we conferred in person about his book. I like the direction he's taking, but I have some ideas to make it stronger." He paused for a long moment, then said in a voice she couldn't quite read, "And since I have some vacation time coming, I thought I'd combine business and pleasure. I look forward to seeing you again, Ashley."

She tried to reply, but panic tightened in her throat.

"Ashley? Are you still there?"

"Yes," she managed. "I'm here. But not for long. I'm leaving Kona. Today."

"Leaving? Why?"

"Please, Ben, don't ask. It's too complicated to explain."

"You can't leave yet," he admonished. "You've become vital to this project. Stay at least through my visit. It'll be a few days at most. Then we can fly home together."

She was too emotionally spent to argue. "All right. I'll stay. Do you want Tonio to pick you up at the airport?"

"No need. I'll take a taxi. I should be there late tomorrow afternoon."

After hanging up the phone, Ashley left a note for Tonio, then went to the kitchen where Mika was polishing the silver. Ashley told her to expect an extra houseguest, then announced that she had a headache and was going back to the cottage to rest. "Tell Tonio I'm skipping dinner. I'm not feeling well."

"I'll tell him, Miss Ashley. Later I'll bring you some tea and toast. You get some rest now. You look white as a ghost."

Ashley smiled grimly. "I've definitely had better days, Mika."

As she tramped back to the cottage, Ashley mused that she would be spending the next few days with two men she loved—one had broken her heart, and the other was living a lie. How on earth was she going to keep her sanity intact?

Chapter 11

I'll be seeing Ben again. . .seeing Ben again. Ashley woke the next morning with that refrain playing in her mind. It had been over three months since their fateful wedding day. Three months since their painful breakup on the beach. *How will I feel, seeing him again? How will he feel about me?*

She didn't want to admit that she was looking forward to seeing her ex-fiancé. Since their breakup, she had struggled to shut the door on her memories of Ben. She had locked her grief away in a little room in her heart—a spot she refused to visit these days lest the pain rush back and overwhelm her. But now she would have to confront those feelings. The idea terrified and tantalized her at the same time. *What's wrong with you, girl?* she chided herself as she scoured her closet for her most flattering outfit. *Get yourself together. Ben's out of your life for good. Why are you trying to impress him?*

"I don't know," she said aloud. "I just am. So there!"

She tried on a tropical-print slip dress and decided it was too dressy. She pulled on a cotton jersey shirt and white jeans and decided they were too casual. She finally settled on a blue tie-shoulder top and white cotton gauze skirt. Blue was Ben's favorite color.

Ashley skipped breakfast so she wouldn't have to face Tonio. By the time she arrived at the main house, he was already busy preparing for Ben's arrival. She cleared Tonio's desktop and organized the latest draft of his novel, hoping he wouldn't notice she was avoiding him. As much as she wanted him to explain his part in his wife's death, she knew she couldn't handle a confrontation with Tonio when she was about to see Ben again.

Late that afternoon she found herself watching out the window for Ben's taxi. Tonio noticed and said, "If his plane was delayed it could be another hour yet."

"I wasn't watching for him," she said quickly, as if she needed to explain herself.

"He'll probably call on his cell when he lands."

She played with the tie on her shoulder strap. "Right. I hadn't thought of that."

Tonio gave her a look she couldn't quite decipher—concern, irritation, jealousy? "Is this going to be hard on you, having him here?"

She looked away. "No, why should it?"

"You were about to marry the guy—until he made the biggest blunder of his life and walked away."

"That's over. In the past. I'll be fine. It's certainly not your problem."

His expression hardened. "You're right. It's not my problem. But we have a lot of work to do, and the last thing I need is a distracted assistant."

She bristled. "Have I ever allowed my personal life to interfere with my work?"

He backed down, his blue eyes warming with unmistakable affection. "I apologize, Ashley. You've done an extraordinary job. I don't know what I would have done without you."

"Thank you, Tonio." Her indignation evaporated, leaving her feeling suddenly vulnerable to his charms. She looked back out the window. "I think I see him. A taxi—coming up the drive."

A minute later she was opening the door to Ben, greeting him as if it were the most natural thing in the world. In his gray pinstripe suit he looked taller than she remembered. His short blond hair was stylishly tousled and his hazel eyes twinkled behind his trendy wire-rim glasses.

"Ashley, you look beautiful!" He embraced her with greater vigor than she anticipated. For an instant she felt as if she had never left his arms. But almost as quickly, the pain over their broken romance flooded back. "You look great, too, Ben," she said, gently extricating herself from his grasp.

Stepping between them, Tonio gripped Ben's hand and gave him a comradely slap on the back. "Welcome, ol' man. Great to see you again. How was your flight?"

Ben chuckled. "I suppose any flight you walk away from is a good one. But I'm not crazy about all those long hours over the ocean."

"We're a long way from the mainland. Well, I hope you're hungry. Mika is putting on a feast tonight."

"Are you kidding? After all those cold meals at the local delicatessen, I'm always ready for Mika's home cooking."

Tonio stepped out on the porch and gathered up Ben's suitcase, laptop, and briefcase. "I've got your luggage. Let's get you settled in your room."

Ben reached for the suitcase. "Thanks, Tonio. I'll take it."

"No trouble, Ben. I've got it. I'll take it upstairs. Then you can get yourself out of that monkey suit and into some Hawaiian duds. One thing we like around here is comfort. Right, Ashley?"

"Right. If you didn't bring your aloha shirt, Tonio has plenty."

"A whole closet full, if I remember right," said Ben.

"Anything to keep from being strangled by a dress shirt and tie," said Tonio.

As the two men strode on down the hall, laughing and making small talk, Ashley sensed a friendly, unspoken rivalry between them. She couldn't help wondering: Was it because of her?

Dinner that evening was bizarre, surreal. Ashley felt a little like Alice in

Wonderland at the Mad Hatter's tea party. Sitting at the same table with the two men she cared so much about, she felt somehow on trial, her every word and action scrutinized. Most curious of all, she had the distinct impression that both men were vying for her attention like capricious schoolboys. She had never heard them tell so many jokes or share so many stories, each seemingly trying to outdo the other.

"Ben, do you remember that offbeat awards show?" said Tonio. "I can't even remember the name of it now—where they gave me that gold-plated statuette that must have weighed fifty pounds?"

Ben nodded. "And after the show we went to that little diner off Fifth Avenue and you left the award sitting in the booth."

"Right. And the waitress—"

"Thought it was a tip."

Tonio chuckled. "She was downright indignant when I asked for it back. Can you believe that, Ashley?"

She looked up from her plate. "I'm sorry. My mind wandered. What did you say?"

"Never mind," said Tonio with a wry smile. "You had to be there."

Ben leaned over and patted her hand. "Are you feeling all right, Ashley? You're so quiet tonight. And you look a little pale."

She set her napkin on the table. "The truth is, I have a headache. Would you two mind if I excused myself and went back to the cottage?"

Tonio pushed his chair back. "We should all make an early evening of it. Ben, you're still on New York time. It's six hours later there."

"Don't remind me."

"Then let's all call it a night," said Tonio. "We'll have an early breakfast and a full schedule tomorrow."

Ashley jumped up, almost toppling her chair. "Good night, then, Ben, Tonio. I'll see you both in the morning." Before either of them could reply, she turned on her heel and hurried from the room. Perhaps she was foolish to run off like that, but how could she go on pretending everything was normal, when one man had rejected her and the other was hiding a deadly secret?

The next day Ashley focused on the work at hand with such diligence that she managed to keep her mind off her personal life. Both Tonio and Ben congratulated her on her sharp editorial skills and extraordinary intuition.

"Ashley, you're a gem," said Tonio approvingly. "You have an innate sense about these characters. It's as if you had created them yourself."

Ben agreed. "I tell you, Tonio, she has a knack for pinpointing exactly what's wrong with a plotline or reworking a character who's false or inconsistent. She's transformed every book she's edited. Do you see why I hated to lose her?"

An uneasy silence settled over them. Ashley wanted to cry out, *If you hated to lose me, Ben, why did you break up with me?*

Ben cleared his throat. "Like I said, Ashley was a hard assistant to lose. Her replacement doesn't have half the talent she has."

"And now you know why I don't want to let her go," said Tonio. "She's challenged me in ways I never expected—creatively, I mean."

"Hello already. You don't have to talk about me in the third person," said Ashley dryly. "I'm still here in the room."

They both laughed, prompting a reluctant chuckle from her.

Over the next few days they worked exhaustively on Tonio's novel, debating plot points, polishing scenes, and tightening the writing. Ashley could see that Ben was more than pleased with the results.

"Well, our marathon editing session has proved amazingly fruitful." He patted the stack of manuscript pages on the desk. "Tonio, this book is your best by far. The way you've explored the emotional lives of your characters and revealed their vulnerabilities is superb. I think it's time we discuss a sequel, maybe several sequels."

Tonio raked his fingers through his tousled hair. "Let's get this one into galleys first, Ben."

"I know you'll need some breathing room. But I'm ready to talk contracts with your agent. I think you'll find the terms impressive. More to the point, presales are looking good, so Haricott is ready to put some solid backing behind this novel. Talk shows, book tours, print and TV ads, reviews in the top newspapers and magazines."

Tonio rubbed his jaw thoughtfully. "Sounds good."

"That's only the half of it," said Ben. "I don't know if your agent has notified you yet, but based on the synopsis he distributed to several major Hollywood producers, at least three are ready to bid on the movie rights. Think of it, Tonio. Another motion picture deal."

Tonio's countenance darkened. "I don't know, Ben. I'm not sure I can handle a production company messing with my work again. You know how bad it was last time."

"You can't judge everything by that experience, Tonio. You need this. Your career needs it."

"Why don't we take a break? I'm famished," said Ashley, sensing Tonio's unease. "Then we can talk again after dinner."

"Good idea," said Ben, his eyes brightening. "Let's celebrate. Tonio, you pick your favorite restaurant in Kona, and we'll make an evening of it. My treat. No work, all play."

"Now that's a deal I can't refuse," said Ashley, looking to Tonio for his response.

He nodded. "Guess I'd better make it unanimous."

"If you know what's good for you," said Ben with a grin.

"Is this party formal or come as you are?" asked Ashley.

"Your call," said Tonio. "Do you want to walk on the beach with the sand between your toes or strut around in your three-inch heels and dressiest dress?"

Usually Ashley would have opted for the beach, but tonight she heard herself reply, "Let's go dressy."

"Then I know just the place," said Tonio. "We'll drive up the coast to Waikoloa, to one of the largest, fanciest oceanfront resorts on the Big Island. Sixty acres of paradise. They have a variety of restaurants, but my favorite has Italian cuisine."

"Naturally, you'd love it," said Ashley. "You're Italian."

"You'll love it, too. It's a fantastic place."

Ashley sprang to her feet. "Then what are we waiting for?"

An hour later they met in Tonio's marble entryway and gazed at one another with approving smiles.

"Hey, we clean up pretty good," said Ben. He was wearing a black suit with a lavender shirt and paisley tie.

Tonio had on black trousers, a white dinner jacket, and black bow tie. "But when it comes to looking fine," he noted, "Ashley wins, hands down."

"No question about it," said Ben. "You look gorgeous, Ashley."

"Thank you, gentlemen." She did a spontaneous little pirouette in her powder blue empire-waist gown and stiletto heels.

"So let's get this show on the road," said Tonio, stepping in front of Ben to escort Ashley out the door. "We have reservations for eight o'clock sharp."

From the moment they stepped into the dazzling resort at Waikoloa, Ashley knew the evening was going to be magical. To her surprise, her earlier uneasiness around Tonio and Ben was gone. She felt happy, relaxed, simply enjoying the company of two men she cared about and who obviously cared about her. Nothing heavy or complicated. Just three good friends enjoying one another's company.

They walked through the enormous lobby with its rows of huge potted palms and a centerpiece of dolphin sculptures. They watched bullet-shaped Swiss trams whiz by and stood on a bridge over a winding waterway watching canal boats take guests from one end of the resort to the other. They scaled the grand staircase and gazed down at the sprawling lagoon with its crystal pools, sparkling waterfalls, and tropical gardens. Beyond the white sand beach, a blue-velvet ocean cut a swath across an azure, star-studded sky.

"I'm on top of the world!" Ashley exclaimed, spreading her arms.

And as she descended the wide marble stairs with her handsome escorts, one on each arm, she felt like Cinderella at the ball. *I don't care if I go back to rags and cinders tomorrow; I'm going to have the time of my life tonight!*

They were seated at a linen-draped table on the lanai along the waterway; a bouquet of tropical flowers graced the table; a guitarist strummed romantic melodies nearby.

"This place is amazing," said Ashley as the waiter placed her linen napkin on her lap. "A little taste of heaven on earth."

"Wait 'til you taste the food," said Tonio, opening his menu.

Ashley ordered the fried calamari with saffron pepper sauce; Ben selected the veal scallopini with sautéed mushrooms in asparagus cream sauce; and Tonio decided on the cannelloni stuffed with veal, spinach, and ricotta cheese.

After a leisurely dinner with spumoni ice cream for dessert, they browsed the quaint shops. But the guys seemed bored, so she suggested a walk along the lagoon. Before leaving the shop, Tonio bought her a shell necklace and Ben, not wanting to be outdone, bought her a stuffed dolphin. Hugging her treasures to her chest, Ashley thanked them both. "You two are making me feel like a pampered child."

"Just a small token of our appreciation," said Tonio with a wink.

"If I'd known a stuffed dolphin would make you happy, I'd have bought you one a long time ago," said Ben.

She grinned impishly. "No, it'll take more than that."

Tonio nudged Ben. "Guess she put you in your place. Last of the big-time spenders."

"You think you scored points with your little string of seashells?" countered Ben. "They're a dime a dozen."

Ashley broke in. "Stop it, you guys. I love my gifts. They'll always remind me of tonight and your good company."

"See, Tonio?" said Ben. "She likes our company."

"What choice does she have? She's stuck with us for the evening."

She wove her arms through theirs. "There's nowhere I'd rather be than right here with the two of you. We've just finished a huge project—a literary masterpiece, no less—so we have every right to celebrate."

"Well put," said Ben.

They walked in step, arms linked. "If we keep this up, they'll call us the Three Musketeers," said Tonio.

Ben chuckled. "Did you say, Mouseketeers?"

"You've been watching too much kiddie TV," said Tonio.

"You guys are spoiling the mood," said Ashley. "Let's just walk around quietly and enjoy the scenery."

"You hear that, Tonio?" said Ben. "You're spoiling the mood."

"Not me. It's you."

"It's both of you," said Ashley. "No one would guess one of you is a temperamental author and the other a stuffy editor."

"Stuffy, am I?" Ben shot back.

"I don't have a temperamental bone in my body," declared Tonio.

"Okay, okay. You're both paragons of virtue. Now can we just go watch the dolphins?"

For the next hour they strolled around the lagoon, watching the dolphins and listening to the rhythmic, rushing roar of the waves. Dozens of towering palm trees were silhouetted against the sky, and tiki torches lighted the pathway. Wide hammocks were strung between trees on the grassy area by the beach with white sand pits beneath them.

"Look! I love these!" Ashley sat down tentatively on one of the hammocks and kicked off her shoes. She put her feet up and lay back. "Okay, you guys, I've found my perfect spot."

Tonio gave the hammock a push. It rocked gently from side to side. "Looks good to me. What do you think, Ben?"

"Looks perfect. Let's try it."

Tonio climbed in on one side and Ben on the other.

"What are you guys doing?" cried Ashley. "Get your own hammock."

"We like this one," said Ben. They both lay back, sandwiching Ashley in the middle. They rocked the hammock, making it sway.

"This is crazy," Ashley protested. "We're like sardines. I can't breathe."

Tonio shifted his weight, making the hammock swing harder, faster. Ashley started to laugh. She couldn't stop, even though her stomach ached and her eyes teared. The threesome rollicked with laughter until the hammock shuddered and rolled. Suddenly it tipped and the three of them toppled out, one after another, sprawling in the sand like rag dolls in formal wear. Tonio and Ben scrambled to their feet and helped her up. She straightened her gown, retrieved her shoes, and gathered up her shell necklace and stuffed dolphin. Tonio brushed sand from her chin and smoothed back her mussed hair.

"I must look like I got in a fight with a hammock, and the hammock won," she said, still on the verge of laughter. "Is my mascara running?"

Tonio rubbed his thumb under her eyes. "You could look like a raccoon, and you'd still be beautiful."

"Not exactly Shakespeare," said Ben, "but a good try, Tonio."

"Think you can do better, Ben? Let's hear your feeble attempts at poetry."

"Come on, you guys," said Ashley. "It's been a wonderful night. But isn't it time to go home?"

The three of them headed back to the car, making silly jokes and laughing all the way, as if they had imbibed more than sparkling cider, the two men behaving more like suitors than colleagues. Ashley sensed there would never be another night like this in her life. Someday, when she was a little old lady, she would still recall with yearning and delight this marvelous evening she had shared with two such extraordinary men.

Chapter 12

"I hope the two of you don't mind keeping each other company tonight," Tonio told Ashley and Ben at lunch the next day. "I have an appointment in town tonight. A dinner meeting. I may be late."

Ashley's heart sank at the idea of Tonio going off to another of his mysterious meetings. "Do you have to go tonight?" she asked. "This is Ben's last night here."

"I'm sorry, Ashley. It can't be helped."

"Don't sweat it, Tonio," said Ben with a sidelong glance at Ashley. "We'll get by just fine. We could watch a movie, take a swim, or even drive into town. What do you say, Ashley?"

She shrugged, swallowing her disappointment. "Since you're leaving tomorrow, Ben, it should be your decision."

"All right, maybe we'll relax on the lanai and listen to the ocean. That's something I can't do this time of the year in New York."

Tonio gave Ben a squint-eyed glance, as if to say, *Don't get too cozy.* Or was Ashley just reading into Tonio's expression what she wanted to see?

That evening, with Tonio gone, dinner felt almost like a date. She and Ben sat across from each other while Mika served them a delectable meal of barbecued chicken, fried potatoes, green beans, and fresh pineapple. Ashley had mixed feelings about being alone with Ben. She couldn't help remembering the many times they had dined together at some of New York's poshest restaurants. Ben had always showered her with the best—long-stemmed red roses, expensive perfume, rare chocolate delicacies, the most popular concerts and plays in town. But mingled with the happy memories were the tears she had shed and the humiliation she had felt when he left her at the altar.

After dinner, Ben suggested they take a swim.

She thought a minute then said, "I'd rather just relax by the pool."

He smiled affably. "We can do that, too. I'll put on some music and we can sit on the lanai and catch up on our lives. Maybe swap stories about what's happened over the past few months."

You mean, you want to know what I've been doing since you dumped me? She dismissed her silent retort. "You know what I've been doing. Working for Tonio."

They walked out to the lanai and sat down on adjoining lounge chairs near the pool. "I'm talking about your personal life, Ashley."

She stretched out her legs, smoothed her sundress, and rested her head against the back of the chair. "There hasn't been much of a personal life, Ben."

"I know Tonio has kept you busy."

"Yes, he has. But I've enjoyed working on his book."

"It's a great read. He owes you a debt of gratitude. He's achieved an emotional resonance I haven't seen in his earlier work."

"It wasn't all me. He finally allowed himself to tap into his buried feelings about his wife's death."

"That wouldn't have happened without you, Ashley."

"I like to think that's true." She looked over at Ben. "Why didn't you tell me his wife died in a car crash?"

"I guess the subject never came up."

"I never thought to ask. I assumed it was an illness or something."

"From the beginning Tonio made it clear he didn't want to discuss his wife's death, so we at Haricott respected his wishes."

Ashley ran her fingers over the arm of her chair. "Did you know he was in the car? He had been drinking. The authorities even considered pressing manslaughter charges against him."

"He wasn't driving," said Ben.

"How do you know?"

"He told me."

She gazed out at the bright orange sun hovering over the glistening sea. "And you believed him?"

"I had no reason not to. What did he tell you?"

"Nothing. I read it on the Internet. He doesn't know I know."

"Why not?"

She shrugged. "He's such a private man. I didn't know how to bring it up. And I didn't want him to feel obligated to tell me when he's tried so hard to forget."

"He is a private man, that's for sure," agreed Ben. "Where do you suppose he is tonight?"

"I don't know. He goes out like this a couple of nights a week. I think maybe he's seeing someone."

"Dating?"

Ashley tried to sound nonchalant. "Is that so hard to believe?"

After a long pause, Ben said, "Frankly, I think he has quite a crush on you."

Ashley laughed. "Ben, you're imagining things. He's still madly in love with his wife. If he is seeing someone, it's because he's trying to forget Brianna."

"You may be right."

"The truth is," she said, her voice tremulous, "I was so disturbed about Tonio's past and his secretive behavior, I was ready to leave here. I would have, too, but then you called to say you were coming to Kona."

"Yes, I remember you mentioned leaving. What do you mean by Tonio's secretive behavior?"

She examined the cuticle of one polished nail, debating whether to broach the subject with Ben.

"Ashley?" he prompted.

Before she knew it, the words came tumbling out. "Oh Ben, it's so frightening—Tonio's so tormented with guilt. It's a terrible thing to live with—the idea that he killed the love of his life."

"What are you saying, Ashley?"

"I've followed him, Ben." She brushed sudden tears from her cheeks. "Tonio goes to his wife's grave on the cliff near here. Sometimes he just stands and stares out at the ocean, as if in a trance. One night I was afraid he was going to. . ." She couldn't say the word.

Ben's eyebrows shot up. "Jump?"

"I don't think he would have. But for a moment I was petrified. And when he realized I was watching, he became enraged. I had never seen him like that."

Ben put his hand on hers. "Maybe it is time for you to go home."

"I can't." She was trembling. "I'm afraid for him, Ben. I'm afraid he's going to get so caught up in his grief he'll throw himself over the cliff. He's so closed up; he doesn't want anyone to know who he really is inside. I've learned the only way anyone can know him is through his writing, and even then it's through a veil of fiction."

"Ashley, listen to me," said Ben. "You can't rush in and save him from himself. His problems are too complicated for you to solve."

"I know." She leaned her head back and closed her eyes. "I know there's nothing I can do for Tonio, except help him with his writing. I've got to stay until his book is done."

"You can finish the editing in New York. We can always find a place for you again at Haricott."

She wanted to ask, *What am I going home to? A broken romance? Working beside the man who hurt me so deeply?*

He seemed to read her mind, for he said, "I know I made a mess of things. And if you don't want to work with me, I'm sure we can make other arrangements."

She withdrew her hand. "I don't know what I want, Ben. I don't know what God wants for me. At first I thought He wanted me to marry you. Then I thought He wanted me to be here in Kona to help Tonio. I've prayed and prayed about it, but I have no idea what I'm supposed to do."

Gently Ben turned her face toward his. "Listen, Ashley. Maybe I have some answers for you."

The intensity in his eyes made her uneasy. "What answers, Ben?"

His gaze was riveting, his hazel eyes crinkling at the corners the way she had once adored. "I want you back, Ashley. I was crazy to let you go." For an instant he was the old Ben, the one who had courted her and won her heart. But just as quickly she recalled the day on the beach he betrayed her trust.

"Ashley, did you hear me? I still love you."

No, no! This wasn't what she wanted to hear now. She jumped up and walked over to the edge of the pool. A breeze was gusting in from the ocean. She hugged herself, shivering.

Ben came up behind her and placed his hands on her shoulders. "Ashley, I didn't come to Hawaii just to work on Tonio's manuscript. Or even for a vacation. You must have known. I came here to see you, to find out if there's still a chance for the two of us."

She shook her head, stunned. "Ben, are you serious?"

He turned her around to face him. The lowering sun cast a burnished glow on his handsome features. "When I got back to New York, I couldn't believe how empty my life felt without you. Everywhere I went I kept expecting to see you. I kept going to church, because it made me feel close to you. And finally it started getting through to me. What I loved about you was your faith, your trust in God, and the way His love shone through you. I wanted that kind of life for myself."

Tears of frustration welled in her eyes. "You should have realized that before our wedding day, Ben, before you humiliated me in front of the whole world."

He brushed a tear from her cheek. "I know. It took losing you for me to realize what I really wanted." He rubbed her arm, his sturdy hand warm and soothing on her cold skin. "I've committed my life to Christ, Ashley," he said softly, "not just for you, but for myself. I'm not pretending anymore. I'm not just playing church."

"Stop it, Ben! You're just telling me what you think I want to hear."

"I'm not, Ashley, I promise you. Because no matter what you decide to do, I'm building a relationship with God. At church, I'm involved in the weekly Bible study and Men's Fellowship. Spiritually, I'm still a newborn. I know I've got so much to learn, but I'm reading the Bible and praying. And now I'm beginning to understand what you were trying to tell me all along."

Ashley stared at him, her mind whirling.

"You believe me, don't you, Ashley?"

She pushed his hand away, anger turning sour in her throat. "How can you use my faith to twist the dagger deeper? This is just a game you're playing. You think by saying all the right things I'll forget what happened and rush back into your arms."

"No, sweetheart, I don't think that. I won't blame you if you want nothing to do with me. But I had to let you know I've changed."

She inhaled deeply, steadying her breath. "If you've truly accepted Christ into your life, I'm happy for you. I've prayed that God would speak to your heart and bring you to faith in Him. But it doesn't change anything between us. It's over, Ben. It was over when you walked away from me on our wedding day."

He removed his glasses and lowered his gaze; a muscle twitched beside his mouth. "It's Tonio, isn't it?"

"Don't, Ben."

"It's true." He rubbed the bridge of his nose and replaced his glasses. "I can feel the connection between you two. I see it even if you don't admit it. You're in love with him."

Chapter 13

Early the next morning Ashley got up, showered, and dressed, all the while thinking of the two men in her life. A few months ago she had loved Ben and was ready to spend her life with him, but now her heart was drawn to Tonio. But the most important question was: What did God want for her now?

Lost in thought, she went to her kitchenette, made coffee, and took it out to the little table on her lanai. She sat watching the sky as vibrant colors of morning washed over the rocky shoals—soft lavenders, pinks, and powder blues. Birds twittered and rustled the leaves of the plumeria trees. A gentle breeze wafted through distant date palms like a whisper from God.

"Lord, I need to hear Your voice," she murmured. "My life seems to be going in so many directions at once. What do You want me to do? Where do You want me to go? And who do You want me to be with?"

Maybe she was asking the wrong questions. Maybe God didn't want her with Tonio or Ben. Maybe He wanted her to be alone. At least for now. Or maybe His plan for her life was something she hadn't even dreamed of yet. "Father, it's so hard not knowing what I'm supposed to do. Sometimes I feel cut adrift, aimless, going nowhere. Help me to do what pleases You. Right now I have no idea what that is."

She sipped her coffee, her thoughts swinging back and forth between Ben and Tonio. When she thought of Ben, she thought of all they had meant to each other. She remembered their dates in New York, their days of working together at the publishing house. Their minds were always in sync; they looked at things the same way, always knowing what to expect from the other. There was a lovely security in being with someone she knew so well.

But you didn't know him as well as you thought. He gave no advance warning when he walked away from you on your wedding day.

"That's true," she admitted aloud, "but otherwise, Ben was always someone I could depend on—rational, reliable, outgoing, secure in himself, a safe haven, never out of control."

And then there was Tonio, the exact opposite of Ben—volatile, complicated, unpredictable, stubborn, moody, secretive. Not the sort of man who would make a good husband. His mistress would always be his writing. But that didn't make him any less appealing.

Ashley drained her coffee cup and pushed back her chair. She went inside, picked up her thumb-worn Bible, and hugged it to her chest. *Look at you, Ashley.*

You're getting so caught up in these two men, you're forgetting the real love of your life: Jesus. When you can't figure out what you're supposed to do, just focus on Him. Love Jesus, and God will take care of everything else.

She returned to the lanai, sat down, and read several chapters of the Gospel of Mark. She loved the verses about loving God with all your heart, soul, mind, and strength. How she yearned to love Him that way. "Instead, I go around acting like a silly, foolish, lovesick girl. I let everything in my life distract me from You, Lord. I get so obsessed with what I want, what I think I need. It's all about me. Forgive me, Jesus. Keep my mind stayed on You. Help me to love You more."

She looked out toward the main house and saw Harry approaching the cottage, a tattered straw hat shading his timeworn face. "Aloha, Harry."

He stooped down and started working on the flower bed by the lanai. "Aloha, sistah."

"How are you doing today?"

"Ev'ryting's jus' fine. Dat nice young man goin' home today?"

"You mean Ben?"

"Yeah, dat's da fella."

"Yes, he's leaving this morning."

"Tell him Harry from da garden sends his aloha."

"I will, Harry. Thanks."

It's true. Ben is going home today, she reflected, *and a part of me wants to go with him. But I can't leave Tonio yet, with only the first draft of his novel finished.*

She looked at her watch. Time for breakfast. She'd better get over to the main house. *And put on a happy face, Ashley, so no one suspects how shaky your emotions are today.*

She entered the dining room just as Ben and Tonio were about to sit down. Ben came around and pulled back her chair, making a gallant flourish as she sat down. "Good morning, milady."

"Thank you, kind sir," she said with forced brightness.

"Good morning, Ashley," said Tonio, eyeing her curiously. "I hope you slept well."

"Very well, thank you." *And I hope you feel guilty for ditching us last night.*

Mika greeted them and poured their coffee.

"Thanks, Mika," said Ben. "Nothing like a cup of strong Kona coffee first thing in the morning. I'm going to miss this back in New York."

"Ben and I had a very pleasant evening last night," Ashley told Tonio. "We sat out on the lanai and watched the most gorgeous sunset."

"And caught up on old times," said Ben. "It was a perfect final evening in Hawaii."

"Of course, it went by too fast," said Ashley. *But not fast enough if you were with some other woman, Tonio.*

"Yes, way too fast," said Ben. "You know, I tried to talk your girl Friday into coming back to New York, but she insists on being true blue to you."

Tonio gave Ashley a pleased glance. "Is that so? I'm glad to hear it. We still have a lot of work to do on the book."

Always the book, thought Ashley. *What about me?*

Ben drummed his fingers on the table. "Well, maybe when the work is done, she'll change her tune. What do you say, Ashley? Is there a chance I'll see you back in New York one of these days?"

"There's always a chance, Ben," she said demurely.

"I'll hold you to that." Ben glanced at his watch. "Looks like it's time to call a taxi."

"Forget the taxi, Ben. Ashley and I can drive you to the airport."

"No need, Tonio. You two have work to do. A quiet taxi ride will give me time to change hats from vacation to work mode."

Tonio chuckled. "If this was your vacation, I'd hate to see what your normal workday looks like."

Ben's gaze flitted to Ashley, then back to Tonio. "The truth is, I thoroughly enjoyed working with you and Ashley on your book. It was a profitable week for all of us."

Ben got up from the table and called for a taxi on his cell phone.

A half hour later, Ashley, keeping watch at the window, spotted the taxi approaching on the circular driveway. "It's here, Ben."

Tonio helped carry Ben's luggage out to the vehicle, then the two shook hands. "Good-bye, ol' man, it's been real," said Ben.

"We'll have to do this again," said Tonio. "On the next book."

"You're on." Ben slapped Tonio's arm then turned to Ashley and opened his arms to her.

Tonio stepped back as Ashley and Ben embraced.

"I'll miss you, Ash," Ben whispered against her cheek. "I meant it about you coming home."

"I can't make any promises, Ben."

"I know. I'm not asking you to. Just remember, I love you."

"I care about you, too, but. . ."

"No buts. I want you back, but it's in God's hands. He'll show you what to do. Just pray about it, okay?"

"I'll be praying for you—that God will bless your life and help you to grow in Him. Good-bye, Ben." She was about to step away when he drew her closer and kissed her soundly on the lips. For a moment she was caught up in the sweet warmth of his touch, his closeness. The rest of the world receded, and they were the only two on earth. Then, suddenly she remembered Tonio was watching. Flustered, she broke away from Ben and stumbled backward. . .into Tonio's arms.

As Tonio steadied her, Ben climbed into the taxi and called back, "Take good care of my girl, Tonio."

Tonio kept his arm firmly around her. "Don't worry, Ben. She's in good hands."

After Ben's taxi disappeared down the road, Tonio looked down at Ashley. "Guess it's time for us to get to work, huh?"

"Yes, I suppose it is."

In silence they walked to the office, took their usual places at his desk, and began going through paperwork. "Do you want me to answer some of your fan mail?" she asked, picking up a stack of unopened letters.

"Sure, go ahead. I'll go over the rewrite of my last chapter."

They began working, but Ashley could tell Tonio's heart was no more into it than hers was. They were both feeling distracted, unmotivated.

After a half hour, Tonio said, "That's it. I'm worthless today."

She pushed the fan letters aside. "Me, too. What's wrong with us?"

Tonio gave her a long, hard look. "I guess there's just way too much going on under the surface."

She gave him a quizzical glance. "What do you mean?"

"You know what I mean."

"No, Tonio, I don't. I can't read your mind, as much as I would like to at times."

"I'm talking about us, Ashley."

"Us? There is no *us*, except in a very general sense."

He cracked his knuckles. "Well, there should be."

"You're talking in riddles."

"Don't you feel the undercurrent? All the stuff we're feeling that we're not saying? All the emotions we keep pushing away?"

Her mouth went dry. She felt suddenly threatened, exposed. What was Tonio trying to say? Had he guessed how she felt about him? Why in the world was he determined to scrutinize their relationship now when she had just said good-bye to Ben?

"Are you still in love with him?" he asked, his frosty blue eyes drilling into hers.

"In love? You mean, with Ben?"

"Yes, Ben. Who else?"

"I care about him, yes. You know that."

Tonio's brows knitted together; his eyes narrowed. "Are you *in* love with him?"

She broke away from his relentless gaze. Her stomach was churning more now than when Ben had left. "I don't know." Her voice quavered. "That's a question I'm still asking myself."

"He kissed you. You seemed to be enjoying it."

"I'm sorry. I didn't expect him to—he just—"

Tonio waved her off. "I know. You don't have to explain."

She looked back at him. "Then what is this all about?"

Tonio stood up and walked around the room, rubbing his chin. After a minute he sat down on the sofa and patted the spot beside him. "Come sit down. We need to talk."

She looked down at the stack of fan mail.

"Forget the work for now. We have more important things to talk about."

She got up and crossed the room to the sofa. She sat down warily and straightened her teal cotton shirt over her white capris. "Okay, I'm listening."

He combed his fingers through his thick curly hair. "You're not making this easy, Ashley."

"And you're making this—whatever it is—clear as mud. If you have something to say, Tonio, just say it."

He took her hand and wove his fingers between hers.

"What are you doing, Tonio?"

He squeezed her hand tighter. "I feel so awkward in moments like these. I'm a writer and now I can't even put a string of words together. Listen to me—I'm rambling incoherently."

"It's okay. Please, just say what's on your mind."

He swiveled to face her. His tanned, rugged face had never looked more vulnerable. "All right, here's the truth. I love you, Ashley. I adore you. I want you here with me always."

Had she heard right? "You love me?"

"I've loved you since the moment I saw you on the cruise. I've fought it, I've argued with myself, I've told myself you still belong to Ben. It doesn't matter. When I saw him kissing you this morning, I knew I couldn't keep silent another minute. Don't get me wrong. I like and respect Ben. He's a fine man and I'm sure he will make someone a decent husband. But not you. You don't belong with him. You belong with me. Do you hear me, Ashley?"

She sank back against the couch, her mind somersaulting. *This isn't happening. I must be crazy as a loon. Tonio wouldn't say—couldn't possibly say—he loves me!*

He touched her cheek. "I've shocked you, haven't I?"

"No, not at all. I'm just—"

"Shocked?"

She nodded. "Shocked. I don't know what to say."

"Don't say anything. Just let it all sink in."

"It's not sinking in. *I'm* sinking." She tried to stand, but her ankles gave out, so she sat back down.

Tonio sat back and inhaled sharply. "I shouldn't have just blurted it out. I should have built up to it. I've completely unnerved you, haven't I?"

"Maybe a little." She rubbed her stomach. "I do feel a little queasy."

"Are you going to be sick?"

She put her hand over her mouth. "I might."

"Do you want to go back to the cottage?"

"Do you mind?"

"No, not at all. We–we'll talk later."

She nodded, still holding her mouth. He helped her up and walked her to the door. "Are you going to be okay?"

"Yes, I just need to take something to settle my stomach."

"Let me know if you'd like Mika to bring you some tea and toast."

"I will."

She ran back to the cottage. Once inside, she collapsed on her bed, closed her eyes, and tried some slow-breathing exercises. Visions of Tonio danced in her head—his words, his face, his touch. Gradually the frantic images subsided; she was regaining control. After a few minutes her stomach relaxed and her head stopped spinning. Looking up at the ceiling, she said, "Ashley Bancroft, what are you doing? Anthony Adler just told you he loved you, and you as much as told him you had to throw up!"

She sat up on the bed and covered her face with her hands. "What have I done? I just turned an incredibly romantic moment into a travesty, a joke, a charade. Tonio must think I'm an idiot."

She paused and let the silence wash over her. She could feel the tension draining out of her body; her mind was clearing, absorbing what had just happened.

Tonio loves me. A little thrill of delight spiraled through her chest. *He loves me! That's all I need to know. And I love him, too. I have to tell him so.*

She sprang from her bed and went to the mirror to inspect her makeup. She ran a brush through her hair and did a little pirouette to check her outfit. But as she headed for the door, another thought brought her up short. *Hold on, Ashley. No matter what Tonio said, he's a man of mystery, a man with problems, and he's kept secrets from you. You can't let yourself fall in love with a man you don't really know. Didn't you learn from Ben? You can't have a relationship with someone unless he's the man God wants for you.*

"And that's not Tonio, is it, Lord? He's not the one You want for me." She whistled through her teeth. "Why does this keep happening to me? I feel like I'm jumping from the frying pan into the fire. What am I supposed to do now, Lord?"

She walked back to the main house, scouring her mind for the right words. *Tonio, I appreciate you sharing your feelings with me. . . . Tonio, let's just forget what you said and pretend nothing happened. . . . Tonio, I do care about you and want to be friends, but. . .*

"I sound so lame. Help me, Lord. I'm stuck. I don't know what to say or do. It's Your call, Father. Please, please, just let me do the right thing!"

Chapter 14

"This is awkward," said Ashley as she joined Tonio in the dining room for lunch. It had taken every ounce of courage she had to face him again. "I'm sorry I ran out like such a crazy person. I really did think I was going to be sick."

"Don't apologize," said Tonio, pulling back her chair. "I have to admit you looked a bit green around the gills. How are you feeling?"

"A little better. But I think I'll go with the tea and toast you mentioned earlier."

"Good idea. And please let me be the one to apologize."

"Why? You didn't do anything wrong."

"I'm the one who put my foot in my mouth—confronting you with my feelings when you had just said good-bye to Ben."

She sat down. "And I'm the one who nearly upchucked on all your sincere sentiments."

"I'm sure it wasn't deliberate."

"No, but it was totally embarrassing."

He sat down across from her. "Well, since we're both feeling duly chagrined, shall we just call it even?"

She managed a smile. "I'm willing if you are."

He winked. "Maybe we should tell Mika we want humble pie for dessert."

Just then Mika appeared with tuna sandwiches and a fruit salad. "You want humble pie, Mr. Adler? What kind of fruit is that?"

They both laughed. "Maybe fruit of the Spirit," said Tonio. "Never mind, Mika. This will do just fine."

"Just tea and toast for me," said Ashley. "My stomach's a little upset."

Mika's round face clouded with concern. "Is it something you ate?"

"No, Mika. A little too much emotion for one day."

"Yes, I see. You looked sad when Mr. Radison left. He's a very nice man."

"Yes, he is," Ashley agreed, avoiding Tonio's gaze.

Mika smiled. "Mr. Adler, while I get the tea and toast, you cheer up Miss Ashley and make her forget Mr. Radison."

Tonio cast Ashley a knowing grin. "I'm trying, Mika. Believe me, I'm trying."

"I'm fine," Ashley insisted. "Please, both of you stop fussing over me."

"I won't say another word," said Tonio. He put his fingers to his mouth and pretended to turn a key. "My lips are sealed."

"Thank you, kind sir."

Ashley ate her tea and toast in silence, but it did no good. Her thoughts were all over the place. She kept hearing Tonio's words, *"I love you, Ashley. I love you!"* Every time she glanced at him across the table, she felt her face flame. She couldn't pretend nothing had happened between them. Their relationship was different now. Tonio knew it, and so did she.

That afternoon, when they had finished reworking a scene from his novel, Ashley broached the subject that had been weighing on her mind all afternoon. "Tonio, we—we both know there's an elephant in the room."

He nodded. "I know. He's sitting right between us. A pink one. Bright pink. Wearing purple polka dots. And he's laughing. If elephants laugh, that is."

"Stop it, Tonio. Don't make fun of me. You know what I mean. We need to talk about what you said this morning. It's like a neon sign. I can't just ignore it."

"Wonderful. I had my say this morning. Now it's your turn."

She twisted a strand of her hair. "It's not that easy, Tonio. You know I care about you. On some level I suppose I love you. But after my broken romance with Ben, I realize I can't rush ahead of God. I can't force my own agenda. Or follow anyone else's. Only God's. And right now I have no idea what He wants for me. Or for you. I don't know if there could ever be an *us*."

Tonio rubbed his jaw thoughtfully. "I agree, Ashley. Neither of us wants to do anything unless we sense God's approval. All I'm asking is this: Are you willing to pray about it and explore the possibilities?"

"Maybe. In time."

"Why not now?"

She was silent a moment, her folded hands pressed against her lips. Finally she said, "Because there's so much I don't know about you. You're such a private man. I understand that. But people who love each other need to share their hearts, the truth about themselves, the good and the bad."

Tonio stiffened. "What is it you think you need to know about me? What truth are you talking about?"

"I—I need to know. . ." Ashley's mouth went dry, but she forced out the words. "I need to know about your wife."

"You mean, how she died—is that what you want to know?" His tone was mildly accusing.

"Yes, that's part of it," she admitted in a small, breathless voice.

Tonio stood up and paced the room. "Have you read the newspaper accounts?"

When she didn't answer, he repeated the question. "You've read about the accident, haven't you? All the lurid details?"

"Yes, I've read some of the stories. But I need to hear it from you."

He turned to face her, his eyes blazing, his face wrenched with agony. "Hear what? That I killed my wife? It's true. If it wasn't for me, my wife would still be alive!"

❧

Later, Ashley kicked herself for not insisting that Tonio explain his shocking confession. At the time she had been too stunned to speak. And when he made no effort to clarify his words, she had mumbled something about feeling sick again and fled the room, trembling.

That evening when she joined him for dinner, he acted as if everything were normal, as if he had never uttered such a shattering revelation.

Over the next few days, as they resumed their usual routine of writing and editing, Ashley shuddered at the thought of broaching the subject of Tonio's wife. She never again wanted to see that look of anguish in Tonio's eyes.

Chicken, she chided herself. *You're letting Tonio off too easily. You deserve an answer. Make him tell you what happened.*

But whenever she considered inquiring about the accident, her mouth went dry and her heart pounded furiously. She knew in her heart of hearts that she didn't want to know the truth. It could destroy everything she had ever felt for Tonio.

On Friday evening Tonio didn't show up for dinner. "He went to a meeting in town, Miss Ashley," said Mika. "But he forgot his wallet. He called and asked Harry to take it to him."

"I can do it," said Ashley. "No sense in Harry going out after a hard day of work."

"Harry don't mind."

"No, really, Mika. I'd be glad to take it. Where is Tonio's meeting?"

"The Royal Kona Resort. On Ali'i Drive."

"Great. I'll leave right now. I know Tonio wouldn't want to drive home without his license."

Mika handed her the wallet. "Give it to Mr. Ramiriz. He's at the front desk. Mr. Adler says he will pick it up after his meeting."

"Will do," said Ashley, trying not to sound overly enthusiastic. At last she would have a chance to discover what Tonio was doing at his mysterious meetings.

Guilt nudged her as she made the short drive to the hotel. *What gives you the right to spy on Tonio? It's his business where he goes and what he does. What would he say if he knew you were tracking him down?*

"I'm not tracking him down," she said aloud. "I'm doing him a favor."

Doing yourself a favor, you mean. You've been dying to know where he goes on his secret jaunts.

"What else am I supposed to do? He's the most mystifying man I've ever met!"

She was still arguing with herself as she arrived at the luxurious multi-tiered resort and parked near the entrance. She crossed a lush tropical lagoon to the expansive lobby with its rows of white pillars flanking a tropical garden. Grasping the wallet, she walked the length of the white marble floor until she found the appropriate desk. In her sneakers and jeans, she felt a little like a beggar in a palace. But it was worth it if she could discover what drew Tonio to this place so often. *But what if I don't even see Tonio here? What if I don't learn a thing from this trip?*

"Excuse me. Are you Mr. Ramiriz?" she asked the thin, dark-haired man behind the desk. When he nodded, she held out the wallet. "Mr. Anthony Adler wanted me to deliver this to him. If you could tell me where to find him. . ."

"Thank you, miss. I will give it to him."

"I really don't mind," she murmured, knowing she had already lost the battle. Beady-eyed Mr. Ramiriz wasn't going to tell her a thing. With a sigh of defeat, she relinquished the wallet. Turning to go, she paused to gaze up and down the lobby. Maybe, just maybe, she would spot Tonio among the passing tourists.

As if on cue, her eyes settled on a familiar figure standing near the tiki-style open-air restaurant. Tonio! Ashley was about to cross the room to him when she noticed an attractive, stylishly dressed woman approach him. In her midtwenties, with flowing, platinum blond hair, the woman greeted Tonio and went into his arms as if she belonged there. They embraced for a long moment; then, with his arm comfortably around her waist, he escorted her toward the elevators. Ashley watched as they stepped inside and the doors closed.

Something closed in Ashley's heart, as well. *He has someone else. How can it be? A few days ago he was proclaiming his love for me, but all along he's been having secret rendezvous with another woman!*

Ashley could hardly see to drive home. She kept swatting away hot, angry tears, but more kept coming. *You fool! How could you have trusted a man as devious as Tonio? Finish your work and get back to New York as fast as you can.*

Chapter 15

Dixie? Dixie Salinger? Where are you, girl? Pick up!" Ashley clutched her cell phone to her ear as if grasping a lifeline. "Come on, Dixie. I need to talk to you, pronto."

Ashley's heart sank when the line went to voice mail. "Sorry I missed your call," came Dixie's lilting, singsong patter. "I'm out skydiving, bungee jumping, or just giving someone a fabulous makeover with my new line of cosmetics. Leave me a message and I'll—" Dixie's voice broke through the recorded message. "Ash, is that you? I'm here!"

Ashley let out a sigh of relief. "Oh, Dixie, am I glad to hear your voice!"

"What's wrong, girl? You sound stressed out."

Ashley sat down on her bed and crossed her legs. "You wouldn't believe what's been happening around here."

"Give me the details," said Dixie.

"I don't even know where to start."

"The beginning works for me."

"Okay, here goes." Ashley drew in a deep breath. "You'll never believe this. Tonio told me he loves me."

"He loves you? Wow! That's amazing. What did you say?"

"Nothing. I almost threw up on him."

Dixie chuckled. "That's probably not the reaction he was looking for."

"I couldn't help it, Dix. My emotions were all over the place. He told me the same day Ben left, right after he kissed me."

"Who kissed you? Tonio?"

"No, Ben."

"Ben kissed you?"

"Yes. Right after he said he wanted to marry me."

"Tonio?"

"No, Ben."

"Ben wants you back?"

"Yes, and when Tonio saw us kissing—"

"Tonio was there?"

"Yes, we were saying good-bye to Ben."

"Listen, girl, my head is spinning."

"Mine is, too, Dixie. I'm so confused."

"Hold on. You're telling me two amazing guys are in love with you?"

"That's only part of it. You haven't heard the rest."

"Something tells me it's not good news."

"It's awful, Dixie." Ashley lay back on her bed and hugged her pillow. "Like something out of one of Tonio's novels."

"Tell me, girl, before curiosity kills this cat."

Ashley searched for the right words. There were none.

"Just spill it," urged Dixie. "It's bad, isn't it?"

"The worst," said Ashley. "It's Tonio. He told me it was his fault his wife died."

Dixie whistled through her teeth. "Wow, I wasn't expecting that."

"Me either. I couldn't believe my ears, Dixie."

"He actually said those words—'it was my fault'?"

"It was something like that. He was responsible. I don't know, Dixie. What does it matter how he said it? He admitted he was to blame."

"How did she die? And are you safe around him? You'd better get on the next plane, girl!"

"Wait, Dixie. I'm running ahead of myself. Tonio's wife died in a car crash." Ashley repeated the grisly details she had gleaned from the Internet stories. "So, you see, it was an accident. But he still feels guilty."

"Whew!" said Dixie. "There's a difference between 'I deliberately killed my wife' and 'I feel guilty that my wife died in a terrible accident.' Did he explain what happened?"

"No. I couldn't bear to hear it. And now I don't know if it matters anyway."

"Why not? You just told me Tonio loves you. So you need to know the truth about his wife."

"There's more," said Ashley.

"More? What more could there be? Your life already sounds like a soap opera."

"Wait 'til you hear this. Tonight I—I saw Tonio with another woman. He's been going to these mysterious meetings in town. I saw them. They looked very cozy together."

"You've got to be kidding!" exclaimed Dixie. "You're making all this stuff up, right, Ash? This is the plot of your next novel."

Ashley sat up and swung her feet off the bed. "I promise you, Dixie, every word is true. I couldn't put all this in a novel. No one would believe it."

"All right, tell me this," said Dixie. "Why would Tonio tell you he loves you if he's seeing another woman? What's the point of that?"

Ashley shook her head. "Like I said, Dixie, nothing makes sense around here."

"Sounds like it's time for you to come home."

"I can't. Not yet. The final rewrite on Tonio's novel isn't finished yet."

"Forget the novel. Just come home."

"I will. Soon." Ashley's voice quavered. "I just wish you were here, Dixie."

"Me, too."

"But I know you wouldn't want to come to Hawaii again so soon." Ashley let the tantalizing idea linger in the air between them like a moth circling a light.

Dixie took the bait. "I wouldn't? Why not? I love doing crazy, unexpected things. I'll be there. I'm catching the next plane to Kona!"

The next morning, when Ashley told Tonio he would be having another houseguest, she felt a bit guilty for manipulating the situation. It wasn't as if she had twisted Dixie's arm, but she had known just what to say to convince her best friend to come to her rescue.

To Ashley's surprise, Tonio actually seemed pleased that Dixie was coming to visit. "Good for you, Ashley. You've been working so hard, you deserve some relaxation. You girls take a few days off and go have fun."

Why? she challenged silently. *So you can spend more time with your secret love?* Immediately shame flooded her heart, washing away her unspoken accusation. She had no right to condemn Tonio when all she had were suspicions. Maybe Tonio had a good explanation for everything—his wife's death, his elusiveness, his clandestine meetings with the beautiful stranger, his volatile emotions. Surely Dixie would help Ashley put everything into proper perspective.

That afternoon Ashley picked Dixie up at the Kona airport in Tonio's SUV. The two hugged and talked at once, babbling like long-lost friends. "I can't believe it's only been four months since I was in Hawaii," said Dixie as they drove back to Tonio's estate. "It seems like we've been apart for years."

Ashley nodded. "So much has happened, I feel the same way." She glanced over at Dixie. "I like the magenta streaks in your hair. Very spicy."

She tossed her head jauntily. "I got tired of plain auburn."

"I wouldn't care if you showed up bald; I'm thrilled to have you here."

Dixie laughed. "Well, that's a style I hadn't considered." She put her hand out the open window. "I can't believe this is nearly November. It still feels like summer here. You can't imagine how glad I was to have an excuse to leave the drizzly cold of New York."

"Forget the cold weather," said Ashley. "For the next few days you're going to bake in the sun and swim in the pool 'til you're waterlogged."

Dixie clapped her hands in glee. "I can't wait to show all the pale people back home my gorgeous tan!"

As they followed the circular drive to the main house, Dixie let out a whistle. "Don't tell me, Ashley! *This* is where you've been hanging out for the past few months? Talk about living in the lap of luxury!"

Ashley nodded. "Sweet, isn't it? Sometimes when I wake up in the morning,

I think I must be dreaming, it's so beautiful around here. Tomorrow I'll show you around the estate."

"So tell me the truth," said Dixie. "Is Tonio bummed that I'm intruding on his privacy?"

"Not at all," said Ashley. "He seems quite pleased that you're visiting. In fact, in spite of everything that's happened, he acts like things are perfectly normal. It's infuriating."

"Well, let's see how things look to this objective bystander. Okay, so I'm not so objective. But at least I'll give you my honest opinion."

"That's what I need, Dixie. Someone with a clear head and a discerning spirit."

Dixie chuckled. "That's me, all right. A regular eagle-eyed Sherlock Holmes."

That evening Mika pulled out all the stops and served a lavish seafood dinner of salmon pâte, fried calamari, and shrimp curry with cashews and mango chutney.

"Dixie, I hope you like fish," said Tonio. "These dishes are Mika's specialties. They're out of this world. Right, Ashley?"

"Absolutely!" She passed the salmon pâte and curry to Dixie.

"It's delicious, Mika," said Dixie, sampling the pâte. "If I didn't like seafood before, I do now."

"Save room," urged Mika. "There's passion fruit and macadamia nut pie for dessert."

Dixie licked her lips. "Given half a chance, I could learn to eat like this every day. It sure beats my usual frozen pizza and boxed macaroni and cheese."

Everyone laughed.

"What's so funny?" said Dixie with a shrug. "What's more American than pizza and macaroni?"

"American or not, we're skipping your old favorites this week," said Ashley. "With Mika cooking, you're going to get the best Hawaiian cuisine anywhere."

Dixie helped herself to more curry. "Girl, you may have to roll me onto the plane when it's time to go."

Over the next few days Ashley and Dixie behaved like typical tourists—driving around Kona, seeing all the sights Dixie had missed on her cruise ship visit, shopping, snorkeling, swimming, and sunbathing around the pool. They visited museums and historic sites until they doubted they could cram another bit of island trivia into their brains. Tonio joined them one day for a kayaking excursion through the rain forest—"*flumin da ditch*," as he called it—and a whale-watching cruise the next day. It was all good fun. But most of all, Ashley and Dixie relished their private, late-night gabfests in her little cottage.

"I feel like a teenager again," said Ashley one evening as they curled up on her bed with sodas and brimming bowls of popcorn.

"Remember all the slumber parties we used to have," said Dixie, "when we'd stay up 'til dawn laughing and talking?"

"And lamenting our latest boyfriend crises," mused Ashley.

"Oh yes! The boyfriend crises. Was there ever *not* a crisis?"

"Never! We always thought it was the end of the world. Life would never be the same without—whoever."

Dixie rolled her soda can between her palms. "We've come a long way, girlfriend. Look at us, sitting here in this exotic estate, with the ocean just a stone's throw away. How great is this?"

"And we're still lamenting our boyfriend problems! What's with that?"

"Some things never change," said Dixie.

Ashley tossed a kernel of corn, hitting Dixie's nose. "Since you got here, I've done all the talking. What about you, Dix? There must be some special guy in your life."

Dixie shrugged. "Not so much. Lots of buddies, but no one special."

"You're not seeing anyone?"

"Not really. I have guy friends. We hang out once in a while. That's all. But I'm content. I don't know if I could handle the drama of a relationship right now."

"You mean, like I'm going through with Tonio?"

"Exactly. So we're back to Tonio."

"Afraid so," agreed Ashley, sitting back on the bed. "And you still haven't told me what you think. You've had a chance to observe him these past few days. What's your opinion?"

"I think he's crazy about you. But he's a hard one to figure out. He doesn't let anyone see the real guy under all the charm and swagger."

"I can't get him to talk about himself," said Ashley. "But then again, I'm not very good at drawing him out. I guess I'd rather not know the bad things."

"You won't know if he's right for you until you take off those rose-colored glasses."

"I know. I just wish the Lord would give me some direction."

"I'm sure you've been praying about it."

"Of course." Ashley twisted a strand of hair around her finger. "But sometimes I feel like I'm just giving God a shopping list. 'Give me this, Lord, give me that. Make Tonio fall in love with me. Make everything perfect for us.' It sounds so selfish, doesn't it, Dixie?"

"It sounds *human*. I do that, too. I think we all do. It's the natural thing to do."

"I don't want to be satisfied with a faith that's always saying 'give me.' I want to grow closer to God, but I get so caught up in all the other things—Tonio, his book, our daily routine, my feelings for him. I hate to say it, but sometimes God is an afterthought."

Dixie nodded. "Every day is a new chance to show Jesus how much we love Him. But sometimes I get halfway through the day before I even think of Him."

Ashley grimaced. "Doesn't sound like we're doing too well spiritually, are we?"

"We could pray right now," said Dixie.

"I'd like that," said Ashley. "Remember the Bible verse about God's strength being made perfect in weakness? Well, God can have a field day with all my weaknesses."

"Stand in line, Ash. I've probably got you beat by a mile."

They both laughed. "We'll let God sort it out," said Dixie.

They took turns praying conversationally, expressing their gratitude and making requests or sitting in companionable silence for a few moments of private worship. After a while Dixie began singing a familiar chorus and Ashley joined in. When they had finished they both had tears rolling down their cheeks.

"This is like the old days," said Ashley.

"It sure is," said Dixie. "Remember how we'd both be a mess emotionally? Upset about one thing or another. But after we prayed together, everything looked different. God felt so close. I miss those days."

"Me, too."

Dixie squeezed Ashley's hand. "I have a feeling God's going to do something amazing in the next few days."

"I feel it, too," said Ashley. "Things are going to change in a big way. I just pray I'm ready for whatever happens."

"You will be, Ash. God is with us, and He never fails."

Ashley nodded. "I just pray I won't fail Him."

The next day, after Ashley and Dixie returned home from an afternoon of shopping, they found Tonio in his office, at his desk, dressed in a tan sport jacket. He was talking on the phone, speaking in hushed tones. "It's still the Royal Kona Resort. But it's a different room, Lydia. The Empire Room. That's right. I'll see you shortly."

When he looked up and saw Ashley and Dixie standing there, he said a quick good-bye and hung up the receiver. He looked like a man who had been found out.

He was talking with her—that woman at the hotel! Ashley realized with a sinking sensation.

He stood up and said, almost too brightly, "Well, look who's home. Looks like you girls had a great day shopping."

They set their packages on the sofa. "I'm sorry, Tonio," said Ashley, fighting her disappointment. "We didn't mean to interrupt."

"No problem. I was finished talking anyway." He strode over and gazed down at their purchases. "So did you get some great buys? If I remember right, Dixie, you went home with half of Hawaii the last time you were here."

"I sure did. And this time I got the other half."

"Terrific. What did you girls buy?"

Ashley let Dixie do the talking. "I bought some more of those plastic plumeria leis for my cosmetics customers, some limited edition lithographs of the ocean for my apartment, a conch shell for my bathroom shelf, and, of course, more Kona coffee."

"What about you, Ashley?" asked Tonio. "What did you buy?"

"Some clothes. Nothing important." She kept her gaze fixed on him. "You're dressed up tonight. Are you going out?"

"I have a meeting tonight."

"Then you won't be here for dinner?"

"No, afraid not. But I won't be out late."

"It doesn't matter." Ashley gathered up her purchases and said a curt good-bye to Tonio. With a little wave, Dixie scooped up her packages and followed Ashley back to the cottage.

"I can't believe it," Ashley lamented as she tossed her purchases on the bed. "He's going to the resort to be with that woman! And after I prayed so hard last night."

Dixie set her bags on the chair. "As I remember it, Ash, you asked God to do things His way, not yours."

"Whose side are you on anyway?" Ashley shot back.

"There's only one side that matters, and that's God's."

Ashley sat down on the bed and wiped away an offending tear. "I know you're right, Dixie, but right now I just want to wallow in my misery."

Dixie sat down beside her. "What can I do to help?"

"There's nothing anyone can do. I just wish I knew what was going on. Why doesn't he come right out and tell me he's found someone else? Then I could accept it and move on. It's the not knowing that's killing me."

"You could ask him."

"No, I can't. I get tongue-tied just thinking about it."

"Then you're going to have to leave it with the Lord."

"I'm trying, but. . ." Ashley paused. "Wait a minute. He told her he's meeting her in the Empire Room at the Royal Kona Resort. We could go there, Dixie."

"Go there? You mean spy on them?"

"Not spy exactly. Just take a peek inside and see what's happening."

"Ash, I'm usually the first to try some new adventure. But this would be wrong."

"Why? It's surely not a private hotel room. It sounds like a conference room. Anyone can probably go in."

"I still don't have a good feeling about it," said Dixie.

"You said you wanted to help me. Come with me, Dixie. I don't want to do this alone."

Dixie shook her head. "I'll go, but I hope we don't regret it."

"How can we regret it? If I get some answers about Tonio, it'll be a good thing."

Ashley was still telling herself that as they drove Tonio's other car—a blue sedan—to the Royal Kona Resort. They parked near the entrance, made their way into the lobby, and checked the hotel directory for the Empire Room.

"It's on the second floor," said Ashley.

As they headed for the elevators, Dixie whispered, "Are you sure you want to do this?"

"We've come this far. I've got to know."

They took the elevator to the second floor, got off, and walked down the hall past several conference rooms. At last they came to the Empire Room. The door was closed.

"It's not too late to turn back," Dixie whispered.

"No way!" Quietly Ashley turned the knob and opened the door a crack. She could see people inside the room. She opened the door wider and stepped inside. Thirty or more people sat in a semicircle facing the front. The blond on the far right was the woman Tonio had met in the lobby, the woman he had called *Lydia*.

Ashley's eyes were drawn to a tall man standing up and taking the microphone. It was Tonio. What was he doing? Giving a speech?

He cleared his throat, then spoke, his booming baritone sounding loud and clear in the high-ceilinged room. "Good evening, everyone. My name is Tonio. . .and I'm an alcoholic."

Chapter 16

Just as Tonio said the words, "I'm an alcoholic," his gaze flitted to the back of the room, to the doorway where Ashley and Dixie stood. The moment his eyes met Ashley's, everything in his face changed. He looked stunned, incredulous, betrayed.

Her heart wrenched at the shock and pain in his eyes. She pivoted on her heel and ran from the room, Dixie right behind her. They hurried out to the car and headed home, Ashley sobbing her regrets.

"Why didn't he tell me, Dixie? I never would have gone there tonight if I'd known he was at an AA meeting. How can he be an alcoholic? I never saw him drink, not once."

"He must have known he didn't dare drink," said Dixie, "or he'd be a slave to it again."

"He's carried that burden all this time, and he never told me about it. Why didn't he tell me?"

"Maybe because you put him on a pedestal. He didn't want you to know he was a mere man with weaknesses like anyone else."

Ashley sat forward, trying to see the road through her tears. "I thought I knew him, Dixie. But I don't know him at all!"

"Watch the road, Ash. Want me to drive?"

Ashley blinked back her tears. "No, I'm okay. But I've ruined everything with Tonio. He'll never want to see me again."

"Yes, he will. You'll get through this. Watch that curve, Ashley. It's a steep drop to the ocean below."

The vehicle veered onto the shoulder of the narrow road and skidded, spewing gravel everywhere. The tires squealed as Ashley turned the wheel sharply and got the car back on the pavement. Her heart pounded as she gasped, "Sorry."

Dixie was holding on for dear life. "I said I'd drive."

"I'm okay. We're almost home."

"That's a relief. Are you going to wait up for Tonio?"

"Are you kidding? I couldn't bear to face him tonight."

"You're going to have to face him sometime."

"Tomorrow. After I've had time to get my bearings and summon some courage." Ashley heaved a sigh. "I don't know whether to be angrier with Tonio or myself. He didn't trust me enough to reveal his true self to me. I didn't trust him enough to accept his desire for privacy. We're a fine pair, aren't we?"

Dixie nodded. "I'd say the relationship needs some work. But maybe now you can take things to a new level of trust."

"Thanks, Dixie. You always manage to see the silver lining in every disaster. But I think it's too late for Tonio and me. I think that ship has sailed."

"Maybe, maybe not. We prayed about it last night. Let's wait and see what God's going to do."

When they got back to the cottage, Ashley went straight to bed. At least if she was asleep, she wouldn't be seeing that look of devastation on Tonio's face. But she was wrong. Her dreams were filled with Tonio announcing he was an alcoholic and then staring her down with those sad, wounded, accusing eyes.

The next morning Ashley slept in. When Dixie woke her and said it was time for breakfast, Ashley told her to go on without her. "I hardly slept a wink last night. Tell Mika I'll get something later."

"No way," said Dixie. "If you're not going to breakfast, I'm certainly not going to face Tonio alone. We'll both stay here and have coffee and whatever I can find in the cupboards to snack on."

"You'll find some stale granola cereal, half a grapefruit, and a few brown bananas."

"Okay. That's a start."

But by lunchtime Ashley knew she couldn't hide out in the cottage any longer. She had no choice but to march over to the main house and face Tonio. Look him straight in the eye and take her punishment. And then give him a taste of his own medicine. Insist on knowing why he kept something so important from her for so long. Did he think she wouldn't understand? Then again, she *didn't* understand. How could Tonio be an alcoholic?

The question still weighed on Ashley's mind as she and Dixie entered the dining room and greeted Mika and Tonio. Mika was serving bowls of fresh fruit and tuna salad sandwiches. Tonio was in his usual spot, reading the newspaper. When they took their seats, he put his paper down and gave them a thin smile. "We missed you at breakfast," he said.

"We slept in," said Dixie.

"Not good to skip breakfast," said Mika, filling their glasses with iced tea.

"We had breakfast in the cottage," said Ashley. *Stale cereal and overripe bananas.*

Tonio cleared his throat. "When I saw you girls at my meeting last night, I thought there must have been an emergency at home. But Mika assured me everything was all right."

"About your meeting, Tonio," said Ashley, lowering her gaze. "I'm sorry. We shouldn't have barged in like that. It was all my idea. I hope you'll forgive me."

"I still don't understand what you were doing there, Ashley."

She stole a sideways glance at Dixie, but Dixie's look said, *You're on your own here, girl!*

"I don't know what to say, Tonio," said Ashley, her throat tightening. "It's just that you were gone so often to your mysterious meetings, I—I was dying to know where you were going. But you never said a word. And then last night I heard you on the phone talking to someone named Lydia, and you mentioned the Empire Room at the Royal Kona Resort. So, on a lark, Dixie and I decided to. . .to—"

"Spy on me?"

"Something like that."

"Let me get this straight," said Tonio, his brows lowering. "You thought I was having a secret tryst with someone named Lydia? And you wanted to find out what was going on?"

She nodded.

"You thought I was having a romantic fling?"

Ashley picked at her tuna salad. "I didn't know."

"How could you think that, Ashley? Especially after I just told you how I felt about you."

Tears welled in her eyes. "I'm sorry."

They all ate in silence for a moment.

Finally Tonio said, "For your information, Ashley, Lydia is a longtime friend. We've both battled the same demon. She got me started in AA when my life was falling apart. I'll be forever indebted to her. I care about her, just as I care about her husband and children. But there's no romance."

"I'm sorry, Tonio," Ashley said through her tears. "I didn't know. I feel so stupid."

He handed her his handkerchief. "Don't cry about it. I hate to see a woman cry."

In her most lilting voice, Dixie said, "Did you hear it's snowing in New York? Imagine! We're sitting here in all this sunshine, and—"

"It's my fault, too," Tonio broke in.

Ashley dried her eyes. "Your fault?"

He put down his fork. "I should have told you I was going to AA meetings. I tried to several times, but I couldn't bear to tarnish your image of me."

"All I wanted was to know the real you."

"All right, that's what you're going to do." He tossed his napkin on his plate. "Are you finished eating?"

"Almost. Why?"

"We're going for a long walk and having an even longer talk. You're going to hear it all, Ashley. Every last detail of my life. And we'll see how you feel about me then."

"I'm ready," she said, pushing back her plate.

Tonio stood up and pulled her chair out. As she stood, she glanced over at Dixie.

"Hey, don't worry about me," Dixie said quickly. "You two go off and have fun. I'll stay here and help Mika with the dishes."

"Where do you want to go?" Tonio asked as they left the main house. "The woods, the orchards, the beach?"

"The beach." As she fell into step beside him, a cool breeze rustled her apple-green sundress. Tonio held her hand as they descended the rocky slope to the beach. She removed her sandals as they walked across the sand to a smooth outcropping of rocks near the ocean. He climbed up, then offered his hand and pulled her up beside him. They were close enough to the water to feel the salt spray when the surf came in, surging over the rocky ledge below them. Yet the water was clear enough to see the ocean floor and large sea turtles washing in with the current and back out again.

They both leaned back against the rocks and gazed at the fleecy clouds stretching from Kailua Bay to the edge of Mauna Loa in the far distance.

"This is beautiful," said Ashley. "And so peaceful. Why haven't we come here before?"

"I'm wondering the same thing," said Tonio. "We get so busy with our lives we can't see beyond our own noses. But a view like this really makes you stop and appreciate God's world."

"It does," she agreed. "It kind of puts our little problems in perspective, doesn't it?"

Tonio rubbed his jaw, his lips firmly set. Ashley studied his sturdy, bronzed profile. A faint stubble of beard covered his sculpted chin, and the salty breeze ruffled his sable hair. He looked like a man who wasn't ready to talk.

"We don't have to do this," she murmured. "You don't owe me any explanations. We can just enjoy the ocean and go back home."

He looked at her, his blue eyes gleaming like crystal in the sunlight. "Don't give me a way out, Ashley. I've tried to summon the courage to do this for months now. I want you to know everything."

"Okay. I'm listening."

He crossed his arms on his chest and put his head back. "I met Brianna at a media party just after my first book was made into a movie. She was a press agent and wanted to represent me. She had all these big plans for making me a star, even though writers don't typically end up in the limelight like actors and musicians.

"Anyway, I admired her energy and enthusiasm. I felt flattered that she was willing to take me on as a client when she already had some big-name actors in her stable. One thing led to another and we decided to get married. I suppose it was her idea, but I figured I'd achieved a good measure of success. The one thing missing was a wife."

"It sounds like you made a good team," said Ashley. "You had someone in your corner fighting for you."

Tonio's jaw tightened. "That's what I thought. At first. But when the movie studio passed on the option for one of my books, Brianna was outraged. Coming from a wealthy family, she loved all the trappings of fame—the luxury homes and cars, the travel, the fancy parties, and gala events. She insisted we build this estate with all its pricey amenities. She wasn't happy unless my books were on the bestseller lists. She kept after me to produce another hit, then complained about being bored when I spent long hours writing. She threw herself back into her own career, taking on more clients than she could handle. She was rarely home. She had no time for me or my writing."

Ashley shook her head. "I had no idea, Tonio. I thought Brianna was the love of your life."

He managed a dry chuckle. "The love of my life? Ha! I didn't have a clue what love was all about. Whatever Brianna and I shared, it wasn't love."

"I didn't think anyone could measure up to what you felt for her."

"I'm not proud of my feelings," Tonio admitted. "I hated what our lives had become, and I think she did, too. I started drinking heavily. I had never been a drinking man, but alcohol became an escape. I didn't realize what a destructive power it held until I was caught in its vise grip."

"What about the accident?" Ashley probed gently.

Tonio massaged his knuckles until they were bone white. "Not a day goes by that I don't relive that horrific night."

"If it's too painful, you don't have to talk about it."

He looked at her, his eyes glinting with torment. "Do you think keeping silent has diminished the pain?"

"I suppose not."

"The accident happened on the road along the cliffs near here. It was over five years ago, but I remember it as if it were yesterday." Tonio picked up a pebble and tossed it into the water. "I'd finally optioned another book, and it had been made into a movie. Brianna and I were attending a celebration party at a private estate south of Kona.

"The evening started out well enough. Brianna was excited about the release of the movie. She was sure I was going to be on top again—an A-list celebrity. All I could think of was how badly they had butchered my novel. I was in no mood for a party. If we had just stayed home that night. . ."

"But you didn't."

"No, we didn't," Tonio conceded. "As soon as I got there, I started drinking. I wanted to drink myself into oblivion. I knew the movie would propel me into the spotlight again, and Brianna wouldn't be content until we had exhausted every media opportunity. All I wanted to do was stay home and write. All Brianna wanted to do was surf the crowd and play every publicity angle.

"Finally, I'd had enough. I told her I was going home, and she was going with me. She refused. We practically had a knock-down, drag-out fight right there in front of everyone. Finally I stalked out to the car and she ran after me. I climbed in the driver's seat, but she wouldn't let me shut the door. She kept telling me to get out and let her drive."

Tonio shifted his torso and lowered his chin to his chest. His voice came out in a hoarse whisper. "Brianna hated driving. Especially at night. Especially on the narrow, winding roads by the cliffs. But she knew I was drunk and couldn't drive. Finally I gave in and let her get behind the wheel. But all the way home we kept arguing. I don't remember now what we said, but the atmosphere was heated, explosive. Neither of us was paying attention to the road."

Tonio paused, his breathing labored. Ashley put her hand on his arm and waited.

After a moment he cleared his throat and squared his shoulders. "I don't remember exactly what happened next. I just know somehow our car veered off the road, crashed through the guardrail, and plunged over the cliff into the ocean below. The whole thing was surreal—the car hitting the water, slowly sinking, water pouring in through the open sunroof, and finally the jarring sensation as we hit the ocean floor. As the car flooded, I held my breath, undid my seat belt, and reached for Brianna. She was unconscious. I tried to pull her free, but she was wedged in against the steering wheel. When I couldn't hold my breath any longer, I forced my way up through the sunroof against the inrush of water. I swam to the surface, took in all the air I could, then dove back down for Brianna.

"By the time I dislodged her from the car and swam with her to shore, I could hardly breathe. I tried CPR, but it was too late. She was gone."

Ashley squeezed Tonio's arm. "I'm so sorry."

With his fingertips he rubbed the moisture from his eyes. "If I hadn't been so drunk, maybe I could have saved her. My mind would have been clearer, my reactions faster. And if I hadn't been drinking in the first place, the crash never would have happened. It was my fault, Ashley. I killed Brianna as surely as if I'd strangled her with my own hands."

"Tonio, you can't blame yourself."

"Who else can I blame?"

"It was an accident."

"An accident that never needed to happen." He looked at her with imploring eyes. "I'll never forgive myself, Ashley. Never! I should have died, not Brianna!"

Chapter 17

"Where is God in all of this?" asked Ashley.

"What do you mean?" said Tonio.

The tide was coming in around them, frothy waves crashing below the rocky ledge where they sat. The sun was lowering, and the breeze had picked up and turned cool.

Shivering, Ashley replied, "You sound like a man without hope."

Tonio reached for her hand, intertwining his fingers with hers. "I don't mean to sound that way. I do have faith. Since the accident I've come to know Christ in a personal way. Even though I was raised in the church and have been a believer most of my life, I took my faith for granted. Having a personal walk with God wasn't my priority. But after the accident I reexamined everything in my life, and I hated what I saw. I threw myself on God's mercy and begged Him to help me stop drinking. He did. He led me to AA. The Lord and AA have kept me sober ever since. But to this day I still struggle with my guilt over Brianna. It shadows every emotion and robs me of the joy I know I should feel in Christ."

"Have you prayed about it? Asked God to forgive you?"

"Every day. But I can't forgive myself. I don't know how to turn off the guilt. A voice in my head keeps accusing me, reminding me I have no right to enjoy such a good life when I robbed Brianna of hers."

"You can't change the past. You can't bring Brianna back."

"I know. I guess that's why I feel so helpless. There's nothing I can do to redeem myself."

"God's the only One who can redeem any of us, Tonio."

He nodded. "I know you're right. But I can't seem to exorcise those demons of the mind that keep reminding me of my guilt. It sounds crazy, I know—I shouldn't even be telling you this—but it's as if the devil himself keeps drawing me to the cliff and taunting me to jump into the ocean to make atonement for my sin; it's as if the only way I'll ever be at peace is to die the way she died."

Ashley stared up at him. "Don't even think such a thing! You're letting the devil's lies destroy you!"

Tonio shook his head. "I knew I shouldn't have said anything. You must think I'm ready for the loony bin."

"I'd never think that. But I am frightened for you."

He squeezed her hand. "Don't worry, I'm not going to do anything drastic.

I'm too chicken to go stepping off cliffs. I just wanted to be completely honest with you about how I feel sometimes."

They were both silent for a moment, gazing out at the sea.

Finally Ashley said, "We all have things in our past we regret. We're all just sinners saved by grace. I wish I knew my Bible better. There's a verse in Romans, I think, that says there's no condemnation for those who are in Christ Jesus. While we were still sinners, Christ died for us. We're under grace, Tonio, not guilt."

He smiled. "I know, Ashley. God loves us unconditionally. And that's a beautiful thing."

"Exactly. There's nothing we can do to diminish His love for us, because He loved us when we were already sinners."

"You're preaching to the choir, sweetheart." He brushed his fingers across her cheek. "I believe everything you've said. Nothing can separate us from the love of God. . .except maybe our own guilt. Who knows? Maybe the devil's greatest tool against Christians is to spoil our fellowship with God by making us feel guilty."

"It's true."

"But what if we feel guilty because we *are* guilty?"

She swiveled to face him. "Tonio, may I make an observation?"

"Go on. I'd like to hear this."

"I think I know the answer to your problem."

He managed a curious smile. "My problem? You have the answer?"

Retrieving her hand from his, she drew in a deep breath, gathering her courage. "Your problem is. . ."

"I'm listening."

"It's your pride. The problem is your pride."

"My pride?" His eyes widened. "Okay, little lady, how did you get to that conclusion?"

"It just came to me." She marched her fingers along his arm. "You're one of those macho men, a rugged individualist, captain of his own destiny, who insists on doing everything himself, right?"

"I don't know if I'd use those words, but. . .okay, so what if I am?"

Her hand rested on his wrist. "I remember something my mom used to tell me. If you tell a woman a problem, she'll offer comfort and sympathy. If you tell a man a problem, he'll immediately try to fix it. That's what you're doing, Tonio. Trying to fix your life on your own terms, atone for your sins in your own strength."

He chuckled. "You amaze me. One minute you're an aspiring preacher, the next you're an armchair psychologist."

"I know I'm saying it badly, but someone has to get through to you." She thought a minute, searching for the right words. "It's like salvation. It's not as if we start the process by doing something good, and then God notices and finishes the job. Nothing we do can start the act of redemption. It begins and ends with God. All we can do is acknowledge our unworthiness and accept His grace."

Tonio slipped his arm around her shoulder. "You're actually quite eloquent at times, Ashley."

"Really? You think so?"

"Of course. My admiration for you just keeps increasing."

She shivered again. "You're teasing me, aren't you?"

"No, my darling. I am deeply touched by your concern."

She met his gaze squarely. "The truth is, I care about you, Tonio. It breaks my heart to see you in such pain."

He grinned. "I guess you're an amateur nurse, too, because I'm feeling better already." He drew her closer and rubbed her bare arm. "You're getting chilled. Maybe we'd better head back to the house."

"I suppose so."

"But first—we've had such a special time together, Ashley—I'd like to thank the Lord for it."

She smiled. "I'd like that."

He cleared his throat and gazed out at the sea. "Father, thank You for bringing Ashley into my life. In spite of my stubborn, prideful heart, You've blessed me in so many ways. And one of the best blessings is this darling girl who keeps me on my toes and makes me take a hard, honest look at myself. Help me to be the man she believes I can be. I know I can't do it by myself. It's up to You, Lord. Thanks for all You're going to do in both our lives—by the grace of Jesus, amen."

"Amen," Ashley whispered.

Tonio scrambled to his feet, pulled her up beside him, then helped her navigate the rocky shoal back to the wet sand. She slipped her sandals on, and they walked back to the house arm in arm.

As they climbed the steps to the wraparound porch, his grip tightened on her arm. He turned her shoulders to face him and searched her eyes. "Ashley, I can't tell you what it means to me to get this whole thing about my past off my chest and know you don't hate me."

She touched his cheek. "I could never hate you, Tonio."

He leaned down and lightly kissed her lips. "I love you, Ashley."

"I love you, too." Had she actually said those words? Tonio looked as surprised as she was.

"You do? You love me?"

Her face flamed. "Yes. I do."

"That's the best medicine yet!"

She moved her fingertips over his chin. "I'll be praying for you tonight. I pray you'll stop condemning yourself long enough to hear God's voice and feel His love."

He pulled her into his arms and held her so tight, she gasped. He smoothed back her windblown hair and whispered into her ear, "If anyone can help me hear His voice again, it's you, Ashley."

At dinner that evening Tonio was in the best of moods—talkative, happy, relaxed. As Mika served grilled porterhouse steaks and baked potatoes, he and Ashley exchanged private smiles across the table. Once or twice she was afraid she would succumb to a fit of giggles. As Dixie chatted about her afternoon shopping spree with Mika, Ashley replayed that magical moment when she told Tonio she loved him. The two of them shared a delicious secret—a blossoming love that made her feel downright giddy. She wanted to shout her feelings to the rooftop but refrained, in case Tonio intended to keep their budding romance confidential for now.

While they were still eating dessert, the phone rang. Mika answered and brought the phone to Tonio. "It's Mr. Ben Radison," she announced.

With a grin, Tonio took the receiver and put it on speakerphone. "Hey, Ben, we're all here. Say hello to Ashley and Dixie. We're having a great time. Wish you were here, ol' man. Or then again, maybe not."

"This isn't a call I wanted to make, Tonio." Ben's voice sounded heavy, strained. "But I've got to give you the heads-up."

Tonio grew serious. "What's going on, Ben?"

"You know we put out a lot of advance publicity on your new book. It's been great for presales."

"That's good news. Why so glum?"

"All the publicity has generated some action among the tabloids. I thought you'd better hear it from me."

"Hear what?"

"That network tabloid show that digs up all the dirt on celebrities is doing a retrospective on you. They're dredging up the accident, doing an investigative report, asking, 'Whatever happened to Brianna Adler, beautiful wife of best-selling author Anthony Adler?' I saw it here on New York time; it'll be coming on your TV in a few minutes."

After a long moment of silence, Tonio said, "Thanks for letting me know, Ben." He hung up the phone, strode to the great room, and turned on the television set. As Ashley joined him on the sofa, she could read the tension and submerged fury in his face. The air was charged with an aura of foreboding. Mika disappeared, busying herself in the kitchen. Dixie quietly excused herself and went back to the cottage.

This is bad, Ashley kept thinking. *Really bad!* Her heart pounded as a long string of commercials gave way to the offending tabloid show. Photos and film clips of Tonio and Brianna flashed on the screen as a resonant voice-over declared, "Was Brianna Adler's death really an accident? Or was something more sinister at play here? In spite of his denials, speculation still runs rampant as to whether Anthony Adler was driving the car that killed his wife that fateful autumn night five years ago. Is it possible this renowned author has gotten away with murder?"

The program droned on with its scathing commentary. "Reclusive author Anthony Adler has been out of the spotlight in recent years, but with the literary world already buzzing over his soon-to-be-released novel, long-buried questions about his wife's tragic death have resurfaced."

Ashley cast a sidelong glance at Tonio. His face was livid, the tendons in his neck taut. His fingernails dug into the sofa arm. "Why did I ever think I could wake up from this nightmare?" he muttered under his breath.

At one point the reporter acknowledged a medical examiner's report that confirmed Brianna's chest injuries were consistent with the impact of the steering wheel. "Tonio, that proves you weren't driving," said Ashley.

He nodded. "That was proved from the beginning, but no one paid any attention. The media would rather distort and sensationalize a story than present the facts."

He was right. The reporter was already suggesting that the medical examiner might have been involved in a cover-up, but then added, almost as an afterthought, "So far there has been no evidence of any impropriety."

"You see that?" said Tonio. "They say just enough to put doubt in people's minds, then cover themselves by admitting there's no real evidence to back up their claims."

Ashley clasped his arm. "You know the truth, Tonio, and I know the truth. The people who matter know the truth. That's what counts."

Tonio stood up and turned off the TV, then paced the room. "The truth is, I still feel responsible for Brianna's death. The reporters are right. No matter how you juggle the facts, if it wasn't for me, Brianna would still be alive!"

"Are you saying you had more power over Brianna's life than God did?" countered Ashley. "Tonio, none of us has that kind of power. It's in God's hands who lives and who dies. Every day we live is an undeserved gift from Him."

Tonio waved her off. "Don't, Ashley. No more sermons, please!"

She got up, went to him, and took his hands in hers. "Okay, no more sermons. But listen, Tonio. Forget about that sleazy program. Forget about the past. Concentrate on today, the good things, the special time we had at the beach."

He turned away, his tone brusque. "I can't, Ashley. I need to be alone. Do you mind?"

She pulled him back. "Are you sure? You look like you could use a friendly face right now."

He looked down at her, his brow furrowed, his eyes blazing. "Please, leave me alone! Go back to the cottage!"

Ashley ran from the room in tears. At the moment, she hated the infuriating Anthony Adler as much as she loved him.

Chapter 18

When Ashley arrived back at the cottage, she found Dixie sitting cross-legged on the bed, working on her laptop. She looked up and asked, "How's it going, Ash?"

"Don't ask." Ashley walked over to the bureau, picked up her brush, and ran it through her hair. Her lower lip was trembling. She didn't want Dixie to see she was about to burst into tears.

But Dixie knew her all too well. She set her laptop aside, scooted off the bed, and approached with a gentle, "I *am* asking. Talk to me, Ash. Tell me what happened."

The two sat down side by side on the bed. "It was awful, Dixie." Between sobs, Ashley poured out the whole story—her conversation with Tonio on the beach, the loving words they had shared, the joy she felt being with him at dinner, and then his explosive reaction to the tabloid show's accusations. "The way he spoke to me tonight, telling me to leave him alone—it was almost as if he wanted me to hate him, as if he was trying to drive me away. Why would he do that when I just told him I loved him?"

"Maybe he realizes things are getting too serious," said Dixie. "He's probably afraid of making another commitment after what happened with his wife."

"He's making me afraid, too. I never know what to expect from him. What should I do?"

"I hate to say this, Ash, but maybe it's time to go home."

Ashley gave Dixie a questioning glance. "You think so?"

Dixie shrugged. "It has to be your decision, but if you want to know how I see it. . ."

"I do. You always have a way of seeing the truth about things."

"Okay. The way I see it, you've gotten so emotionally involved in Tonio's problems, it's distracting you from your own life, maybe even affecting your walk with the Lord."

Ashley was silent for a long moment before replying, "I suppose you're right. I've been anxious and upset over what's happening with Tonio. I guess that means I'm not really trusting God for the future."

Dixie squeezed Ashley's shoulder. "There's nothing more you can do here to help Tonio. Think about getting on with your own life."

Ashley stifled another sob. "I want to, but I can't leave him like this. He's hurting so much. How can I just walk away?"

"I know it won't be easy, but you can do it. You have to think of yourself now, Ash. Tell me, how long before you're finished editing his novel?"

Ashley picked up her pillow and hugged it against her chest. "I'll finish the final edit in a couple of days. Then it's off to the publisher."

"That's about the time I'm going home," said Dixie. "Why don't you fly home with me?"

Ashley pressed her cheek against the down-feathered pillow. Visions of Tonio's tormented blue eyes lingered in her mind like remnants of a dream. "I can't promise anything, but I–I'll think about it."

Dixie sat back on the bed and drew her legs up under her. "Don't just think. Pray. Why don't we pray about it right now?"

Ashley laughed through her tears. "Girl, what would I do without you?" She swung the pillow at Dixie. "You keep me on the straight and narrow."

"I sure do." Dixie tossed the pillow back at Ashley. "And I'm good for a few laughs, too!"

❧

Ashley felt better after her prayer time with Dixie, but she still couldn't sleep. Too many questions tumbled in her brain; too many conflicting emotions tugged at her heart. *Should I go or stay? Love Tonio or leave him?*

After tossing and turning for an hour, she got up, pulled on her robe, and slipped out to the lanai. The wind was rising off the ocean, rustling the trees, and stirring the grasses with hushed whispers. The lanai groaned and the screened windows creaked as if unseen hands were shaking the cottage.

Ashley gazed out toward the main house. All was quiet and dark. Was Tonio sleeping? Or was he pacing the floor, thinking of her?

Or has he gone to the cliffs again?

A sudden sense of foreboding chilled her. She hugged herself, shivering. The more she thought about it, the more likely it seemed that he would go there tonight. The tabloid show had left him distraught, and perhaps he was regretting the way he had sent her away so harshly. She recalled his words that afternoon on the beach. "*It's as if the devil himself keeps drawing me to the cliff and taunting me to jump into the ocean to make atonement for my sin.*"

"Dear Lord, no," she whispered. "Don't let him do it!"

With growing urgency, she rushed back inside, threw on a shirt, jeans, and sandals, and set out through the woods to the cliffs. As she made her way through palm and mango trees and the thick undergrowth of tropical ferns, the wind whistled through swaying branches and sent little eddies of leaves whirling at her feet. She stepped gingerly among the brambles and twigs, following slivers of moonlight that pierced the dense foliage. Twice she stumbled and caught herself, her breathing labored, her mind playing tricks on her. The forest seemed alive with whispers, its spreading limbs moving, stirring, swaying as if in a hushed requiem of lament. Did all of nature know what she was just beginning to fear—that Tonio's life hung in the balance tonight?

When she finally emerged into the clearing, her first glimpse was of a full moon casting a silver ribbon of light over the rocky cliffs. But her heart caught in her throat as she spotted a dark figure standing at the edge of the precipice.

Tonio!

He stood facing the sea, his arms raised, a liquor bottle in one hand, the wind howling around him.

Ashley moved toward him, slowly, silently, one agonizing step after another. At any moment he could jump and be gone. She resisted the urge to call out to him. If she startled him, he could lose his balance and fall. A twig snapped under her foot. She stopped, holding her breath. But the sound was lost in the eerie whine and moan of the wind.

When she got closer, she spoke his name gently. "Tonio."

He pivoted and stared at her as if waking from a dream. Moonlight and shadows accented his rugged features. His voice was husky with surprise. "Ashley?"

She held out her hands to him. "Please, Tonio, don't do it."

He shook his head, looking bewildered. "Don't do what?"

"Don't listen to the devil's lies. You can't give your life to atone for Brianna's death."

He accepted her outstretched hand. "Is that what you think? That I'm going to jump?"

She searched his shadowed eyes. "Yes. Weren't you?"

The wind whipped his ebony hair and rippled his shirt. "I came here to throw this bottle of booze into the sea. I almost gave in and drank it tonight. All these years I kept it just in case I needed it. I really needed it tonight, but God gave me the strength to resist. Now I'm giving it to Him once and for all." As if to prove his point, he turned and heaved the bottle into the ocean. "There. It's gone. Forever!"

He turned back and opened his arms to her. She eagerly entered his embrace, pressing her head against his strong chest, savoring the delicious warmth of his sturdy arms. "I love you, dearest one," he whispered against her hair.

"Oh Tonio, I love you, too."

A capricious wind wrapped around them, groaning a disquieting siren song. As they steeled themselves against its gusty blast, Tonio's foot slipped on loose lava rocks lining the craggy shelf. A scream tore from Ashley's throat as the earth beneath their feet gave way. They both scrambled to regain their footing on the cascading gravel. Tonio pushed her hard, propelling her backward, sprawling and dazed, onto the grass.

"Tonio!" Her eyes searched the darkness, her heart jack-hammering. *Did he go over? No, no, no!*

"I'm here, Ashley!"

She crawled toward the flinty edge, the taste of salt spray and grit in her mouth. Tonio was there, a shadowed figure grasping a moon-washed boulder, his feet kicking at sheer air. "Get back," he rasped. "It's not stable. It's all going to go!"

"No! Let me help you."

"Go!"

She held out her hand.

As his fingers circled her wrist, the thunder of falling rocks echoed against the roar of the restless ocean below them. His grip was so tight she winced. "Hold on to the rock," he told her, his breathing ragged. With monumental effort, he swung one leg onto the bluff, hoisted himself up onto the rock, and climbed back to solid ground.

They clung to each other for a long moment, trembling. She wept. He kissed her hair. "I think you just saved my life."

"You saved mine first."

He slipped his arm around her shoulders and walked her back to the cottage. Pausing outside her door, he looked down at her and said, "We're both exhausted tonight. But tomorrow we'll talk. We both have a lot to say. For now, good night, love."

❧

At breakfast the next morning, Ashley and Tonio exchanged private glances across the table while Dixie chatted about the souvenirs she wanted to purchase before leaving Hawaii. "I'm going to spend all day in town. You two don't mind, do you? You can come with me, Ashley, if you like. I've mapped out all the stores. I'm getting some more of those chocolate-covered macadamia nuts—they're absolutely delicious!—and I'm dying to get one of those hot pink sarongs to match my bathing suit. And I love those little koa wood bowls. They're great for salads and popcorn. And, of course, I can't leave without some more Kona coffee. What do you think, Ashley? Do you want to come, or would you be totally bored? You've been here so long, you've probably seen everything already, right?"

"I've seen a lot," Ashley agreed. "The truth is, Tonio and I really need to spend the day finishing the edits on his novel."

"Oh, sure, sure you do." Dixie took one last swallow of coffee and stood up. "So I'll get out of your hair and let you guys work, work, work." She paused. "You don't mind if I borrow your car, do you, Tonio?"

"Not at all." He reached in his pocket and handed her the keys. "Have fun. Take all the time you need."

"Thanks, Tonio. I'll bring you guys some sushi or pineapples or coconuts or something."

"Don't worry about us," said Ashley. "Just go!"

Dixie gave a little wave as she headed for the door. "Shop 'til you drop, that's my motto."

When she had gone, Tonio sat back in his chair and laughed. "I know she's your best friend, but I didn't think she'd ever stop talking."

Ashley sipped her coffee. "I know. I felt the same way."

"All I could think about was how much I wanted to be alone with you, free to talk, free to share what's on my heart."

Ashley nodded. "Me, too."

Tonio pushed his plate aside. "I know we have to work on the book, but first we talk, okay?"

She loved the merry glint in his eyes today. "Sounds good to me."

He got up from the table and called into the kitchen, "Thanks for breakfast, Mika. It was great, as usual." He took Ashley's hand and helped her up. "Now let's head for the office for some private time together."

After closing the door behind them, they settled on the sofa facing the wall of windows overlooking the pool area. The sun shone in, suffusing the room with a rosy warmth. Tonio reached over and took her hand. "It's been quite a roller-coaster ride, hasn't it?"

"You mean, our relationship? Or are you talking about the last few days?"

"Both."

He rubbed the back of her hand. "Last night was a wake-up call for me. I was so stupid to go to the cliff like that, as if it were some necessary ritual or rite of passage. When I think that we both could have been killed, I shudder inside."

"I thought you were going to. . ." She let her words drop off.

"Ashley, I would never do that. I'm sorry I put that idea into your head. I realize our relationship has been unconventional, to say the least. You've had to put up with a lot from me. But God has used you in so many ways to reach into my heart and change me. I don't know what I would do without you."

Ashley glanced out toward the pool, where rivers of sunlit diamonds sparkled on its surface. She didn't know what to say to Tonio. She was still struggling for answers. Did God want them together, or did He want her to go back to New York? How could she be sure she was following His will and not just her own wishes?

"You look lost in thought," Tonio noted.

She met his gaze. "I'm sorry. I guess I have a lot on my mind."

He squeezed her hand. "I hope I'm uppermost in your thoughts."

She smiled. "You are. You know you are. But things are so complicated."

"They don't have to be."

"What are you saying?"

He released her hand, sat forward, and massaged his knuckles. "I just want you to know that all the things you've been trying to drum into my thick skull are finally making sense. Last night when I got back to the house I had some time to think. . .and pray. I got out my Bible and read several passages in the Gospel of Mark, especially Mark 12:30, the Great Commandment."

"That's my favorite verse," said Ashley. "It amazes me that God desires our love. He has all of heaven, all of creation, and yet He still wants us to love Him."

"Quite a challenge," said Tonio. "Loving God with all our heart, soul, mind, and strength. I thought a lot about that last night, and I realized what you said about my pride was absolutely correct."

Ashley settled back into the corner of the sofa and tucked her legs under her. "Really?"

"Yeah, really. As long as I kept my eyes focused on myself and my failures, I was putting myself first. And that's selfish. And wrong. That's what I've been doing. And it's kept me from feeling close to God. I couldn't experience His forgiveness when I refused to forgive myself, because in a perverse way I was thinking only of myself, not Him."

"Exactly."

He reached over and rubbed her shoulder. "So now I'm trying to do what you suggested. And what the scripture says. Focus on Jesus. Love Him with everything in me. And everything else is simply in His hands."

"And how does that make you feel?"

He thought a moment. "It makes me feel. . .free. Forgiven. Joyful. As if a huge boulder had rolled off my shoulders into the ocean, never to be seen again. My mind is clear for the first time in years."

"I am so happy for you." He was still massaging her neck. She placed her hand over his, savoring the warmth. She wished they could be together like this forever.

"I owe it all to you, Ashley," he said, his deep voice resonating with emotion. "You didn't give up on me. You helped me get back on track."

"It wasn't me, Tonio. God wooed you back."

"He used you to show me the truth."

She smiled. "I'm grateful I could help."

"There's so much more I want to say, Ashley." He pulled her over beside him, his arm circling her shoulders, his fingertips lightly drumming her arm. Her head rested easily on his chest. She loved being close to him like this, savoring the warmth of his touch, the fresh scent of his aftershave, the nubby texture of his shirt against her cheek. But what would happen to this sweet fellowship when she told him she might go home?

"Ashley, did you hear me?" He pressed his chin against the top of her head.

"What?" With her ear against his chest, she could hear his heartbeat and feel the rumbling, reassuring vibration of his voice.

"I said, we have so much more to talk about. Before, I was so consumed with keeping secrets from you—about Brianna, my drinking, the accident—I couldn't allow myself to think of a future together. But now—now you know everything. And you're still here. Even last night on the cliff you said you loved me, as I love you. You meant it, didn't you?"

"Yes," she murmured, "I do love you."

His arm tightened around her. "And I love you more than I can say." He lifted her face to his and gently kissed her lips. "This is only the beginning, Ashley. It came to me this morning how perfect we are for each other. Maybe it's too soon to speak of marriage—I don't know—but I pray that someday you might consider becoming my wife."

Ashley pulled away from his embrace. She brushed her tousled hair back from her face. "Your wife?"

His brow furrowed. "I spoke too soon, didn't I? Like a fool, I'm rushing headlong into this. Too fast. Too soon. I can see you're upset."

"Not upset. Surprised. A little overwhelmed."

"I'm not asking you today, Ashley. This isn't an official proposal. It's just something to think and pray about."

"I will. I'll pray about it."

"But you are upset. I can see it in your eyes."

Ashley looked away. "It's just—I don't know what God wants me to do. Since coming to Hawaii, I've let so many things distract me from my relationship with Him."

"You mean me?"

"You. Ben. My work. Everything. It's so easy for everyday life to get in the way. Just like you, Tonio, I'm trying to focus again on my walk with Christ."

"Can't we do that together, Ashley? I can't imagine a better life than that—the two of us serving God together."

She folded her hands under her chin. "It sounds wonderful, but. . ."

"But what?"

"God may have other plans for me."

"What other plans? What are you talking about?"

"I don't know how to tell you this—"

Impatience crept into his voice. "Just say it, Ashley."

"Okay. Here's the thing. I–I've been thinking about going back to New York."

"New York?" Tonio's tone was sharp, incredulous. "You can't be serious."

"It's the truth." She forced out the words. "I'm thinking of flying home with Dixie."

"Is this her idea? Did she talk you into it?"

"No. It's just something I've been thinking about, something I feel the Lord is leading me to do. Our work is done. You've worked through your problems. There's no reason for me to stay."

"There's every reason!" A vein throbbed in Tonio's temple. "I love you, Ashley. You love me."

Hot tears scalded her eyes. "It's not enough, Tonio."

"You're telling me love isn't enough to build a future on? Then what is?"

She brushed away her tears. "I've got to know it's God's will."

Tonio raked his fingers through his hair. "Of course it's His will. Why else do you think He brought us together? He's orchestrated every step of the way."

"I want to believe that, Tonio. I want us to be together. But I don't know if it's God plan or just my own wishful thinking. I made a mistake with Ben. I don't want to make the same mistake again."

He shot her a wounded glance. "I'm not Ben."

"I know."

"Is that the problem? You still want Ben?"

"No, I didn't say that."

"But if God wanted you with Ben, you'd go back to him?"

"I suppose. But this isn't about Ben. It's about us—about what God wants for us."

Tonio stood up and walked over to the window. "All right," he said, an edge in his voice. "Maybe we've both said enough for now. Pray about it, Ashley. I'll pray, too. We'll see what happens. Meanwhile, if you're thinking about going home in a few days, we'd better get back to work on those final edits."

Over the next two days Tonio said nothing about his proposal or their future together. Everything was strictly business. He and Ashley finished the work on his novel and e-mailed the completed manuscript to Ben. Ben replied with a brief e-mail:

> *Congratulations, Tonio! This is a winner. Your best work yet! Good work, Ashley. You've brought out the best in Tonio. You're a great team*

Reading Ben's e-mail, Ashley couldn't miss the irony in his remarks. If she and Tonio were really such a great team, why was she feeling so conflicted over their relationship? As much as she wanted to stay in Hawaii, and as hard as she prayed that God would give her the peace to stay, she nevertheless found herself packing up her belongings and preparing to go home with Dixie.

Until the very hour that she and Dixie were to leave for the airport, Ashley continued bombarding heaven with prayers that God would show her she belonged with Tonio. But no signs from heaven appeared, no angel of light revealed the road best taken, no vision captured her senses with a certainty that Tonio was the man for her.

In the wake of God's apparent silence, Ashley said good-bye to Anthony Adler and the lovely, romantic, turbulent, mercurial life she had known in Kona. They said good-bye at the airport with a restrained embrace, a minimum of words, and an undercurrent of emotion as tempestuous as a storm-whipped sea.

Ashley's heart broke as Tonio said, "I'll never forget you. You'll always be a part of me."

Fighting back tears, she replied, "You'll always be in my heart, too."

All the way home on the six-hour flight to New York, Ashley's thoughts raged with recriminations and second thoughts. *What on earth are you doing leaving the man you love? What more do you want than a genuine, amazing, fascinating man like Tonio? What more do you expect—a letter of permission from God written in the clouds? What if you've just thrown away your last chance at happiness?*

But as her plane touched down at Kennedy International Airport, Ashley's pulse raced. She was home, in the world she had known for so many years, about to resume the life she had left behind after Ben broke her heart. God was still in charge. He knew her heart. No matter what the future held, she desired to be obedient to Him.

Chapter 19

Over the next six months, as Ashley settled back into life in New York City, she and Tonio kept in touch by e-mail.

December 23

Tonio, I can hardly believe I've been away from Hawaii for nearly a month. I got my job back at Haricott, working now for another editor. Not Ben—although we pass in the halls and share a cup of coffee in the cafeteria now and then. The snow is falling here in New York, and the streets are strung with festive lights. I'm sitting here in my little apartment with my miniature Christmas tree while icicles hang like crystal stalactites from my windows and two-foot snowdrifts blanket the yard. How I miss Hawaii's sun and surf, the tropical flowers, and all the greenery. Most of all, I miss you.

December 25

Merry Christmas, Ashley. How I wish you were here. I keep looking out at the cottage and expecting to see you there. This big old house feels so empty without you bustling about the office or sitting across from me at dinner or walking with me along the beach. I'm still attending AA, but I'm also getting more involved in my church. I've joined the men's prayer group, and even though I'm a loner at heart, I'm enjoying the fellowship and discovering the power and blessings that come from praying for one another. And, of course, every moment of every day you have my prayers, dear Ashley. . .and my heart.

January 13

Tonio, I can't believe it's a new year already. The snow is still here, deeper than ever. But Hawaii is in my heart. At various times during the day I try to picture what you are doing. Then I remember it's six hours earlier there and you're half a world away. I miss you! By the way, be praying for Ben. We've talked things out. I've vented; he's listened. We've both had to do a reality check on our lives. He seems to be taking his faith seriously. He's often at church these days. Pray that he continues to grow in the Lord.

January 19

Ashley, is there more about Ben you're not telling me? Or don't I have the right to ask?

January 20

Ben and I are in the process of making peace with each other. The wounds are healing. We've agreed to be friends—friends who keep their distance.

February 6

Ashley, it amazes me that I still feel your presence here in this house. Sometimes I walk around my estate and imagine you beside me, enjoying the sunsets, gazing out at the sea, burrowing your toes in the sand. I resist the urge to phone you lest, hearing your voice, I throw caution to the wind and rush to New York to bring you home with me.

February 10

Oh Tonio, I haven't called you for the same reason. As long as I don't hear your voice, I can pretend you aren't quite real. How I miss you! But God is teaching me to be patient, to wait on Him, to trust that He knows best. My work at Haricott is going well, but it's not as much fun as working for a certain renowned novelist living in Hawaii. I'm working again on my novel and sending out proposals to Christian publishers. Pray that my novel will find a happy home somewhere.

March 18

Ashley, I'm so pleased you're back at work on your novel. It's a beautiful story, and I pray it will be embraced by just the right publisher. My novel, Cliffs over Kona, *will be on store shelves next week. For the most part, the reviews are good and presales are strong. I keep thinking about how much you poured yourself into this book. You encouraged me to reach deep within myself and search for truth, no matter how painful. Not only is this a better book because of you—I'm a better person for having known you. I'll forever be indebted to you, my love.*

March 29

Tonio, thank you for the autographed copy of your book. It looks beautiful. And I never dreamed that you would dedicate it to me. Thank you! I will treasure it always. . .as I treasure you.

April 4

Ashley, I'll be starting a six-week, multi-city book tour next week. I'll be doing lots of media interviews and book signings. I admit I'm dreading the whole ghastly experience, but 'tis the life I've chosen, so I'd better not complain too loudly. Naturally I'd rather be home writing than living out of dreary hotels and drearier airports. Say a prayer for me. Wherever I may be in the weeks ahead, my heart is still there with you.

May 1

Tonio, I just heard the news. Congratulations on winning the National Golden Pen Award! It looks like our paths will be crossing here in New York City when you come to accept your award. I can't wait to see you again.

May 3

Dear girl, no award will mean half as much to me as seeing you again. I'm counting the days.

May 27

News item in the New York Times*: The National Golden Pen Awards ceremony will be held at the Waldorf Astoria at 6:00 p.m., Saturday, May 30th. The literary community will gather to honor bestselling author Anthony Adler with first prize for his latest novel,* Cliffs over Kona. *Adler, who just completed a national book tour, will give the keynote address. His novel, which has won rave reviews even among his harshest critics, is being made into a major motion picture scheduled for release next year.*

For weeks Ashley had looked forward to this evening. At times she had awakened in the middle of the night, her heart pounding at the thought of seeing Tonio again. Now here she was at the world-famous Waldorf-Astoria Hotel, sitting beside Ben and Dixie in an opulent ballroom, watching Tonio receive his award. She hadn't had a chance to talk with him yet. His plane had been late, so he had come here directly from the airport, with just enough time to take the stage for his speech. But they would be together again at the gala reception after the ceremony. What would she say to him after all this time?

The ceremony lasted less than two hours, but for Ashley it seemed eternal. When the final applause died out, she was the first on her feet. She slipped through the crowd ahead of Ben and Dixie. Even in her flowing, mint green strapless gown, with her blond hair styled in a cascade of crimped curls, she felt tongue-tied and self-conscious as a schoolgirl.

"Wait up, Ash," said Dixie. "We're right here with you, okay?"

"I know. What I don't know is what I'll say or how I'll feel when I see Tonio again. I just might swoon at his feet."

Dixie chuckled. "At least that would make a memorable impression."

"That's not the kind of impression I'm hoping for."

"I know. You want him to take one look at you and wonder why he ever let you out of his sight."

Ashley grimaced. "You know me way too well, Dixie."

"I sure do. You're hoping he'll sweep in and whisk you back to Hawaii on his white steed. Or a jet airplane. Whatever."

"You think?"

"Only you're really afraid when you see him again, nothing will happen, and you'll each keep going your separate ways."

Ashley clasped Dixie's hand. "You guessed it, girlfriend. I walked away from him when I left Hawaii. What if he walks away from me now?"

"It's in God's hands, Ash. He knows what's best for both of you."

"I know. I keep holding on to that thought."

The party was well under way as they entered the festive reception hall. An orchestra was playing and people were mingling and laughing. It promised to be a beautiful night to remember.

"I'm heading for the hors d'oeuvres," said Dixie. "I hope they have some of those little crispy things with cream cheese. Want me to get you guys something?"

"No, I'm fine for now," said Ben.

"Me, too." Ashley scanned the crowd for Tonio. Just as she was about to give up, she turned, and there he was, bigger than life, more handsome than ever in his black tuxedo and tails.

"Tonio!" Her ankles were suddenly weak in her three-inch heels.

"Hello, Ashley." His blue eyes flashed with admiration. "You look stunning as usual."

Her face warmed. "Thank you. So do you."

He embraced her, then handed her a long-stemmed goblet. "I brought you a ginger ale."

She accepted the glass with a little titter of laughter. His closeness left her feeling light-headed and giddy. "You didn't have to do that, Tonio. I should bring you a drink. You're the man of the hour."

"She's right, ol' man," said Ben, extending his hand. "Congratulations on the award. It was well deserved."

"And thank you again for dedicating the book to me," said Ashley. "I never expected that."

"It wouldn't be the book it is today without you, Ashley," said Tonio. "And you, Ben. You two deserve the acclaim as much as I do."

"Now you're being unduly modest," said Ben. "That's not like you, Tonio."

He grinned. "Let's say it's been quite a year of change for all of us."

"Yes, it has," said Ben. "Mostly changes for the good."

Ben turned to Ashley. "Listen, I'm going to go find Dixie and help her carry back those heaping plates of goodies she's no doubt collected."

As Ben walked away, Tonio said, "He's a good man."

Ashley nodded. "Yes, he is."

Tonio's voice deepened. "It's been a long time."

She nodded again. "Six months."

"You never called."

I couldn't bear the pain of hearing your voice again. "Neither did you," she said.

"So many times I almost called you, but, frankly, hearing your voice would have stirred up all the loneliness again." He touched her arm, his eyes looking deep into hers. "I've got to know. Are you happy living in New York? Really happy?"

She looked away, flustered. "Happy? Why wouldn't I be happy?"

He rubbed her arm gently. "I just need to be sure. There's nothing more I want for you than your happiness."

She studied him. "What about you? Are you happy?"

"Sure. I'm content." He cleared his throat. "I've come a long way since last year. God has done a lot of work in my life. I'm not the tormented man I used to be. In fact, I can't complain about anything. God has given me the peace and fellowship with Him I've always longed for."

Ashley's eyes filled. "I'm happy for you, Tonio. That's been my prayer for you every day."

"And I'm happy for you," he said. "It looks like you have the stable life you've always wanted."

She nodded. "I suppose I do. I finished writing my novel."

"Wonderful. The first of many, I hope."

"It's coming out next year with a Christian publishing house in the Midwest. I just found out two days ago. It probably won't be the blockbuster yours is, but I'll be reaching people with the message the Lord has given me."

He squeezed her arm. "I'm so proud of you, Ashley. It sounds like you're living a rather perfect life these days."

"I don't know if I'd call it perfect, but I have a pleasant routine—work, writing, friends, family, church."

He smiled. "What more could you want?"

She sipped her ginger ale. "It's not set in stone, of course. My life, I mean. It could change."

"It could?"

"Yes. I may not always stay in New York."

"Really? You might consider going somewhere else?"

"Of course. I'm always open to a little adventure in my life." *What kind of banal conversation is this?* she wondered. Why couldn't she say what she wanted to say?

Tonio rubbed his jaw. "I'm glad to hear that, Ashley. I am, too. Open, I mean. To a little adventure."

"Your life in Hawaii is quite adventurous, I'd say."

"Yes, I'd say so. Hawaii is a wonderful place for adventure—assuming that's what you're looking for."

"Yes, assuming that, Hawaii is a wonderful place. I loved it there."

"I'm glad you loved it there. I love it, too."

"Quite a coincidence, isn't it?" she murmured.

"A coincidence?"

"Both of us loving Hawaii so much."

A hearty chuckle rose from Tonio's throat. "This is the most confounding conversation I've ever had. Do either of us have the slightest idea what we're talking about?"

The humor in the moment struck Ashley, too. She stifled an urge to grin foolishly. "You're right. We're not expressing ourselves very well. We sound like dunderheads."

"Now there's a word I haven't heard lately. If you mean we're acting like a couple of fools, I heartily agree. Neither of us is admitting what's really on our minds."

He stepped forward and drew her into his arms. He held her close and whispered into her ear, "Here's what I really want to say. Is there still a chance for us?"

She rested her head against his chest. For the first time in over six months she felt at home, in exactly the place she was meant to be. "Yes, Tonio, there's every chance," she replied with a sigh. "I love you more than words can say."

He pressed his lips against her hair. "I never stopped loving you, Ashley. Not for a moment. You were in my heart wherever I went. No matter what I did, you were there."

"I felt the same way," she confessed. "You know I didn't want to leave Hawaii, but I had to. It wasn't God's time for us."

"You were so sure of that."

"No, I wasn't sure at all. It's taken all this time for me to understand why God was holding me back."

"And now you understand?"

"Yes, Tonio. I do. We were two very wounded people back then. We both needed time to heal. We needed to let God make us whole again without leaning on each other as a crutch."

"If you were a crutch, you were a very lovely one."

She smiled. "You know what I mean. God had special work to do in us. And I think we both let Him do it."

He tipped her face up to his, his eyes twinkling. "Are you saying what I think you're saying, love? Is this God's time for us?"

A smile started in her heart and spread to her lips. "Yes, Tonio, I believe it is."

He cut off her words with a kiss, slow and tender and exquisite. For one glorious moment Ashley forgot they were standing in a banquet hall surrounded by party guests. Then she heard a patter of applause. She looked around, her face heating with embarrassment. Several guests were watching, smiling, clapping.

Amid the applause, Tonio slipped his arm around her waist and held her as if he would never let her go. "I was just thinking, my love," he murmured against her ear, "God willing, September is a wonderful time of year for a wedding in Hawaii."

She looked up at him, thrilling to the love she saw in his eyes. "Yes, sweetheart, God willing, September is a perfect time!"

TO LOVE A GENTLE STRANGER

Dedication

To my son, David Aldon Page—my only son! I love you with all my heart and am so proud of you. How thankful I am that you have always walked faithfully with the Lord.

Prologue

Hey, my cute little snuggle-bunny, wake up!"

Marnie rolled over and stretched languorously. She wasn't ready to let go of her lovely, pastel dreams. But, as usual, her dear husband wasn't about to let her sleep. "One more minute, Jeff," she pleaded.

"Thirty seconds."

"Forty-five." She pressed one foot against his leg.

"Hey, babe, stop that. Your feet are cold."

"I know. Aren't you my personal foot warmer?"

He raised up on one elbow. "So that's why you married me!"

"That and a million other reasons, Mr. Jordan."

"Really, Mrs. Jordan?" He pulled her into his arms. "I'd love to hear every one."

"It would take a lifetime."

"That's okay." He kissed the top of her head. "I'm yours for a lifetime."

"Me, too." She loved snuggling like this in the mornings—lying in the curve of her husband's arms, her head on his chest, his heart beating against her cheek. It was like being in a warm, safe harbor. Jeff was the kindest, most handsome man she had ever known. And he was hers, all hers. "Jeff, I dreamed about our wedding," she murmured lazily. "We were there on Keauhou Beach under a trellis of plumeria and roses, and the sun had turned the ocean a shimmering gold. Everyone was there cheering us on—our families from the mainland, Nate and Jenny and all our other friends from church and the university. It was perfect."

"That wasn't a dream, honey. That's how it really was."

"I know. Can you believe it's been six whole months? It seems like yesterday. And I was reliving every delicious moment. Until you woke me up!" She sat up, grabbed her pillow, and gave him a playful swat.

"So it's a pillow fight you want? Well, you've met your match!" He seized his pillow and flung it at her. She caught it, but before she could throw it back, he grabbed her around the waist and tickled her.

"Not fair!" she cried between fits of giggles.

"All's fair in love and war! And this is both!"

She wriggled out of his grasp. "Truce! Truce!"

He released her, and they both lay back laughing. She looked over at her smiling husband. His chestnut brown hair was mussed, with several wayward strands curling over his forehead. His blue eyes were twinkling. He reminded her of a mischievous little boy. "Look at us, Jeff, acting like children! I haven't even gotten out of bed yet, and I'm already exhausted."

"Well, catch your breath, babe, because we're driving to Hilo for a day of fun in the sun. I want to be on the road in an hour."

"Fun in the sun? Isn't it always raining in Hilo?"

"I guess you're right. So we'll play in the rain."

She scrambled out of bed. "Speaking of getting wet, last one to the shower fixes breakfast!"

He was right behind her. "I'll fix scrambled eggs if you do the French toast."

"Go put the coffee on, and you've got a deal!"

After breakfast, Jeff opened his thumb-worn Bible for morning devotions. She loved hearing him read the scriptures, but she loved him most when he held her hands across the table and prayed. He had such a natural, spontaneous intimacy with God. Her relationship with the Lord had always seemed more restrained and formal, perhaps because that's how she had been raised. But Jeff was teaching her to relax in God's presence and simply enjoy His fellowship.

The sound of a sudden downpour nearly drowned out their prayers. Jeff went to the window of their small apartment and looked out. "Can you believe it? It's raining buckets. Maybe we should postpone our trip to Hilo."

She ambled over and hugged his arm. "Come on, Jeff. We won't melt. Besides, we're going to the rainforest where it rains all the time anyway. And we've been planning this trip for days. You know how much I want to see the botanical gardens and Rainbow Falls again. It's where we first kissed, remember?"

"Do you think I could ever forget an amazing event like that?" He jingled his car keys. "Then let's go, babe. Rain or shine, we're on our way."

Minutes later, they were heading along the upper road toward Waimea in their small sedan, affectionately tagged "Old Reliable." Jeff often joked that the car was nearly as old as they were. But it got them where they needed to go. Eventually.

Marnie sighed. "With this rain, it may take all day to get to Hilo."

Jeff leaned forward, white-knuckling the wheel. Traffic was at a standstill. Torrents of water pelted the windshield. "I had planned on getting home early tonight. I have a research paper due for Old Testament Hebrew on Monday."

"Turn around if you like," said Marnie. "I have a paper to write for my journalism class. I guess we'd be better off at home studying."

"But you had your heart set on Rainbow Falls."

"We can go another time, Jeff. Let's just go home, okay?"

"Fine with me."

They were twenty miles short of Waimea when Jeff found a place to turn around on the winding, two-lane road. Traffic was lighter now, but the rain was unrelenting. Jeff glanced over at Marnie. "Sure you don't mind going home?"

She tucked her arm in his. "No, I can't wait to snuggle up on the couch with our laptops."

He laughed. "Now that's a romantic image!"

"You know what I mean. I love studying together."

"And I love our little breaks from studying, when I can steal a few kisses."

She nodded. "That's the best part."

"Totally, babe!"

Marnie stiffened. "Oh Jeff, be careful!" A truck was approaching on the narrow road, going too fast on the rain-slick pavement. Her hand tightened on his arm.

She watched, transfixed with horror, as the truck hydroplaned across the road into their lane. It bore down on them like a crazed, glassy-eyed behemoth, spewing gravel, out of control. Jeff wrenched his steering wheel to the right. As the truck whizzed by, their vehicle rode the edge of the pavement. Its wheels spun helplessly on the collapsing, mud-soaked shoulder, Marnie's screams mixing with the shrill of squealing tires. With a violent, dizzying shudder, Old Reliable plunged down the steep embankment to the volcanic rocks below. The impact brought convulsive jolts and the shattering, ear-splitting cacophony of metal crushing metal. And then, silence—except for the pelting rain—and utter, all-embracing darkness.

Chapter 1

Pounding, relentless rain drenched his face, blinding him. He was sandwiched between upholstery and a twisted steel frame. He tried to move. Everything hurt. Tangled metal was everywhere. Something was clamping his leg like a vise. His chest hurt. Hard to breathe. The taste of blood in his mouth, blood and rainwater mixing in his throat, gagging him. He tried turning his head. Couldn't see much with the rain and blood in his eyes. "Marnie?" he rasped. "Marnie, you okay?"

He looked over where the passenger seat had been. It was covered with debris. The windshield was gone. Marnie was lying across the dashboard, her head facedown on the crumpled hood. He wouldn't have known it was Marnie, for all the blood. *She's dead! My baby's dead!*

He stretched his hand out to her, but the world was suddenly spinning, sucking him into a vortex of darkness. From somewhere far away, he heard a siren screaming, or maybe he was the one screaming. He had to stay alert. Had to help the woman he loved. With consciousness ebbing, he fought to stay awake. At last, his eyes closed and his hand fell to his side, while the rain, the screams, and the blood dissolved into blackness.

When he woke, he was lying in a hospital bed, hooked up to tubes and IVs. His parents were sitting beside his bed, looking more worried than he had ever seen them. He tried to talk, but his tongue felt like cotton. His mother got up and leaned over him, touching his cheek with her fingertips. "Jeff, honey, I love you, baby!" Her face looked pinched and her hair grayer than he remembered. She looked older than her fifty-two years.

His father came around to the other side of the bed and squeezed his shoulder. "Hey boy, you gave us quite a scare!"

"What. . .happened?"

His mother stifled a sob. "You were in an accident, honey."

Jeff forced out the words over the pain in his chest. "How bad. . .is it?"

"You're banged up pretty good," said his father. "Got a cracked rib and torn ligaments in your leg. But, knowing you, you'll be back on your feet in no time."

Jeff managed a crooked grin. "But probably not today, huh?"

"No, not today, son." The lines in his dad's face were deeper, his hair a little thinner, his frame heavier. How long since Jeff had seen his parents? Was it only six months? Yes, they had flown in from California for the wedding last summer.

The wedding. Marnie!

Jeff tried to raise himself up, but his chest hurt too much; he couldn't move his torso. "Where's Marnie?" he cried. "Is she okay?"

His parents exchanged wary glances.

"Mom? Dad? She's okay, isn't she? I gotta see her—now!"

"You can't, honey." His mother ran a cool, soothing hand over his forehead. "She's in surgery, sweetheart."

Jeff's body tightened with alarm. "She's not gonna die, is she?"

"We don't know, son," said his father. "All we can do is pray. And trust God to watch over her."

Jeff sank back and closed his eyes. "Please, God, don't let her die!"

Darkness.

Heavy.

Oppressive.

All-encompassing.

And then, a glimmer of light.

She felt herself rising through layers of blackness toward it, sloughing off fingers of night reluctant to let her go. She opened her eyes to stark whiteness, too bright, nearly painful with brightness. She closed her lids and focused on her own breathing—the ragged intake of air—her chest rising then falling as the air escaped her nostrils. The steady rhythm of her breathing comforted her, although she had no idea why she needed comfort.

She wasn't in pain. Except for the sensation of her own breathing, she wasn't sure she was even connected to her body. She couldn't feel her hands, fingers, legs, toes. She was floating somewhere in space, unfettered by earth.

Was this what it was like to die?

She blinked against the light, slowly adjusting to the brightness. As the physical parameters of the room took shape, her vision swept over foreign pieces of equipment, tubes, and wires—odd contraptions that held no meaning for her—and anonymous paintings of unfamiliar places framed against blank, white walls. Machines whirred and pinged around her with a persistent drone. And the smells assaulting her nostrils were medicinal, sterile, heavily antiseptic.

This isn't heaven!

Then, where am I?

She closed her eyes and waited. It was as if something important had been on the tip of her tongue, at the very edge of her mind, and now it had escaped, had receded from her consciousness into a massive fog bank. She couldn't retrieve it, and yet, she was aware of it, aware of its loss, just as she was aware of a vast store of information—memories, feelings, impressions—stealing away into the murkiness, like a dream that fades on waking, just beyond her grasp.

Her mouth tasted stale, musty, as if she had been asleep for eons. Yes, that was it. She had overslept. That was why she felt so sluggish, so disconnected from her body, her thoughts so jumbled. She tried to move, but her arms and legs refused to respond. How could she have slept so long that she couldn't rouse her own body? It had to be the bed. It was too firm, not her bed. Why was she in someone else's bed?

She heard a voice speaking from a great distance away. A man's voice. Sounding urgent, agitated. "Marnie? Marnie! Thank God, you're awake!"

She stared up into the face of a stranger. He was tall and broad-shouldered, with curly, dark brown hair and thick brows over gentle blue eyes. He was bending over her, his strong hands on her shoulders, his sturdy, chiseled face wet with tears. She opened her mouth to scream, but no sound emerged. The man released her and ran from the room. She sank back against her pillow, her heart hammering.

Just when she thought she was safe, several people—apparitions in white—burst into the room and scurried around her, doing things that made no sense. One woman leaned over her and clasped her hand. "Mrs. Jordan, can you hear me?"

Who's Mrs. Jordan?

The dark-haired man had returned, too. He was touching her face. "Marnie, are you okay?"

At last, she found her voice. "Where. . .am I?" she rasped.

"She's trying to speak," said the man. "That's a good sign, isn't it?"

"Yes," said the woman. "I'll get the doctor."

When she tried to speak again, an incredible exhaustion overtook her, and she felt herself slip back into the soothing darkness.

Sometime later—whether minutes, hours, or days, she had no idea—she woke again and saw the stranger sitting beside her bed. He was reading something—was it a Bible?—and his lanky frame was bent over in the chair as he murmured something under his breath. He appeared to be praying.

Swallowing over the dry, acrid taste in her mouth, she whispered, "What. . . happened?"

The man swiveled in his chair, suddenly alert, and gazed intently at her. The shadow of a beard covered his sculpted chin. "What are you trying to say, Marnie?"

She repeated the words. "What. . .happened?"

"I don't understand. Are you asking about the accident?"

Accident? I don't remember any accident.

"Don't try to talk, Marnie. Just concentrate on getting well."

Getting well? Am I sick? How could I be sick and not know it? "You. . .my doctor?" she asked, struggling to form the words.

He gave her a look of surprise and incredulity, as if she had asked, *Are you the man in the moon?* "No, Marnie, I'm not your doctor," he said with a slight tremor in his voice. "I'm Jeff. Jeffrey Jordan. Your husband!"

She flinched, fear rising in her throat. *I don't know you! Why are you doing this to me?*

The door opened, and a short, round man with olive skin and small, half-moon eyes entered the room and approached the bed. He asked, "How's our girl doing?"

The stranger said, "She's awake. She tried to speak."

"Excellent." The stout man jotted something on his chart. "For the past few days, she's tracked us with her eyes, but this is the first time she's spoken."

"Her words were slurred, garbled," said the younger man, "but I understood. She thought I was the doctor."

The older man nodded. "Some confusion is to be expected. The fact that she's trying to communicate is a significant step." He pulled a chair over beside the bed, sat down, and took her hand. "Hello, Mrs. Jordan. I'm Dr. Forlani. Can you squeeze my hand? That's it. Keep your eyes open. Look at me, Mrs. Jordan. Stay awake. Squeeze my hand, dear. That's it. Can you squeeze harder? Wonderful." He looked at the young man. "She's following commands. That's a good sign."

The stranger's voice broke with emotion. "Dr. Forlani, you have no idea how hard I've prayed!"

"Yes, I think I do, Mr. Jordan." The doctor lifted her hand. "Can you show me two fingers, Mrs. Jordan? Hold up two fingers, dear. Wake up, Mrs. Jordan. Open your eyes. Can you hear me? Stay with me, dear. . . ."

It had taken every ounce of energy and strength she had to squeeze the doctor's hand. But she couldn't focus on him any longer. Sleep beckoned— deep, consoling slumber.

When she woke again, the room was shrouded in shadows. The dark-haired stranger was sitting beside her bed, his head back, as if he had dozed off. She turned her head toward him and said hoarsely, "It's. . .dark."

He sat up with a start. "Marnie, you're awake again. Did you say it's dark? It's nighttime, sweetheart." He got up and turned on a light. "There. Is that better?"

She squinted against the brightness. "Who. . .are. . .you?"

His expression fell. "I'm Jeff. Your husband. Don't you remember?"

She shook her head. She wanted to lash out at him for making such an absurd claim, but her body wouldn't cooperate. Her legs felt limp and unresponsive. She was swaddled in coarse blankets and sheets. She could hardly lift her hand.

He reached over and rubbed her bare arm. "It's okay if you don't remember. You've been through a lot. I love you, Marnie."

She flinched. Why did he keep calling her that? "Who. . .is. . .Marnie?"

He flashed a tentative smile. "It's your name. Marnie Jordan."

The name wasn't familiar to her.

He sat back in his chair, eyeing her curiously. "Okay, honey, if you're not Marnie Jordan, then what is your name?"

She closed her eyes to block out the intrusive stranger. Try as she might, she couldn't summon a name for herself. How could it be? She had no idea who she was. She bit her lower lip, fighting back tears. "Go. . .away," she said at last.

The man stood up. "I'll go, Marnie. Just don't get upset. I'll be outside your room if you need me."

A sob tore at her throat. "I don't. . .need. . .anyone!"

The man slipped out the door with a subdued, "I'll be back, honey."

After he had gone, she realized she felt no better, only more confused. She had said, *I don't need anyone.* And it was true. She couldn't picture anyone she knew. She couldn't even summon the image of her own face.

Who am I? And why can't I remember anything?

A nurse—a young honey-skinned woman with short black hair—entered and checked her blood pressure. "Are you feeling better, Mrs. Jordan?"

"I'm not. . .Mrs. Jordan."

The nurse smiled, as if humoring a child. "Dr. Forlani is making his rounds. He'll be in shortly to see you. We're all very pleased that you're awake."

"Where. . .am I?" Suddenly, it was urgent that she know where she was.

"You're in the hospital, Mrs. Jordan."

"What hospital?"

"Kona Community."

"Hawaii?"

"Yes. You live in Hawaii. Remember?"

"No." She tried to move but didn't have the strength. For the first time, she realized she was tethered to an array of tubes and IVs. "A mirror. Please! Get me. . .a mirror!"

"All right, Mrs. Jordan. I'll be right back." The nurse returned a minute later with a mirror and placed it in her hand.

Clasping it with uncertain fingers, she gazed intently at her reflection. The eyes that stared back at her were not familiar. Dark, haunted eyes in an oval face. A full, pale mouth. Porcelain white skin. Tangled, reddish brown hair cascading over lean shoulders. It was a young, almost attractive face, except for the dark circles under the vacant eyes. It was not a face she recognized. She let the mirror fall onto the bed.

"That's not me!" she cried, her agitation growing. "That's not me!"

The nurse patted her arm. "It's okay, Mrs. Jordan. You've been in a coma. It's common to have temporary memory lapses."

She looked up beseechingly. "Coma?"

"The doctor will explain everything to you. My name is Elena. If you need anything, you ask for Elena. Meanwhile, you just relax, Mrs. Jordan. Please, just relax." The nurse turned and bustled out of the room, as if eager to escape.

She was alone again, alone with her muddled hodgepodge of thoughts. She laid her head back on the pillow and tried to steady her breathing. *Something terrible happened to me! Why can't I remember?*

Dr. Forlani entered the room, a chart tucked under his arm. "Hello, Mrs. Jordan. You're looking better this evening."

"I'm not. . .Mrs. Jordan," she murmured under her breath.

"Would you prefer I call you Marnie?"

She carefully enunciated each word. "I. . .don't. . .know. . .her. . .either."

"Then what would you like me to call you?"

She looked away. "I can't. . .remember my name."

Dr. Forlani sat down beside her and smiled. "For a young lady who can't remember her name, you've made a lot of people around here very happy these past few days."

She gave him a begrudging glance. "Why?"

"Because you've returned to the land of the living after a very long sleep."

"How long?"

"Approximately two weeks. But the important question now is, what are we going to do to bring you back to the life you had before the accident?"

She struggled for the right words, her tongue thick in her mouth. "Tell me. . .about the accident."

Dr. Forlani paused a moment then replied, "You were in a car crash, Mrs. Jordan. You sustained a brain injury. You've spent the past several days waking from a coma. And now we need to run some tests to determine how we can best help you recover."

She closed her eyes. The doctor's words were too much for her. This whole alien world was too painful and overwhelming. *Go away! Leave me alone! I'm not who you think I am! I don't want to be here!* At the moment, all she wanted to do was return to the sweet, soothing oblivion of sleep.

Chapter 2

When Marnie woke again, the room was filled with sunlight. She noticed two people sitting beside her bed—an older couple in conservative, midwestern-style clothing. Plaid short-sleeved shirt and khaki pants on the man, white blouse and tailored skirt on the woman. They definitely weren't Hawaiian. The woman had short, gray blond hair and delicate features; the man had a weatherworn face and straight brown hair with gray sideburns. Most important, they looked familiar to her.

"Mom? Dad?"

The woman jumped up and rushed to her. "Marnie, oh, sweetheart, you're awake! And you remember us!"

They took turns hugging and kissing her. She wanted to respond with the same enthusiasm, but her thoughts were still jumbled and confused. Almost instinctively, she had acknowledged them as her parents, and yet, her mind fed her no information, no memories or details to confirm such an assumption. She couldn't remember their names or anything about them, except that she knew she shared an enormous emotional bond with them.

The woman sat down beside her and chatted excitedly, speaking so fast Marnie couldn't comprehend what she was saying. "Your dad and I flew in last night from Detroit, Marnie. Long, tiring flight, but at least we made it okay. We were here right after the accident, of course, just as Jeff's parents were here for him. We sat by your bedside for days. Some wonderful people from your church looked after us and made sure we had a place to stay and were well fed. We'll forever be indebted to them. And it was so sweet and touching—some of your girlfriends sat with you and read the Bible and even sang to you. But when over a week went by and you showed no response, we felt we needed to go home and get back to work. You know how your dad's boss is—doesn't want to give him any extra time off. Then, when Jeff phoned yesterday and said you were awake and talking, we were beside ourselves with joy. We immediately made plane reservations, and here we are, dear."

The man stood at the end of the bed, smiling at her with tear-filled eyes. "Marnie girl, you are a sight for sore eyes. We wondered if you'd ever come back to us. I guess the good Lord was watching over you."

"How are you feeling, sweetheart?" asked the woman. "The doctor says you'll need several weeks of treatment—physical therapy and who knows what all—but everyone's optimistic, honey. You'll be up and walking in no time. Your old self, good as new!"

Marnie laid her head back and closed her eyes. Her mind was shutting down, blocking out the noise, the voices, the chatter that she couldn't quite grasp. "I'm tired," she murmured.

"Of course you are, dear," said the woman. "You've been through a terrible ordeal. We'll go now and let you get some rest."

"If you need anything, honey, let us know," said the man. "We're here for you."

Marnie looked over at the glass of water on her tray. "I want. . .lightbulb."

"What, dear? A lightbulb? What are you saying?"

"Lightbulb," Marnie said again. What was wrong with them? Didn't they understand that she wanted a drink of water? She nodded toward the glass.

"Water? Is that it, dear?" said her mother. "Why didn't you say so?" She took the glass and put the straw to Marnie's lips. Marnie swallowed the tepid water, but an unsettling feeling gripped her. She hadn't said what she had meant to say. The words were somehow scrambled in her brain. Frustration welled up inside her, but there was nothing she could do to alleviate it.

The shattering truth stunned her. She could no longer speak well enough to express her feelings, her arms and legs had become useless appendages, and she couldn't even trust her mind to feed her the right information. Whoever she was, she was better off dead.

She began to weep.

The woman leaned down and embraced her. "It's going to be okay, Marnie. I know how hard it must be, waking and finding yourself like this. But we're all here for you, sweetheart—your dad and me—and Jeff. He's been by your side every moment. He loves you so much. And all your friends from the university and the dear people from your church—they've been here every day, praying for you and encouraging us. I don't know what we would have done without them. You're fortunate to have so many wonderful people who love you. With their prayers, you're going to get better. I know it, Marnie. Just keep telling yourself that, okay?"

She wanted to scream, *How can I get better when I don't know who I am or who any of you are? I can't even walk or speak correctly! I'm damaged and useless! Why didn't God just let me die?*

Dr. Forlani entered the room and offered his greetings. "How are you today, Mr. and Mrs. Rockwell?"

Rockwell? Is that my name? It doesn't sound familiar. But then, I didn't recognize the name Marnie *either. I'm just starting to get used to people calling me that.*

Dr. Forlani pulled a chair over beside the bed. "And how are you feeling today, Marnie?"

She looked away.

"She's having a little trouble with her words," said the woman.

The doctor nodded. "That's to be expected with a brain injury like this. We'll be bringing in a speech therapist to help her. Did she recognize the two of you?"

"Yes, she seemed to." The woman looked back at Marnie. "You do remember us, dear, don't you?"

Marnie nodded. It was what the woman wanted to hear.

Dr. Forlani checked her pulse. "Are you saying you can recall specific memories from your childhood, Marnie?"

She closed her eyes and scoured her mind for memories. There were none.

"Hey, little girl," said the man, "do you remember when we used to make snowmen in the backyard? You always insisted that we make an entire snow family—the papa with his top hat and cane, mama with a flowered hat and apron, and baby with a rattle and bib. We made their arms with branches from the old oak tree you loved to climb. Don't you remember, baby?" He choked up. Grabbing a handkerchief from his pocket, he wiped his eyes and sniffed. "You always gave them funny names. Mergatroid and Marmaduke for the mama and papa. Sassy Britches for the baby. You loved coming up with crazy names for them. And when the first thaw came and they melted away, you always cried, like you'd lost a good friend. Remember, honey?"

No, no, no! I don't remember.

Dr. Forlani stood up. "Marnie, we're going to let you rest for now. Someone will be coming shortly to help you out of bed. We want to give your legs a chance to regain a little strength. And we'll be running a few more tests. We hope to start your physical therapy this afternoon."

Marnie was glad when the doctor and her parents had gone. As long as she was alone, she didn't have to worry about meeting someone's expectations. She didn't have to pretend to recognize people she didn't know. She relaxed, allowing herself to drift into slumber.

She dreamed. She was rolling a ball of snow across a yard. She could feel the cold through her wet mittens. She could see the little white puffs of vapor in the air as she exhaled. She could taste snowflakes on her tongue. She could hear the crunch of her black rubber boots making footprints in the snowdrifts.

She opened her eyes. *I remember!* The images were broken and disjointed, but at least they were there. Actual memories that belonged to her. She had an identity. It was there somewhere. It wasn't lost forever. She was a real person with a real history. Retrieving it would be like putting a puzzle together. She had the first piece—a little girl in the snow.

She opened her eyes. She needed more of the pieces. "Mom. . .Dad! Where are you?"

A nurse poked her head in the door. "Did you need something, Mrs. Jordan?"

"My. . .parents."

"I'll get them."

The couple returned and sat by her bed. Although she still didn't remember them, she felt their love, and she knew that somehow she loved them, too. "Tell me more. . .about myself."

"Sure, honey," said the man. "What do you want to know?"

"Anything. Everything."

For the next hour, the couple took turns telling her stories—what she was like as a baby, her favorite hobbies and subjects in school, what they did for holidays. Marnie listened intently, creating, piece by piece, an image of herself in her mind.

"You loved making up stories," said the woman. "You pretended there was a family in the attic, and you were always telling us what they were doing."

The man chuckled. "Yeah, lots of kids make up an imaginary friend. You created an entire family."

"Family was very important to you, Marnie," said the woman. "You always wanted brothers and sisters, but we weren't able to have more children. I had several miscarriages. Each time I was pregnant, you got your hopes up. You picked out names and made little drawings for the baby. Losing those children was very painful for your dad and me. But it grieved us even more to see you so heartbroken and disappointed."

Marnie began to weep. "I wanted you to adopt a baby."

"Yes, you did, honey. We checked into it, but we were older. . . ."

The man reached for her hand. "Honey, are you saying you remember?"

Marnie's eyes widened. Yes, the memories were clicking into place like video clips on a screen. She remembered her childhood. She remembered her parents! "Mommy!" she sobbed.

The woman—her mother—gathered her into her arms and held her tight. The two rocked together, weeping. Her father embraced her, too. The emotions she felt were delicious, deep, overpowering. She belonged to someone, to these two people who loved her and had known her for her entire life. She wasn't some anonymous soul existing in a vacuum. She was someone's daughter. She was Marnie Rockwell. She had a history and emotional connections. She would survive after all!

Chapter 3

"Hi, Marnie. Your mom says you're remembering things." It was the young man who called himself Jeff or John or something like that. He stood at the end of her hospital bed, his fingers drumming the rail. "Does that mean you remember *us*?" He pointed at himself then at her.

She shook her head. "I don't know you."

He came around, pulled up a straight-back chair, and sat down. "That's okay. They say it'll take time. I'm just glad you're starting to get your memory back. Do you remember anything about Hawaii—about our lives here?"

She glanced out the window at the palm trees and tropical greenery. "No. I remember Michigan. I'm Marnie Rockwell, and I live in Michigan."

"You're Marnie Jordan now. And you did live in Michigan. Several years ago."

"I still do."

"Really? How old do you think you are, Marnie?"

She frowned, struggling to make sense of his question. "I don't know. Am I twelve? Yes, I'm twelve."

"No, honey. You're twenty-two. Like me. You came to Hawaii when you were nineteen." He brushed a shock of curly brown hair back from his forehead. "You've lived here in Kona for three years now."

"Why did I come here?" She was finding it easier to gather her words and form sentences, but what she was hearing left her more confused than ever. "Why Hawaii, so far away?"

"You came here to attend the University of the Nations. Remember?"

"No."

"It's a school where they train people to become missionaries. They're part of YWAM—Youth With A Mission—a cool worldwide mission organization with bases all over the world—in over 160 countries. You know what a missionary is, don't you?"

"Yes." She knew, but she didn't know how she knew. "They tell people about God."

"Right. That's what we want to do, Marnie. Tell people that Jesus died to save them. You remember Jesus, don't you?"

She smiled. Of course she knew about Jesus. " 'Jesus loves me, this I know, for the Bible tells me so.' "

"Yeah, you probably sang that in Sunday school when you were little."

"I don't remember."

"That's okay. You remember Jesus. That's the important thing."

But what did she remember about Him? She had no rational memory of Jesus, and yet she sensed an emotional connection with Him just as she had felt with her parents before she knew who they were.

"Tell me more," she said.

"What do you want to know?"

She shrugged. "I don't know."

"Well, okay, let's see." He shifted in his chair. "We met as students at the university. I'm majoring in biblical studies. You're majoring in journalism and ESL—English as a Second Language. I want to preach. You want to teach people in other countries how to write and publish Christian magazines."

"I want to be a teacher?"

"Right. And you're going to be a great teacher, too. But we've both had to do lots of other things on campus to help pay our way, though most of our support comes from our parents and our churches back home. These days, I do carpentry work and campus maintenance, and you babysit faculty kids. At first, we both worked in the kitchen at U of N. The first time I saw you, you had just dropped a huge bowl of salad on the floor. And you were on your hands and knees scooping up lettuce and tomatoes and carrots and stuff. You looked so flustered and upset. You even got pieces of lettuce and carrots in your hair."

Marnie chuckled. "I'm glad I don't remember that."

"Anyway, you looked so funny and cute. I got down and helped you clean up the mess. I guess you were grateful because you agreed to hang out with me."

She gazed down at her hands. "I don't remember."

"I know."

They were both silent for a long moment.

Jeff craned his neck then scratched the back of his head.

Marnie waited, wishing he would get up and go. It was painful talking with a stranger who knew things about her she didn't know.

He cleared his throat. "I hear they had you up walking today. That's terrific."

She nodded. "I walked down the hall."

"That's great! I wish I'd been here. I had to get back to my classes. Since your folks were here with you, I figured you wouldn't miss me." He paused, his expression darkening. "I guess, since you don't remember me, you wouldn't miss me anyway."

"I'm sorry."

"Don't be. It's not your fault." He sat back and crossed his legs. "Everyone at our church and the university is praying for you. After the accident, they held a prayer meeting just for us."

She stared at him. "You were in the accident, too?"

"Yeah. I was driving the car. I swerved to miss a truck and went over the embankment right into a lava bed."

"Were you hurt?"

"Just some bumps and bruises and a cracked rib. It's okay now."

She nodded. It hadn't occurred to her that anyone else was in the accident.

"It nearly killed me to see you hurt so bad," he said unevenly. "I don't know what I would have done if you. . ." His words trailed off. He swiped at a tear. "I'm just so thankful to God that you're alive, babe."

She recoiled at his words. She wasn't his babe, and she wasn't thankful to be alive. Not like this—without a working mind and body. If she ever prayed again, it would be to die.

"Do you want to hear more?" he asked. "More about our life here in Hawaii?"

"I guess so." She knew already that whatever he said wouldn't mean anything to her. He might as well be talking about complete strangers.

"We're in our third year at the university, Marnie. Our first year, we completed DTS—Discipleship Training School. It's a twelve-week lecture program, followed by an eight-week overseas field assignment. We were both sent to Cambodia. We worked in a teen center in Battambang. We became good friends. By the time we returned to Kona to start our course work for our degrees, we knew we were in love. We got married last summer. We had our wedding on the beach. It was awesome."

Marnie wanted to protest. Surely if she was married to this man, she would remember. How could anyone forget something like that? Maybe he was making up the entire story. Maybe he had fooled everyone, telling people he was her husband. He'd know that with her memory loss, she couldn't contradict him. What kind of man was he—taking advantage of a helpless girl?

"Were my parents there. . .at the wedding?" she asked. They would know the truth.

"Sure. So were mine. We didn't have money for a honeymoon, but we went on a mission trip to Nigeria last summer. We called that our honeymoon. It was amazing. We had a chance to minister to some really neat people. The ladies loved you. You held prayer meetings with them and had a chance to lead several to Christ. You still get e-mails from them, telling how they're growing in the Lord."

Marnie bit her lower lip. She didn't want to hear any more about the woman this eager young man—this John or Jack or Jeffrey, whoever—was talking about. For Marnie, that woman didn't exist.

He pulled a folded piece of paper from his shirt pocket, opened it, and handed it to Marnie. "You got an e-mail just this morning from Nigeria—a girl named Ubong Ibe. I thought you might like to read it."

She glanced down at the paper then thrust it back at Jeffrey. "I can't!"

He set the paper on the nightstand. "That's okay. I'll leave it here. You can read it another time."

She covered her face with her hands. "No! I can't read the words! They're gibberish to me!"

He retrieved the paper. "I'm sorry, Marnie. I didn't know."

She looked imploringly at him. "What's wrong with me? I'm not a real person anymore! I can't even read."

He clasped her hand. "Yes, you are, babe. You hang in there. It'll all come back. You wait and see."

She pulled her hand away. "Go. Please go."

"Not until I've read you Ubong's e-mail. I think it'll cheer you up. It says, 'Dear Sister Jordan, I was very happy to have you as my mentor last summer. We have just come through the most harsh weather of our country—the harmattan season with its dry, cold winds. I read my Bible every day, in good weather and bad. I love you for caring about me. I thank you for helping me know God better. Sorry I don't write often. It's different here. We don't own our own computers. We go to centers away from home. Please write me soon. And remember me in your prayers. Your friend, Ubong Ibe.' "

Tears ran down Marnie's cheeks. "How can I help someone like that when I can't even help myself?"

Jeff's eyes glazed with tears. "I know it's hard, sweetheart. This is the hardest thing you've ever had to do. But you'll get through it. God is with you every moment, and I'll be here for you every day."

She shook her head. "No one can be where I am. Inside my head. Feeling what I feel."

"I know, honey. But give us a chance to try." He folded the paper and tucked it back in his pocket. "Would you like me to send Ubong an e-mail for you?"

Marnie flexed her fingers. "I can write. My hand is better. Get me a sandwich."

"A sandwich? Are you hungry?"

She scowled. "No, I want to write. Get me a sandwich. And a pen."

"You mean a tablet? Paper?"

"Yes, that's what I said!"

He brought her a pen and tablet from the bureau.

She clutched the pen in her hand. It felt foreign, unnatural. She closed her fingers around it and began to write. The pen slid off the paper. She tried again, pursing her lips tightly. Nothing but chicken scratches! She threw the pen across the room. "I can't write! I can't do anything!"

Jeff reached out to embrace her. She pushed him away. "Leave me alone! Let me die! I want to die!"

He stared at her for a long moment, looking helpless and baffled. Finally, he left the room and returned with a nurse. "Elena, my wife's upset," he explained. "Can you do something to help her?"

The nurse approached her bed. "What's the problem, Mrs. Jordan? What do you need?"

Marnie held out her hands, fingers splayed. "I—I can't read or write!"

"Try to relax, Mrs. Jordan. Lie back and breathe slowly." The nurse picked up Marnie's water glass from her meal tray. "Take a drink of water. You'll feel better."

Marnie knocked the glass from the woman's hand. It flew across the room and shattered against the wall. Marnie buried her face in her pillow. "Go away! Everyone go away!"

Jeff paced the hospital lobby, pummeling his fist against his palm. His stomach was in knots, his head pounding. He had to get out of this place, away somewhere, anywhere. But there was nowhere he could go to erase the image of Marnie looking at him like he was a stranger, worse than a stranger. He pulled his cell phone out of his pocket and punched in a number.

"Hey, Nate, it's me, Jeff. I'm here at the hospital. Where else? You know Marnie's awake now."

"Yeah, that's great news. How is she?"

"She's doing okay, I guess. But listen, I gotta get out of here for a while. With my car totaled, it's kinda hard to get around without imposing on people. I'm looking for new wheels, but the insurance money won't cover much. Would you mind giving me a ride?"

"No problem, bro."

"Really? Great. Pick me up at the front entrance."

A half hour later, Nate Anderson pulled up in his red pickup. Jeff jumped in the cab and buckled his seat belt. "Man, am I glad to see you."

"You okay, buddy?" Nate's ruddy face was pinched with concern.

"Yeah, sure."

"You don't look it."

"Neither do you. New shirt?" The guys were always kidding Nate about his crazy aloha shirts. He was lean as a matchstick, but he sure loved big prints and vivid colors.

"You like my shirt?"

"Looks like an explosion in a paint factory."

"I can get you one just like it."

"Thanks but no thanks."

Nate pulled out of the parking lot. "Where to?"

"You hungry? Wanna go grab a burger?"

"Sure. How about that little place around the corner?"

Jeff waited until they had settled into a booth and placed their order before mentioning Marnie. "She's awake now, you know, but she's not the same."

Nate sipped his soda. "Well, she was in a coma for two weeks. That's gotta affect a person."

"I know. The doctor warned me about that. He said there'd likely be some cognitive impairment. They throw around these big terms like that's how people talk every day. Coordination loss. Muscle regression. Processing difficulties. What he means is, Marnie can't walk or talk right, and she doesn't know who in the world she is. Or who I am, for that matter."

"That's gotta hurt."

"Man, it does. You have no idea. She looks at me like she's looking through me, like I'm invisible. I mean nothing to her. Zip. Nada."

"I'm sorry, buddy."

"I'm not looking for pity."

"But I still feel bad."

"I know you do." Jeff traced a water ring on the table. Like Marnie, he was having a hard time finding the right words. "When she didn't wake up after the accident, I was a mess. I sat by her bed day and night, praying for God to take me instead of her. When she started waking up, I was the happiest guy on earth. But now, when I see her, everything's different. I can tell she doesn't even want me in the room. I'm just an intruder, someone hanging around. When I try to tell her about our life together, she gets this glazed look in her eyes. She doesn't remember a thing. I look at this girl, and I see a helpless, lost little waif. I keep looking in her eyes, looking for Marnie, but she's not there." Jeff snapped his straw between his fingers. "What am I supposed to do, Nate?"

"What do you wanna do?"

"I don't know." The waitress brought them their burgers and fries. Jeff popped a fry into his mouth, but it was too hot. "What if she never comes back to me? What if she stays like this forever? How can I take care of her? What kind of life are we going to have?"

Nate shrugged. "I know it sounds like a cliché, but God can get you through this. He'll give you the strength you need. Hold on to Him, no matter what. And when you can't hold on any longer, He'll still be holding you."

Over the next two weeks, Jeff clung to those words as he juggled his university classes with work and long hours at the hospital. He was at Marnie's side as she began an exhausting regimen of rehabilitation. He encouraged her as she endured the grueling routine of speech, cognitive, and physical therapy. He cheered her on as, like a child, she learned to walk, speak, read, and write again. He pored over every book he could find on brain injuries and amnesia, arming himself with all the information he could get. And even then, he knew it wouldn't be enough.

One afternoon, as he sat in Marnie's hospital room reading, the nurse wheeled her in from a therapy session. It always shocked him to see her again. She looked like a poor imitation of the Marnie he knew and loved—pale, fragile, lost, remote. Even though she was getting better, he still didn't see *his* Marnie in her eyes.

"Well, Mr. Jordan," said the nurse, "your wife did very well today."

He looked up and forced a smile. "A good session, huh, babe?"

She looked down at her clasped hands. "I walk like a two-year-old and read like a five-year-old. And I'm so tired I can't think straight."

Jeff got up and helped the nurse get Marnie out of the wheelchair and into bed. At least—thanks to her mom's suggestion—Marnie was wearing her own pretty pajamas now instead of those ugly hospital gowns.

"You rest now, young lady," said the nurse. "You've had a big day. And don't let her fool you, Mr. Jordan. She's making real progress. One of these days, you're gonna see her skipping down these halls. Nobody's gonna keep her down."

Jeff flashed an appreciative smile. "I'm counting on that, ma'am." He reached over and pulled the covers up around Marnie. It was like tucking in a child. "You're looking good, honey. Even got a little color in your cheeks."

She touched her face. "That's makeup. It's called blush. My mom put it on me this morning. She says I've got to start thinking about my looks."

"You look good to me, no matter what," said Jeff. *Lord, forgive my little white lies.*

"I don't like looking in the mirror," said Marnie, jutting out her lower lip. "It's weird. I don't know that girl."

"Well, I do, and she's pretty awesome." *The old Marnie was awesome.*

She looked over at his book. "What are you reading?"

"This?" He held up the thick textbook. "I'm reading about amnesia."

"So you can figure me out?"

"Something like that." He opened the book and scanned several pages. "Did you know there are several kinds of memory?"

Marnie smoothed the sheet under her chin. "My memory is full of holes."

"But it's getting better," said Jeff. "Listen to this. There's short-term memory, like remembering where you put your car keys. And there's long-term memory—remembering what happened years ago. There's episodic memory. That means you remember your own experiences. And there's semantic memory—storing facts about history and stuff."

She put her hands over her ears. "I don't want to hear it. It doesn't make sense to me."

"Okay. How about this? There are two types of amnesia. Anterograde amnesia means you remember the past but can't form new memories. Retrograde amnesia means you've forgotten what happened before your injury."

"I remember Michigan, when I was a little girl."

"But not Hawaii, right?"

"I don't remember Hawaii."

He tried to keep his voice steady, nonchalant. "Which means you still don't remember anything about us."

She shook her head.

"That's no good." He looked back at the book, fighting the taste of disappointment in his throat. "I think you have both kinds of amnesia, because you forget things now."

"What things?"

"My name. Do you remember my name?"

"John?"

"Jeff!" He hated it when she did that, calling him some other guy's name. "What day is it, Marnie?"

"I don't know."

"What month?"

"Summer? The sun is shining."

He sighed. "It's February. The accident happened in January." He wasn't ready to give up yet. "What did you have for breakfast?"

"I don't know. Did I have breakfast?"

"You had cereal with bananas and milk. And orange juice and toast."

She scowled. "How do you know?"

"I was there."

She rolled over and buried her face in her pillow. "I don't like this game. Go away."

Jeff sat back and shook his head. *What's the use? It's hopeless! I can't get through to her.*

The door opened just then, and Marnie's mother peeked inside. "Is this a private party, or is everyone invited?"

Jeff got up and opened the door wide, relief sweeping over him. Reinforcements! "I don't know about everyone, Barbara, but you're sure welcome." He pulled over the comfortable, overstuffed chair for her. "Sit down. Spend some time with your daughter. I'll go for a little walk."

"You don't have to leave, Jeff."

He headed for the door, his book tucked under his arm. "No, that's okay. You two ladies need some private time together. I have some work to do at the library."

Marnie's mother nodded. Her face looked weary, strained. "Okay, Jeff, if you insist."

He was out of there before anyone could say another word. *Gotta get away. Gotta get out of here. Gotta clear my head and catch my breath.* As he strode down the hospital corridor, guilt stabbed him. What kind of husband was he? He couldn't get away from Marnie fast enough. She was the love of his life; yet at times, he could hardly stand to be in the same room with her.

Marnie watched in silence as the young man named Jeff or John left the room and shut the door behind him. She was glad he was gone. He made her nervous with his incessant questions. Always wanting to know how she was. Did she remember this or that? Always talking, telling her stories that meant nothing to her.

"Marnie, dear, I have a surprise for you." Her mother sat down beside her and smiled.

"I like surprises."

"Good. Because I brought along some scissors, rollers, and mousse. I thought it was time for you to have a nice hairstyle again."

Marnie put her hands on her head. "My hair's fine."

Her mother ran her fingers through the long strands. "The Marnie I know wouldn't let anyone see her with hair like this."

Marnie pushed her mother's hand away. "I don't know that Marnie!"

Her mother clasped her arm. "I'm sorry, sweetheart. I shouldn't have said that. I just thought you might like to have pretty hair again. We couldn't do much with your hair before, because of the bandage."

"What bandage?"

"You know, honey. Where they put the catheter in your head to relieve the swelling."

"I don't remember."

"There's a word for it. A whopper of a word. Ventri—ventriculostomy. It saved your life, honey. The doctor told us most damage comes not from the original injury, but from the brain swelling during the first week. We're very fortunate to have doctors who knew just what to do to help you."

Marnie pointed at the little cloth bag her mother was holding. "What's that?"

Her mother handed her the bag. "These are the rollers I'm going to put in your hair. They'll make your hair look pretty."

Marnie removed several plastic rollers and stuck them in her hair. She shook her head, but they held firm. She started to laugh. "Now I'm pretty!"

Her father entered just then and grinned at her. "Well, look at my girl with a head full of curlers!"

"Am I pretty, Daddy?"

"The most beautiful girl in the world, sweetheart."

"But the point isn't to wear the curlers, but to wrap your hair around them," said her mother, pulling a curler from Marnie's tangled hair.

"No, I like them like this!" said Marnie.

Her mother removed a brush from her purse and began brushing Marnie's hair. "Do you remember what I called the snarls in your hair when you were little?"

Marnie thought a moment. "Rats! You said I had rats in my hair."

Her mother beamed. "That's right. That's exactly what I called them."

"See? I remember."

"And you'll be remembering more all the time, honey."

"That's what that boy says, too."

"Boy?"

"The one who's always here. Jack?"

"Jeff."

"Right. He's always here."

"Because he loves you, sweetheart."

"He bugs me."

"Why?"

"I don't know. He just does."

Her father came around and put his hand on her mother's shoulder. "Have you told her yet?"

"Not yet. I was waiting for you."

"Leave the dirty work for me," he murmured under his breath.

"I just thought we should tell her together."

"Tell me what? Is it a secret?" asked Marnie. "A riddle?"

"No, dear," said her mother. "It's time for your dad and me—"

"What your mother's trying to say is, we've been away from home a long time, Marnie. Weeks now. And we both have jobs to get back to."

"The thing is, Marnie, your dad and I are flying home to Michigan tomorrow."

She stared from one to the other. "No, don't go!"

"I can't take any more time off from work, sweetheart," said her father, his eyes tearing.

"I want to go to Michigan, too."

"You can't, honey. You're right in the middle of your rehabilitation program. You need to stay here and get better."

She clutched her mother's arm. "Take me, too. Please, Mommy!"

Her mother pressed Marnie's hand against her cheek. "We can't, honey. You need special care. Care your dad and I can't give you."

"Yes, you can. I'm your little girl. I'll be good!"

Tears streamed from her mother's eyes. "Oh honey, of course you're good. You're our beautiful, wonderful daughter. But you need to stay here and get well."

"If I get well, can I come home?"

Her father sidled over and rubbed the back of her neck. "You will go home soon, honey. To your home with Jeff. He's so eager for you to come home."

Marnie scowled. "I don't know him. I don't like him."

"He's your husband, Marnie," said her mother. "You promised to love him always."

"I love you and Daddy. I'm your little girl."

Her father kissed the top of her head. "You'll always be our little girl. But you're also Jeff's wife, and you belong with him."

Marnie began to weep. "Take me with you. Please! Pretty please! Take me with you!"

"We want you to get your life back, honey. We want you to be whole again. That won't happen if you go back to being our little girl. Give Jeff a chance to show you how much he loves you."

"No, no, no!"

Amid her tears, they took turns hugging and kissing her good-bye. As they left the room, she pounded her tray with a spoon, screaming, "Mommy! Daddy! Don't go! Don't leave me!"

Chapter 4

Jeff paced the floor outside Marnie's hospital room, waiting for her to dress and pack up her things. It was exactly two months since the day of the accident, and she was being released today into his care. She would continue her therapy as an outpatient, but he would be the one taking care of her now. He wasn't sure he was up for the job. And he knew Marnie wasn't eager to go home with him. He couldn't blame her. She still didn't have a clue who he was. Well, that wasn't true. She had been told often enough that he was her husband, but it didn't sink in. She didn't believe it in her heart of hearts.

The nurse appeared with a wheelchair. "Your wife is all checked out, Mr. Jordan. I'll get her, and you can be on your way. I know this has to be a wonderful day for the two of you."

"Yeah, Elena, it sure is." Guilt nudged him. Sure, this should be one of the happiest days of his life. He was taking Marnie home. Then, why was he scared out of his wits? Why would he rather be almost anywhere else?

"We're ready, Mr. Jordan." Elena squeezed his hand as she handed him a plastic hospital bag of Marnie's things. "I just want you to know, I said a lot of prayers for the two of you. And I know so many of your friends have been here every day praying. God answered our prayers. I know you're going to have a wonderful life together."

"Thanks. Everyone's been so supportive—our family and friends, the doctors and nurses. We appreciate everything." He couldn't think of what else to say, so he simply followed the nurse as she wheeled Marnie out to the car. He helped her into the passenger seat and tossed her things into the backseat. Marnie looked almost like herself in her green knit top and denim capris. It felt strange, like he was taking someone home who looked like Marnie but was really someone he hadn't quite gotten to know yet.

"Am I well?" she kept asking as he headed back to their apartment near the university.

"You're getting there, honey." He always had to couch his replies in simple, positive words, as if he were answering a child. "You're a hundred percent better than you were a month ago."

"Will I go back to the hospital?"

"Yeah, but you won't sleep there. You'll go three days a week for your therapy sessions."

"Where will I sleep?"

"At our place."

"Where are we going?"

"Home."

"To Michigan?"

He sighed. Would she ever get over the idea that she belonged in Michigan? "No, not Michigan. To our apartment. You'll like it. Why wouldn't you? You decorated it. Most everything in the place is your stuff, except for my favorite beanbag chair and my sports trophies."

"Sports trophies?"

"Yeah. I ran track. I was the fastest runner in my high school. Six years later, my record still stands for the hundred meters." *Why am I rattling on like this? I'm going to overwhelm her. Why can't I just shut up!*

"Where did you go to high school?"

"California. Burbank. It's where I was born and raised."

"Oh." She gazed out the window at the passing scenery. "Are we there yet?"

"Getting there." He was miffed. She wasn't listening to him. She was like a little kid. Distracted, impatient. There had to be something they could talk about, something to engage her attention. "How do you like our new car?"

"It's new?"

"Actually, it's eight years old. But I got a great deal on it. We needed another car. Old Reliable was totaled in the accident."

She gave him a bewildered glance. "Old who?"

"Old Reliable." Why would he think she'd remember that when she had forgotten everything else? "It's the nickname we gave our car. I know it sounds dumb, but the old rattletrap was sort of like a member of our family."

"I like a car with a name."

"Me, too."

"What is this car called?"

He gave her a quick smile. "I haven't named it yet. I was waiting for you to help me."

She crossed her arms on her chest. "I'm not good at names. I can't even remember yours."

"Jeff."

"And I'm Marnie."

"Right. See, you're getting it."

"I am?"

"I bet you'll come up with the perfect name for this hunk of metal." He turned onto Kuakini Highway. He had an idea, the perfect thing to stir her memory. "Would you like to see where we go to school?"

She shrugged. "Whatever."

"It's a beautiful campus. Forty-five acres. It looks out over Kailua Bay. You can stand on the campus and look out at the ocean and see cruise ships in the harbor. The sunsets are breathtaking."

She tugged on his arm. "John, I'm hungry."

"Jeff." He saw red every time she called him the wrong name. Why was it so hard to get a simple name right?

"I'm hungry, Jeff."

"We could grab a burger at a fast-food place."

"I want macaroni and cheese."

"You hate macaroni and cheese."

"I love it."

"You ate it at the hospital all the time, but before that, you hated the stuff. You'd make it for me once in a while, but you never ate any of it."

"I want macaroni and cheese."

"Okay, we'll fix some when we get home. But it'll be out of a box."

She smiled. "I'd love a box of macaroni and cheese."

"But first, I want you to see the university. Maybe it'll jog your memory." He made a left turn onto the campus. *Lord, please let her recognize something. Let me know the old Marnie is still in there somewhere.* "See those buildings over there on the right?"

"I guess so."

"See the sign with the red 'Aloha' on it? That's the Visitors Center. Next is the Global Outreach Center." They passed a row of umber brown, two-story buildings. "Keep watching, Marnie. See that circle of flags with the fountain in the center? That's the Plaza of the Nations. Those are the national flags of all the students on campus. And the stepping-stones around the fountain were gathered from every nation on earth. Cool, huh?"

Marnie slumped down in her seat. "I'm tired, Jack."

"Jeff," he muttered. His hopes were nosediving like paper airplanes in a downdraft. "Do you remember any of it, Marnie? Anything at all?"

"No." She laid her head back and closed her eyes. "I should go back to the hospital. My bed is there."

"We're not going back to the hospital. We're going home, Marnie. To our apartment. Right now!" His sudden anger surprised him. Where did it come from? This was supposed to be a happy day. Marnie couldn't help it that she wasn't herself. *Lord, help me! Don't let me spoil this day just because it's not the way I wanted it.* He turned the car around and headed back to Kuakini Highway. "Our apartment is just on the other side of the highway. We'll be there before you know it."

❧

Marnie couldn't stifle her feeling of dread. It had been growing steadily, spreading through every cell of her body, making her palms sweat and her heart pound harder. She had been away from the hospital for less than an hour, and already, she wanted to go back. Everything about it was familiar. Everything in this new world was strange. She recognized nothing. And she had no desire to get acquainted with it. What little independence she had managed to achieve at the hospital was slipping away. The familiar white room, the daily routine, and the people who took care of her were gone now. She had no idea what to expect next.

She watched in wary silence as the man who called himself her husband pulled into a parking lot beside a tan, two-story building with a red tile roof. It was an attractive complex surrounded by towering palms and lush, tropical greenery, but it looked no more familiar than the far side of the world.

"Not bad, huh, Marnie? There's even a courtyard with a pool," the man—her husband—said as he helped her out of the car. "We could go swimming later. It would help get the strength back in your legs."

She hugged her arms to her chest. "I don't know how to swim."

"Yes, you do. You're a better swimmer than I am."

"I am?"

"You wait and see. Swimming is like riding a bike. You never forget how."

"I had a bike. I remember riding my bike." The memory helped soothe her dread.

"Well, you keep those memories coming, babe." He led her up the walk to the nearest unit and unlocked the door. "Good thing we have a downstairs apartment. No steps to climb." He pushed the door open and moved aside. "Go on in, hon. It's been waiting for you for a long time."

She held back. "You go."

He took her hand and led her inside. Something in his face changed. His voice filled with emotion. "Wow! This brings back memories, seeing you in this room again. I almost feel like I should carry you over the threshold or something."

She gave him a puzzled glance. "Why? I can walk."

"Never mind." He released her hand and opened the blinds, letting the sunlight in. She looked around. This wasn't so bad. Nothing scary or threatening. The room was cozy and inviting, with wicker furniture and a red tile floor with white throw rugs. At the far end of the room was a small kitchen with a glass-top table and wicker chairs.

"Do you recognize it?" he asked.

"No, but it's pretty."

"You lived here for six months."

She ambled into the kitchen and ran her hand over the granite countertop. It felt smooth and cold. She lifted the top off a ceramic cookie jar shaped like a fat brown bear.

"No cookies," he said. "That was your department. You always baked those chocolate chip cookies that come in a tube."

"Cookies in a tube?"

"Yep. We'll make them sometime. Assuming you still like cookies."

"I love cookies."

"Good. Me, too." He went over to the refrigerator and opened the door. "See all these casseroles? We have plenty to eat. The ladies at church have been keeping me well fed."

"Is there macaroni and cheese?"

"No, there's chicken and rice, ham and scalloped potatoes, meat loaf—"

"I want macaroni and cheese."

He shrugged. "Okay, there's probably a box in the cupboard."

She looked around. "Where's the bedroom?"

"I'll show you." He walked to the end of the hall and opened a door. She followed him inside. It was a small room with shuttered windows, a double bed, small glass lamp stands, and a ceiling fan that looked like palm leaves. "Your clothes are in the closet and drawers," he told her. "Do you want to rest while I fix lunch?"

She studied the oak bureau for a moment then tentatively pulled open a drawer. It was filled with a man's clothing.

"That's my drawer," he said. "You have the top three; I have the bottom three."

She nodded and tried another one. It contained lingerie and undergarments. She quickly closed the drawer.

Jeff rubbed the back of his neck. "I'll leave you alone while you settle in." He started out the door then paused and looked back at her. "Just so you know. I set up a cot in the other bedroom. I figured that's the way you would want it for now."

Relief swept over her. "Thank you." She sat down on the bed and bounced a little. "I like this. It's softer than my other bed."

"Yeah. We always thought it was pretty comfortable." He gave her a little wave and headed out the door. "Guess I'd better get busy on that macaroni and cheese."

She was quickly on his heels. "I'll help you, Jack." She wasn't ready yet to be left alone in this strange new place.

"Great. Come on."

He got a box out of the cupboard and handed it to her. "You open this while I get a pan and start the water boiling."

She pulled at the box, but her fingers wouldn't work right. Infuriated, she tried several more times to open it then gave up and slammed the box against the countertop. It broke open, and dry macaroni flew everywhere.

"Way to go, Marnie!" Jeff turned off the spigot and set down the iron kettle he was filling. He sounded frustrated, too. "There goes our lunch!"

She began to cry. She didn't want to be here. She didn't want any of this, and yet, here she was, forced to do things that had nothing to do with her. And it was all going badly, just as she had feared.

"It's okay, babe." Jeff gave her a quick hug. Without emotion, she accepted the embrace, her arms at her sides. "No use crying over spilled macaroni. We'll try one of those casseroles."

After Marnie nixed the casseroles, they ended up eating peanut butter and jelly sandwiches. She loved them. When she had finished her sandwich, she stuck her finger in the jar, scooped out a gob of peanut butter, and licked it off her finger. "This is so good!"

"Better drink a lot of milk with that, or it'll get stuck in your throat." He refilled her glass. "There. Wash it down with that."

She drained the glass.

"Hold on," he said. "We forgot to pray."

"We did?"

"Yeah, we always say grace before meals. It's been so long since we've sat together at our table like this I completely forgot to ask God's blessing." He reached across the table and took her hands. "We have so much to be thankful for, babe. God brought you back to me. There were times when I didn't think the two of us would ever be here like this again."

He bowed his head and began praying. Marnie began to hum. She hummed the entire time he was praying. After he had said, "Amen," he looked up at her and asked, "What was that all about?"

She looked puzzled. "What?"

"The humming. Why were you humming?"

"I like to hum."

"But not while I'm praying."

"Why not, Jack? God doesn't like humming?"

"I don't know if He does or not. It's just not polite to hum when someone's praying."

"I could hum with words. We did that in the hospital sometimes, remember? People came and sang to me. You sang, too."

"We were singing praise songs, Marnie. That's different."

"Why?" She sensed she had displeased him.

"I don't know. It just is."

He got up and started clearing the dishes. "You know, you can pray whenever you want, Marnie. I used to love to hear you pray."

"I don't think so." Why did he keep asking her to do things she didn't know how to do?

"Why not?"

"I don't remember what to say."

"Just say whatever's on your heart. Whatever comes to mind."

"I'll pray later."

"You don't have to pray out loud. You can talk to God anytime in your thoughts. Just you and God."

She twirled her milk glass between her palms. "He's listening in, isn't He?"

Jeff filled the sink with soapy water. "He's with us every minute, hon. He never leaves us."

"Or forsakes us."

"Right. That was one of your favorite verses." He put the plates in the sink. "Would you like me to read you some more verses?"

Marnie got up from the table and looked toward the door. "Is it time to go back to the hospital?"

Jeff took her glass and washed off the table. "No, hon, not until tomorrow."

Her shoulders sagged. "How long is that?"

"About nineteen hours before your physical therapy."

"I should get ready."

"You'll have plenty of time to get ready tomorrow morning."

"What about my hair?"

"What about it?"

"My mom puts my hair in rollers."

Jeff laughed. "Yeah, I remember how you looked in those rollers in the hospital. But I don't think you use rollers, Marnie. I've seen you using a flat iron or a curling iron."

"I iron my hair?"

"Yeah, I guess you could call it that. Come to the bathroom. I'll show you what I'm talking about."

She followed him into the bathroom. He took two appliances out of the cabinet. "See these? One makes your hair straight, and the other makes it curly."

"That's confusing. Which way should it be, Jack? Straight or curly?"

"Either way. It's your choice."

She held the two irons, one in each hand, trying to decide what to do. She sensed that this was an important thing to know. It held the secret to pretty hair. She looked up at him. "Show me how to work them, Jack. Pretty please."

He chuckled. "Sure, babe. And, by the way, it's Jeff. But I guess you won't remember that two minutes from now anyway." He plugged in the flat iron and turned it on. "We've got to wait a few minutes for it to get hot. When it does, be careful, because it gets superhot. Like a stove, you know? Don't burn yourself."

"I won't. There's no fire."

"You don't need flames to get burned. Maybe you should let me do it for you."

"No, Jack. I can do it."

"Jeff."

"I can do it, Jeff. Just show me how."

"Okay, now that it's hot, you take the flat iron, put a small section of hair in it, and pull it all the way down to the end. There. See? Now it's straight." He took another section and clamped the iron down on it. "Now you try it."

The phone rang in the living room. "I'll get that. You practice, okay?"

She forced herself to remain stone still while the flat iron did its work. She held her breath, waiting, wondering how long it would take. *I can do this. I can take care of myself. I can do it!* She smelled something hot. It was working, making her hair straight, making it pretty. The iron began to smoke. Something wasn't right. She opened the tongs, and a tuft of singed hair fell into her hand. She dropped the iron. It clattered on the counter. She let out a shrill scream and ran out of the bathroom, still clutching the tuft of scorched hair.

Jeff was on the phone. It was Marnie's mother, the last person on earth he wanted to talk to right now. So far, the day had been a comedy of errors. Or maybe *tragedy* was a better word. The way things were going, Marnie's parents would be whisking her off to Michigan in no time flat. And maybe that wasn't such a bad idea after all—if today was any example.

"That's right, Barbara," he replied calmly, even though he heard a commotion in the bathroom. "Everything's, uh, going great. Your daughter's settling in just fine. Um, yeah, that was Marnie screaming, but it's okay." He turned around and looked at his distraught wife, standing there, bawling like a baby, a bunch of burned hair in her hand. "She's just a little upset about her hair. Can we call you back in a few minutes? Thanks. Bye."

Marnie waved the clump of hair in his face. "It didn't work!"

He drew her into his arms and gave her a comforting embrace. "I'm sorry, honey. Don't be upset. Give yourself time. You'll get the hang of it."

Between sobs, she lamented, "I can't do anything right!"

He kissed the top of her head and murmured, "You're still beautiful to me."

She stopped crying and tried to pull away. His arms tightened around her. Holding her like this brought back all the old feelings, the closeness they had shared, the yearnings, the sweet intimacies. This was his wife, the woman he loved like no other. At last, she was in his arms again. "Please, Marnie, it's been so long. . . ."

She placed her hands against his chest and gave him a hard shove.

He stumbled backward and caught himself. "What'd you do that for?"

"You wouldn't let go." With her singed hair still in her hand, she ran to the bedroom and slammed the door behind her.

Jeff dropped down on the sofa and put his head in his hands. It was only Marnie's first day home, and he was already at the end of his rope. Was he wrong to have brought her home? Was there anything left of their relationship? He had promised to love and cherish this woman for the rest of his life. But nothing had prepared him for a situation like this. *Lord, Lord, where do we go from here?*

Chapter 5

When Marnie woke the next morning, she was still wearing yesterday's denim capris and knit top. She rolled over and hugged her pillow. Something wasn't right. This wasn't the hospital. She was in a strange place. It felt different, smelled different. She sat up and looked around the room. It was someone's bedroom. Slowly the details clicked into place. This was where that man Jack lived—the man who claimed to be her husband. He had insisted it was her home, too, but she didn't really believe him. He said a lot of things that she just let fly over her head because they made no sense to her.

She swung her legs off the bed and planted her feet on the cold, hardwood floor. She drew her feet back up, curling her toes. There was something she was supposed to do today. Someplace she was supposed to go.

The hospital! Of course! They were helping her learn to read and write again, and get her strength back. It was a good place. Except for scattered memories of her life in Michigan with her parents, her only memories were of the hospital and her new friends there—the doctors, nurses, technicians, and therapists.

And then there was Jack. He was always hanging around.

She got up and went to the bathroom. The flat iron and curling iron were still there on the counter. She stared at herself in the mirror. No matter how many times she looked at her reflection, she was always surprised to see someone she didn't recognize. She ran her fingers through her long, auburn brown hair. Maybe no one would notice that a clump of hair was missing.

She ambled out to the kitchen where Jack or Jeff or whoever was standing at the stove, cooking something. He looked at her and smiled. "Good morning, sleepyhead. I was wondering if I was going to have to come wake you up. You've got to be at the hospital in an hour."

"I'm ready," she said.

He laughed. "I don't think so. Did you sleep in those clothes?"

She nodded.

"You have nightgowns and pajamas in the drawer."

She looked down at her capris and top. "I like these."

"You can't wear them to the hospital."

"Yes, I can."

He shook his head. "The old Marnie wouldn't wear something she had slept in."

She shrugged. "I don't care. She isn't here."

"You can say that again." He flipped a pancake on the griddle. "Are you hungry?"

"Yes. I love pancakes."

"Good. I made plenty."

She watched as he poured the batter. "I like pancakes like my mother makes. She makes little animals, with heads and legs and tails."

"Sorry, babe. I just make circles." He set a stack of hotcakes on the table then took syrup and butter from the refrigerator. "Sit down. Help yourself."

She sat down and looked at her plate. "I like sour cream on my pancakes."

He put a pitcher of orange juice on the table. "Really? Sour cream?"

"Yes. Sour cream."

"Are you sure you don't mean whipped cream?"

"Yes! Whipped cream."

He sat down and filled their glasses with juice. "Sorry, honey. We have lots of casseroles, but we're out of whipped cream. The church ladies kept me fed, so I haven't done much grocery shopping since you've been gone. Besides, you were the one who always knew what we needed."

"We need whipped cream."

"We'll go shopping after your therapy session today. Okay? You can buy whatever you like." He reached across the table for her hand. "Let's say grace before we forget again, okay?"

"Okay." She bowed her head and closed her eyes.

"How about you praying this time, Marnie?"

She looked up. "Me? I can't."

"Sure you can. Just say whatever's on your heart."

She closed her eyes again and gnawed her lower lip. Finally, in a small voice, she said, "Hi, God. It's me. Marnie Rockwell. I like pancakes, even if they're not little animals like my mother makes. Thank You for the pancakes. Amen."

"That's great, Marnie, even though you're actually Marnie Jordan now. I bet God loved that prayer." He helped her spread butter on her hotcakes then handed her the syrup. She held the open bottle over her plate until the pancakes were swimming. "That's enough, Marnie. Save some for me."

She tried cutting her hotcakes. When that didn't work, she speared one on her fork and tried eating it whole. That didn't work, either.

"Here, babe, let me help." Jeff reached over with his knife and fork and cut the stack into bite-size pieces.

When they had finished eating, he asked, "How were the pancakes?"

"They were boring little circles," she replied. "But they tasted good."

He sighed. "You win. Next time, we make little animals." He got up and carried their dishes over to the sink. "Why don't you go take a shower while I clean up the kitchen?"

"Okay." She got up and headed for the bathroom, but once inside, she stared blankly at the shower fixtures. How did the water come out? She turned one handle, but when nothing happened, she pulled another. Still, no water. She went to the doorway and called, "Jack, there's no water!"

He came sauntering down the hall, wiping his hands on a dish towel. "You can't turn the water on?"

"No, it won't work."

He stepped into the shower. "You've got to turn on the faucet. This one's hot; this one's cold."

"Like this?" She reached in and turned the handle. A geyser of cold water shot out.

Drenched, Jeff stumbled out, wiping water from his eyes. "Why'd you go and do that?"

Marnie broke into laughter. "You're all wet, Jack. You look so funny!"

"It's not funny, Marnie." He towel dried his hair. "Now, I've got to go change." Suddenly, he grabbed her and pulled her against him. "There! Now you're wet, too."

She wriggled out of his grasp, stepped back, and ran her hand over her damp shirt. "It's okay if I'm all wet. I'm taking a shower anyway."

"Yeah? You can't take a shower with your clothes on."

"I know. I'll take these things off."

Jeff looked away. "There's a robe in the closet. While you're at it, find something suitable to put on for your therapy session."

A half hour later, Marnie stepped out of the bathroom, showered and dressed. "I'm ready," she told Jeff.

He was busy putting away the last of the dishes and didn't pay any attention to her at first. When he finally looked up, he did a double take. "What are you wearing, Marnie?"

"Clothes."

"You're wearing *my* clothes. My plaid flannel shirt and my black corduroy pants! You can't wear them!"

"Why not? I like them."

"First of all, they're for a man. And they're way too big on you."

"Girls wear big shirts. They're in style."

"Maybe ten years ago, but not now. Why didn't you pick something from *your* side of the closet?"

"I didn't like anything."

He took her hand and led her to the bedroom. He slid open the door to her side of the closet. "Now, pick out something to wear. If you want me to, I'll pick something for you."

She gave him a pouting glance. "You pick. I can't decide."

He grabbed a pair of patch-pocket jeans and a green pullover shirt. "Put these on, Marnie. You like green. Come on. We've got to get going."

Neither of them spoke during the drive to the hospital. She was glad when he dropped her off and went on to his classes at the university after promising to pick her up after her therapy. If there was anything worse than living under the same roof with a stranger, it was living with a grouchy stranger. She had been too proud to admit she had no idea how to find the rehabilitation department, but after wandering the hospital corridors for a long while, she encountered a kind nurse named Elena who showed her the way.

That afternoon, when she was finished with her therapy sessions, she found Jeff waiting to take her home. As he walked her to the car, he said, "I'm sorry I got mad at you this morning. Forgive me?"

She nodded. "I forgive you, Jack."

He opened the passenger door and helped her inside. "Guess where we're going."

"For a ride?"

"We're going shopping. For food! Any kind of food you like!"

She clapped her hands. "Macaroni and cheese?"

"All the macaroni and cheese you can eat."

But grocery shopping turned out to be more daunting than Marnie had expected. As he led her up one aisle and down another, she clung to his arm, overwhelmed by the choices. When he told her to pick out the cereal she wanted, she stared in astonishment at the towering boxes. She seized one colorful package and tried to read the words. "Corn. . .flakes."

"Just pick one," he said.

She selected another box. "Oat. . .bran. Whole. . .grain."

He seized the box and tossed it into the cart. "At this rate, we'll starve. We'll be shopping until next week!"

Tears welled in her eyes. She hated that tone of voice. "I'm sorry, Jack."

He squeezed her arm. "There's nothing to be sorry about, Marnie. You just can't stand there reading everything on all the boxes. Just pick out what looks good to you and put it in the cart."

That sounded easy enough. She went up the aisle, selected several colorful items, and brought them back to the cart, dropping them in one by one.

He raised an eyebrow. "What did you get?"

She held up a small object.

"Denture cream?" He scanned the other items. "Diapers? Wart remover? Hair dye? Marnie, we don't need any of these things!"

"The boxes are pretty."

He shook his head. "Next time, I'm shopping alone."

She silently trudged behind him for the rest of their shopping trip. She hated the grocery store. It was way too confusing. Too many choices. Too many people. Too much commotion. It made her head hurt.

When they arrived back at the apartment, she insisted on helping with the groceries. At least she would show him she could do something. She wasn't completely helpless. But the paper sack she was carrying ripped open, dumping cans of tomatoes and beans on the kitchen floor. When she stooped down to retrieve them, she dropped them again.

He bent down and gathered up the cans. "It's okay, Marnie. It'll take time for you to regain your strength. You've had a big day. Why don't you go lie down for a while."

"I want to help."

"I know you do. But you don't know where things go."

"Tell me."

He heaved a sigh. "Okay, that bag of rice goes in the lower cupboard. The box of cereal goes on the top shelf. The hamburger goes in the fridge."

She stared at him for a long moment. His words were already scrambled in her head. She couldn't make them fall into place. "Okay, I'll go rest." She went over to the sofa and sat down.

"Do you wanna watch TV?"

She nodded. "I like the show about the judge who tells people what to do."

He continued putting away the groceries. "The remote's right there by the couch."

She picked it up and stared at it. There were a zillion buttons to press. She turned it over in her hand. It looked mysterious and alarming. She set it back down. "I'll just sit here, Jack."

"I'll turn it on, hon." He came over, picked up the remote, and aimed it at the television. "There. You're all set."

"Where's the judge?"

"I think she comes on later. You can watch the news."

"I don't like the news. They talk about bad stuff all the time."

"Hey, I have a great idea. How would you like to see the video of our wedding?" He strode over, removed a videotape from the shelf, and inserted it in the video player. "I don't know why I didn't think of this before." He sat down beside her and pressed the remote. "You're going to like this, Marnie. It was the most beautiful wedding ever."

She fastened her eyes on the screen, her anticipation rising. If Jack said it was beautiful, he must be right. A beach scene flashed on the screen. People were milling around, music was playing, and the sun was setting. The people filed into rows of chairs and sat down. "There's my mom," said Marnie, sitting forward. "And my dad."

"Right!" He clasped her hand. "Look, Marnie. Your folks were right there. Keep watching, babe. You'll see yourself in your wedding dress."

She watched as the bride walked along the beach in time to the music. She looked so graceful and happy. Marnie nodded. "She's beautiful."

"That's you, babe. And me. See? I'm standing there waiting for you with

Pastor Maluhia. I couldn't take my eyes off you. That was the best day of my life." He made a coughing sound in his throat and looked away. When he looked back at her, his eyes were glazed with tears. His hand tightened on hers. "Do you remember, Marnie? Do you remember our wedding day?"

She pulled her hand away. He was doing it again—expecting her to recall something that had nothing to do with her. She twisted a strand of her hair. "I like watching your wedding. The bride is pretty."

"That's you, Marnie. *You're* pretty."

"No, *she's* pretty."

"You really don't see any connection between you and the girl on the screen, do you?"

Marnie shook her head. "I'm not that girl. I'm me."

He turned off the television and tossed the remote on the coffee table.

"Is it over, Jack?"

"Yeah, Marnie, it's over." He sat back, closed his eyes, and raked his fingers through his hair. For a long while, neither of them spoke. Marnie stared at the blank television screen, waiting. She curled a strand of hair around her finger, then uncurled it, and then curled it again. Why wasn't Jack saying anything? She was used to taking her cues from him, letting him lead their conversations. Her own thoughts were still too random and higgledy-piggledy. Was that a word? It described how her brain felt much of the time.

At last, he stood up and removed the videotape from the machine, put it back on the shelf, and then looked down at Marnie. "Tomorrow is Sunday. Are you up to going to church?" When she didn't answer right away, he said, "I know it's been a couple of months since you were there. But now that you're out of the hospital, I think it would be good for you to go. It's a little open-air church. Very informal. A great bunch of people. They've been praying for us every day. Many of them took turns sitting by your bedside when you didn't even know they were there. I know they'd love to see you again."

She folded her hands under her chin. "What would I wear?"

"A dress and some flip-flops, I guess. Nothing fancy."

"Will I know anyone?"

"I don't know. But they'll know you. They've been in and out of the hospital visiting you. They all care about you, Marnie. They've been pulling for you. They're thrilled that you're getting better."

She gave him a faint smile. "Okay, Jack. I'll go."

The next morning, from the moment Marnie awoke, she felt a knot of anxiety in the pit of her stomach. Any activity out of the ordinary struck her with fear. She hated being placed in a situation where she didn't know what to do, and that seemed to be happening all the time lately.

Even though he'd made pancakes in the shapes of little animals, she was too nervous to eat much breakfast. She drank her juice, ate the heads and legs off her hotcakes, then pushed the plate away. "I'm done. Let's go."

"But you're not ready yet. You're still in your robe. And your hair's a mess."

"Oh."

He helped her style her hair with the flat iron and rubbed the redness from her cheeks where she had put on too much blush. He tied the ribbon around her mint green cotton dress and made sure her flip-flops matched. He was wearing a green polo shirt and khaki slacks.

"Look, we match," she said as they headed out the door.

On the way to church, she bombarded him with questions. "What will we do in church, Jack?"

"Sing, pray, read the Bible, listen to Pastor Maluhia's message, visit with our friends."

"Do I have friends there, Jack?"

"Of course you do. You just don't remember them."

"Will you stay with me?"

"Right by your side every minute."

"Will I have to talk?"

"Just smile and say hello and let everyone else do the talking."

"Okay. Smile—hello. Smile—hello."

But by the time they pulled into the parking lot, Marnie couldn't remember any advice he had given her. She knew only that she was terrified. Oh, if only she could be back at the hospital—or even at the apartment—where she knew what to expect.

"Where's the church?" she asked as he led her toward a structure with a roof but no sides.

"This is it. Like I said, it's an open-air church. We love to worship in the great outdoors."

She had expected to see a huge church with a steeple and stained-glass windows, like the one she had attended in Michigan. This church was more like a garden with lots of trees and greenery surrounding a cozy meeting area.

From the moment they arrived, they were greeted like royalty. "Oh Marnie and Jeff, how wonderful to see you both again," said a small Asian woman who gripped Marnie's hand and seemed unwilling to let it go.

Marnie smiled. "Hello."

An elderly couple approached and took turns embracing Marnie. They both talked at once with such excitement that she couldn't understand a word they said. She smiled and said, "Hello."

Soon, a group of people had gathered around them, everyone talking and laughing and hugging Marnie.

"*Pehea `oe?* How are you, dear?"

"We've prayed for you at every service, Marnie."

"Aloha, Marnie. It's so good to have you back."

"We sat with you in the hospital. Do you remember, Marnie?"

"Your husband has been a gem. He never left your side."

"We'll be bringing in more meals until you're up to cooking again, Marnie. Let us know what you like."

"I don't know," she murmured. "Maybe macaroni and cheese. And peanut butter and jelly sandwiches."

"Oh, we can do better than that, dear."

"You look like your old self again, Marnie. What a wonderful answer to prayer!"

Marnie's head started spinning. She felt the way she had at the supermarket—dizzy, breathless, overwhelmed. She wanted to run away, but her legs felt wobbly as noodles. She clutched Jeff's arm. He slipped his arm around her, thanked everyone for their loving concern, then led her through rows of white plastic lawn chairs to a seat near the front, where a keyboard, guitars, and a small lectern stood.

Marnie was never so glad to sit down. She was even happier when the service started. That meant no one else would be coming up and hugging her and chattering about things she couldn't comprehend.

While she loved the praise and worship music, her mind wandered during prayer time. And shortly into the pastor's sermon, she found herself fidgeting. She kicked off her flip-flops and tapped her feet against the cold cement floor. As hard as she tried to concentrate on his words, her thoughts kept flitting off to distant places.

"When can we go?" she asked.

He put his finger to his lips. "Soon. Be quiet and listen."

She didn't want to listen. As far as she was concerned, the words were gobbledygook. They were gone long before she could catch their meaning. Why sit and listen to something she didn't understand?

"I want to go home, Jack," she whispered.

He shushed her again.

She crossed her arms, scooted down in her chair, and tapped her fingers on her elbows. Her eyes fixated on a bright green gecko crawling over the lawn chair in front of her. She reached for it, but it jumped to the floor and scurried away. Then she sat back again and started humming.

Jeff scowled at her. "Stop it, Marnie. You're in church!"

"I want to go home."

"It's not time yet."

"Why not? I'm tired."

"Please stop complaining!" He looked around. Marnie followed his gaze. People were watching. Even the minister had paused. There was dead silence. Before Marnie realized what was happening, her angry companion stood up, grabbed her hand, and pulled her to her feet. Without a backward glance, he led her down the aisle and out to the car.

As he opened the door for her, he snapped, "I hope you're happy. That's the last time I'm taking you to church!"

She jutted out her lower lip. "Good! I don't want to come back."

His angry scowl faded. Tears glazed his blue eyes. "Baby, I'm sorry. Of course I'll bring you back to church." He took her in his arms. "You just make me so crazy I say things I don't mean. Forgive me?"

She turned her face away from his. "Just take me home, Jack."

Chapter 6

Hey, Nate—is that a new shirt?" Shielding his eyes from the sun, Jeff watched his buddy sauntering toward him along Ali'i Drive, a two-lane road that curved around Kona's Kailua Bay. They had agreed to meet at the gift shop beside Hulihe'e Palace, a historic two-story mansion on an expansive, manicured lawn. The palace was next to the seawall, Jeff's favorite spot in Kona.

"So you like my shirt?" Nate asked. The two exchanged friendly cuffs on the arm. "I got it at that little shop on Waterfront Row."

"Man, that shirt must have every kind of flower in Hawaii in there somewhere."

Nate flicked his silk collar. He didn't seem to mind that the shirt hung loose on his lanky frame. "Yeah, I thought it was pretty cool. Lots of color, huh?"

Jeff nodded, stifling a grin. "More colors than I knew existed."

"So what's up, bro?"

Jeff shrugged. "Nothing much. I've been walking all morning, trying to clear my head." On a lark, he had phoned Nate and asked him to meet him here, but now, he was having second thoughts. He felt awkward, at a loss for words.

Nate fell into step beside him. They passed a row of banyan trees then the palace and headed for the seawall. "There's gotta be more. What's going on?"

"Nothing," Jeff insisted. Nothing he could put into words anyway.

"You sure? On the phone, you sounded pretty upset."

"I don't know why I called you. It was stupid. You're probably deep into studying for tests or something."

"No more than you."

They ducked under a low-hanging tree, sidestepped the standing puddles of seawater, and hopped up onto the jagged lava rock wall. It was smooth on top, its four-foot-wide surface covered with a layer of cement. Jeff liked walking the seawall; he came here whenever he wanted to get away from his studies and soak up some sun and local culture. He always stopped at the quaint little shop across the street for some Hawaiian "shave ice" with coconut ice cream in the middle. Then he would sit on the wall and ponder the world, watching tourists and sea turtles at the same time.

"So are you gonna tell me what's going on, Jeff, or do I have to drag it out of you?"

"It's nothing, man. Nothing and everything." They walked north, passing several fishermen bent over their poles, until they reached a spot where the waves weren't crashing as hard against the wall. They sat down, facing the ocean. A balmy April breeze ruffled the cerulean waters. Jeff could almost taste the salt spray on his lips. Fleecy cotton-ball clouds dotted the blue sky. It was the kind of day he and Marnie used to love. They had sat here just like this, talking, daydreaming, watching the sunset, planning their future. *What future?* he wondered now. Who knew it would turn out like this?

"Is this about Marnie?" asked Nate, his eyes fixed on the horizon.

"What else?" Jeff kept his gaze straight ahead, too. It was easier not making eye contact. Several outrigger canoes rolled over the waves. The sea was so clear he could spot schools of fish zigzagging through the water and large sea turtles bucking the current.

"Has she had a setback?"

"No, nothing like that." They were talking over the din of roaring breakers, blaring traffic, and laughing children.

"What then?" said Nate. "From what I've seen, she's amazing. She's back in school. Catching up on her classes. Looking and acting like the old Marnie."

"I know. It's going on two months since she came home, and I've never seen anyone work harder than she has. Classes, rehab, counseling, therapy—she's trying to do it all. Of course, the mental stimulation is more important for her recovery than whether she gets the credits. She still has trouble with her short-term memory. She makes lists constantly—everything she does goes on a list. And she can't find her way out of a paper bag. Worst of all, she still doesn't remember me. But otherwise, she's gone from being a helpless, confused child to a practically normal woman again."

"Isn't that what you want?"

"Sure it is." Jeff cracked his knuckles. "But everything's different. Marnie. Me. Our marriage."

Nate gave him a sidelong glance. "You saying your marriage is in trouble?"

"That's just it," said Jeff. "There is no marriage. We're coexisting like strangers forced to share the same living space. Polite but distant. She's wary of me. I don't even think she likes me."

"Come on, man. She loves you. Um, she just doesn't remember you."

"And that's supposed to reassure me? What if she never remembers me?"

"But she's there. Living in your apartment. That has to count for something."

"Truth is, I don't know how long she'll stay. I have a feeling someday I'll come home and she'll be gone."

"Where would she go?"

"I don't know. Michigan maybe. I really think she'd like to go back to the mainland and live with her parents."

"Have you tried talking things out with her? Maybe something will jog her memory."

"I've talked till I'm blue in the face. Nothing gets through to her. I'm telling you, Nate; in our wedding vows we said, 'for better, for worse. . .in sickness and in health.' To me, they were just nice words. I didn't think about what they meant. But they're heavy-duty. There's a whole lot hanging on those words. I don't know if I can live up to them."

Nate swiveled and looked him square in the face. "You thinking of ending your marriage?"

Jeff picked up a chipped piece of concrete and pitched it into the ocean. "I'm saying there is no marriage. Not in Marnie's eyes. It's like I don't even have a wife. These days, it's all in name only. I'm still sleeping on a hard cot in the spare bedroom. How does a guy deal with that?"

"I don't know what to say, buddy."

"The trouble is, there's no chance to work things out. We hardly even see each other anymore. She's always in class or rehab. I'm busy with my classes or putting in additional hours doing carpentry or maintenance work to bring in a little extra cash. Our medical bills are astronomical."

"I thought your car insurance covered the medical expenses."

"It has paid a lot of them, but it doesn't cover everything."

"Sorry, man."

Jeff ran his hand over the wall's smooth surface. "There's something else that gets to me."

"Yeah? What's that?"

"Marnie doesn't like to go to church anymore. She says she doesn't know anyone, and she has no desire to get reacquainted. It drives me up a wall, Nate. She doesn't remember all the people she used to care so much about, even though they're still dropping in and bringing us food now and then. She has no interest in reading the Bible or praying. And when I talk about us going to the mission field someday, she says she doesn't want to go. I'm telling you, man, my whole life's hanging in the balance. Marnie and I were totally committed to becoming missionaries. That's why we're here at University of the Nations. Do I have to give up my dreams because my wife can't remember what God called us to do?"

Nate let out a sigh. "Wow, that is heavy. I don't have any answers for you, Jeff—except for the standard advice you already know. Trust God. Keep praying. Be a good husband even if Marnie doesn't see herself as your wife."

Jeff nodded. "Yeah, I know what you're saying. I was just hoping there might be some easy answers out there."

"None that I know of." Nate leaned back on his hands and gazed up at the sky. "What about Marnie's girlfriends? Has she made any connections with them?"

"You know Marnie. She was friends with just about everyone. When we were dating, she had so many friends I could hardly get her undivided attention. Of course, once we got married, we spent a lot of time together, just the two of us. But she still kept in touch with her friends."

"And now?"

"Now when they drop by, she's polite, but I can tell she doesn't feel any connection with them anymore. When they invite her out, she always says no."

"There was one girl she hung out with a lot," said Nate. "She was in your wedding. What was her name?"

"Jenny. Jenny Purkeypile."

"Is that her last name?"

"Yeah, I think it's German."

"Don't they call her Perky—or something like that?"

"Yep. Perky. The name fits her to a tee. Her family came from Germany, and she's hoping to go back as a missionary someday. She and Marnie were as close as sisters."

"That's good," said Nate. "As I recall, Jenny—or Perky—is pretty upbeat, with a good sense of humor. I think she'd be great for Marnie."

"True." Jeff gazed out at a cruise ship docked in the harbor. Its white hull glistened in the sunlight. He wouldn't mind sailing off somewhere and forgetting his troubles. "The thing is, Jenny's been on a mission trip to Cambodia for the past few months. But I heard she's due back any day now."

"Get in touch with her, bro. I'm sure she'll want to see Marnie. And maybe, she can stir up a few memories."

Jeff nodded. "It's worth a try. Nothing else has worked."

Marnie stood staring into her closet, her latest list in her hand. She was wearing her comfy chemise top and lounge pants, but Jeff would be home soon to take her to her therapy session, so she must select something appropriate to wear. Making decisions was one of the hardest tasks she faced these days. It was easier when Jeff picked something out of her closet and told her to put it on, but he had insisted she start making her own choices. Choosing something to wear was almost as daunting as selecting the right items at the grocery store.

She looked at her list. Yesterday she had worn her skinny jeans and red drawstring top; the day before, her blue-striped tee and tan cargo pants. What should she wear today? She took down her yellow kimono top and khaki skirt. Did they go together? She had no idea.

She laid the outfit on her bed, then she stooped down and foraged among her shoes for a matching pair. More than once, she had left the house with mismatched shoes. She found a pair of canvas wedges, sat down on the bed, and examined them. Yes, they were the same.

So much of her time was spent making lists of things and diagrams of places, and reading material over and over again. Would her mind ever work right? Would she ever feel like a whole person again?

The doorbell rang, so she dropped the shoes and scurried to answer it, hoping it wouldn't be someone she was supposed to know. She opened the door to an attractive woman about her age, with short brown hair and a smile that lit up her round pixie face.

"Marnie, hi!"

The girl grabbed her in a bear hug, but Marnie gently disengaged herself, wondering, *Who on earth is this person?*

"Marnie, it's me. Jenny. Do you remember me?"

Marnie shook her head. "I don't remember anybody. Nobody here in Hawaii anyway."

The girl flashed a sympathetic smile. "I know. Jeff told me."

"He did?"

"Yes. He phoned me. I just got home from Cambodia yesterday. Great timing, huh? I had heard about your accident and was planning to call you. But after Jeff phoned, I decided to come right over. Do you have time to visit?"

"I have a therapy session."

"Maybe I could stay for just a minute."

"I guess so." Marnie reluctantly stepped aside and let her enter. The girl followed her inside and sat down beside her on the wicker sofa.

"How are you feeling, Marnie?"

"Okay. I forget things. Are we friends?"

The girl beamed. "Best friends. I was maid of honor in your wedding."

Marnie twisted a raveling on her chemise top. "I don't remember. I saw the video. It was very pretty."

"You were the most beautiful bride ever. Jeff was the happiest man alive."

"I don't remember him, either."

"I know. But someday you will. He loves you so much. I hope I find a guy like him someday."

Marnie pulled at the ravel. She hated trying to make conversation. There never seemed to be anything to say. She looked up at the girl. "What is your name?"

"Jenny. Jenny Purkeypile."

"That's a funny name."

"I know. Everyone teases me. They call me Perky. But you call me Jenny."

"Jenny. I'll write it on my list." She picked up a small tablet on the coffee table and wrote down the name. "I keep lists of everything, or else I'll forget."

"Good idea. I should try that myself."

"Why? Do you forget?"

"Sometimes. We all do."

"I feel like I'm the only one."

"Well, you're not. And from what Jeff says, you've done a fantastic job with your therapy and getting back into your classes."

"I have to read my assignments over and over again."

"Not many of us would be that diligent," said Jenny.

Marnie smiled. "You're nice. I like you."

Jenny clasped her hand. "I like you, too. We always have a great time together."

"Were you here before?"

"Not since before your accident," said Jenny. "I've been in Cambodia."

"What were you doing there?"

"I was taking care of children who were abused or mistreated."

"That's a nice thing to do."

"I think I was blessed more than the children. They were so eager for love and attention. Families there are so poor, and young girls there are often sold into slavery. It's very sad."

Marnie nodded. She had been on a mission trip, but she couldn't remember where.

Jenny was still flashing her radiant smile. "We held day camps and vacation Bible schools. I had the chance to lead lots of little children to Jesus. It was beautiful to see their faith growing."

Marnie looked down at her hands. "I don't talk to Jesus anymore."

Jenny looked intently at her. "Why not?"

Marnie shrugged. "I don't know."

"He still loves you, Marnie. He wants to be there for you."

"Then why did He let the accident happen?"

"I don't know." Jenny drew in a deep breath. "Some things we'll never understand until we're in heaven with Him. But whatever God does, it's because He loves us."

"That's what Jack—uh, I mean Jeff—says."

"He's right." Jenny stood up. "I guess I'd better go and let you get ready for your therapy session."

Marnie got up and walked her to the door. "Will you come back?"

"I'd love to. Whether you remember me or not, we're still friends."

"Friends," Marnie repeated. "I have your name on my list. I won't forget you."

"I'll never forget you, either." Jenny gave her a quick hug. Marnie didn't pull back this time. Jenny's eyes glistened. "We have a lot to catch up on, my friend. Take care of yourself." She blinked then turned away. "I'll see you soon!"

After watching the slender girl go down the sidewalk to her car, Marnie shut the door and returned to her wicker sofa. She looked at the tablet where she had written in large letters: J-E-N-N-Y. She repeated the name several times.

She was determined to remember this girl with the smiling face the next time they met. It wouldn't be easy. Dr. Forlani had told her she suffered from a condition called "face blindness." Even when she got acquainted with people, she wouldn't necessarily recognize them the next time they met.

"I will remember. I will!" Clutching her pen, she traced Jenny's name over and over, until the letters were thick and black and the pen dug through the paper. "Jenny," she said again, enunciating each syllable. "My friend. . .Jenny."

Chapter 7

"I have a new friend," Marnie told Jeff when he arrived home to drive her to her therapy session.

"A new friend?" He came inside and gave her a quick kiss on the cheek. "Who is it?"

Marnie retrieved her tablet from the coffee table. "Here. Look. Her name is Jenny."

Jeff smiled. "So she gave you a call, huh? I was hoping she would."

"No. She came over. She sat right here, and we talked. I like her. She's really nice."

"Of course you like her. She's your best friend. She was even in our wedding."

"She told me. I'll look for her when you show me the video again."

"Great. We'll do that. You'll have to invite her back again."

"I'd like that."

Jeff sat down in his black beanbag chair. "Maybe we could have her over for dinner sometime. I'd like to hear how she liked Cambodia."

Holding up the tablet, Marnie carefully ran her finger over Jenny's name. "When can we have her over?"

"Anytime you want. How about tomorrow night?"

Marnie set the tablet aside. "Yes! Tomorrow night! What day is that?"

"Tuesday."

"Do I have classes on Tuesday?"

"Yes. And I work. But we can get home in time for dinner."

"Great! Call Jenny. Tell her to come over tomorrow for dinner."

"Sure. I think I have her number on my cell phone."

"What will we eat?"

"We can order a pizza."

"No pizza, Jack—I mean, Jeff." Marnie walked over to their little kitchenette and browsed through the cupboards. She pulled out a cookbook. "I'm going to cook dinner myself."

He gave her a searching glance. "Are you sure? You're still just finding your way around the kitchen."

"I make macaroni and cheese. I can cook lots of things now."

"Yeah, with a little help from yours truly."

"Call her, Jeff. Call her now."

"Right now, I've got to get you to therapy. I'll call her this evening, okay?"

Marnie jutted out her lower lip. "Okay. I guess I can wait."

But she had a hard time concentrating on her therapy that afternoon. Her mind kept wandering to her new friend and the dinner she would fix. Marnie would show both Jeff and Jenny that she was becoming a capable person again. She could do things on her own. She could cook a simple dinner. She could be like other people who did things without even having to think about them.

That evening, after Jeff confirmed that Jenny would be joining them tomorrow for dinner, Marnie sat down at the kitchen table and thumbed through her cookbook. "What can I fix? It has to be really good."

Jeff sat down, too. "How about spaghetti? That's pretty easy. You can't go wrong with spaghetti."

Marnie nodded. "I like spaghetti. But what about dessert?"

"I can buy something."

"No, I'm making it myself."

"How about cookies in a tube? You always like them."

"Okay. I can do that."

"We'll go shopping tomorrow." He reached for her hand. "We'll get some salad fixings, too. It'll be a great dinner, Marnie."

"You can't help me."

"I won't. It's your party, okay?"

"I love parties."

He grinned. "That's right. You always loved parties."

But Marnie didn't feel quite so confident the next afternoon as she stood in her kitchen trying to decide where to begin. She had insisted that Jeff go run errands and let her work alone. She was so tired of having to depend on other people for help. She needed to do this by herself. How hard could it be—spaghetti, a salad, and cookies?

She got out her cookbook and looked up spaghetti. She must have made it a dozen times, but she had no memory of it. She would follow the recipe step by step. That way she couldn't go wrong. She found the recipe. Okay, so far so good. She looked around the kitchen. She would have to remember where everything was—pans, utensils, spices, pasta, tomato sauce.

She opened the bottom cupboard. Yes, the pans were there. She removed a large kettle for the pasta and another one for the sauce. She would be making a salad, too. She would need lettuce, tomatoes, and dressing. They would all be in the fridge. Yes, they were there. And the cookies. A tube of chocolate chip cookies sat on the shelf above the head of lettuce.

But it was too soon for the lettuce and cookies.

She looked around. She needed to preheat the oven. Okay, that was done. There was the table to set, too. Three place settings. Dishes were on the top shelf on the right. No, those were glasses and mugs. She tried the cupboard on the left. Yes, plates and bowls. She took out three place settings and arranged them on the table. Silverware next. She looked in one drawer then another. The third drawer was the charm. But did the knife go on the left or right? And the fork? Oh well, she would put them all on the plate.

She looked at the clock. Was dinner supposed to be at five or six? When would Jeff be home? When would Jenny arrive? She couldn't remember.

They could be here at any moment! She had better get the spaghetti started. She took the kettle to the sink, filled it nearly to the brim, and set it on the stove. She turned the burner on high.

Now for the sauce. She read over the recipe again. She needed olive oil, an onion, a clove of garlic, a large can of Italian tomatoes, fresh basil, oregano, ground round steak, and tomato paste. She had forgotten how many ingredients a simple dish like spaghetti required.

She gathered the ingredients from the refrigerator and cupboards and set them on the countertop. She started chopping the onion and garlic then noticed that the water was already boiling. She dropped in the dry pasta, stirred it, then returned to her chopped onion. A whiff of onion juice stung her eyes, sending tears coursing down her cheeks. She grabbed a dish towel and wiped her eyes, but when she looked back at the cookbook, her tears blurred the words. She blinked until the words finally came into focus.

Simmer ground round, onion, and garlic in olive oil in heavy skillet.

She got out a skillet, poured in the olive oil and stirred in the ground round and half-chopped onion and garlic. She was adding the basil and oregano when she noticed the pasta boiling over. With one hand, she tossed the spices into the pan; with the other, she grabbed the knob and turned off the pasta. But it was too late. The white billowing foam had surged over the edge of the kettle, drenching the stovetop and streaming onto the floor.

No, no, no!

She grabbed several paper towels and wiped up the floor. Then she drained the pasta. This wasn't going the way she had planned. Why did so many things have to be done all at once? *Focus, Marnie, focus!*

While the meat simmered, she worked on the sauce, adding tomatoes and seasonings. As she turned on the flame under the sauce, she thought of the cookies. They would take awhile to bake. She got the tube out of the fridge, sliced the dough onto a cookie sheet, and put them in the oven.

Her head was hurting, so she sat down at the table and closed her eyes. *What do I do next?* She looked down at her clothes. She had spilled tomato sauce on her top. She got up and headed for her closet. She would pick something special to put on.

She stood for a long while staring into the closet. Whenever she faced too many choices, her mind shut down. She had to make a decision. Finally, after trying on half a dozen outfits, she reached in and selected a simple green shirtdress.

As she slipped it on, she smelled something burning. At the same moment, the smoke alarm broke the silence with its shrill, high-pitched scream. She ran back to the kitchen and grabbed the skillet off the stove. The meat was scorched, but that wasn't what she smelled. The cookies! As she opened the oven, black smoke billowed out. She stepped back and coughed. Her chocolate chip cookies had become little black, smoldering lumps of coal! With a pot holder, she gingerly removed the cookie sheet and dumped it into the sink. So much for dessert!

With the smoke alarm still blasting, she checked the spaghetti sauce. It was bubbling fiercely, so she stirred it and lowered the flame. Then she checked the scorched meat. If she carefully removed the top layer, she could still salvage part of it. First, she had to do something about that deafening alarm. She pulled a chair over, stepped up, and finally found the button that turned it off. Returning to the stove, she picked up the skillet and with a spatula removed all the meat that wasn't burned and dumped it into the sauce. She put the burned meat and cookies down the disposal. Maybe Jeff wouldn't notice there was no dessert.

But what about the pasta? You couldn't have spaghetti without it. She stuck a fork into the white, glistening mound. It was a congealed mass. Maybe a little water and butter would unstick it. After a few minutes, the strands separated. The pasta might be gummy and chewy, but it would have to do.

She tackled the salad next, breaking up the lettuce and slicing the tomatoes. Her head still pounded. Why hadn't she agreed to order in pizza? Because too much was at stake—the chance to feel normal again, to be like other people who took their minds for granted.

She heard a car pull up outside. Jeff! Or maybe it was her new friend, Jenny. She headed for the door. *Please let everything go right. Please don't let me feel like a broken person anymore!*

❧

Jeff was just returning home from his errands when he spotted Jenny pulling into the parking area by his apartment. After parking his car, he walked over and greeted her as she was getting out of hers. "Thanks, Jen, for coming. You're a lifesaver. I think you're going to do wonders for Marnie."

Jenny reached into her car and retrieved a brown grocery bag. "I brought her favorite chocolate cake. She's got to remember that."

"She doesn't remember anything that happened in Hawaii. Or anyone."

Jenny looked up at him, concern etched on her face. "I know. It was really spooky coming here yesterday and having her look at me like I was just some door-to-door saleslady or something. I couldn't believe she didn't recognize me. I'm sure glad you gave me the heads-up beforehand."

"Even though she's been talking about nothing else but your visit, she still may not recognize you again. She has this condition called 'face blindness.' The doctor's hoping it will get better as the rest of her brain function improves."

"So she is continually improving?"

"Yeah. She's a hundred percent better now than she was a month ago."

"But she still doesn't remember you're her husband?"

"Oh, she knows it in her head but not in her heart. I'm just the guy who hangs around and makes sure she's on track with her classes and therapy and stuff."

"That must be awfully hard for you."

"Tell me about it. I'm virtually a bachelor these days, with a slightly wacky roommate. Whoops, I didn't mean to say that."

"That's okay. I'm sure you need to vent sometime. If there's anything I can do to help, let me know."

"You're doing it. I haven't seen Marnie this excited since the accident. Somewhere in that foggy mind of hers, she senses how important you are to her. I just wish she felt the same way about me."

Jenny took his arm as they walked toward the apartment. "She does, Jeff. You have to believe that. Someday, the old Marnie will come back to you."

"The old Marnie doesn't exist anymore, Jen, and the sooner I learn to live with it, the better."

Jen smiled up at him. "Well, I'm just starting to get acquainted with the new Marnie. This should be an interesting evening."

"You can say that again. Marnie insisted on fixing dinner all on her own. Usually, I'm there to make sure she gets it right, so this is her first solo. I have no idea what to expect."

"Well, maybe we can both help her pull it together."

Jeff chuckled. "No matter what happens, just keep smiling."

"Will do."

He opened the door and stepped aside, letting Jen enter first. Marnie was right there by the door, smiling expectantly. Even though she looked tired, there was something cute and vulnerable in her face that wrenched his heart. Her long, auburn brown hair was a little mussed, but he hadn't seen her look this happy in months.

"Hello, Jenny." Marnie crossed her arms, as if not sure what to do next.

"Hi, Marnie." Jenny gave her a hug. "I like your dress."

"It was in my closet. I couldn't decide what to wear, so I just reached in and picked this."

"You look great, hon." Jeff was about to kiss her cheek when he noticed a smoky haze filling the house. He wrinkled his nose at the acrid smell. *Great! I knew I shouldn't have left her alone.* "What's burning, Marnie?"

She gave him a frown. "Nothing. Everything's okay, Jeff."

"Is it the spaghetti?" He strode over to the stove. "It smells like you burned it."

Marnie ignored him. "Do you like spaghetti, Jenny?"

"I love spaghetti."

Jeff's voice rose in intensity. "The smoke is thick enough in here to cut. What burned, Marnie?"

She looked at him in exasperation. "It was the cookies. They didn't make it."

"That's okay." Jenny held up her grocery sack. "I brought dessert. Your favorite chocolate cake."

Marnie took the bag over to the counter. "Look, Jeff. Chocolate cake."

"Yeah, that's great." He was having a hard time handling his irritation. Why couldn't he be married to a normal girl like Jenny? Guilt punched him like a blow to the stomach. Marnie couldn't help how she was. If he were the right kind of husband, he wouldn't let things like this bother him. He turned on the fan over the range then went around and opened the windows.

"I'm sorry about the cookies." Marnie's voice sounded like a little girl's.

He took a deep breath. He was being a jerk, and here he had such high hopes for tonight. "It's okay. Don't worry about it."

"Can I help you with anything, Marnie?" asked Jenny.

"Everything's done. I did it all myself."

"I see that. I'd be glad to help you put the food on."

They held hands around the table as Jeff said grace. He was pleasantly surprised that the spaghetti tasted better than he had anticipated.

"Good dinner, Marnie." He squeezed her hand. "You did a good job."

She beamed. "Thank you, Jeff."

As they ate, Jenny talked about her experiences in Cambodia. "I loved going to the little villages and helping with the children. There's such poverty there, and the children are so grateful for such little acts of kindness. Braiding their hair. Telling them a story. Teaching them a song. I loved seeing their faces when they came to know Jesus. Their eyes lit up, and they looked so happy. It made me know I was doing exactly what God had called me to do."

Jeff nodded. "Marnie and I felt the same way when we were in Cambodia. We worked in a teen center in Battambang."

"That's right," said Jenny. "I remember."

"I don't," said Marnie, lowering her gaze. "I don't remember it at all."

Jenny squeezed her hand. "That doesn't change the fact that you helped a lot of people over there, Marnie. God used you in a wonderful way."

"I can't wait to go again," said Jeff. "Whether it's Cambodia or Nigeria or someplace else. I can't wait to be in full-time ministry." He stole a glance at Marnie. She was twirling pasta on her fork. Did she have the slightest interest in what he and Jenny were saying? His enthusiasm waned. There was no use pretending that everything was normal. Marnie had no memory of the most important events of their lives. How could they build a future together if she couldn't remember the past?

Chapter 8

Jeff heard birds chirping outside his window long before his alarm went off. Without opening his eyes, he could see the brightness of the June sun against his lids and feel its heat on his skin. It promised to be a beautiful day, but it wasn't starting out that way for him. He rolled over, kicked off his covers, and groaned. This hard cot was giving him aches and pains in muscles he didn't even know he had. He dragged himself out of bed, stretched, and rolled his shoulders. These days, he was going around with a permanent crick in his back.

He headed for the bathroom, but since Marnie was already there showering, he made his way to the kitchen instead and put on the coffee. He was setting the table when she came out in her terry robe, her hair wrapped in a towel. She looked as cute as a button. In the old days, they would have had a fun little skirmish with the towel and ended up back in the bedroom. But no more.

"Your turn," she said.

"Do you want oatmeal or eggs? Or both?"

"Both. But you go take your shower. I'll fix them after I get dressed."

"Sounds good to me." As he passed her, he flicked the towel. "You look cute, babe."

She laughed. "Right. No makeup. My hair in a turban. If this is cute, you need glasses."

"So I like the natural look." He took a step then winced and drew in a sharp breath.

Marnie's brow furrowed. "Are you okay?"

He reached back and rubbed the small of his back. "Yeah, it's just that cot. It's killing my back. I don't know how much longer I can take it." He wasn't talking just about the cot now, but that was another story.

She gave him a sympathetic smile. "I'm sorry, Jeff. I know you miss your comfortable bed."

He tried for a solemn martyr's tone. "Yes, I do. More than I can say."

She looked thoughtful. "Well, maybe we can fix that."

Was it possible? Was she saying what he hoped and prayed she was saying? His voice rose on a wave of excitement. "Marnie, you mean it? I can come back to our bed?"

She slapped his arm. "No, silly. I'll switch places with you. I'll take the cot from now on."

He continued on to the bathroom, grumbling, "That's not what I had in mind."

At breakfast, the subject of their sleeping arrangements still played in his thoughts. For months, he had avoided discussing their relationship. Marnie had been too sick, confused, and overwhelmed to make decisions about their marriage. But now, she was almost like her old self again. Even since April, her memory was better; her confidence was growing. More and more, she seemed like the Marnie he remembered. And he was tired of treating her like a sister.

But how to find the words to plead his case? He poked mindlessly at his scrambled eggs. Might as well just jump in. "Marnie, we gotta talk."

"About what?"

"Us."

"Oh."

"I think I've been more than patient, sweetheart. I don't know any guy who would go five months living in the same house with his wife and not expect her to be, you know, his wife! How long do you think we can keep up this 'look, but don't touch' policy? I love you, babe. And I need you more than I can say."

Marnie continued eating her oatmeal, her eyes downcast.

"Are you listening, hon? Am I getting through to you?"

"I hear you," she murmured. "I know it's not fair to you, but I just can't think of you like that, Jeff."

"Like what? Your husband? That's what I am."

"I know. And you have every right to expect your wife to be. . .a wife. But I don't feel it inside. I can't imagine us being more than. . .friends."

Jeff raked his fingers through his hair. This was the last thing he wanted to hear. The old "just friends" rejection. Especially coming from his wife, whom he had promised to love and cherish for the rest of his life. "So what do we do, Marnie, if all you want to be is friends? You want to spend a lifetime together just being friends?"

She looked up at him, her eyes wide and solemn. "No, Jeff. I've been thinking a lot about us. And I've made a decision."

"You have?" That sounded like progress. Usually, Marnie couldn't even decide between brown sugar or maple syrup on her oatmeal. "So what's your decision, hon?"

"I'm going home to Michigan."

His heart skipped a beat. "Michigan? You gotta be kidding."

"No, I'm serious. Our classes will be finished in about a month. It would be the perfect time."

"Perfect for who?"

"Okay, so nothing's perfect about our situation, Jeff. So we have to come up with something that's at least fair."

Anger and indignation were getting the best of him. "You're gonna decide what's fair for us? This I've gotta hear."

Several emotions played out on her face—distress, concern, determination, gratitude. But not love. How he missed that look of adoration he used to see in her eyes. "You've been wonderful, Jeff. Since the accident, you've taken such good care of me. I appreciate everything you've done. But even you have to agree we can't keep living in limbo like this."

Now she was using his own argument against him! "But I never meant that you should go home to your parents. Are you talking about a short visit? Maybe we could both go. I know they must be dying to see you again."

She raised her chin resolutely. "No, not a short visit. I plan to stay."

He was coming unglued. He had to hold it together, or she'd tune him out for sure. "But what about our marriage, babe? We have a serious commitment here."

She hesitated, as if weighing what to say next. "I'm sorry, Jeff. I don't feel married. I have no memories of ever being married. We may have a piece of paper that says we're married, but I can't be intimate with someone I have no memories of. It would go against everything I feel inside. It would feel *wrong*. I know you—we—don't believe in divorce, but maybe we should consider getting, uh, an annulment."

Jeff sat back and inhaled sharply. No matter how deeply he breathed, he couldn't get enough air to deal with Marnie's crazy talk. "You gotta be kidding me! After all these months, now that you're well again, you wanna get an annulment and just take off and go traipsing back to your parents? Give me a break!"

Her lower lip jutted out. "Now you're getting mad. I knew I shouldn't have said anything."

Jeff got up and paced the floor. He picked up a newspaper, rolled it, and swatted his palm. What he really felt like doing right now was putting his fist through the wall. "I can't believe we're having this discussion! All this time, I figured, okay, give her some space. Let her get well. Then she'll come back to me, and things will be like they used to be. But you're not even willing to try, are you, Marnie? You don't have the slightest desire to fight for this marriage!"

She looked up at him with the saddest eyes he had ever seen.

"Don't you see, Jeff? Our history started the day I woke up at the hospital. As far as I'm concerned, there is no marriage. I don't know how many ways I can say it. I don't feel that way about you—the way a wife should feel about her husband. I wish I did. It would make everything so much easier. I see you as a devoted, trustworthy friend. That's all. I can't imagine us ever being anything else. I'm sorry."

All his anger dissolved in those big, sad, earnest eyes. He went to her, pulled her up into his arms, and held on for dear life. Burying his face in her long, silky hair, he broke into sobs—big, racking sobs that shocked him. What kind of man was he, weeping like a child? He felt Marnie's body shudder and realized she was weeping, too. Was this a watershed moment for them—a beginning, a new direction? More likely, an ending. They stood like that, crying like babies, until neither had any more tears.

Finally, he let her go. His emotions were spent. He felt weak in the knees. They sat back down at the table. He heaved a sigh. His mouth tasted dark, bitter all the way to his throat. "Okay, Marnie, you win. Go call your mom. Tell her you wanna go home. We'll do whatever you say."

"I didn't mean I was going to call her right this minute."

"You might as well just go call her and get it over with."

Wiping away her tears, she went and got her cell phone and started punching in the numbers. "Jeff, is it 3541 or 5341?"

"The number's stored in your phone."

"I can't remember how to find it."

He took the phone and found the number for her.

"Thanks." She took the phone and sat down on the sofa.

He sat down beside her, his head in his hands. *Lord, please don't let her go. I can't bear to lose her. You brought her back from the edge of death. Are You going to take her from me now?*

Marnie's voice sliced into his prayers. "Hi, Mom? It's me. . . . No, nothing's wrong. I'm doing fine. My classes are coming easier. My memory's a lot better. And I only need to read things twice instead of three or four times. . . . Yes, Jeff's doing fine, too." She looked over at him. "My mom says hi."

"Tell her I said hi."

"Mom, Jeff says hi. . . . Yeah, we're doing okay. That's what I want to talk to you about. Not about us exactly, but about me. I want to come home, Mom. . . . No, it would be for more than just a visit." Her voice filled with emotion. "I want to come home to stay—permanently. . . . Yes, I've thought a lot about it. . . . No, Jeff doesn't agree, but it's my decision, Mom."

For several minutes, Marnie was silent, listening. Jeff could tell, whatever her mother was saying, Marnie wasn't happy about it. She started twisting a strand of hair around her finger. She twisted it, let it go, then twisted it again.

"Mom, that's not fair. I tried it your way. I've been here for months. It's not going to work. It's not fair to Jeff or me to prolong the agony."

He stared at her. *Is that what it's been for you, Marnie—agony staying here with me?*

She looked at him, as if realizing what she had said. "I don't mean agony. It's just not fair—I can't be his wife—I can't change how I feel. Yes, Mom, I'm listening. I know you have my best interests at heart. Yes, Mom, I know you love me. Okay, if that's how it has to be, I'll give it a few more weeks. But then, I'm coming home, okay?" She handed the phone to Jeff. "She wants to talk to you."

Jeff took the phone. "Hello, Barbara."

A mature, melodic voice replied with a note of sympathy, "Hello, Jeff. I'm sorry Marnie's insisting on coming home."

"Me, too."

"She still has no memory of your life together?"

"We're not even a blip on the radar screen."

"Well, I bought you a little time. Marnie's not coming home yet."

Jeff propped his feet up on the coffee table. "Thanks, Barbara. But I think it's just a matter of time before she's outta here."

"Please don't give up on her, Jeff. She needs you, even if she doesn't realize it."

"It's not me who's giving up, Barbara. Your daughter just doesn't want to be married to me."

Marnie elbowed him. "Don't blame it all on me."

"Who then?" he shot back. "This definitely isn't my idea."

She stood up and put her hands on her hips. "I'm not going to sit here and listen to you bad-mouth me to my mother."

"I'm not bad-mouthing you, babe!" As Marnie stalked off to the bedroom, Jeff turned his attention back to the phone. "Barbara, you still there?"

"I'm here, Jeff. I have some advice. Can Marnie hear me?"

"No, it's just me now."

"Okay, I have an idea."

"I'm listening."

"I think you should start courting your wife all over again."

"Courting her? You mean, dating? Stuff like that?"

"Exactly. Treat her as if the two of you had just met."

Jeff shrugged. "That's kind of hard to do when we're living under the same roof."

"Then move out. You know that old saying 'Familiarity breeds contempt.' Give her some space. Be a mysterious, romantic suitor. Send her flowers. Bring her candy. Write her little love notes. Sweep her off her feet. She fell in love with you once. Make her fall in love with you all over again."

Jeff scratched his head. "Wow, I never thought of that. I was so busy trying to make her remember the past. You're saying I should start over and build brand-new memories?"

"That's what I'm saying, Jeff. I don't know if it'll work, but it's worth a try."

Jeff was already warming to the idea. Why hadn't he thought of it himself? He swung his feet off the coffee table and stood up. "Barbara, you're an angel! I gotta go make some phone calls and put this plan into action!"

He spent the next ten minutes on the phone. Then, he went to the bedroom and knocked on the door. Marnie appeared, looking red eyed. "Are you through ragging on me to my mother?" she asked in a small, wounded voice.

"I wasn't ragging on you." He went to the closet and pulled down a large suitcase.

She stepped back, her arms folded on her chest. "What are you doing?"

He opened the suitcase on the bed. "Packing."

"Are we going somewhere?"

He emptied a dresser drawer into the case. "Not us. Me."

"Where are you going?"

He dumped another drawer into the bag. "I'm moving in with Nate."

"Nate?" She started straightening the pile of socks, underwear, and shirts. "You're going to live in campus housing with Nate?"

"Why not? He and his roomie have a spare bed."

"I never said you had to leave. I said *I* wanted to go."

"I know. But your mom says you can't go home yet. So I'm leaving."

"Are you mad at me?" she asked warily. "I didn't mean our life is agony. It just came out like that. You know I still have trouble saying the right word."

Facing her, he placed his hands squarely on her shoulders and looked deep into her eyes. What he saw broke his heart. His beautiful Marnie looked so sad, so fragile, so utterly appealing. He desperately wanted to take her in his arms and kiss her until all their problems faded away. But he quelled the impulse. It would only make matters worse.

"It has to be this way, Marnie," he said, returning to his packing. "Like you said, we can't live in limbo. What we had in the past is gone. It's time we both got on with our lives."

She looked flustered, dismayed. "But earlier you said—"

"It doesn't matter what I said. I've come to my senses. For the first time in a long time, I see how things really are." He took a duffel bag from the closet and stuffed in his shoes and jeans. "I'll be around if you need me. I'll still take you to therapy and stuff like that. You can reach me at Nate's place."

"Write down the number for me."

"I will." He carried his luggage out to the front door. "I'll be back tomorrow to pick up the rest of my things." He scrawled several numbers on a sheet of paper and put it on the refrigerator. "If you need anything, here's my cell phone and Nate's and Jenny's."

"Okay. Thanks." She was still hugging her arms, looking bewildered.

He gave her a quick embrace and kissed her cheek. This was tearing him up inside, but it had to be done. "Bye, Marnie. Take care of yourself, okay?"

As he walked out the door, he memorized his last glimpse of her—a wide-eyed, sad-faced girl standing alone in the doorway, a lost soul trying to find her way home. Someday—if he had anything to say about it—she would be the love of his life again.

Chapter 9

Marnie awoke and sat up in bed, listening. She hugged her arms and inhaled slowly then exhaled. There was no sound except for the clock ticking and birds twittering outside the window. The rooms of her apartment were eerily silent, as if the silence itself possessed a sound, a reality. It was the sound of aloneness.

When Jeff was here, there was always noise—the shower running, a door banging, dishes rattling, the news channel blaring on television. And there were good smells, too—coffee perking, bacon frying, his aftershave wafting from the bathroom.

Marnie climbed out of bed, pulled on her terry robe, padded to the kitchen, and put on the coffee. She looked around, half-expecting to see Jeff sitting at the table reading his Bible. It had been only three days since he moved out, and already, the apartment seemed empty without him. *It has to be this way*, she told herself. *It's not fair of me to expect him to stay here and be my friend when he wants so much more—more than I can give. I have to let him go. And as soon as I finish my classes, I'll go home to Michigan and put this whole painful chapter of my life behind me.*

She poured herself a bowl of cereal. If Jeff were there, they'd be fixing scrambled eggs and French toast together or pancakes shaped like little animals. Jeff made them that way all the time now, just to please her. She hated cold, soggy cereal, but it made no sense to fix a hot breakfast just for herself.

As she ate, she opened her Bible and scanned a few verses. It was what she and Jeff had done every morning after breakfast, and it seemed only natural to continue the routine. After reading the scriptures, they would hold hands across the table and pray, with Jeff doing most of the praying. She was always content to listen. She loved the sound of Jeff's voice when he was talking to God.

"Lord, are You there?" she said aloud. Her words sounded stark and jarring in the empty room. "Jeff's gone. Father, are You gone, too?"

The silence taunted her.

She read several verses in Matthew 10 about God watching over the fallen sparrows. *That means He's watching over those little birds singing outside my window.* They sounded happy, unconcerned about the future. She wished she could be so trusting. She was like a fallen sparrow—wounded, broken, afraid to fly again. If only she could remember what it felt like to sense God's presence, to converse with Him like an old friend. She knew He was real. He had watched over her and brought her back from the brink of death. But He still seemed like a distant acquaintance—someone she wanted to know better but had no idea how to begin.

As she read, her gaze lingered on the words, *"And even the very hairs of your head are all numbered."* What a curious fact. What did it mean? Why would Jesus make such an unusual statement?

Does God really keep track of how many hairs I have on my head? What difference does it make? No one cares about something like that—unless they're losing their hair! But God cares. He counts every hair. A startling realization came to her. *If God keeps track of something that trivial, then He must care about even the tiniest detail of my life—things I would never expect the God of the universe to be interested in. Amazing! He loves me that much!*

She read further. "So don't be afraid; you are worth more than many sparrows." She smiled. The room no longer felt quite so empty. Sunlight poured in the windows where, on the sills, chirping birds sang of God's caring compassion. "You are here, aren't You, heavenly Father?" she whispered. "Help me to feel Your closeness again."

She continued reading for another twenty minutes, until a knock on the door caught her attention. She jumped up from the table, her heart pounding. Who could it be? She wasn't expecting anyone. Or was she? She went to the refrigerator and quickly scanned her latest list. "Nine o'clock Jenny coming to visit."

Another knock sounded. Marnie scurried across the room and threw open the door. Her best friend stood there smiling back at her. Marnie grabbed her hand and pulled her inside. "Oh Jenny, I'm sorry. Come in. I forgot you were coming. I'm not even dressed yet."

"No problem." Jenny crossed the room and sat down on the sofa. "We're just going to have an old-fashioned gabfest. If I'd brought my robe, it would be like one of our famous sleepovers."

Marnie sat down in Jeff's favorite beanbag chair. "I don't remember our slumber parties."

"One of these days when we have lots of time, I'll fill you in on all the details. We had some really crazy, fun times when we lived on campus."

"That's where Jeff is now. He's staying with his friend Nate."

"Yes, I heard. I remember Nate. Great guy. Always wearing the wild aloha shirts."

"That's him."

"So how does Jeff like living back on campus again?"

Marnie shrugged. "I don't know. I haven't heard from him."

Jenny raised one eyebrow. "Really? I figured he'd be here every day taking you to classes or therapy."

"I'm walking to my classes now. It's a good workout for me."

"Right. The campus is just up the hill on the other side of Kuakini Highway.

But what about your therapy sessions? I'd be glad to take you if you need me."

"No, Jeff set it up with the people at church. They're taking turns driving me to the hospital. He gave them my schedule. I never know who's coming until they show up."

Jenny eyed her curiously. "So how do you feel about Jeff cutting himself out of your life like this?"

Marnie thought a moment. "I feel—strange. Every day, I wake up and think he should be here. The apartment feels so empty without him. But I can't blame him. He doesn't want to be my friend. He wants to be my husband. But I can't think of being anyone's wife right now. I've got to get my own life back again."

"Does that mean that someday you may want to be his wife again?"

Marnie gazed off into the distance, absently twisting a strand of her hair. "When I was a little girl, I dreamed I'd be madly in love with the man I married. We'd be the perfect couple and live happily ever after."

"You were madly in love with Jeff," said Jenny. "Take my word for it. I was there at your wedding."

"But the person who married Jeff isn't me. Not the me I am now. I can't relate to her. I can't bring her back. I can't make myself feel what she felt."

"Are you saying there's no hope for you and Jeff?"

"I don't know what I'm saying," Marnie admitted. "I'm still trying to figure out who I am and where I fit in these days." She sat forward, her hands pushing against the beanbag. "I forgot to ask. Can I get you something to drink? A soda or something?"

"No thanks. I've got my bottled water in my bag." They were both silent for a moment. Finally, Jenny said, "I don't think any of us realize what you've been through, Marnie—how hard your recovery has been for you. We can't begin to understand it, because we haven't experienced it ourselves."

Tears welled in Marnie's eyes. At last, someone understood.

"Don't cry," said Jenny. "I just want you to know you're not alone."

"But that's how I've felt—how I still feel." Marnie swiped at a tear. "No one knows how hard it's been. I feel like, after the accident, I was a newborn. I had to learn everything all over again—how to walk and talk and think clearly. I had to learn how to do things everybody else takes for granted—how to open a can of soup or write a letter or use a computer. Only I didn't have years to learn, like a baby does. I had to learn it all in weeks and months. I'm still learning. Sometimes, I feel like such an idiot. I keep forgetting the simplest things—words, names, places, appointments, faces. . . . And I don't think I'll ever figure out how to balance my checkbook or drive a car again or use the remote control."

Jenny smiled. "I'm still trying to figure out the remote myself."

"And I still don't remember anything that happened since I came to Hawaii. Sometimes I still feel like that twelve-year-old girl back in Michigan. That's why I want to go home. I remember my parents and my life there. I want so desperately to be in a place where I remember my past."

Jenny nodded. "I can understand that. But what about the future?"

Marnie shifted. Her head was starting to ache, and the beanbag no longer felt comfortable. "What do you mean?"

"I mean, what will you do in Michigan? Will you work or finish your education or what?"

"I haven't thought that far ahead."

"You left Michigan three years ago because you wanted to become a missionary. You felt God had called you here to U of N."

Marnie chewed on her lower lip. Why did everybody keep talking about her becoming a missionary? "That girl died in the accident, Jenny. She's gone."

"I don't think so." Jenny fixed her gaze on Marnie. "I'm still looking at her."

"You see the outside, not the inside."

"I think the old Marnie is still inside; just give her a chance to find her way back to the surface."

Marnie pushed herself out of the beanbag and went over and sat down on the wicker sofa beside Jenny. "But what if you're wrong?" she asked, searching Jenny's eyes for answers. "What if this is all I'll ever be—a person without a past, a person too broken to have a real future?" A sob tore at her throat. "Jeff is always telling me what a passion I had for sharing my faith with others. He says I wanted to devote my entire life to reaching people for Christ. But I feel such a disconnect with that person. Sometimes I even hate her—the old Marnie—because I know I'll never be like her."

Jenny reached over and patted Marnie's shoulder. "You're being too hard on yourself. Don't worry about the person you were; just concentrate on the person you are becoming. All the good things about you are still there."

Marnie smiled grimly. "Jeff would say I think too much about myself. And maybe he's right."

"Why would you say that?"

"Because, since the accident, I've been totally consumed with myself. I can't think of anything or anyone else. My recovery has taken every ounce of strength and concentration I have. And—I don't know—maybe it's made me a selfish person."

"Not selfish. Self-focused maybe. I think it's more a matter of self-preservation."

"Whatever you call it, somehow I need to find out who I am and what I can do with my life. I don't know where to start, Jenny, except to go back to the home and family I remember."

Jenny paused then asked solemnly, "Have you asked God what He wants you to do?"

Marnie lowered her gaze. "I pray sometimes, but I don't feel very close to God. Most of the time, He's like a stranger to me—someone I know about but don't know personally."

"Then it's time to get reacquainted. Do you mind if I pray for you?"

"Right here? Right now?"

"Why not?"

Marnie didn't want to admit how self-conscious she felt as Jenny clasped her hand and began entreating God to restore the life Marnie had had before the accident. "Make it an even better, more glorious life, Lord," Jenny said with an urgency that made Marnie catch her breath a little. "If the old Marnie would have won a thousand souls to Jesus, let the new Marnie win ten thousand. Restore Marnie's passion for lost souls and give her back her love for Jeff, tenfold. Give them a marriage that honors You and a love that reflects Christ's love for us."

Just as Jenny said, "Amen," the doorbell rang. Marnie jumped up and headed for the door. "I hope I didn't forget another appointment."

A deliveryman greeted her with a long box tied with a large white bow. "Mrs. Marnie Jordan?"

"Yes," she said, stifling the impulse to say no.

He handed her the box then thrust a clipboard at her. "Sign here, please."

Without thinking, she signed *Marnie Rockwell*.

"Have a good day, Mrs. Jordan." Tucking the clipboard under his arm, the man pivoted and strode back to his vehicle.

Marnie carried the box inside and set it on the kitchen counter. "I don't know what this is. I don't think I ordered anything."

Jenny joined her at the counter. "It looks like a gift. Open it up."

Marnie removed the lid and gazed down at a dozen red roses nestled in white tissue paper. "Wow! These are the most beautiful roses I've ever seen." Realizing what she had said, she chuckled and added, "At least, as far as I can remember."

"Well, they're certainly the most gorgeous roses I've ever seen," said Jenny. "Is there a card?"

Marnie picked up a small white envelope and opened it. "It says, 'From someone who cares more than you will ever know.' "

"They must be from Jeff," said Jenny.

"Why would he send me flowers?"

"Because he loves you."

"No, I think he's had enough of me. Why else would he move out?"

"I don't know, but who else would send you flowers?"

"I got lots of flowers when I was in the hospital."

"Not like these. These roses speak of love, not sympathy or get-well wishes." Jenny looked around. "Do you have a vase?"

"I don't remember."

"Let's look and see." Opening one cupboard door after another, Jenny finally found a clear glass vase on a top shelf. "Here we go. I'll fill it with water. You put the roses in."

They both worked at arranging the roses just so. "Have you smelled them?" asked Jenny.

Marnie put her face close to the bouquet, closed her eyes, and breathed in deeply. The most heavenly fragrance filled her nostrils. She sighed with pleasure. "I love them. They're like a promise of new life." She carried the vase over to her glass dinette table and set it beside her Bible. "This will be the first thing I see when I come to the kitchen in the morning."

"Those roses are sure to brighten your day," said Jenny. "Wish I had someone who cared about me like that."

"It's not Jeff," said Marnie.

"Are you sure?"

"He's too practical to spend money on flowers. He'd say we should pay a bill or give the money to missions."

Jenny smiled knowingly. "I thought you didn't know Jeff very well."

"I don't. I'm just guessing."

"Well, he might surprise you. He's that kind of guy."

"It doesn't matter who sent the roses. I'm just going to enjoy them."

Marnie's cell phone rang. It sounded muffled, far away. She looked around. "I can never remember where I put that phone."

Jenny traced the sound to a kitchen drawer. "Here it is, by the silverware." She handed the phone to Marnie.

"Hello?"

There was silence then a familiar voice. "Marnie? This is Jeff."

"Hi, Jeff." It seemed longer than three days since she'd heard his voice.

"Did you get my surprise?"

"You mean the roses?"

"Yeah. So you got them?"

"Yes. They're beautiful!"

"I'm glad you like them."

"It's not my birthday. . .is it?"

"No. I just wanted you to know I was thinking about you."

"Why?"

"Just because. Are you busy?"

"Jenny's here. We're talking."

"Good. Are you busy for dinner?"

"No, I'll probably make macaroni and cheese."

"I'd like to take you out, if you're free."

"Out? Where?"

"I don't know. You pick the place. Wherever you want to eat."

"Okay. I'll stay right here and eat macaroni and cheese."

"That's not what I meant, Marnie. Listen, if you're not free for dinner, how about a drive to Hilo tomorrow? We could go see the World Botanical Gardens.

You've wanted to see that place again for a long time."

"I have? Okay, I don't have classes or therapy tomorrow. At least, I don't think I do."

"No, you don't, Marnie. I know your schedule. You're free tomorrow."

"Okay. Then I guess I can go."

"Great. I'll pick you up at ten o'clock sharp. Write it on your list, okay?"

"Okay. Bye, Jeff." She hung up the phone, took her list from the refrigerator door, and wrote down *Jeff tomorrow 10:00 a.m.*

Jenny came over and slipped her arm around Marnie's shoulder. "So, my friend, you have a date with Jeff tomorrow?"

"Not a date. He's driving me somewhere. Hilo, he said."

"Sounds like a date," said Jenny with a lilt in her voice. "First, he sends roses; then, he calls and invites you out for a special day together. That definitely sounds like a man in love to me!"

Chapter 10

Jeff pulled up beside the apartment at 10:00 a.m. sharp, just as he had promised Marnie. As he climbed out of his car and strode to the door, he felt as skittish as a cat on a high-tension wire. What was wrong with him? This was worse than a first date. Come to think of it, he couldn't remember feeling this nervous on any first date. He was usually Mr. Laid-back—calm, cool, and collected.

But not this morning.

Everything was on the line—the life he had shared with Marnie, their love for each other, their marriage, their future. What if he couldn't win her back? What if this whole dating thing turned out to be a fiasco?

He straightened his shoulders and rang the doorbell. Even in his favorite plaid madras shirt and cargo pants, he still felt like a bumbling kid in mismatched shoes. *Lord, I could use a little help here. Please don't let me mess things up with Marnie. You know how to get through to her. Show me, too. Help me to win back her love.*

He was so lost in thought that he jumped when Marnie opened the door.

"Hi, Jeff," she said with a little half smile. "Come on in."

"Thanks." He went inside and glanced around. The place looked the same, but it felt like he'd been gone nearly forever. "So how are you doing, Marnie?"

"Fine." She tucked her clutch purse under her arm. "I remembered you were coming over. I didn't even have to look at my list."

"That's good." He couldn't help noticing how fantastic she looked in her tank top and skinny jeans, with the little canvas wedges that made her legs look amazing. She must have finally mastered her curling iron, too, because her long, auburn brown hair looked perfect. He debated whether or not to compliment her. Would she think he was being too forward? He decided to chance it. "You look absolutely gorgeous."

Was she blushing?

"So do you," she said in a small, polite voice. "Handsome, I mean."

"Thanks. I guess we're ready to go?"

"Guess so."

He walked her out to the car and opened the door for her. It seemed strange that they were being so formal with each other, but that was the ritual of courtship. He was going to have to learn those rules all over again. Man, how he missed the easy, comfortable camaraderie of marriage.

As he pulled out onto Kuakini Highway, Marnie asked, "Have you named your car yet?"

Jeff gave her a sidelong glance to make sure she was serious. She was. "Um, no, I haven't picked out a name. Any ideas?"

"I'll think about it. What was the name of your other car?"

"Old Reliable."

"That's right. You told me that."

"I didn't expect you to remember it."

"Old Reliable was wrecked in the crash, wasn't he?"

"Yep. Totaled."

"We were on our way to Hilo."

"Do you remember that?"

"No. I just know."

"People have talked about it often enough, marveling that we survived."

"Are we going to Hilo now—to the same place we were going then?"

"That's what I was planning—the Botanical Gardens and Rainbow Falls. It's where we first kissed. I guess it was a stupid idea."

"Not stupid. But can we go somewhere else?"

"You wanna visit some places here in Kona?"

She nodded.

"Whatever you want, Marnie. You say the word."

"Which word?"

"No, that's just an expression. Tell me where you wanna go."

She shrugged. "I can't remember how to get anywhere."

"That's okay. I remember."

"How about Sam?"

"Sam? You wanna go to. . .Sam?"

"No, silly. I'm talking about a name for your car. How about Sam?"

"Sam's okay by me. You like Sam?"

"I love Sam. It's short and easy to say. Samsamsamsam."

Jeff patted the dashboard. "So where are you taking us, Sam, ol' man?"

With a spontaneous little chuckle, Marnie patted the dashboard, too. "Take us on an adventure, Sam, ol' man."

"What would you like to see, Marnie?"

"I guess it doesn't matter. It'll all be new to me."

"You want the beach, shops, food, galleries, museums?"

"What would you like?" asked Marnie. "You've probably already been everywhere."

"Not really." He pulled onto Ali'i Drive, heading toward Kailua Pier. "We both came to Hawaii to attend University of the Nations. We've spent most of our time in class, on campus, in church, or in ministry. We haven't had time or money to do all the touristy things most people do."

"What did we do for fun?" asked Marnie.

Jeff resisted the urge to say, *We had fun just being together. We didn't need anything else in the world but each other.* "When we could grab a few minutes away from our studies, we'd come to the pier and walk on the beach at sunset, or sit in the sun on the seawall talking and watching whales and sea turtles and tourists in their wild aloha shirts. Or we'd grab a latte at the coffee shop, or hang out with friends, or go swimming, or wander around a bookstore."

"What did we talk about when we sat on the seawall?" she asked with a hint of wistfulness.

"Lots of things. Mainly about what we wanted to do with the rest of our lives—our hopes and dreams, the places we wanted to go, the things we wanted to see, the people we hoped to help someday. We talked about how incredible it was that God had brought us from two distant places on the mainland to this little island in the middle of the Pacific Ocean, and how amazing it was that we had found each other." His voice trailed off. He was saying too much, making Marnie feel uncomfortable. *This is supposed to be our first date. Keep things light, man. Keep things light!*

Marnie gazed down at her hands folded tightly in her lap. "I don't remember my hopes and dreams."

Jeff swallowed over a lump in his throat. Giving her a sidelong glance, he said with more bravado than he felt, "That's okay, Marnie. You can create new hopes and dreams."

She looked back at him with pleading eyes. "How?"

The sadness in her voice knocked the wind out of his sails. "I don't know, Marnie. You just can. It'll take time. You'll form new hopes and dreams, or maybe some of the old ones will come back to you."

She was quiet for a moment. Then, almost under her breath, she said, "I can't remember the past, and I'm scared to think of the future."

He looked at her, almost forgetting he was driving. "You're scared? Of what?"

"I don't know." She paused for so long that the silence between them felt heavy. Finally, she said in a soft, breathy voice, "It's like my life is a big picture puzzle. I had one like that when I was a little girl. It had a thousand pieces. I can't remember several years of my life, but I can see that puzzle in my mind. It was the picture of a beautiful garden with every kind of flower you can imagine. I worked on that puzzle for months. I wouldn't let anyone else help me."

"Did you get it together?"

"Yes. And my mom laminated it and framed it and put it on my bedroom wall. I loved that garden."

"That's a great memory, Marnie—a special part of your past."

With an unsettling urgency, she said, "But what if I never get all the pieces of my life back together? What if too many pieces are missing?"

He reached over and squeezed her hand. "You'll find all the pieces, sweetheart, and your life will be so beautiful it'll make the garden in that puzzle look like an old weed patch."

Marnie laughed and sobbed at exactly the same moment. "Oh Jeff, you watch the road, okay?"

He had the feeling she wanted to say a lot more, or was it just a vain hope that he was getting through to her? They both lapsed into silence. After a while, Marnie put her head back on the seat and started murmuring in a singsong voice, "Sam, Sam, Sam, ol' man, where are we going today?"

"How about Bubba Gump's?" he suggested. "It's right here on Ali'i Drive. It's a fun place, and they have great shrimp and burgers."

Marnie sat forward and clasped her hands. "I like that name. It sounds silly. Hey, I'm Bubba Gump," she said, faking a slow Southern drawl.

"Then that's the place for us." He pulled into a parking lot across the street from the bustling, movie-themed restaurant. "After we eat, if you like, we can head over to the Kona International Market. You used to love that place. You could spend hours looking at the handmade jewelry and woodcarvings and the local arts and crafts. Once you found these wind chimes that looked like little silver doves. You sent them to your mother for Christmas."

"Did she like them?"

"She loved them. You were always great at picking out gifts for people. You always knew just what people liked."

"Not anymore," she said quietly. "I don't even know what I like."

"I know what you like," said Jeff. "Burgers piled high with tomatoes and onions and lots of catsup. You love Bubba's burgers, take my word for it."

He got out of the car, went around, and opened her door. "And you like french fries thin as shoestrings and so hot and crispy they snap when you break them. I know, because I love them like that, too." He took her hand, helped her out of the car, and they crossed the street. "So for now, we won't think about the past or the future. We'll just concentrate on how much of Bubba's great food we can eat right now." As they entered the restaurant, he added, "And if you want to make a contest out of it, I'll show you I can eat more fries than you."

"No way."

"I will, babe. I'm the french fry king of the world. But they gotta be hot. No cold fries for me."

She stifled a giggle as the hostess showed them to a booth.

"What's so funny?" he asked as they sat down.

"Nothing. Everything. You make me laugh."

He grinned. "That's a start, at least."

She studied him from across the table, her expression hard to read. She looked so much like the old Marnie. This could be a routine lunch date with his wife if so much weren't at stake. He leaned forward, his gaze fixed on her. "What are you looking at, babe?"

"I was imagining a crown of french fries on your head."

"You making fun of me?" He reached across the table for her hand. "You don't believe I'm the french fry king?"

"Not for long."

"Okay, that's it. You're on, babe. Prepare to do battle."

As soon as the waitress brought their order, they tackled the brimming basket of fries, but not before Jeff doused them with plenty of catsup. "The main thing is to eat them while they're hot. That takes total concentration. As soon as they're cold, it's all over."

They devoured the fries between bursts of laughter as the catsup smeared over their faces and fingers. Marnie looked totally vulnerable and appealing with catsup on her face. Jeff fed her the last fry, then he leaned over and wiped her chin with his napkin. "A little too much catsup," he murmured, "but I gladly give up my crown to the new french fry queen."

She smiled. "Is that me? I'm the queen?"

"You're the queen, babe. For real."

She touched her head. "Where's my crown?"

"I'll make you one—the next time we have fries."

"That's too late. I want one now."

"Okay." He grabbed a napkin from the dispenser, made a makeshift crown, and placed it on her head. "There. I declare you Queen of the Fries."

She adjusted the fragile tiara. "It's perfect. I'll wear it always."

Jeff chuckled. "You've already embellished it with some tasty red markings."

"I have?" She looked at her hands. They were streaked with catsup.

She quickly licked her fingertips then looked around self-consciously.

He followed her gaze, knowing she was wondering if anyone was watching their silly antics. No one was. He felt his own tension ease as she put her head back and relaxed against the booth. The old chemistry was still there, in spite of everything.

"You're so funny, Jeff," she said, so softly he could hardly hear her. "I like it when you're funny."

"And I love you like this," he replied, struggling to keep his voice steady.

Marnie touched her paper crown again. She looked the happiest he had seen her in a long time. "Tell me what else I like, Jeff."

"What else you like? You mean, besides burgers and fries?"

She nodded. "Yes. What else? I want to know."

He thought a minute. "Okay, it's probably stuff you already know. You like old black-and-white movies. But only the ones with lots of romance, with girls in long dresses and men in tuxedos, and lots of sentimental music. And when they get mushy, you cry."

"I do not."

"Yes, you do."

"Okay, maybe I do. What else?"

"You like country music, but not the twangy, noisy stuff. You like the old ballads. Let's face it, Marnie, you're an old-fashioned romantic."

"I am? Am I really?" She smiled as if she liked the idea.

He traced a water ring on the table. "You're the most romantic girl I ever knew. And the most sentimental. You cry over a sunset, or a lost puppy, or a sad song. You have a heart as big as the ocean. That's why you'll make such a great missionary someday."

She lowered her gaze. "I don't see myself that way."

"That's because you're still discovering who you are. Take my word for it, Marnie. I know the real you. You're one of the most beautiful people I've ever known—both inside and out."

She removed her paper crown. "Maybe it's time to go home."

He reached for the bill. "Sure, if that's what you want."

The drive home was more solemn than Jeff had expected. He sensed that Marnie was mulling over a lot of things she wasn't ready to confide yet—if ever. He had almost convinced himself that everything was on its way back to normal, but he could see that wasn't the case. He and Marnie might share some light, fun moments together, but she still wasn't ready to let him back into her world.

When they reached their apartment, he walked her to the door and kissed her lightly on the cheek. He felt awkward, and he sensed she did, too. "May I see you again?" he asked, even though everything inside him shouted, *She's my wife! I shouldn't even have to ask.*

She opened the door. "Sure. Give me a call."

"I will. Good night, Marnie."

"Good night, Jeff."

He waited until she went inside, then he turned and strode back down the walk to his car. As he drove back to the campus, he noticed his hands were shaking and a painful lump had formed in his throat. It was all he could do to keep from turning around and going back to the apartment and reclaiming his life with the woman he loved.

Chapter 11

Over the next few days, Marnie didn't hear a word from Jeff. Then, just when she was wondering if she should phone to make sure he was okay, she received an orchid lei and a handmade card inviting her to join him on an adventure to the Mauna Kea volcano. She called immediately and told him she would be happy to go. Her eagerness to see him again took her by surprise.

"I'll pick you up on Saturday at two o'clock," he told her. "Wear warm clothes and some good hiking shoes."

She was wearing a long-sleeved, animal print shirt, cargo pants, and her sneakers when she greeted Jeff at the door on Saturday afternoon. He was wearing a crewneck sweatshirt, stonewashed jeans, black tennis shoes, and a hooded Windbreaker.

"Ready for an adventure?" he asked with a wink.

She grabbed her sunglasses. "I'm ready if you are."

"Got your digital camera?"

"I don't know. Do I own one?"

"You sure do. It should be on the top shelf of our, uh, your bedroom closet. While you're at it, grab a warm jacket. It'll be cold and maybe rainy on the mountain. To be on the safe side, I've got some snacks and bottled water in the car."

She smiled. "You think of everything."

"I try."

She was back shortly with her coat and camera. "I don't know how to work it."

"Don't worry. I'll show you," he said as they headed to the car.

After a brief drive, he pulled up beside a bakery in Kona's Lanihau Center.

"Hey, I thought we were going to the volcano," she said as he parked and turned off the ignition. "Or do we need more sugary snacks before we head up the mountain?"

"Surprise, babe. We're letting someone else do the driving. We're taking a sunset stargazing tour. We're meeting the van here."

She eyed him solemnly. "That must be awfully expensive."

"Only an arm and a leg. But I've been saving up for it. And I had a little extra help besides. It's something we've wanted to do since we got married."

"You don't have to do this, Jeff. I don't even recall wanting to see the volcano. I'm happy with just a walk on the beach or a burger at Bubba Gump's."

He laughed. "We're not having a replay of all those catsup-soaked fries we stuffed down our throats at Bubba's. Listen, babe, this is going to be a night you'll remember. And I don't mean that facetiously—about remembering. They say you haven't seen real beauty until you've seen the sunset from the top of Mauna Kea." His voice softened. "Of course, whoever said that hasn't seen *you*."

She looked away. "Don't, Jeff. I don't know what to say when you talk like that."

"That's okay. Forget I said it. Let's go. Looks like our ride is here."

They boarded what Jeff described as a four-wheel drive, turbo-diesel coach that seated thirteen people. Whatever it was, Marnie was glad to get a seat near the front where the huge windows provided a panoramic view.

"*E komo mai*," said the guide, a stout, weathered man with twinkling black eyes. "Welcome to the experience of a lifetime. *Mauna Kea Kuahiwi ku ha'o iku malie*—Mauna Kea is the astonishing mountain that stands in the calm. It rises 13,796 feet above the sea. But if you measure it from its base on the ocean floor, it reaches 32,000 feet. That makes it the tallest mountain in the world. Does anyone know what *Mauna Kea* means?"

Someone shouted, "White mountain."

"That is correct," said the guide, his eyes crinkling merrily. "Tonight, from its pinnacle, you will see the most dramatic sunset on earth. After dark, you will view the skies through powerful telescopes. Over the next few hours, I will share with you many fascinating facts about Hawaii, its history, and its culture, so please sit back, relax, and enjoy the drive to majestic Mauna Kea."

Marnie did as the guide suggested. She put her head back and breathed deeply. She had told Jeff she didn't care about visiting the volcano, but already, she could feel an excitement building inside her. Obviously, the new Marnie wanted this as much as the old Marnie. Maybe Jeff really did know her better than she knew herself.

No, that's not possible! He doesn't know me that well. I can't even let myself think such a thing. She promptly turned her attention back to the guide.

"How many of you know how Hawaii was formed?" asked the solid, leather-faced man, as the van traveled along Highway 190 north toward Waimea. He answered his own question. "These islands are the tops of gigantic mountains rising from the ocean floor. Heat from deep inside the earth created magma—molten rock—that rose up through the earth's crust and. . ."

Jeff reached over and squeezed her hand. "Having fun?"

She nodded. But she didn't want to give Jeff the idea that having fun in any way changed their relationship. She couldn't let her defenses down. He was just her friend now. Nothing more. No matter what a piece of paper said, surely her marriage could be annulled, and she would soon be free to go home to her parents. That was the plan that kept her secure, on track. No matter how her emotions wavered, she had to remain focused on her plan.

The guide was still speaking in his pleasant, thickly accented voice. "Mauna

Kea is an inactive volcano, while neighboring Mauna Loa is active. The ancient Hawaiians believed the top of Mauna Kea was heaven itself. Legend has it that Poli'ahu, the icy snow goddess of Mauna Kea, often clashes with her rival Pele, the fire goddess of Mauna Loa, who spews her anger in fiery lava eruptions."

Marnie gazed out the window, her mind drifting, random prayers forming. She was just getting used to praying again. Talking to Jesus comforted her like nothing else did. She was still just beginning to get reacquainted with Him, just as she was slowly getting to know herself again. She still had a long way to go on both counts.

Lord, what's wrong with me? she prayed silently. *My emotions are all over the place these days. Like right now, I'm enjoying sitting here with Jeff. I'm actually looking forward to our day together. I even missed him those few days when he didn't call. I like him, Lord. And yet I can't be what he wants me to be. I can't be his wife. Right now, I don't want to be anyone's wife. Dear Lord, my life is in such limbo. Jeff is part of the past—a past I can't even recall. Please don't ask me to pretend to be something I'm not. Please let him let me go. How can I face the future if I'm still tied to the past?*

"You looking at the scenery, Marnie?"

Startled, she glanced over at Jeff and said, "Yes, I guess so." She felt guilty thinking of leaving him when he was gazing at her with such affection and trust.

"We're on Highway 200—Saddle Road—now," he said, leaning against her shoulder to look out the window. "This narrow, winding road cuts across the island between Mauna Loa and Mauna Kea. Better hold on to your hat."

"I don't have a hat."

"I mean, it's going to be a bumpy ride. Keep watching. We'll be going through Parker Ranch, one of the largest cattle ranches in the United States."

Pushing aside her troubled thoughts, Marnie focused on the passing scenery—rolling green hills dotted with farms and ranch houses. "It's beautiful—and so peaceful," she murmured. "Almost like a painting that goes on and on."

"It is beautiful, but I'm sure the view from Mauna Kea will beat this by a mile."

"Will we see some actual lava flow?" she asked.

"No. Like the guide said, Mauna Kea is inactive. I thought of taking you to the national park near here to see Kilauea. It's the world's most active volcano. But the park's closed for a few days. The sulfur dioxide levels are too high. We'll go there one of these days though, okay?"

She nodded. It would have to be soon. She would be on her way to Michigan in a few weeks.

The guide was still talking. "Over fifteen hundred years ago, the Polynesians came to Hawaii from Tahiti. They gave Hawaii her name. The Hawaiian Islands were unknown to the rest of the world until January 18, 1778, when English explorer Captain James Cook first laid eyes on Oahu and Kauai. He named them the Sandwich Islands after the Earl of Sandwich."

With a little chuckle, Marnie whispered to Jeff, "What kind of sandwich was it—ham? Peanut butter and jelly?"

"My guess is bologna."

They both covered their mouths to stifle their laughter. The guide didn't seem to notice. He was saying, "In 1810, King Kamehameha the Great united the Hawaiian islands into one kingdom. . . ."

Marnie looked back out the window. She still wasn't able to track what people were saying when they were long-winded. By the time she had made sense of the last thing they said, she had forgotten the first thing. She watched as the van passed a military base then entered a lava field. All the greenery gave way to charcoal gray mounds that seemed to go on forever. Finally, they turned onto the Mauna Kea Access Road—a winding, bumpy road up the mountain, where land formations looked like pyramids. As they ascended the mountain, Marnie noticed that the cloud layer was below them.

"Look, Jeff! We're above the clouds. They look like ocean waves, only they're white."

Jeff moved closer to her and gazed out the window. "Awesome! I haven't seen anything like that since we flew in from our trip to Nigeria last summer."

"Did the clouds look like that then, too?"

"They sure did." His face was so close to hers she could feel his warm breath on her cheek. "You were as excited as a little kid. You kept saying it was like we were in heaven. We imagined ourselves running and jumping on the clouds and doing somersaults."

"I wish I could remember."

"So do I," he said wistfully.

"Ladies and gentlemen," said the guide, "we are approaching the Onizuka Visitor Information Station. We are 9,300 feet above sea level. We will stay here for an hour while you become acclimated to the high altitude. You will be served a hot meal and issued arctic parkas with hoods and thick ski gloves. Then we will proceed up to the summit in time to view the sunset."

A little cheer went up from the passengers around them. Marnie sat forward and clasped her hands. "This is so neat, Jeff. I can't wait to see the sunset."

He squeezed her shoulder. "I'm glad you're having a good time, babe."

As they exited the van, a cold, dry wind hit them full in the face. People bundled in heavy coats and hats milled around with their telescopes, looking for the best place to stargaze.

"Good thing we brought our jackets," said Marnie with a shiver.

Jeff slipped his arm around her as they entered the visitor center. "If the jacket's not enough, I've got my love to keep you warm."

She rolled her eyes and wrinkled her nose.

"Okay, it's a silly old song my grandmother used to sing when I was a kid. It just popped out. I can't believe I even said it."

She patted his arm. "It's okay. I like silly old songs."

"Good. Then maybe I'll sing it to you someday."

She raised her brows. "Do you sing?"

"Yeah, sometimes. I took voice in high school and even sang with a praise band for a while. Haven't you noticed my old guitar in the closet?"

"Yes, but I didn't think anything of it."

"I'll play it for you sometime."

She smiled. "You surprise me, Jeffrey Jordan."

"Just hang out with me long enough, and you'll learn all kinds of things."

They spent a few minutes browsing the visitor center's interactive displays, information panels, and exhibits. In the small bookstore, they thumbed through astronomy texts and slick paperbacks on Hawaiian culture; they bought nutrition bars and cans of soda at the snack counter, passed over the expensive souvenirs, and helped themselves to free brochures on the volcanoes.

When their guide announced that supper was being served, they sat down with their fellow passengers to tasty meals of glazed beef ribs, teriyaki chicken, jasmine rice, and cucumber salad, with fudge brownies for dessert.

"Wow, I was hungry," said Marnie as she finished her last bite of brownie.

"The cold air does that to you," said Jeff. "Come on. Looks like the van is ready to head up the mountain."

Their guide handed them parkas and gloves as they boarded the coach. Jeff helped her with hers and tied the hood under her chin.

"I feel like an Eskimo," she said as she pulled on the heavy gloves.

Jeff nudged her chin. "Cutest Eskimo I ever saw."

They took their original seats. "I'm so padded I can hardly sit down," said Marnie as she lowered herself onto the leather cushion.

"When we're standing on the top of Mauna Kea, you'll be glad you're wearing lots of layers."

Everyone was surprisingly quiet as the van chugged up the steep gravel road. The ride was bumpy, with jarring twists and turns. "See why we're taking the tour van?" Jeff whispered to Marnie. "Ol' Sam could never make this drive."

"I'm not sure *we* can. This road is scary."

"It'll be worth it. You wait and see."

A half hour later, just before they reached the top, the rough gravel road gave way to a smooth paved road. They had climbed four thousand feet.

"The air is thin up here," said the guide, "so we won't be staying long. With 40 percent less oxygen here at the top than at sea level, you may experience a headache or some nausea. You may feel light-headed, giddy, drowsy, or breathless." He flashed a wry smile. "You may even find yourself using poor judgment. Don't be alarmed. It's not unusual to experience some of those symptoms. Drink plenty of water. We also provide some hot drinks and shortbread cookies. Stay with your group. And enjoy the beautiful sunset."

Someone asked, "Will we be able to enter the observatories up here?"

"No," said the guide. "Here on the mountaintop, you will see the observatories open their domes and swing their telescopes into position. Mauna Kea has eleven telescopes representing thirteen countries watching the heavens. Mauna Kea is an astronomer's dream—some of the clearest skies in the world. Scientists are able to see the faintest galaxies in the observable universe. But modern telescopes are not made for viewing by the human eye. The astronomers, who, by the way, live in a lodge next to the visitor center, make digital images."

"Then, how will we see the stars?" asked Jeff.

"We have our own portable, computerized telescopes. And you'll find additional telescopes on the visitor center lanai. Your eyes work better at a lower altitude. Don't worry. You'll see star clusters, nebulae, planets, galaxies, and supernovas." With a little flourish, he opened the van door. "Ladies and gentlemen, as the sun goes down, the show begins!"

Jeff took Marnie's hand. "I guess it's time to see that sunset."

Marnie drew in a deep breath. Already, she could feel the effects of the high altitude. He held her hand as she stepped out of the van. Wide-eyed, she gazed around at an eerie moonscape—a dark, rolling wasteland dotted with huge, luminous globes like objects from another planet. The observatories could have been glistening white mushrooms sprouting from black mounds of lava rock. It was an ebony desert studded with black rhinestones. The blue sky was rimmed at the horizon by a rosy white ribbon of light. Beyond the barren rocks was a layer of cotton candy clouds that allowed only fleeting glimpses of the ocean below.

Hand in hand, they walked along the rocky terrain. A silence surrounded them, almost of awe. Fellow tourists spoke in respectful whispers.

Ascending a hill, Marnie stretched out her arms and raised her face to the heavens. "We're on top of the world, Jeff."

He pulled her against him. "I'm always on top of the world with you."

They stood watching the clouds take on whimsical shapes as a changing rainbow of vibrant colors splashed across the blue sky—magenta reds mingling with burnished copper, vivid orange, and slashes of brilliant purple. The view took Marnie's breath away. As the molten white sun hugged the horizon, dazzling beams spiked in every direction.

"When Jesus returns, it will be in a sky just like this," whispered Jeff.

"Even so, come, Lord Jesus," she murmured. It was a verse from scripture, but she couldn't remember how she knew it.

She laid her head against his shoulder. Whether it was the altitude or the amazing view, she felt breathless and light-headed, even a little giddy. She couldn't remember ever feeling happier than she was at this moment. She raised her face to Jeff's. "I feel like laughing."

"Then laugh."

"I'll make too much noise."

"Who cares?"

"Then you've got to laugh with me."

He managed a chuckle.

"You can do better than that."

"So can you."

She laughed nervously. He joined her. The laughter warmed her cold cheeks and brought tears to her eyes. Between laughs she said, "We've got to stop. People are looking at us."

"Let them look."

The more she tried to stop, the harder she laughed. "I can't stop, Jeff."

"I'll help you." He turned her face up to his, his eyes reflecting the colors of the sunset, and brought his lips down firmly on hers.

Her first instinct was to pull away, but something in the kiss struck a response deep inside her. To her astonishment, she found herself returning the kiss, as if it were the most natural thing in the world.

Later, as they shared a telescope at the visitor center and gazed through the black night at a sequined blanket of stars, her thoughts kept going back to that kiss. While Jeff pointed out the rings of Saturn, Orion's Belt, and the Milky Way, she pondered her conflicting emotions. Was it possible she cared more for Jeff than she was willing to admit? Or was it the seductive enchantment of the mountaintop and the lightness of the atmosphere that stole her breath away and left her head reeling?

Chapter 12

Jeff was whistling a happy tune these days. Marnie's mother had given him the best advice in the world: *Date Marnie as if you had just met. Help her fall in love with you all over again.*

It seemed to be working. In the weeks since their amazing date at Mauna Kea, he had finally persuaded her to go with him to the World Botanical Gardens near Hilo, where they once strolled through the rainforest and first kissed beside Rainbow Falls. Although she had no recollection of that earlier date, she let him kiss her again beside the falls. They shared more kisses during evening strolls along the moonlit beach at Kailua Bay, during intimate conversations on the seawall, and following a Polynesian feast at a luau on the historic estate of King Kamehameha.

He even found the courage to write her a sappy little love song and serenade her with his guitar on the beach. They walked on the boardwalk and shared their MP3 player, listening to Nat King Cole, Frank Sinatra, and countless syrupy, sentimental tunes. They had dessert at the Four Seasons Hotel—chocolate soufflés and fruit sorbet served in the rind of the fruit. When he held her hand in church, she no longer pulled away. More and more, she seemed like the old Marnie he knew and loved. Surely, it was only a matter of time before she invited him back into their home and into their bed.

Tonight might be the night. He was taking her on a sunset dinner cruise on a sixty-foot catamaran along the Kohala Coast. It wouldn't be an inexpensive date, especially for a ministry student, but fortunately, his parents and Marnie's had chipped in some cash to help out. At first, he had refused their offers, but when they had assured him they had a stake in the outcome, he had reluctantly accepted their generosity. He had to agree it would take more than burgers at Bubba Gump's to create an aura of romance that would win Marnie's heart.

He was still whistling that afternoon as he left campus and drove to their apartment. He felt hopeful and confident in his favorite blue oxford shirt and dress slacks. The guys in the dorm had teased him about getting all spiffed up and smelling like a perfume factory. He didn't care. He was willing to do whatever it took to become the man of Marnie's dreams again. He had even come prepared with a single long-stemmed red rose and Marnie's favorite chocolates with the caramel centers.

When she greeted him at the door, he had to stop and catch his breath. She looked stunning in a simple black empire dress and platform sandals. Her auburn hair was crimped in little curls around her face, and her big brown eyes made him melt inside. It was all he could do to keep from gathering her into his arms and kissing her.

He forgot about the flower and candy until she held out her hands and asked, "Are those for me?"

"Who else?" He realized instantly that was a dumb thing to say and kicked himself for dropping the ball in the romance department. He should have made some gallant gesture or said something clever like, *Sweets for the sweet* or *A rose by any other name*—or whatever that saying was. No, he was probably better off keeping it short and simple. He was no Romeo or Don Juan. The old Marnie had accepted that about him; he wasn't so sure about the new Marnie.

"Are these the chocolates with the caramel centers?" she asked as they went inside.

"Absolutely. Would you eat any other kind?"

She shrugged. "I don't know. Would I?"

"Not on your life."

"Then I thank you for knowing what I like even when I don't."

He picked up her black silk wrap from the sofa. "Are you ready to go?"

"I think so," she said as he slipped it around her shoulders. "I had a little headache earlier. But it's better now."

"Listen, if you're not feeling well, we don't have to go."

"Are you kidding? A sunset dinner cruise?" She tucked her small clutch bag under her arm. "You're not getting out of it that easily, mister."

He grinned. "Then, let's get going. Sam Ol' Man is waiting to take us to Anaeho 'Omalu Bay."

"Where?"

"Don't ask me to say it twice."

"Can you?"

"I can, but it won't sound the same."

"Where is it—this bay we can't pronounce?"

"North of Kona. About a half-hour drive. Maybe an hour considering Ol' Sam's seen better days. We board the catamaran at Waikoloa Beach."

"I can't wait."

"Me neither. Guess we'd better get a move on so we don't miss the boat."

"You smell good," she told him as they walked to the car.

He opened the door for her. "So do you."

She slipped inside. "It's the perfume in the fancy green bottle on the bureau. Did you buy it for me?"

"I gave it to you when we got engaged. How'd you guess?"

"I don't know. I just had a feeling."

As he shut the door and walked around to his side, he started whistling again. It was going to be an awesome night.

The cruise turned out to be everything he had anticipated, except for an unexpected hitch at the beginning. He and Marnie were overdressed. They should have worn casual beach attire. They had to remove their shoes and wade in ankle-deep water to board the sleek vessel. Marnie laughed as he sheepishly pulled off his shoes and socks and rolled up his pant legs.

But spending the evening barefoot wasn't a problem. He and Marnie were having too much fun watching the colorful Tahitian show; gazing at dolphins, manta rays, and tropical fish through glass-bottom wells; and sampling the *ono grinds*—the tasty food. They were served a scrumptious dinner—fresh fish, London broil with shiitake mushroom sauce, smoked-turkey wraps, hand-rolled sushi, and a tropical fruit platter, with cream puffs for dessert.

"If we ate like this every day, we'd both be blimps," she told him.

He licked the last bite of filling from his fingers. "But what a way to go."

Just before sunset, they found a spot by the railing at the front of the vessel. While Hawaiian music played in the background, couples strolled along the deck arm in arm. The sky was aflame with vivid reds and oranges. A gentle breeze ruffled their hair, and salt spray cooled their skin.

Jeff drew Marnie close and whispered, "If God can paint earthly skies like this, imagine what heaven must look like."

"It reminds me of the sunset at Mauna Kea. I'll never forget that night."

He nuzzled her hair. "Me neither."

She rested her head against his chest. "I believe God gives us skies like this as a silent reminder of what He's preparing for us."

"It's like a teaser," Jeff agreed. "A little sample to whet our appetite for more."

Marnie moved her fingers over the shiny mahogany railing. "People go about their business and never think about the beautiful world God paints for them every day—sunrise and sunset, oceans and mountains, flowers and trees. When I woke up from my coma, I saw everything with new eyes. I came out of such a dark place into so much color and light. Every day, I notice things I haven't seen before. I never want to take anything for granted again."

He hugged her close and pressed his chin against the top of her head. "I never want to take *you* for granted, Marnie. Every day, I thank God that He spared your life."

They were both silent as the vibrant clouds gave way to a cloudless, deep blue sky and the blazing sun shrank to a bubble of light on the horizon then disappeared. With darkness came a chill in the air. Marnie stiffened.

"You cold?" asked Jeff.

"No. My headache's back."

"Anything I can do to help?"

"No, it'll go away in time."

He held her at arm's length and searched her face. Shadows kept him from reading her eyes. "How long have you been getting headaches?"

She shrugged. "I don't know. A few days. A week maybe."

"Why didn't you tell me?"

"What could you do—except look worried like you do now?"

"Is it because of your injury? What does the doctor say?"

"He says headaches aren't unusual with a brain injury. Not to mention the hole they drilled in my skull. Just thinking of that gives me a headache. But he says I'm doing great considering all I've been through."

Jeff hugged her again. "I think so, too. More than great. Amazingly great."

"Greatgreatgreat," she repeated. "If you say it enough, it doesn't make sense anymore."

They tried it—*greatgreatgreatgreat*—and dissolved in laughter.

"Oh great! I can't even say that word anymore. Oh wait, I just did."

"Then just say I'm terrific. Or fantastic. Or marvelous. Or stupendous. Is that a word?"

"I don't know, but you're all of those. And more."

"Look," said Marnie. "We're back already."

Jeff nodded. The catamaran was approaching the pier. Their magical evening was almost over. "It's ending too soon."

"We still have the drive home."

Home. She said the word almost as if she still considered it his home, too.

She wrapped her arm in his. "I have something to show you."

His curiosity was piqued. "What? Something at home?"

"Yes."

"What is it?"

"I found two boxes in the cupboard—one marked CAMBODIA and one marked NIGERIA."

"Oh yes, I remember those."

"They're filled with letters and pictures and e-mails. And cute little souvenirs."

"They're from our mission trips. We took the pictures. The e-mails, letters, and little gifts are from the people we ministered to. We saved everything they sent. We couldn't wait to go back again someday."

"Is that where you want to go—to Cambodia or Nigeria?"

"Maybe. Wherever the Lord leads. Wherever there are hurting people who need to hear about Jesus' love for them."

Marnie lowered her head. "I've been reading the letters and e-mails. I can't read fast yet, so it will take me a long time. But when I read them, I don't want to stop. I want so much to remember those people and the times we spent with them. I search their letters for details to make the experiences come alive for me. I feel so hungry to know more. It's like all those people hold a key to unlock a secret part of me. They're buried somewhere in my heart, and I need to find them again."

Jeff caught his breath. *This is the old Marnie talking—the woman with such amazing love and passion for ministry. She's back! Thank You, Father. Thank You!*

"Listen, sweetheart, I can help you. I can sit down and read the letters with you and tell you everything I remember about those days. That way, you can make my memories your memories."

She looked up at him. "Do you think it'll work?"

"We can give it a try."

"Okay. When we get home, I'll show you the boxes. We might have time to read a few letters tonight."

"Sounds good to me. As long as you feel like it."

"I do. My headache is better."

"Good. And if it comes back, I'll rub your temples. That's what I used to do when you had a headache or were stressed out."

"I don't remember."

"I know. It doesn't matter."

"You can still rub my temples."

"Great."

She stifled a giggle. "Not that word again!"

He held up his hand. "I promise not to say it again tonight. We'll just talk about our marvelous, fabulous, magnificent days on the mission field."

Jeff was true to his word. He didn't say *that* word, but he kept the drive home filled with conversation about their days in Cambodia and Nigeria. He told her everything that came to mind. He knew the letters and e-mails would prompt more memories. It was only a matter of time before Marnie's yearning for the mission field would be reborn. And if that love returned, why not her love for him as well?

They arrived back at their apartment shortly before nine o'clock. "Do you still want to read a few letters?" she asked as he walked her to the door.

"I'd love to, if it's not too late for you."

"No, it's not too late." She unlocked the door, and they went inside. "Being out on the ocean invigorated me. Believe it or not, I'm even hungry. I didn't think I'd ever want to eat again after that big meal."

He turned on the lights. "I hate to admit it, but I'm hungry, too. We could have our old standby—popcorn and sodas. If you like, I'll pop the corn while you get the letters out."

She kicked off her shoes. "Sounds good to me."

After removing his shoes, Jeff went to the kitchen and found the microwave popcorn in the same cupboard where it had always been. Everything seemed just as he had left it. He was home again, and it felt so good. *Lord, please let me stay. Let me have my life with Marnie back again.*

By the time the popcorn and sodas were ready, Marnie had the boxes of memorabilia open and letters spread out on the kitchen table. He handed her a soda and set the brimming bowl of popcorn on the table. The aroma of freshly popped corn made him feel even more at home.

"Only one thing is missing," said Marnie.

Jeff looked around. "What? Music?" They had always loved having praise music playing in the background.

"No, but that's a good idea." She turned on the stereo then reached for the box of chocolates he had brought. "I love chocolate with my popcorn."

He chuckled. "That's right. You love eating sweet and salty things together."

She sat down and popped a chocolate into her mouth. "You knew that?"

"Sure. You always eat potato chips with your ice cream and chocolate shakes with your fries."

She shook her head. "I didn't even realize that. But you're right. That's what I do. It's scary when somebody else knows you better than you know yourself."

Jeff helped himself to the popcorn. "It doesn't have to be scary. . .when that someone loves you like I do."

Her face blanching, Marnie quickly turned her attention to the letters on the table.

Idiot! Jeff said to himself. *You can't push her. When you come on too strong, she retreats like a startled deer. Just let things happen naturally.* He reached for a stack of photographs. "Look. These are pictures we took in Cambodia. Even though we hung out together after the spilled-salad incident, it was in Cambodia where we first became close friends." He wanted to say, *That's where we fell in love,* but he didn't want to alarm her again.

He handed her a photo. "Here we are at an open-air market. You loved all the beautiful baskets. And look at all the colorful fruits and vegetables and raw fish spread out on the wicker mats." He handed her another picture. "See, here you are buying a basket. Look how busy the marketplace is—all the little shops crammed together, merchants wearing wide-brimmed hats and stooping over their baskets, hundreds of bikes lined up along the road, and people everywhere."

Marnie looked at the pictures. "I see myself there, but I have no memory of it. It's so frustrating."

"Cambodia is where the Killing Fields are," Jeff said solemnly. "In the seventies, the Khmer Rouge killed nearly two million people—over one-fifth of Cambodia's population."

Marnie's eyes welled with tears. "That's so sad. Is that why we went there?"

"We went there because the people are poor and need medicine and education and training. But mostly, we went to tell them about Jesus. We worked at a teen center in Battambang. But we also traveled to nearby villages with a health-care team. They treated sick children and immunized people. Children over there often die of diseases before they're five. We couldn't treat anyone ourselves, but we held the children and played with them. They really loved us."

Marnie studied him for a long moment, her dark eyes shiny with unshed tears. "You really do care about the people over there, don't you?"

He wasn't sure how to respond. "Sure I do. Once you've been there, you never forget what it's like." He stopped abruptly, realizing what he had said—*you never forget.* "You couldn't help forgetting, Marnie. You were injured. Otherwise, you'd still be remembering what it was like over there, too."

She pushed her chair back and stood up. "My headache's back."

He got up and went to her. "Can I help? Should I go? Do you want me to rub your temples?"

She paused a moment then said, "Okay."

He followed her over to the wicker sofa, and they sat down. She put her feet up and lay back against his chest. Gently he stroked her temples. They had sat like this a hundred times before. Marnie felt so warm and good in his arms. Being close like this was as natural to him as breathing. He could almost make himself believe this was like any other night before the accident—the two of them cuddling on the sofa, grateful to be together and so deeply in love. Yes, that's exactly how it was. He had his wife back in his arms again, back where she belonged. Almost dozing now, she looked so trusting and content. He lowered his face to hers and lightly kissed her lips. "I love you, Marnie."

"Me, too," she murmured sleepily.

Joy spiraled through his chest. *She still loves me!* He kissed her again. She didn't resist.

Impulsively he gathered Marnie up in his arms and carried her to their bedroom. He laid her on the bed and smothered her face and neck with kisses. "I need you, Marnie," he whispered. "I need you to be my wife again." He was so caught up in the moment that it shocked him when she gave him a hard shove backward.

"Stop it! Leave me alone!" Sobbing, she scrambled to the far side of the bed and hugged her arms, looking like a frightened kitten.

He stumbled and grabbed the bedpost to keep from falling. In exasperation he uttered, "What's wrong with you, Marnie?"

She was trembling. "I was half asleep. You surprised me."

He raked his fingers through his hair. "When I kissed you today, you kissed me back. You liked it; I know you did. I thought that meant you were ready to be my wife again."

"I can't." She rubbed her mouth with the back of her hand. "I can't be with you like that. I'm not ready. I thought you understood."

He was still white-knuckling the bedpost. "I want to understand, but you keep giving me mixed signals. Which is it, Marnie? Do you want a husband—or a buddy?"

"That's not fair." She pushed her tangled hair back from her face. "You know how it is for me. I don't feel—married."

"But I thought—I thought tonight was different." His heart was pounding like a tom-tom, and the bitter taste of gall seared the back of his throat. "I thought you loved me again."

"I do," she said in a small, sad voice. "But not that way."

Jeff paced the floor, rubbing the back of his neck. He couldn't wrap his mind around what had just happened. Everything had been going so well. Now it was all up in smoke. "I can't do this anymore," he said under his breath.

"Do what?" Her gaze was silently accusing.

He looked her straight in the eyes. "I can't keep playing the devoted suitor, Marnie." He tried to sound forceful and strong, but his voice came out tremulous, uneven. "I can't pretend we're just dating like some single couple. I'm a husband who yearns to hold and caress and cherish his wife."

She bit her lower lip. "I told you I'm not ready. I don't know if I ever will be. Why do you keep pressuring me?"

"I don't know." He heaved a sigh. "I guess because I had this crazy idea that with a little romance I could make you fall in love with me again. Your mom even thought so. I guess we were both wrong."

"My mom put you up to this?" She sat hugging herself, looking like a sad little waif with her smeared makeup and mussed hair. "This was all a crazy scheme you two cooked up?"

"Don't blame her. She was just trying to help."

"I don't need her help," Marnie shot back tearfully. "Or yours, either. Just go! Leave me alone!"

"That's one wish I can grant." He strode to the door, his breath ragged in his throat, his voice raw with emotion. "I'm outta here, Marnie. And don't worry. I won't be back."

Chapter 13

Marnie's head pulsed with pain. Over and over, the words throbbed in her mind: *What have I done? What have I done?* She lay curled on her bed, hugging her pillow. In the hours since Jeff had walked out promising never to return, the apartment was accusingly silent. Only her own desolate sobs echoed against the bleak walls. She had never felt so alone.

How could things have fallen apart so quickly? She and Jeff had had a wonderful day together. Her feelings for him were stronger than ever. She was beginning to see why she had fallen in love with him in the first place. She was even entertaining the idea that it could happen again.

And then. . .

And then he had demanded more than she could give.

He had taken her by surprise, and instinctively she had resisted.

And now he was gone forever.

She didn't know who to be angrier with—Jeff for spoiling their perfect day with his sudden ardor or herself for overreacting and driving him away.

Already, she missed him. How could she be so upset with him one moment and so lost without him the next? Was it possible she was in love with him after all? But even if that was so, she couldn't risk another incident like tonight. Her emotions were too fragile, too volatile, too unpredictable. And Jeff—she couldn't bear to see that look of pain and disappointment in his eyes again. He deserved someone who knew how to be a proper wife.

After a while, between sobs, Marnie slipped into a restless slumber. She dreamed of Jeff. He was holding his arms out to her, beckoning her to come to him. Just when she was about to rush into his embrace, he disappeared. She woke up with a start and called his name. No one was there.

She sat up and swung her legs over the bed. She was still wearing her black empire dress. The night air was so warm and humid that the garment clung to her skin. She didn't care. She stared into the shadows and watched the moonlight from the open window cast faint streamers along the floor. She listened to the clock ticking on the nightstand and the shutters rattling in response to a stirring breeze.

She welcomed the breeze. Maybe it would blow away the gloom and lift the heaviness from her heart. With a sigh, she got up, pulled off her dress, and slipped into an old tank top and cotton shorts. It was three o'clock in the morning, but maybe she could still catch a few more hours of sleep.

She lay back down and stared up at the ceiling. She was wide awake now, and her mind was running in every direction at once. How had she come to this precise moment in time? And where did God want her to go from here? She replayed the long months since she had awakened from the coma. She relived the past couple of weeks with Jeff—their dates, the fun they had had. She went back over every detail of the past evening, trying to understand how things had gone so wrong.

She couldn't blame Jeff for wanting his wife back. And yet, in her heart of hearts, she still didn't see him as her husband. Maybe if he had given her more time. But she couldn't fault him for his lack of patience. If anything, he had been more patient than anyone had a right to expect. He had stood by her through all the craziness, the ups and downs, when she was learning to walk and talk again, when she didn't have a clue who he was or, for that matter, who she herself was. He was always there for her.

Until now.

Now he was gone. For good. He had had enough, and she couldn't blame him. Now it was time for her to find her way alone.

"But I'm not alone, am I, Lord?" she said aloud, her voice filling the darkness. "You're still with me, aren't You? I need You so much. You said that You will never leave me nor forsake me. I'm holding You to that, heavenly Father." She brushed away a tear. "Help me to be strong. Help me to make the right choices. Help me to know I'm not alone."

A fresh breeze ruffled the curtains and brought goose bumps to her bare arms. "You are here, aren't You, Father? I can almost feel You wrapping Your arms around me. I love You, Jesus."

She lay back down and fluffed her pillow under her head. She wasn't alone. Jesus was with her, watching over her. No matter what happened tomorrow, He would be with her every step of the way.

It was after nine o'clock when Marnie awoke to bright, golden sunlight streaming in her window. She got up and stretched. Her body ached from lack of sleep, but at least her headache was gone. It was a new day. Maybe Jeff would call. Maybe he would come back. Maybe last night wasn't as bad as she remembered. Surely Jeff wouldn't leave her after all they had been through together. Even the memory of his kisses was sweet now. She did enjoy being close to him. If it hadn't been for her headache and the way he took her by surprise, perhaps the evening would have ended differently.

She went to the kitchen, fixed a bowl of oatmeal, and poured herself a glass of orange juice. As she ate, she opened her laptop and checked her e-mail. Maybe Jeff had sent a note. She sighed in disappointment. The only note was from a lady at church reminding Marnie she would pick her up at two o'clock for her therapy session.

She checked her cell phone to see if she had missed any calls. She hadn't.

Checking her appointment calendar on the fridge, she let out a groan. She was scheduled to give an oral presentation in her ESL class the day after tomorrow. It was her final project. Her grade depended on it. And she wasn't ready. She had spent too much time lately dating—and daydreaming.

If Jeff were here, he would go over her notes and help her organize her material. When it came to her classes, she still had a hard time making her brain work right. And she still felt uneasy about giving a speech in class. She didn't always say what she intended to say. Sometimes, her words got jumbled and her mind went blank.

"No excuses, Marnie." She got out her textbook and notes. "If I start now, maybe I can get a head start on this before my therapy session."

Over the next four hours, she pored over her textbook and took copious notes even though she had a hard time concentrating. Every few minutes, she would glance at her cell phone and wonder when Jeff would call or text message her. She kept checking her e-mails, certain that he would write one of his brief, funny little notes. Several times she got up and looked outside the door in case Jeff had left her a little gift or flower or handwritten note.

There was nothing.

She went to her therapy session feeling discouraged. As much as she appreciated the ladies at church taking turns driving her to the hospital, she missed the days when Jeff had taken her. His caring smile had always prompted her to try harder and go the extra mile, no matter how difficult the task was.

When she got home that afternoon, she returned to her studies. She kept reading the same words over and over, but nothing made sense. After an hour or so, she gave up in frustration. She felt restless, distracted, at her wit's end.

Finally, she reached for her Bible and let it fall open at random. It opened to 1 Corinthians 13. "The love chapter," she mused. "How ironic is that?" She scanned the verses. " 'Love is patient, love is kind; love. . .rejoices with the truth. It always protects, always trusts, always hopes, always perseveres. Love never fails.' " She brushed at an unwelcome tear. "That's how Jeff has loved me, isn't it, Lord—just the way You told him to?"

She closed the Bible and ran her palm over the leather cover. "And, Father, that's the way You wanted me to love Jeff, too, isn't it? I'm sorry, Lord. I couldn't do it. But it's a strange thing. The closer I feel to You, Jesus, the closer I feel to Jeff. It's as if by loving You more I'm loving him, too. Is this the kind of love that comes only by knowing You?"

She felt as if she were on the verge of comprehending something she hadn't understood before—the connection between loving God and loving others. The realization was only half formed and still too nebulous to grasp fully. But what she did understand was mind-blowing. True love wasn't something she could generate in her own flawed human heart; it was born out of her love and devotion to Christ. The more she loved God and experienced His love for her, the more she could love others—the more she could love Jeff!

Still mulling over the implications of what she had read, she fixed herself a box of macaroni and cheese for dinner. "If only I had someone wiser than I am to help me understand this whole love thing," she murmured as she finished her macaroni. Suddenly, she thought of Jenny. Jenny was wise and had a close walk with God. She would be the perfect one to go to for advice. Marnie hadn't seen her best friend in what seemed like ages, except for a few minutes here and there at school. She had been too busy doing all the touristy things with Jeff.

With eager fingers, she punched in Jenny's number and waited. Her shoulders sagged when she got Jenny's voice mail. "Give me a call when you have a chance, Jen," she said, trying to sound lighthearted. "I miss you."

After dinner, she forced herself to tackle her presentation again. She had only one more day to prepare. Somehow she had to be ready.

About an hour later, a familiar melody rang from her cell phone. She grabbed it and said hello. Surely it would be Jeff. He hadn't called all day.

It was Jenny. She sounded worried. "Marnie, I just got home from work. I've been wanting to call you all day. I heard about Jeff."

"Jeff?" Now Marnie was confused. Surely he wouldn't tell Jenny about last night. "What about Jeff?" she asked.

"I heard he's leaving the island."

"Leaving?"

"Yes. I ran into his friend Nate—Nate Anderson—and he said Jeff's moving out."

"Moving out?" Marnie's mouth went dry. "Where is he going?"

"Cambodia."

"Cambodia?"

"That's what Nate said."

"How could he be going to Cambodia?"

"On a mission trip. You mean you didn't know?"

"No. I mean, he didn't mention it—yet. When is he going?"

"I heard he leaves tomorrow. I thought for sure he would have told you."

Marnie swallowed over a lump in her throat. "How could this happen so suddenly? It takes weeks to plan a mission trip."

"Usually, it does," Jenny agreed. "But Nate said someone on the outreach team got sick. Jeff is taking his place. The plane leaves tomorrow. I guess it all just fell into place all of a sudden."

Marnie's head spun. How could Jeff do this to her—leave without so much as a word? Did he hate her that much?

"Jeff didn't tell you he was going?" Jenny asked with a hint of concern.

"No, he didn't."

"Well, it all happened so quickly; he must be frantic trying to finish up his classes and get ready. But I'm sure he'll call you."

Marnie tried to hold back the emotional fireworks exploding inside her. "I, uh, I probably just missed his call. I'm sure that's it."

"Are you okay?" asked Jenny. "If you need anything, Marnie, you'll let me know, won't you?"

"Sure. I'm fine." She realized she was writing Jeff's name over and over in the margins of her presentation. "I'm just busy studying."

"Aren't we all? I'm so glad classes end this week."

"Me, too."

"Maybe we can get together when all the pressure's off."

"I'd like that," said Marnie. "But I'll probably be flying home to Michigan next week."

"That soon?"

"As soon as I can get a flight."

"But you are coming back to U of N for the fall quarter, aren't you?"

Marnie paused a long moment, trying to regain her composure. "I—I don't think so, Jen. There are too many sad memories here."

"I understand," said Jenny with a catch in her voice. "You've been through so much this year. I can't blame you for wanting to go home. But I'll miss you like crazy."

Marnie swallowed a sob. "I'll miss you, too, Jen."

"We'll definitely get together before you go. I'll get some of our friends together, and we'll have a girls' night out."

"Great, Jen. That's just—great." *Great* was *their* word—hers and Jeff's—their funny, happy word.

"Talk to you later, Marnie."

"Right, Jen. Have a great night." Marnie snapped her cell phone shut and dropped it on the table then sat back and closed her eyes. She had never felt more abandoned and betrayed. Just when she was beginning to think they had a chance, Jeff had given up on her once and for all. There was no going back and redoing the past. It was finished. Over. The truth was as searing and explosive as an autumn bonfire devouring dead, dry leaves on a windy night. As a girl in Michigan, she had once burned her arm standing too close to the crackling flames. But that pain was nothing compared to the pain she was feeling now.

Tears rolled down her cheeks and into her mouth; they tasted warm and salty. She sat for a long while, letting the tears flow. It was strange how you could feel so miserable, and yet, it felt so good to cry. Then she got the hiccups, which interrupted the rhythm of her weeping, so she dried her tears and concentrated on getting rid of the hiccups. She held her breath, and just when she thought it had worked, she hiccupped again, more noisily than before. They were getting worse—not better. She tried drinking a full glass of water, but that sent her running to the bathroom.

Then—you might know it—her cell phone rang. By the time she got back to the kitchen, it had stopping ringing. But there was a message. It was Jeff. Her heart thundered in her chest so loudly she could hardly hear what he was saying.

"Marnie, it's me. I'm on my way over. I've got something to tell you. See you in a few."

Chapter 14

Marnie ran to the bathroom and stared at her reflection in the mirror. She looked ghastly. Her eyes were red-rimmed from crying, with black mascara-circles smudged under her eyes. Her nose was running and as red as Rudolph's. Too weary to style her hair this morning, she had tied it back in a makeshift ponytail. It looked hideous. With rising panic, she let her hair down and fluffed it with her fingers, but now it stuck out oddly, making her look like some crazy creature in a horror flick.

She couldn't let Jeff see her like this, especially if this was going to be their last time together. If he was leaving her forever, she at least wanted him to carry away a pleasing last impression of her.

But where to begin? He said he was on his way over. How much time did that give her? Five minutes? Ten? Or what if he had called while he was actually en route? He could arrive at any second.

Marnie washed off the mascara, but she couldn't do anything about her red, swollen eyes. Jeff would know she had been crying, and that was the last thing she wanted. He had made his decision to go, and that was that. Let him go. She didn't want his pity.

As she ran a brush through her tangled hair, the doorbell rang. She looked down at her oversized tee and sweatpants. She wished she could change into something more feminine, but there was no time.

She hurried to the door, paused to catch her breath, then opened it, praying that she looked more calm, cool, and collected than she felt. "Hi, Jeff," she said, trying to sound nonchalant.

"Hi, Marnie." He looked a little nervous and unsure of himself. "Can I come in a minute?"

"Sure." She stepped aside.

He entered, rubbing his hands together as if debating what to say. "I won't take much of your time, Marnie."

"That's okay. I'm not going anywhere."

"Can we sit down?"

"I guess." They took opposite ends of the sofa.

He gave her a closer look. "Are you feeling okay?"

She looked away, but there was nowhere to hide. "Yeah. Why?"

"You look like you're coming down with a cold."

"It's nothing. My allergies must be kicking up."

"You don't have allergies."

"Whatever." Why did he have to catch her looking like this? It was bad enough that their relationship was ending. At least she should have been able to say good-bye to him with her hair styled, her makeup on, and her pride intact.

He was still rubbing his hands together. "I have some news, Marnie."

She nodded. "You're going to Cambodia."

He looked startled, taken aback. "How did you know?"

"Jen told me. Nate told her."

"News travels fast."

"Not as fast as your travel plans."

He sat back and drew in a deep breath. "I found out about the opening on the ministry team when I got home last night. Then, this morning, everything just fell into place. I was able to sign up, do all the necessary paperwork, and get a plane ticket. I even squeezed in time to take my last two finals. It just seems like the Lord orchestrated the whole thing."

"How long will you be gone?"

"Two months. I'll be back in time for fall classes." He shifted, turning to face her. "We'll be flying in to Phnom Penh. From there, we'll drive north to do some prison ministry at the maximum-security prison in Ratanakiri. Then, we'll travel south through Stung Treng and Kompong Cham back to Phnom Penh. Do you remember any of those places?"

"No. Should I?"

"We held Bible classes for the children in Kompong Cham. In that box in the cupboard are some photos of us holding the kids. They loved you. They were always flocking around you, wanting you to pick them up. I'm sorry we didn't get to see those pictures last night."

She looked away, tears starting in her eyes. "Me, too."

"Anyway, besides evangelistic meetings, our team will be holding discipleship classes for Christian teens. We're teaching them to minister to their own people. Did you know 80 percent of Cambodians are under the age of thirty?"

"No, I didn't know." Why was he rambling on about everything except what was on both of their minds—the final death throes of their marriage? Gazing down at her hands, she pushed back the cuticle of her thumbnail until it hurt. "So, is that all you came over to say?"

He sat forward and massaged his knuckles. "I came to pick up the rest of my things. I don't have much here—my guitar, a few clothes, some books and papers. I assume you won't still be in Hawaii when I get back from Cambodia."

The casual way he remarked that she wouldn't be here made her wince inside. Plus, her cuticle was bleeding now. She wanted to say, *How do you know where I'll be?* But he was right. She wouldn't be here in the fall. "I'm going home to Michigan in a few days."

"That's what I figured." He cracked his knuckles—first one hand and then the other. "Listen, Marnie. I want you to know I'm not going to stop you if you want to file for an annulment."

Fresh tears filled her eyes, but she turned away so he wouldn't notice.

"Did you hear me, Marnie?"

She blinked rapidly. "Yes, I heard you. Fine. I'll look into it."

He stood up. "I'll go get my stuff."

While he gathered his belongings, she busied herself in the kitchen—washing the same dish over and over. Silently she prayed, *Help me, Lord! I don't know what to do. I don't know what to say. Just when I saw a glimmer of hope for Jeff and me, it's all falling apart. How did things get so bad between us?*

After a while, he came out with his guitar over his shoulder and a duffel bag in each hand. "There are still a few things left." He set his bags by the door. "The rent is paid until the end of the month. Nate will stop by and get the rest of my junk before you leave."

"Okay."

"I'm sorry I won't be able to help you pack up this place. Maybe Nate can round up some of the guys and help you out—you know, packing, cleaning the floors, stuff like that."

Marnie hadn't thought that far ahead. All the pieces of her life were here in this apartment. How was she possibly going to box it all up and take it back to Michigan? "If I need help, I'll call Nate."

"Do that. I don't want you trying to do it all yourself. You're not that strong yet."

"I'm strong enough," she said defensively.

He managed a grim smile. "Yeah, maybe you are." He opened the door then turned back to her. "If you need anything, Marnie—anything at all. . ." His voice trailed off.

"I'm fine," she said, while a little voice in her head screamed, *I'm anything but fine!*

He nodded. "Great."

There was that word again—*their* word.

"Yeah. Great," she repeated.

They stood staring at each other for a long while, neither speaking. Marnie could see the emotion playing out in Jeff's eyes and in the way he flexed his lips, as if he were about to say something and then changed his mind.

Her own heart was crying out, *Let's go back and erase last night and start over. Let's figure out how we can have the kind of love God talks about in the Bible.* But she couldn't bring herself to say the words aloud.

"Marnie—" Jeff clasped her arm. "You take care of yourself, okay? When you go home to Michigan, keep up your therapy and do what the doctor tells you."

She nodded. "My mom will see to that."

"Great. I love that about your mom." He leaned over and kissed her cheek, like a brother would. "You'll always be in my prayers, Marnie."

"Thanks." She licked her dry lips. "You'll be in mine, too."

He glanced around the room as if he didn't know quite what to do next. She followed his gaze, knowing he was remembering the times they had spent together in this apartment—the good times and bad. Finally, he looked back at her, his eyes glazed with unshed tears. It was all she could do to keep herself from rushing into his arms and begging him to stay. But that would be cruel and selfish of her. As much as she wanted to work things out with him right now, tomorrow, she might be pushing him away again, afraid to be the wife he needed. It wasn't fair to keep him on an emotional roller-coaster ride. Besides, Jeff had made his decision. His heart belonged to the missions. She had no right to keep him here when God was calling him to Cambodia.

"We had some special times here," he murmured. "I'll never forget that."

"Me neither." But that was the problem. She had forgotten. The memories were lost forever. And until now, she had been too afraid to build new ones.

Kissing the top of her head, he whispered, "Stay in touch." Then, with a sigh, he opened the door, picked up his bags, and strode outside, letting the door clatter behind him.

Even after he had gone, Marnie stood watching the closed door, certain that Jeff would turn around and come back. It couldn't be over as simply as this. At any moment, he would come striding back inside, laughing and telling her he had no intention of going; this was just his way of making her realize how much they meant to each other.

Finally, she pressed her cheek against the door and let the tears flow. Her headache was back, too, more severe than any she had experienced before. But at least the physical pain helped deaden the emotional pain. When all that remained were dry sobs, she went to her room, stretched out on the bed, and let sleep bring its anesthetizing solace.

Marnie's first thought when she woke the next morning was that Jeff would be flying to Cambodia about the same time she was giving her speech in her ESL class. The thought made her feel even more empty and alone than she had felt last night. Without Jeff, she felt marooned, rudderless. She wanted nothing more than to pull the covers over her head and let slumber obliterate her pain. But that wasn't possible. She had to face the fact that he was gone and she was on her own now.

"But I'm not alone, am I, Lord?" she whispered as she gazed at the sunlight streaming in the window. "You're with me. I can do all things through Christ who strengthens me. Help me to live those words. In my weakness, please show Your strength, Father. I love You, Jesus."

With a prayer on her lips, she forced herself to get out of bed and go about her usual routine of breakfast, devotions, showering, and dressing. She put on her green drawstring top and white denim capris and styled her hair the way Jeff liked—with crimped curls framing her face just so.

She spent the next few hours going over her presentation until it was word perfect. As she grabbed a peanut butter and jelly sandwich for lunch, she realized she'd better phone her mother and let her know she would be coming home next week. Her mom had insisted she stay and try to salvage her marriage, but even her mother couldn't protest her coming home when she learned that Jeff had left for Cambodia.

She managed to get through the first few minutes of their conversation without giving in to her emotions. But when her mother asked how she felt about Jeff's leaving, she burst into tears. "I didn't want him to go, Mom, but I can't blame him. I couldn't be his wife, and he said he doesn't want just a—a buddy."

Her mother's voice came back firm and reassuring. "Listen, honey, I'm not letting you come home alone. Your dad and I will fly over—today if we can get a flight—and help you pack up your apartment. Then we'll bring you home. You just go finish your classes, and I'll call you later with our flight information."

All she could manage to say was "Thanks, Mom." She hadn't mentioned her headaches. Another one was brewing even as they spoke—spiking in her skull like a hot iron striking an anvil. But there was no sense in worrying her mother unnecessarily.

After saying their good-byes, Marnie closed her cell phone, gathered the materials for her presentation, and set off for the campus. It wasn't a long walk, but besides being uphill, the day was warmer and more humid than usual, even for Hawaii.

By the time Marnie walked into her ESL class, she was feeling overheated, light-headed, and breathless. She sat down in her seat and prayed that her headache would abate long enough for her to give her presentation. She was the second student the instructor called on. As she picked up her notes and walked to the lectern, she prayed that God would help her. Her mind felt fuzzy, her thoughts disjointed. She arranged her notes and gazed out at her fellow classmates.

"My name is Marnie Rockwell—um, I mean, Marnie Jordan, and my topic is. . ." She was having a hard time forming her words correctly. The words on the page blurred, and the faces watching her were suddenly transformed into distorted, dizzying, multiplying shapes. She closed her eyes and gripped the lectern. She was feeling nauseated. Her headache was paralyzing now—her skull about to explode while searing, knifelike pain shot down her neck.

"I'm sorry," she murmured. "I—I can't do this."

Even as she said the words, the world started spinning around her—faces blending, colors meshing, the very room turning topsy-turvy like a carnival ride gone terribly wrong. Trapped in a nightmarish vortex of pain, she felt herself sinking down, down, collapsing into a chasm so dark and deep she might never return.

Chapter 15

Jeff set his laptop, carry-on bag, shoes, and the contents of his pockets—keys, wallet, cell phone, and change—on the screening table then handed his passport and plane ticket to the security guard. Ahead of him, his team members had already passed through the metal detectors and were collecting their possessions. They had two hours before their plane would be flying them from the small, open-air Kona airport to Honolulu, and then on to Tokyo for a connecting flight to Bangkok, and another connecting flight to Phnom Penh. From there, they would take a van north to Ratanakiri. It would be over twenty-eight hours before they touched down in Cambodia, so he had come prepared with several books and a bag full of snacks—candy bars, chips, beef jerky, and hastily made ham sandwiches.

Just as he was collecting his belongings, his cell phone rang. Striding away from the security checkpoint, he opened the phone and said a hushed hello. It was Nate. "Hey, bro, what's up?" he asked, keeping an eye on his team members up ahead. They were already halfway to the gate, and he was lagging behind, bringing up the rear. "I can't talk now, man. We're heading to our gate. I'll call you back just before we board."

The reception was bad, and when the phone cut out, Jeff wasn't sure he had heard Nate correctly. "What'd you say—what about Marnie?"

"She collapsed in class," said Nate. "They took her to the hospital. She's being prepped for surgery."

Jeff stopped in his tracks and set his bags at his feet. "Surgery? What happened to her?"

"No one knows. But it looks serious, buddy."

Jeff sucked in a breath. He felt as if the wind had been knocked out of him. "Is she gonna be okay?"

"I have no idea," said Nate. "But I figured you'd wanna know."

"Yeah, I sure do. See if you can get some more information, okay?"

He hung up the phone, his head spinning with questions. What could have happened to Marnie? She was fine last night—except for the headaches. *Lord, help her. Take care of my girl. Let her be okay.*

As he joined his team members at the gate, his mind was in a tailspin. He set his stuff on a chair and turned to Charles, the team leader. "I got a problem," he said, his thoughts running blindly. How could he explain what he himself didn't know?

"What is it, Jeff?" Charles—a big-boned, red-faced Swede with wispy blond hair—had a way of sounding calm and reassuring, no matter what was happening around him.

Jeff needed a little of that composure right now. "It's my wife," he said, his voice catching. "She's in the hospital."

Compassion registered in Charles's eyes. "What can we do for her?"

Jeff was on the verge of tears. The last thing he wanted was to look like a crybaby in front of the guys. "That's just it. I don't know what's wrong. It could be serious."

Charles clasped Jeff's shoulder. "Let's pray for her right now, man." He called the other guys over, and they formed a circle around Jeff. "Heavenly Father," said Charles in his deep, thickly accented voice, "put Your loving arms of protection around Marnie this very minute. We don't know what's wrong, Lord, but You do, and we entrust her to Your care. And give Jeff Your comfort and courage. Help him to know what he needs to do right now."

As they all said, "Amen," Jeff had to steel himself to keep from bawling. He swiped at a tear and spoke over a lump in his throat. "Listen, guys, I don't know how to say this, but I can't go to Cambodia with you. Marnie's my wife, and I've gotta stay here by her side."

Charles shook his hand heartily. "You go take care of your wife, Jeff. We'll trust God to pick up the slack for us. It's His ministry. He's in charge."

Grabbing his bags, Jeff nearly sprinted across the airport to a waiting taxi. "Take me to Kona Community Hospital," he said breathlessly. During the drive, he called Nate back and asked if he had any more information. He didn't, but he was phoning classmates and asking them to pray.

Then Jeff phoned Jenny. "Have you heard about Marnie?" he said, the emotion raw in his voice.

"Yes. I heard she was taken to the hospital. What happened, Jeff?"

"I don't know, Jen. I'm on my way to the hospital now."

"Me, too. I called the church and talked to Pastor Maluhia. He's notifying the prayer chain."

"Good. I'll see you in a few minutes."

When the taxi pulled up at the hospital, Jeff jumped out and nearly forgot his luggage. "Hey, man, don't forget your stuff!" called the driver. Returning to the cab, Jeff thrust several dollars into the man's hand and asked him to drop his bags off at his dormitory at U of N.

Every nerve ending bristled as Jeff ran into the hospital and crossed the lobby. "My wife was brought here to the hospital," he told the woman at the information desk. "Her name's Marnie. Marnie Jordan." He was panting so hard he wasn't sure the woman understood him.

Checking her records, she said, "Your wife has been taken to the surgical suite, Mr. Jordan."

Jeff paced the floor. "Why? What happened? What's wrong with her?"

"You'll have to talk with her doctor."

"Where is he?"

"I'll page him, but he may already be in the operating room. We have some papers for you to sign, Mr. Jordan—permission forms for surgery, since you're her closest relative. Then you may wait for Dr. Forlani in the visitors' lounge."

Jeff signed the forms, but there was no way he was going to sit around waiting for news. He had spent a lot of time in this hospital when he and Marnie were recuperating from the accident. He knew half the nurses on the staff. Now he just had to find one who would give him some answers.

It didn't take him long. He found a surgical nurse named Elena on duty in the emergency room. She greeted Jeff with a big hug. "I'm so relieved you're here, Mr. Jordan. You and your wife were always my favorite patients."

"How's Marnie?" he asked.

The woman's expression darkened. "I was here when they brought her in. She was unconscious. They ran tests—a CT scan, MRI, and ultrasound. I believe they've taken her to surgery."

"What's wrong with her?"

She hesitated. Jeff could see the indecision playing in her olive black eyes. "I should wait and let the doctor tell you."

"Please, Elena—!" He clasped her arm. "I've got to know."

"They—they suspect a ruptured cerebral aneurysm."

Jeff caught his breath. "That's bad, isn't it?"

"It can be."

"People die of those!"

"Yes, but they're acting quickly. We must trust they've caught it in time."

"She was having headaches," said Jeff. "I should have recognized the signs. If anything happens to her. . ."

"You can't blame yourself, Mr. Jordan."

"Why not? She needed me, and I wasn't here."

"You're here now. That's what counts."

"I've got to see her."

"I don't know if that's possible now."

"Jeff!"

He looked around. It was Jenny. She came running up to him, her brown hair flying, her dark eyes filled with concern. "How is she? Do you know anything?"

"They said she might have—" He could hardly get out the words. "She might have an aneurysm, Jen. They've taken her to surgery."

"Why don't you both sit down," said Elena, "and I'll go see if there's any news. Maybe Dr. Forlani hasn't scrubbed yet."

They walked over to the visitors' lounge and sat down on wicker chairs. "What do you know about aneurysms?" Jeff asked Jenny.

"Not much. Isn't it when an artery bulges out like a balloon?"

He nodded. "And if it bursts, it can kill you."

Jenny put her hand over his. "Everyone's praying for her. Students all over campus are setting up little prayer groups."

"But what if God wants to take her home?" He pummeled his fist against his palm. "She's gone through so much already this year, Jen. And now this!"

"She's in God's hands, Jeff. There's no better place to be."

The brisk click of leather shoes on the tile floor caught Jeff's attention. He looked up to see Dr. Forlani striding toward him in his surgical gown. The doctor greeted him with a solemn nod and shook his hand. "Mr. Jordan—Jeffrey—we need to talk. Will you join me in the consultation room?"

"What about Marnie? Is she okay?"

"Come with me."

Jeff gave Jenny a helpless shrug and followed Dr. Forlani to a small room just off the visitors' lounge. The surgeon sat down at a small oak desk; Jeff settled into an overstuffed chair. His heart was pounding so hard he wondered if he'd be able to hear or comprehend the doctor's words.

Dr. Forlani sat forward, folded his hands, and got right to the point. "Jeffrey, we've just completed several tests, including an angiogram, on your wife. They show that an aneurysm has ruptured in her brain at the intersection of her ophthalmic artery and one of her carotid arteries. It may be the result of trauma from her accident last January. Whatever the cause, blood is spilling into surrounding brain tissue and, without treatment, will likely lead to a host of problems."

"What problems? Don't dance around it, Doctor. Tell me the truth."

"Without proper treatment, Marnie may suffer brain damage, paralysis, or a stroke. She could go into another coma and never wake up. She could die."

Jeff's stomach knotted. He was going to be sick. "You've got to save her, Doctor."

"We'll do everything we can. We need your permission to operate."

"I know. I already signed the papers."

"Good. Then there's something else we need to talk about. We have two options. The traditional approach is a craniotomy. The procedure is known as microvascular clipping. We remove a section of the skull and clip off the aneurysm to stop the bleeding."

Jeff shook his head. "Marnie's already had brain surgery. I don't know if she could survive it again."

Dr. Forlani cleared his throat. "The other option eliminates invasive surgery. It's a newer technique called endovascular coiling. A catheter is guided up through the patient's groin into the ruptured blood vessel. Then tiny platinum coils are deployed into the aneurysm to make the blood clot and create a seal."

"That sounds better than drilling into her skull," said Jeff. "Do that one."

"Here's the problem. As a neurosurgeon, I can perform the craniotomy immediately. If you want the noninvasive coiling, we need an interventional radiologist."

"Then get one." Jeff's impatience was growing. Why was Dr. Forlani wasting time talking and throwing around all these tongue-twisting terms? "Do whatever's best for Marnie."

"The closest interventional radiologist is Dr. Iwamoto, in Honolulu," said Dr. Forlani. "I've already contacted him, and he's flying to Kona even as we speak."

"Great. Then he'll be able to fix Marnie's head."

"Here's the dilemma, Jeffrey." Dr. Forlani leaned forward with a quiet, confidential air. "While the coiling method is less risky and offers a much shorter recovery time, your wife's condition could deteriorate while we wait for Dr. Iwamoto to arrive. As I said, Marnie could suffer a stroke. She could die before we have a chance to treat her."

Jeff felt what little strength and composure he had drain right out of him. "Then do the other one—the cranio—"

"Craniotomy. But the risk there is that Marnie might not be strong enough to survive the surgery."

"Then what do we do?" Jeff's voice came out sounding shrill and desperate.

"I suggest we wait for Dr. Iwamoto. He will be able to determine which procedure is best for Marnie. But if you don't choose to wait, I will go ahead with the craniotomy."

Jeff sat back, closed his eyes, and cupped his hands behind his neck. "Lord, I feel like I'm holding Marnie's life in my hands. What do You want me to do?" Tears welled in his eyes. His mouth felt as dry as sand. He could hardly get out the words. "I don't want anyone cutting into Marnie's head again. We'll wait for Dr. Iwamoto."

For Jeff, the next few hours were a blur. Dozens of his classmates joined him in the visitors' lounge and took turns praying for Marnie. Two hours passed before Dr. Iwamoto arrived from Honolulu, and then another hour crept by before the surgeons confirmed they were going with the minimally invasive coiling treatment.

Just before the orderlies wheeled Marnie into the operating room, Dr. Forlani allowed Jeff a few minutes with her. He entered her room with fear and trembling. What would he find? How bad would it be? Seeing her, he uttered a wistful sigh. She was still his Marnie, the girl he adored. She looked like a sleeping princess. Or like a fragile china doll lying so quiet and still in the large hospital bed.

She wasn't aware of his presence, but he sat down, took her hand, and prayed over her. "Father, she's in Your hands now. Take care of her. Please let her be okay." After he had prayed, he got up, leaned over, and kissed her forehead. "I hope we made the right choice for you, Marnie. Please come back to me. I love you so much." The words spilled out between broken sobs. "And I promise—I'll never leave you again—no matter what."

For the next two hours, he sat in the visitors' lounge with Jenny and Nate and all the others from the church and university who had gathered to show their support. As he waited and prayed, he received a phone call from Marnie's parents. Their plane had arrived in Kona—they had come to take their daughter home to Michigan—and they were worried that she wasn't answering her cell phone.

"I tried to reach you," said Jeff, "but I guess you were already in the air." With halting words, he told them about Marnie's aneurysm and tried to reassure them that she was getting the best of care. They stayed on the line with him, urging him to relate every detail while they flagged a cab and headed for the hospital.

They arrived twenty minutes later, worried and exhausted and full of questions. It was irrational, but somehow Jeff felt as if he had let them down—he hadn't taken care of their daughter the way he had promised. He was too emotionally spent to go through the motions of introducing Marnie's parents to everyone, but, to his relief, his friends quickly gathered around and welcomed them. Many remembered the Rockwells from their previous visits after Jeff and Marnie's accident. There was a lot of hugging and weeping and muffled words of comfort.

For Jeff, all the commotion was too much, considering at this very moment Marnie's life hung in the balance. He couldn't handle other people's emotions and neediness right now. He sat forward and buried his face in his hands. If the doctors didn't come with news soon, he was going to explode. If only he could get away by himself and sit in silence and pray.

He was relieved when Jenny put her hand on his shoulder and said, "Jeff, why don't you go get some fresh air. I'll keep Mr. and Mrs. Rockwell company."

He gave her a look that said, *Thank you, thank you!* Aloud he said, "Are you sure?"

"More than sure. Take a little break."

Nate joined in and said, "Hey, bro, I'll come get you if there's any news." Turning to the Rockwells, Nate said, "I'd be glad to go get you two some coffee or bring you back something from the cafeteria if you're hungry."

"Coffee would be good," said Barbara, wiping away a tear, "but we're not moving from here until we know our daughter's okay."

"Excuse me. I'll be right back." Before anyone could say another word, Jeff was on his feet and striding down the hall. Maybe he was being a coward for not wanting to deal with other people's pain, but right now, he was feeling spiritually depleted. He needed a touch from the Lord more at this moment than he ever had in his life. He kept walking until he was outside the hospital.

It surprised him to see that it was dark already. The sky was a deep azure blue, the air still heavy with the heat of the day and the wafting fragrance of bougainvillea. He crossed the thick grass and found a private spot around the corner of the building. Leaning against the wall, he put his head back and wailed. The sound that escaped his lips shocked him. It was more than a moan; it was a deep, guttural lament—primal and raw. He wept, his chest heaving with sobs until there was nothing left.

"Lord," he whispered at last, "no matter what happens, I'm Yours. Marnie is Yours. It's all in Your hands. I give it all to You, Father. I'm holding nothing back. Do what You will. Just don't let us go. Keep us always in Your arms. I love You, Jesus. I'll always love You."

He wiped away his tears, blew his nose, and, after composing himself, went back inside. He felt like he'd just been through the biggest workout of his life. He was physically spent but spiritually stronger. He had connected with the Holy Spirit in a way he couldn't even define with words. God was with Him. He could face anything now.

Returning to the visitors' lounge, he spotted Dr. Forlani talking with the Rockwells. *He's giving them news about Marnie, and I wasn't even here!* After sidestepping a table and nearly colliding with a passing nurse, he joined them, his heart pumping like crazy. He looked the doctor straight in the eye. "How's Marnie?"

Dr. Forlani's small dark eyes were hard to read. "The procedure was successful. I was just telling Mr. and Mrs. Rockwell that Dr. Iwamoto did an excellent job. He was able to identify the aneurysm and fill it with coils of platinum wire. The coils will mesh together, causing the blood to clot and form a seal. We're pleased that we were able to accomplish our goal without highly invasive surgery."

Jeff's hopes soared. "Then Marnie's going to be okay?"

Dr. Forlani raised his hand in a cautionary gesture. "She's not out of the woods yet, Jeffrey. She'll be in intensive care for the next twenty-four hours. There's still the danger of bleeding and of spasms in the blood vessels causing a stroke. We'll be monitoring Marnie's vital signs constantly, and we have her on a heart monitor to watch for abnormal heart rhythms. But if Marnie's recovery progresses as well as Dr. Iwamoto's coil embolization procedure, then I predict you'll have your wife back in your arms in a matter of days."

Chapter 16

She was standing in the midst of a green valley that stretched as far as the eye could see. The color was startling in its intensity—a bright emerald green nearly blinding to the eyes. Purple mountains with a soft velvet sheen surrounded the valley like cardboard cutouts pasted against a pastel blue sky studded with puffball clouds.

She was walking barefoot through tall grass that rustled against her bare legs. Where she walked, the crushed tendrils exuded a fresh, verdant scent. The breeze that kissed her face carried the fragrance of roses and the song of birds soaring overhead. Music played in the air like the patter of raindrops and the flutter of angel wings. It was a beautiful valley—as timeless and entrancing as it was peaceful.

Still, the journey was endless as she forced one foot ahead of the other through thick, clinging brush. The more she walked, the longer the distance grew to the other side of the valley. At times, the sun peeked through the clouds and shot out its blinding rays in little explosions of sheer, pure white. She covered her eyes, but the light kept growing, finally obliterating everything around her.

Weariness was about to consume her when a hand reached out and touched her shoulder. She grasped the willing fingers and held on for dear life. As loving arms embraced her, she felt warmth that transcended physical comfort. She wasn't alone anymore. Someone was with her, holding her close.

Someone else followed her as well—a shadowy figure lingering nearby, whispering words of hope and reassurance. "Marnie, I love you, sweetheart. You're going to be okay."

Of course she was going to be okay. She had this valley. She had never felt more at peace. This valley was taking her home. It was a long, hard journey, but she would get there someday.

"Marnie, can you hear me?"

The voice was familiar. As she turned her face toward it, the valley ebbed away. The music was gone; in its place, a jarring cacophony of noises. The wafting fragrance of roses had given way to an assault of repugnant, antiseptic smells. Everything about the world was suddenly crass and harsh and out of sync with her valley. She opened her eyes as if to ask, *Why did you disturb me? Why did you bring me back to. . .this?*

"Marnie, it's me—Jeff."

"Hi. . .Jeff." Her mouth felt cottony and tasted as stale as week-old chewing gum. Every part of her body was waking to stiffness and discomfort. "Where am I?"

"In the hospital. Do you remember what happened?"

"No." She turned her head away. Somehow, whatever it took, she had to get back to the green valley. But it was too late. It was already a fleeting memory. She was here now, in a sterile hospital room, trapped once again by a ruthless reality that demanded she fight her way back to normalcy. "I thought I was dead," she murmured.

Jeff placed his palm over her forehead. "We wouldn't let you go. God answered our prayers and brought you back to us."

"I'm not. . .back yet." She closed her eyes and let sleep enfold her.

For Marnie, the next few days were a broken mosaic of disrupted slumber, disjointed dreams, and faceless nurses coming and going like silent apparitions, murmuring singsong words that came at her from a distance.

And then one morning, she awoke in her hospital room and realized she felt alive again, almost normal. The headaches were gone, replaced by a sprig of hope in her soul. Whatever had happened, whatever dark, troubling journey she had just come through, God was with her, giving her another chance at life.

She opened her eyes and looked around. Jeff was sitting by her bed in an overstuffed chair, his chin on his chest, sleeping.

"Wake up. . .sleepyhead." Her voice came out husky, hardly there.

But Jeff heard. He sat bolt upright and stared at her. "Marnie, did you just say something?"

"Wake up."

He jumped to his feet. "That's what I thought you said."

She managed a faint half smile. "You're. . .sleeping on the job."

He grinned sheepishly. "Sorry, babe. I just dozed off."

"I need. . .water."

He brought over her glass and held the straw while she sipped, his eyes full of wonder and concern. "How are you, sweetheart?"

She searched his eyes. He really had a rather handsome face. "You tell me."

Sitting down on the edge of the bed, he took her hand and rubbed the back of it with his thumb. "Dr. Forlani says you're going to be fine. You'll need to be on medication for a while, but that's no big deal."

Her mind was still fuzzy. "What happened to me?"

"What's the last thing you remember?"

She thought a minute. The images in her mind were jumbled, out of focus. "I was going to my ESL class. I had to give a presentation."

"It didn't happen, babe."

"Why not? I worked so hard on it."

"You collapsed. They had to take you to the hospital."

"I don't remember."

"Do you remember me?"

"Of course. You're Jack."

He smacked his forehead. "Oh no, not again!"

Marnie started giggling. "I'm only kidding. You're Jeff. My husband."

"Whew! You know how to scare a guy."

"Did you really think I didn't know you?"

"Yeah. I figured you considered me some stranger off the street again."

She shook her head. "No way." She paused for a long moment, trying to gather her thoughts. "So, Jeff, are you going to tell me why I'm here?"

"Sure, babe. It's a long story, but I'll give you the condensed version." In a few short, matter-of-fact sentences, he told her what had happened. But it was all coming at her too fast. She could make sense of only a few words—aneurysm, surgery, everyone praying.

In alarm, she felt her head then sighed in relief. "I still have my hair."

"Yeah, I wasn't about to let them cut into your head again."

"You told them that?"

"Sort of. I'm your closest relative. I had to give my permission. They asked my opinion, so I told them."

She managed a generous smile this time. "Thank you for looking after me."

He reached over and smoothed back her hair. "I'm just so grateful you're going to be okay, babe. I was so worried. I had to keep turning my fears over to the Lord, but He was there for me all the way."

"He was with me, too." She loved the touch of Jeff's palm on her forehead. His closeness brought back a memory from the green valley of her dreams. "I was in this beautiful place. I kept walking, but I couldn't get to the other side. I wasn't afraid because I wasn't alone. Jesus was beside me, holding me up when I couldn't walk."

"That's a cool dream, Marnie."

"There was someone else with me, too, Jeff."

"Yeah? Who?"

"I think it was you. I couldn't see your face, but I knew it was you."

"Yeah, it was me." He walked his fingers through her hair, gently separating the strands. "I was sitting here by your bed day and night—until they kicked me out and told me to go home and get some sleep."

"How long have I been here?"

"Five days. You'd wake up long enough to complain a little then go back to sleep. The doctor said if you didn't come around pretty soon he was going to kick you out and give someone else your bed."

She eyed him suspiciously. "He didn't say that."

"Okay. He didn't. But he will be glad that you're really back with us—all bright-eyed and bushy-tailed, as my mom used to say."

She gave him a bemused smile. "I don't have a tail."

He grinned. "Okay, we'll skip that part. But your beautiful brown eyes are bright again. That's what counts." He turned and looked toward the closed door. "I'd better get the doctor. He'll want to talk to you. And your parents. They've been camping by your bed as much as I have."

"My mom and dad are here?"

"They sure are. In fact, half the students from U of N have been here at one time or another. And Pastor Maluhia and most of the people from church. You're a pretty popular girl."

"I'm afraid I wasn't much company."

"That's okay. You can make up for it. Just seeing your big smile will do it for most of us."

A thought occurred to her. "Jeff, I just remembered. You were going to Cambodia."

He nodded. "I was at the airport waiting to board the plane when I got news about your collapse. There was no way I was going to leave the country with you sick in the hospital."

She lowered her gaze. She was grateful, but she had no words to express it. Finally, she said, "Thanks for staying with me."

Jeff's eyes glistened. "There's nowhere I'd rather be, Marnie."

She pulled at several frayed threads on her blanket. "Now that I'm better, maybe you can still catch up with your mission team." It was the last thing she wanted, but she hoped she sounded convincing, for Jeff's sake.

"No way." He squared his shoulders and tightened his jaw. "I'm not leaving you again, no matter what you say or do. Even if you never remember our life together, you can't make me go."

"I can't?" Something akin to joy rose in her chest. "But you had your heart set on going overseas with the mission team."

He moved his fingers along her hairline to her earlobe. "The only thing I care about right now is helping you get well and back on your feet."

That was exactly what she wanted to hear. She clasped his hand against her cheek. "I want to go home, Jeff."

He gave her a puzzled look. "You mean to Michigan? You wanna go home with your parents?"

"No, not Michigan. I want to go home with *you*."

A light of comprehension swept across his face. "Are you serious? You mean, back to our apartment? You wanna go home—the two of us together?"

She nodded. "Is it too late?"

"It's never too late."

Relief washed over her. "Jeff, that night when you said you were going away forever, I felt so miserable." The words tumbled out, her voice raspy and weak but full of urgency. "I wanted to run after you and beg you to stay. But I was too stubborn and proud. Do you hate me for sending you away?"

"Of course I don't hate you." He was laughing now, his eyes crinkling with merriment. "How could I ever hate you, silly girl?"

She touched his cheek, his chin. "Does this mean you still. . .love me?"

He gathered her into his arms and pressed her head against his chest. "I never stopped loving you, sweetheart. When I thought you were going to die, I realized just how much I love you."

"I love you, too, Jeff."

The words hung in the air for a full moment—dazzling and dancing and full of promise. He stared at her in astonishment. "Does this mean you remember our life together—our wedding, our marriage, the love we shared? Do you finally remember *me*, Marnie?"

She gazed up at him, mentally tracing the solid line of his forehead and jaw. "No, Jeff. I'm sorry. I still don't remember the man you were before the accident."

Disappointment glinted in his gentle blue eyes. "I was hoping—"

"Wait, I'm not finished." Her emotions were rising, catching her by surprise, leaving her breathless. "I know only the man you are right now—the man who stayed by my side even when I didn't know you were here. That's the man I love, Jeff. The man I'll always love."

Chapter 17

Mr. and Mrs. Daniel Rockwell
And Mr. and Mrs. Gerald Jordan
Cordially invite you to share their joy
As their children, Marnie and Jeffrey,
Renew their wedding vows
At five o'clock p.m.
On the third Saturday of August
At Kahaluu State Park
Kailua-Kona, Hawaii
Beach reception following ceremony
R.S.V.P.

A bright orange sun hovered over the crystal waters and salt-and-pepper sand of Kahaluu Beach as Marnie stepped from the pavilion in her *holoku*—a Hawaiian A-line satin gown with a ruffled train, hand-beaded with lace and sequins. Placing the *haku* orchid lei on Marnie's crimped curls, her mother smiled her approval. "You look breathtaking, honey."

"Thanks, Mom. At least my wedding dress still fits."

Her mother clasped her hand. "Are you nervous?"

"Nervous? Look at her, Mrs. Rockwell." Jenny, in her ankle-length taffeta bridesmaid dress, adjusted a white orchid in Marnie's bouquet and handed it to her. "She's absolutely radiant."

"Actually, I am a little nervous," Marnie admitted. "Are you sure I've done this before?" She glanced across the beach at the white, orchid-draped canopy under which dozens of her family and friends sat in plastic chairs waiting for the ceremony to begin. By a jagged outcropping of lava rocks, Jeff and his groomsmen stood talking with Pastor Maluhia. Several ladies from the church, dressed in festive, floral-print silk and organza dresses, were placing glass bowls with orchid blossoms on the buffet tables in the thatched-roof serving area. Musicians were already strumming their guitars and ukuleles in the shade of banyan and plumeria trees and rainbow eucalyptus. In the distance, coconut palms were silhouetted against a vibrant rainbow sky. "I can't remember, Mom. Was I nervous the first time I married Jeff?"

"As nervous as any new bride," said her mother.

"I'm a new bride *now*," said Marnie. "I have no memory of being with Jeff as his wife, so it's as if I'm marrying him for the first time."

Her mother straightened Marnie's train, fanning it out behind her on the loose-packed sand. "I admire Jeff for being willing to wait for you and staying in campus housing until your wedding today."

Jenny, looking as perky as her nickname, smiled at Marnie. "Nate says Jeff's chomping at the bit to carry you across the threshold of your little rose-covered cottage. You have one eager groom there."

Marnie felt her cheeks grow warm. Was she blushing, or was it just Hawaii's tropical heat bringing perspiration to her forehead? It wouldn't be proper to confess that she was nearly as eager as Jeff to start their honeymoon.

Her mother blotted Marnie's face with her lacy handkerchief. "We don't want your makeup to run in this heat."

"It is warm today," said Jenny, "but the air will turn cool once the sun has set."

"Is everything ready?" asked Marnie. "I feel like we're forgetting something."

"Everyone's here," her mother assured her. "All the guests are seated. The musicians are playing. I just checked, and the ladies from your church have done a beautiful job with the buffet. It's an authentic Hawaiian feast—lomi lomi salmon, Kalua pork, fresh pineapple, passion fruit, chicken crepes, mango quiche, rice pilaf." She paused. "Let's see, I've forgotten something. Oh yes. Shrimp dumplings and coconut chutney. Sure different from the wedding dinners in Michigan."

Marnie shook her head. "I can't even think about food right now, Mom."

Leaning close, her mother said, "Take my word for it, sweetheart. After the wedding, your nervousness will vanish and you'll be starved." Confidentially, she added, "Your father has already sampled the jumbo shrimp and teriyaki beef skewers. He says they're out of this world."

"I'll keep that in mind," said Marnie drily.

Jenny pointed at the horizon. "Look, everyone. The sky is already glorious with color. It's going to be a beautiful evening."

"Indeed it is!" Marnie's father came striding toward them looking debonair in his white dinner jacket. "Have you noticed, Barbara? The sky looks like some painter got carried away with his palette."

Marnie chuckled. "Speaking of wild colors, Daddy, you've got a red streak on your chin."

His hand flew to his face. "Uh-oh. Must be the red sauce from the shrimp."

Marnie took her mother's hanky and wiped off the smear. "You stay away from the buffet table, Daddy, until after the wedding."

His brows furrowed. "I just wanted to make sure everything was up to snuff."

"And was it?" Marnie asked with a bemused smile.

"Sure enough. Best wedding buffet I ever saw—or tasted." He turned to

Marnie's mother. "But I was talking about this Hawaiian sky. Look at it. I never saw so many colors. I bet you've been so busy you haven't even noticed."

"How could I not notice, Dan?" said her mother, finding a spot of sauce Marnie had missed and dabbing at it with her hanky. "The closest thing we have in Michigan is the northern lights."

Her father waved his wife away. "Leave me alone, Barb. My chin is perfectly clean, thank you."

"No more samples," she warned. "You might spill something on Marnie's gown."

"Look at your mother, Marnie. She's not happy unless she has something to worry about." He tucked her arm in his. "Well, sweet daughter, are you ready to walk down the aisle to your groom?"

"Yes, Daddy." She leaned over and kissed his cheek. "I'm just glad I can hold on to you when my ankles wobble."

"Mine are wobbling, too, on this uneven sand," he confided as they joined the rest of the wedding party at the back of the festive, open-air tent. At the front, Jeff and his groomsmen stood with the pastor beside an orchid-draped arch.

This is it, Marnie acknowledged silently. *A wedding day I'll always remember. After all these months, I'll finally feel like Jeff's wife.*

A woman in a flowing organza dress stepped forward and blew on a conch shell in four directions; the deep, haunting sound echoed on the gentle ocean breeze. As the musicians' tempo picked up with a contemporary love song, Marnie's father escorted her to the front and placed her hand in Jeff's. He looked more handsome than she had ever seen him in his white, long-sleeved aloha shirt and white linen trousers.

Pastor Maluhia stepped forward and asked them to face each other for the exchange of leis. Holding up his right hand, he declared, "*Ei-Ah Eha-No. Ka Malohia Oh Na Lani. Mea A-Ku A-Pau. . . .* May blessings from above rest upon you and remain with you now and forever."

He held up two orchid leis. "Like the rings you exchange, leis are a circle representing an eternal commitment and undying devotion to each other." He handed them each a lei. Jeff placed his around Marnie's neck and kissed her on the cheek. Marnie placed her lei around Jeff's neck and kissed him, too.

"Jeffrey and Marnie, you are renewing your vows surrounded by God's beauty," said Pastor Maluhia, "the beauty of the land, of the ocean, and of the mountains. You are surrounded also by your *ohana*—your circle of family and friends. May the act of giving and receiving leis represent the continual blossoming of your relationship."

As a caressing breeze stirred around them, the pastor opened his large, worn Bible and read 1 Corinthians 13. Then he set the Bible aside. "My dear friends, Jeff and Marnie have learned the truth of this beautiful love chapter. They have overcome more trials in their brief marriage than most couples face in fifty years. Theirs is a beautiful love story. God has blessed them with a love that has survived incredible odds. Jeffrey has won the woman of his dreams not just once, but twice in a lifetime." He turned to Jeff. "Now we will have the exchange of vows. Jeffrey, please share your heart with Marnie."

Marnie gave her bouquet to Jenny. Jeff clasped her slim hands between his sturdy palms. His strong, sculpted face was dotted with perspiration. His blue eyes reflected the crystal blue of the sea and sky. A tendon along his jaw moved up and down as he said her name. "Marnie, I fell in love with you the first time I saw you on campus at U of N. My love for you deepened when we became friends during our trip to Cambodia. When you married me last summer, I was the happiest man on earth."

He paused and inhaled deeply. "But it wasn't until after our car accident last January that I learned what true love is all about. When I thought you were going to die, I would have given my life for you. When I realized you had no memory of me or our marriage, I was devastated. But I knew you were worth waiting for. I knew, for better or worse, God had brought us together and would work all things out according to His will.

"It was your mom who helped me realize I should concentrate on the future, not the past. Your mom encouraged me to court you as if we had just met. And I am so thankful to God that He helped you come to love me again. I was a pretty clueless, naive guy when we married the first time. But this time, with God's help, I'm ready to be the husband you need for the rest of our lives, no matter what." He smiled, his blue eyes warming her heart and yet sending a little chill up her spine. "I love you, Marnie."

"I love you, too," she whispered back. Now it was her turn. Her hands trembled slightly in Jeff's warm palms. She let herself be drawn into the depths of his adoring eyes. "Jeff, you are an awesome, godly man. When I was sick and unlovable and pushing you away, you held on to me and wouldn't let me go. You were a kind and gentle stranger drawing me back to God and back to you. You showed me unconditional, Christlike love. You helped me reclaim my faith and begin discovering the person I was before the accident. It's no wonder I fell in love with you the first time. I'm sorry I don't remember the man you were then. But I know the man you are now. And I have fallen in love with you all over again. I take you as my husband, my partner, my lover, and my best friend to love and cherish forever."

With a tear rolling down his cheek, Jeff whispered, "Thank you, babe."

Pastor Maluhia held up his hand in a gesture of benediction. "Dear friends, let us pray." After offering a brief prayer of commitment, he gave a hearty "Amen" and announced, "Jeffrey and Marnie Jordan, by the authority entrusted to me by the State of Hawaii, I now reconfirm that you are husband and wife. Jeff, you may kiss your bride."

He swept Marnie into his arms and kissed her soundly. She returned the kiss. It was sweet and tender and full of promise. For the first time in a long while, she knew she was exactly where she was meant to be. She was with the man she loved. She was home.

Epilogue

Two years later. . .

Marnie and Jeffrey Jordan
invite you to share their joy
as they welcome their son
Daniel Gerald Jordan
into their family

Born: June 25 at 3:06 p.m.

Weight: 7 pounds 14 ounces

Length: 21 inches

Who Daniel looks like:
He has his dad's blue eyes
and his mom's reddish brown hair

Where Daniel will reside:
With his parents in
their happy little cottage on the Sangker River
in Battambang, Cambodia

Rejoice with us for all of God's awesome blessings!

SWEET JOY OF MY LIFE

Dedication

To my beautiful daughter, Kimberle Page Bunch. You are a light and a joy in our lives. And my thanks to your handsome husband, Jay, for letting me borrow his name for the hero of this book.

Chapter 1

A child moves through the shadows—a young girl with long, straight ebony hair and wide umber-brown eyes. Her lacy white nightgown swishes around her bare feet as she walks. In her hands she carries a candle, its capricious flame licking at the darkness with an orange undulating glow. "Mama," she calls out in a small, frightened voice, but no one answers. Her hands tremble, making the flames dance with a frantic intensity. To keep the candle steady she holds her breath and presses her arms close to her sides. "Mama," she whispers again.

From somewhere in the gloom she hears a scream. She runs, mindless of the candle, her eyes searching the dark. She can't tell whether the scream is her own or someone else's—her mother's, perhaps? The sound is horrific, ear-splitting. It shatters the silence. The bloodcurdling shriek mingles with a crackling, popping noise that assaults her from every direction. She watches, paralyzed, as the warm airless night explodes in monstrous, clamoring fingers of fire—a deadly, dragon-breathed, earth-scorching conflagration that threatens to snuff out her very breath.

Kayli woke with a start, her heart racing, her fingers gripping the leather armrests.

"Honey, you fell asleep. Are you okay?"

Looking over at Aunt Jessie in the window seat beside her, Kayli Akimo expelled a sigh of relief. There was no fire. They were on an airplane, safe, secure, winging their way to Hawaii. "Yes, I'm okay," she murmured, putting her head back and closing her eyes. She was no longer that terrified little girl caught in a fiery holocaust crying for her mother; she was a rational, competent, twenty-two-year-old woman with a bright future ahead of her. There was nothing to worry about, nothing to fear.

"Was it that dream again?" her aunt asked quietly.

Aunt Jessie was a kind, sturdy, insightful woman who possessed the shrewd wisdom and resourcefulness of her Asian ancestors. She never missed a thing, especially when it came to Kayli, the niece she had raised single-handedly.

Kayli was the first to admit it hadn't been easy for her aunt—a single woman with health problems raising a five-year-old girl after Kayli's parents died in the fire. But Aunt Jessie had never complained. She was the only mother Kayli remembered.

"Yes, it was the dream again," Kayli conceded. "Or should I say the nightmare." She had no conscious memory of the fire that claimed her parents' lives—only the dreams that disrupted her sleep and haunted her waking hours.

Sometimes she went for months without dreaming of the fire, but whenever the nightmares struck again, they left her feeling shaken.

Aunt Jessie clasped her hand. "How long since the last dream, dear?"

"Six months," said Kayli. "I thought maybe they were gone for good."

"It's all the stress from packing up your life and moving away from the mainland. Your whole life is changing—all because of me. Maybe I'm asking too much of you."

Kayli looked squarely at her aunt. Jessica Akimo was a handsome woman—not pretty—but striking with her short black hair and smooth, olive skin. She had an infectious smile, dark almond-shaped eyes that danced with merriment, and the whitest teeth Kayli had ever seen. "How can you say that, Aunt Jessie, after all you've done for me? Besides, you didn't ask me to move to Hawaii with you. It was my idea."

"But you wouldn't be going if you weren't trying to help me fulfill my dream."

"What about all the dreams and goals you helped me reach? Without your support I wouldn't have gotten my degree in art. I'd still be struggling to earn money for college—probably selling my paintings on street corners for pennies instead of traveling to a new job at a prestigious art gallery in Honolulu."

Her aunt smiled knowingly. "You always manage to put the best spin on things. The truth is, you gave up a very pleasant life in California to help me build my dream house on the ocean and recapture my Hawaiian roots."

"Remember, they're my roots, too, Aunt Jessie. Don't you think I'd like to see where my father was born and raised?"

"I suppose so. Of course, he left for California when he was eighteen and never came back to the islands. If, like your dad, you find Hawaii isn't to your liking, I will insist that you go back and reclaim your life in California."

Kayli chuckled. "I'm not leaving that much behind, Aunt Jessie."

"What about your church? You were so devoted to it."

"There are churches in Hawaii."

"And your friends," her aunt persisted, "won't you miss them?"

"Yes, I'll miss my friends. But I'll make new ones. I wasn't really that close to anyone anyway."

Her aunt leaned her head close to Kayli's. "That's the first time I've heard you admit it."

Kayli managed a bemused chuckle. "Admit what, Aunt Jessie? That I've never had really close friends? I haven't needed them. I've always had you."

Her aunt cleared her throat dismissively. "That's a sorry state of affairs for a vibrant young woman like you—hanging out with me when you could be out socializing and having fun."

Kayli rolled her eyes. "Aunt Jessie, you know I'm not the life-of-the-party type. I'm happy being home, working on a painting, trying out a new recipe, or playing Chinese checkers with you."

"That's the most ridiculous thing I've ever heard of. You have a hundred other things you could be doing."

"Like what?"

"Like dating."

"I date."

"When?"

"I don't know. Lots of times."

"You've never brought a nice young man to the house."

Kayli stifled a twinge of defensiveness. "That doesn't mean I haven't had a boyfriend, Aunt Jessie."

"Then you have had a boyfriend?"

"Not a boyfriend exactly. But I've dated lots of guys at school." They had had this conversation before. Why did her aunt have to get into this sticky topic just as they were about to start their new adventure in Hawaii?

"You dated at school? What kind of date?"

"I went out with various guys for coffee or to see a campus play. Sometimes we studied together at the library."

Her aunt folded her arms and lifted her chin. "In my book that's not a date. For a date you get dressed up and go to a fancy restaurant, and he opens the door for you and makes you feel like a princess."

Kayli laughed a little too loudly. She glanced around but no one had noticed. "We don't date like that anymore, Aunt Jessie. We don't even call it dating. We just—hang out."

"Hang out? What kind of nonsense is that? In my day when we went on a date, we knew we were on a date. And it was lovely."

"I'm sure it was, Aunt Jessie. But we do things differently now."

"Different doesn't make it better. Sometimes the old ways are—"

In the midst of her aunt's rebuttal, a woman's voice came over the intercom and announced, "Ladies and gentlemen, we'll be landing in Honolulu in ten minutes. Please fasten your seat belts, stow your tray tables, and return your seats to their upright position. Thank you for flying with us today."

Kayli fastened her seat belt and glanced over to make sure her aunt's was fastened, too. As much as Aunt Jessie still mothered her, Kayli felt equally protective of her aunt. They didn't always see eye to eye, but they had always been there for each other. That would never change.

Aunt Jessie always had an answer for everything. And she was usually right. But not about dating. That was the last thing on Kayli's mind. Establishing a whole new life and career in Hawaii would take all of her time and energy. There would be no time left for some clueless, surfboarding suitor.

Aunt Jessie patted Kayli's hand. "Hawaii will be different; you wait and see."

"Different? How?"

"The young men you've *dated*," Jessie said pointedly, "were too caught up in their educations or careers. But Hawaii is the land of romance and enchantment—one of the most beautiful spots on earth. It's the perfect place to fall in love."

"Then I hope you fall in love with an awesome man, Aunt Jessie."

"That's not what I meant."

"But it's what I meant," said Kayli with a patient smile. She gazed out the window as their plane touched down, bumped jarringly on the tarmac, and finally taxied to a stop on the expansive runway. In the distance she saw palm trees and tropical greenery. Her excitement was growing. A sense of anticipation made her heart flutter. A beautiful new world lay at her fingertips—a lush, exotic land in the middle of the crystal-clear Pacific Ocean. No matter what her aunt said about finding romance, Kayli wasn't about to let a silly infatuation over some man muddy the waters of this pristine paradise.

Chapter 2

Jayden Mahala gathered up the specs for the Kimura project and strode down the hall to his father's plush office. The gold-lettered sign on the ornately carved door read LEOLANI MAHALA, PRESIDENT. It might as well have read LEOLANI MAHALA'S KINGDOM. His father ruled with an iron fist and would have done quite well as a fifteenth-century potentate over his own little empire.

Actually, he did have his own empire. It was named Mahala, Mahala, and Associates. Jay was the second—and nearly invisible—Mahala. For twenty years his father had been one of Honolulu's most esteemed builders of custom oceanfront homes. Five years ago, fresh out of college, Jay had joined the firm as chief architect. He had hoped for a platform to display his own unique vision for creating twenty-first-century homes that were environmentally sound and reflected the best of nature. But he and his father were often at loggerheads over what constituted an optimum design.

It wouldn't be so bad if his father limited his penchant for control to the boardroom, but it carried over to their personal lives, as well. His father couldn't understand why Jay preferred a modest cottage overlooking the sea to living in his father's sprawling mansion. That was the difference between them—Jay loved things that were simple, solid, and down to earth; his father loved things that were lavish, impressive, and expensive. So far they had managed to balance each other out, but one of these days that could all change.

Jay knocked lightly on the office door then turned the knob and looked in. "Dad, you busy?"

His father rolled his chair back from his massive mahogany desk. "Come in, son. I was expecting you."

Jay always felt a trifle intimidated when he entered his father's sumptuous office. The teak walls boasted dozens of architectural awards along with photos of magnificent homes his father had built throughout the islands. Gleaming trophies lined the shelves—silent reminders that Jay would never be as flashy and successful as his dad.

He handed his father the specs. "Here are the drawings for the Kimura project. Do you want to go over them now?"

His father set the drawings on his desk. "No, JJ, they'll wait."

Since Jay was a small boy, his father had called him that. *JJ*. It sounded like the name you would call a child or even a favorite pet. *Here, JJ, come, JJ*. Jay had long since outgrown the name, but try telling that to his father. In fact, he had tried. *Come on, Dad, just call me Jay. I'm not a kid anymore.* His father's reply had been, *Jayden Joseph Mahala is a fine name, but a mouthful. As far as I'm concerned, JJ says it just fine.*

Jay took a step backward. "Well, if there's nothing else, Dad—"

"Wait, son." His father came around and leaned against the front of his desk. He was a charming, gregarious man with a high forehead and a shock of thick black hair that never knew quite where to settle. Even though his jowls and waistline had thickened over time, he looked younger than his fifty-five years.

Jay had inherited his English mother's green eyes, softer classic features, and genteel nature. But sometimes he would have preferred his father's distinctive Hawaiian nose, piercing black eyes, and intractable nature. Sometimes people described his father as overbearing because that was the side he showed the world. But three years ago, when Jay's mother lay dying of cancer, he had glimpsed his father's vulnerable side. He tried to remember that side now when all he sensed was his father's imperviousness. "Tell me, JJ, how was the banquet last night?"

"Fine. A little long, but those architectural events always are. You should have gone. Everyone asked about you."

"I would have been there but my client meeting ran late. Did you go with Liana?"

"Yes. You said you wanted her to go."

"She's our office manager. She loves those glitzy affairs. Did she have a good time?"

"I guess so. Why not ask her?"

"I'm asking *you*, son. Did you take her somewhere nice afterward?"

"I took her home, Dad. It was late and we both had to work today."

His father's brows furrowed with disappointment. "I thought maybe. . ."

"You thought what, Dad? That I would take her out and realize we were made for each other?"

"I'm not saying that, JJ."

"But it's what you're thinking. You want me to find some nice, homespun girl and get married and give you a dozen grandkids."

His father ambled back to his chair and sat down. "You make getting married sound like a death sentence. The thirty years I was married to your mother were the happiest of my life. Not a day goes by that I don't wish she were still alive."

With a little sigh of defeat, Jay sat down in the nearest leather chair. He wasn't going to win this round. "I know, Dad. I miss Mom, too. But that doesn't mean I'm ready to tie the knot with someone just to give you an instant family." He realized as soon as he said it that the words had come out wrong. He could see a flash of pain in his father's eyes. "I'm sorry, Dad. I didn't mean it like that. It's just that I don't need someone to play matchmaker for me. I'm not ready for a wife."

His father didn't appear to hear him or simply wasn't listening. "Liana's a very nice young lady, JJ. Any man would be fortunate to be her husband. She comes from a big family. She'll want lots of children someday."

"But it won't be with me, Dad." Jay stood up. "If there's nothing else, I'd better get back to work."

"Hold on, son." His father stood up again. "There is something else. I have a luncheon appointment with a new client. I'd like you to come along. I want your feedback."

Jay hesitated. Was this another of his father's pointless matchmaking schemes? "Okay, Dad. If it's purely business, I'll go. Who's the client?"

"Jessica Akimo. She and her niece moved here from California a few weeks ago and may hire us to build their dream house overlooking the ocean. I've talked with her on the phone several times this past week, and I think you may be the perfect architect for this project."

"Don't tell me. She's single."

"Yes, but I get the impression she's middle-aged. Not a likely marital candidate for you, JJ."

"What about the niece? Are you playing cupid again, Dad?"

His father crossed his arms on his chest. "For crying out loud, I've never even seen the woman. Please don't read ulterior motives into everything I say or do."

Jay's shoulders relaxed. "I'm sorry, Dad. I don't mean to sound defensive. I'd love to meet with them. If they choose our firm, I'll do my best to come up with a design for a home that captures their dreams."

"That's my boy! We're meeting them at the Aloha Tower Marketplace at noon."

Jay took out his PalmPilot and punched in the appointment. His father always took new clients out to lunch before meeting them in the office. He always said he got a better idea what clients wanted in a relaxed, social atmosphere. Jay suspected his father had long ago discovered it was easier turning strangers into friends over a pleasant table brimming with mouthwatering food.

Jay and his father arrived at Chai's Island Bistro in the Aloha Tower Marketplace shortly before noon. The popular restaurant fronted the Promenade Boat Days Bazaar on Aloha Tower Drive. Its Asian-themed decor, exotic greenery, and white linen-draped tables created an elegant, understated ambiance.

"I'll see if the ladies are here yet, son."

While his father checked with the hostess, Jay scanned the crowd. The restaurant was a busy place at lunchtime. He noticed several people who could have fit the description of a middle-aged aunt and her niece, but they all moved on.

Then, as he was about to rejoin his father, he noticed two women enter. The younger one was striking—slender and graceful as a swan, with flowing, shiny black hair, a long neck, and the heart-shaped face of an angel. She had high cheekbones, full pink lips, translucent skin with a coppery glow, and huge, luminous brown eyes framed by thick black lashes.

Jay didn't realize that he was staring at the woman until she met his gaze and registered a flicker of curiosity before looking away. For a moment he felt flustered, breathless. Just as he was scouring his mind for a proper way to introduce himself, she spoke with the hostess then turned with a smile to his father. He greeted the two women and escorted them over to Jay.

"JJ, I'd like you to meet Miss Jessica Akimo and her niece, Kayli Akimo. Ladies, this is my son, Jayden Joseph Mahala. He's also our firm's chief architect."

The younger woman offered Jay her slim hand. "How do you do, Mr. Mahala?"

"Please call me Jay," he said as he clasped her hand between his palms. Her skin felt as soft and smooth as the downy feathers on a dove. To his chagrin, he realized he'd held her hand a moment too long when she gently withdrew it.

When the older woman held out her hand, Jay shook it politely, but he was still reeling from the presence of the dark-eyed beauty named Kayli.

As the hostess showed them to their table, he chided himself for his clumsy schoolboy reaction. Usually women didn't affect him this way. He had to remember that this was a professional meeting, nothing more, and he must maintain an attitude of dignity and detachment. But when he gazed at the younger Miss Akimo across the table, his resolve faded. He wanted to know more about this exquisite woman who had so quickly captivated his mind and tantalized his senses.

"So how are you enjoying Hawaii?" he inquired. It was the most dim-witted of questions. What he really wanted to ask was, *Who are you, and how have you so swiftly stolen my heart?*

"Oh, I absolutely love Hawaii." Her voice was light and lyrical. Her smile danced all the way to her eyes and brought roses to her cheeks. "My aunt and I have been doing all the usual touristy things. We've taken the trolley to Chinatown and the historical district. We've gone to Waikiki Beach and the North Shore. We tried to find Aunt Jessie's birthplace near the pineapple factory, but unfortunately the neighborhood has been replaced with a hotel."

"I couldn't find a single relative still alive," said her aunt. "It was disappointing. But I haven't let it keep me from having a ball getting reacquainted with my beautiful homeland."

"In the three weeks we've been here," said Kayli, "we even managed to visit Punchbowl Crater and the Pearl Harbor Memorial."

Jessica Akimo joined in. "It was a sobering experience to see the USS *Missouri* and *Arizona* memorials. They even gave us tickets with pictures of the men who had died. It was heart-wrenching to actually look into their faces. It's one thing to read about history; quite another to step into the past and catch a glimpse of it."

"Yes, I've stood at that memorial gazing down into the water at the oil still seeping up from that battered ship," said his father in his usual booming, authoritative tone. "It's an experience you never forget. It reminded me that we must learn from the past if we are going to be prepared for the future."

Jay wasn't sure what his father was trying to say, but Jessica Akimo seemed impressed.

"Yes, Mr. Mahala, I've always felt that way myself."

"Call me Leo, please. Everybody does."

"I will. But I must say *Leolani* is a beautiful Hawaiian name."

Jay noted that Jessica Akimo, in her own way, was as striking as her niece—not a beautiful woman by any means, but noticeable, with short, jet-black hair and snapping black eyes that seemed both tender and shrewd. When she laughed her entire face lit up. Her wide red lips framed sparkling white teeth. She was a large-boned woman who took up just enough room that you couldn't miss her presence. But she was so well proportioned that she didn't appear overweight.

His father seemed quite taken with her; or did he just recognize a wealthy client when he saw one?

Immediately guilt nudged Jay. Why was he always so cynical when it came to his father? Leo Mahala was a good man, an honest man, shrewd and uncompromising, even if his stubbornness made him seem ruthless at times.

As the waiter took their orders, his father suggested the lobster tortellini and Thai chicken curry. The older Miss Akimo agreed, but her niece preferred the papaya salad and vegetarian stir-fry. Jay decided on the grilled Atlantic king salmon.

As they ate, the conversation flowed naturally. The four of them might have been longtime friends, the way they moved easily and pleasantly from one topic to another. All the while Jay couldn't keep his eyes off the graceful, demure Kayli Akimo. "So I assume you've found a comfortable place to stay until your new home is built?" he inquired.

Kayli's smile seemed meant just for him. "Oh yes, a lovely furnished apartment. It's called Waikiki Park Heights—on the eastern end of Kuhio Avenue."

"You must have a beautiful view of the ocean," he noted.

"We do. We have two lanais overlooking Waikiki Beach. We've sat out on our little verandas with our lemonades and watched surfers, sailboats, and passing ships."

Jessica spoke up. "What I like best is that our apartment is within walking distance of nearly everything—restaurants, shops, museums. . . And if we don't feel like walking, we can always call a taxi."

Kayli nodded. "When I get better acquainted with Honolulu, I'll get a car. But for now. . ."

"Oh, and the most interesting thing," said Jessica, "our apartment building was originally a Japanese hotel. It has a Japanese soaking tub. I'd never seen one before."

"That's called a *furo*," said Jay's father with a little sparkle in his eyes.

Jessica returned his smile. "You're a very learned man, Mr. Mahala. I mean, Leo."

"What I know best, Miss Akimo, is houses." He touched his linen napkin to his lips. "I've been in this business for over twenty years, and I'm convinced—if you'll let us—our company can build you the house of your dreams."

"I'm eager to hear more," said Jessica. "Do you agree, Kayli?"

Jay noticed that Kayli's gaze darted fleetingly in his direction as she murmured, "Yes, Aunt Jessie, I want to hear more, too."

"Excellent!" said his father. "We'll chat some more today and get some idea of what you're looking for. Then we'll set up an appointment to meet in our office later in the week. We'll show you some preliminary drawings and bat around some ideas until we've nailed down exactly what you want."

Jessica nodded. "I contacted you because I want someone who can do the whole job—from designing the house to building it—and because your firm has an excellent reputation."

"We do the whole project in-house," said Leo proudly. "We have our own designers, architects, and construction crew. And, as I mentioned when we spoke last week, we work closely with realtors who will be able to find you the perfect lot on which to build."

"I want lots of windows to let in sunlight." Jessica's excitement was growing. "I want my house to have a style that's both Asian and Hawaiian—clean and simple lines with a feeling of openness and light."

"We can do that."

"I'm not a fussy woman, Leo. Or maybe I am, depending on who you ask. But one thing is not negotiable. My house must be on the ocean." She stifled a smile. "Not *on* the ocean. I'm certainly not looking for a houseboat."

"We understand. You want oceanfront property," said Jay. "I'm sure we can find a location that will please you."

"And it must have a breathtaking view. My niece is an accomplished artist, and I want her to be inspired to paint beautiful seascapes and landscapes."

Jay's eyes met Kayli's. "You're an artist, Miss Akimo?"

"Yes, and please call me Kayli."

"Yes," said his father. "Let's all be on a first-name basis. If we're going to build that dream house of yours, we'll be spending a lot of time together in the months to come."

"I imagine you'll want an art studio in your home," said Jay, "especially if you'll be spending all your days at home painting." He liked the idea that she was an artist.

Kayli flushed slightly. "I'm afraid I won't have the luxury of spending all my days painting. I have a job with an art gallery here in Honolulu. I'll be around paintings every day, but they won't be my own. Perhaps someday. But I admit I've always dreamed of having my own studio."

"Then you shall have one." Jay glanced over at Jessica to make sure he hadn't spoken out of turn. "I trust that fits in with your plans, as well."

Jessica beamed. "Oh yes! I plan to cover the walls of my new house with Kayli's paintings. Make her a magnificent studio."

"We're making mental notes even as we speak," said his father.

Jay heard himself saying, "I'd like to see some of your work sometime, Miss Akimo—um, I mean, Kayli."

"I'd be glad to, Jay. Unfortunately, my work is being shipped from California with our furniture and hasn't arrived yet. Then it'll all go into storage until our house is built."

"Well, let me know when it's available to view, and we'll arrange a date."

She gave him a quizzical glance. Had he used the wrong word? Was she wondering if he was asking for a date? He decided it would be more awkward to try to clarify what he meant. Then again, the idea of a date with her was becoming increasingly tantalizing. She was not only gracious and beautiful but apparently a talented artist, as well.

Jay himself had always had a bent for drawing and painting, although he had finally decided that architecture was more financially secure than trying to peddle his paintings to strangers. Selling one's artwork always seemed to him like trying to sell off one's children, for each painting took with it a piece of his soul. Jay was not the type to relinquish his soul, or even bits of it, to anyone.

But gazing now at the beautiful Kayli Akimo, he realized he had already lost a bit of his soul to her.

Chapter 3

Kayli set her book aside and stretched languorously on the padded lounge chair, welcoming the summer sun's balmy rays. Of anything she loved about this little apartment, the best was having two lanais. She and Aunt Jessie often ate their dinner on the one off the living room. But Kayli had adopted the second lanai for herself. It adjoined the third bedroom, which she had turned into a little art studio. Whenever she wanted a break from painting, she simply stepped out onto her lanai and breathed in the fresh ocean air. It was her private oasis—her favorite spot for morning devotions and quiet evening reflections.

To her relief Aunt Jessie—a chatty, fun-loving extrovert at heart—had always respected her niece's need for privacy and time alone. She rarely bothered Kayli when she was on her lanai. While Aunt Jessie was always up and running at the crack of dawn, she recognized that, in the mornings, Kayli needed silence and peace to replenish her spirits. Over all these years they had developed a comfortable rhythm and harmony living together.

A shuffling noise broke Kayli's reverie. Looking around, she gazed up at Aunt Jessie standing in the doorway wearing her most flattering business suit. "Dear, I hate to interrupt you."

"What is it, Aunt Jessie?"

"We have our appointment with Mr. Mahala in half an hour. Are you ready to go?"

Kayli glanced down at her apricot sundress and flip-flops. "I'm ready. But what's the rush? It's only a ten-minute taxi ride."

Her aunt lingered in the doorway. "Don't you want to do something special with your hair? It would look lovely in a chignon with an orchid tucked in it."

"You know I like my hair long and straight. We're going to a business meeting, not some formal affair."

Her aunt came out and sat down beside her. She twisted her pearl necklace for several moments before speaking. "What do you think of Mr. Mahala?"

Kayli shrugged. "He's very distinguished. He comes on a bit strong, but I think he knows his business."

"No, I'm not talking about Leo Mahala. I meant his son."

"His son? He seems okay. I like him."

Her aunt brightened. "I knew it. I sensed the spark between you two."

"Spark? Please, Aunt Jessie, I don't even know him."

"But you'll see him again today. I could tell he liked you. At the restaurant he couldn't take his eyes off you."

Kayli picked up her book and opened it where she had left off. She was determined not to have this conversation with her matchmaking aunt again. "I'm reading about the Hawaiian alphabet," she said pointedly. "Did you know it has only twelve letters—five vowels and seven consonants?"

"Honey, are you listening to me? I did some research online and found out Leo Mahala is a widower and his son has never been married. Think of it! He's an eligible bachelor and such a charming, handsome man."

Gritting her teeth, Kayli kept her gaze focused on her book. "The seven consonants are *h*, *k*, *l*, *m*, *n*, *p*, and *w*. It says the Hawaiian language was an oral tradition until it was written down by missionaries in the nineteenth century."

"I know all that, dear. Your grandparents spoke Hawaiian. I still remember enough of it to get by."

"Really?" She gave her aunt a scrutinizing glance. "I didn't know you knew Hawaiian."

"I've forgotten a lot, but I still remember some things. *Mai e `ai.* 'Come and eat.' My mama always said that in her loudest voice at mealtimes."

"I'm impressed. What else?"

"*Mai poina, kaikamahine.* 'Don't forget, daughter.' My papa often said that when I neglected my chores. And my mama was always saying, *Pa`ahana no au, keiki.* 'I am busy, child.' "

Kayli smiled. "I love hearing you speak Hawaiian. It's such a beautiful language."

"*Mahalo.* 'Thank you.' Do you want to hear my favorite words? *Aloha Au Ia `Oe.* 'I love you.' "

"*Aloha Au*. . .um, you know what I mean." Kayli closed her book and stood up. "Maybe we should get going a few minutes early—in case the traffic's bad."

"A good idea. And I promise not to say another word about you and the young Mr. Mahala."

"And I won't say a word if I see you getting goo-goo-eyed over his father."

They both laughed.

With the traffic sparse, they arrived at the Mahala office with ten minutes to spare. After a short wait, a secretary showed them into Leo Mahala's spacious office. Both father and son were already seated at a large conference table poring over architectural drawings. As Kayli and Jessica entered, the two men got up and extended generous handshakes and ready smiles.

"It's good to see you ladies again," said Leo as he offered them chairs. "My son and I have been going over some house plans I think will interest you."

Jay Mahala urged Kayli to take the chair beside him. As she did, her cheeks warmed. This morning Aunt Jessie had said, *he couldn't take his eyes off you.* Was there any truth to that?

Kayli had to admit that the younger Mahala was a very attractive man. His hair and complexion were lighter than his father's. His mahogany-brown hair was short in back but long enough to curl over his forehead in a casual, disarming way. His skin had the healthy bronze tone of a surfer. His features were gentler than his father's and more precisely cut. And his eyes were an amazing shade of green, like the ocean at certain times of the day. When he smiled his eyes crinkled into little half-moons. In fact, his smile went straight to her toes, tickling her tummy like a carnival ride.

She silently chided herself. What was wrong with her—thinking like that about a practical stranger? Was she actually falling for her aunt's harebrained romantic fantasies? She quickly looked away. There was no way in the world she was going to give Mr. Jay Mahala a second thought. If Aunt Jessie guessed Kayli had the slightest interest in him, she'd never hear the end of it.

Leo handed her a drawing and another one to her aunt. "If you ladies would like to take a few minutes to look over these drawings, I think you'll see we're on the right track for your dream house."

"These are stock drawings," said Jay. "From these we'll prepare the blueprints for your custom home. Let us know what you want and we'll see that you have it."

Jay handed her a thick photo album, as well. "These are some of the homes we've built. Feel free to check our references. We have many satisfied customers."

"Thank you," said Jessie. "That's reassuring."

Leo handed her a sheaf of papers. "Here are some preliminary ideas—a four-bedroom, three-bath split-level house with a wall of sliding glass pocket doors facing the ocean; a great room with a white ash coffered ceiling; a master bath with a traditional Japanese design combo furo and shower; and stainless steel appliances in a gourmet kitchen. Our plans include a wraparound covered lanai, a teak-lined dining room with crystal chandelier, decorative grillwork in the windows, and floor-to-ceiling rock fireplaces in the great room and master bedroom. And, of course, all of the building materials will be appropriate for Hawaii's climate."

"No fireplaces," said Aunt Jessie with an abruptness that startled them all.

Kayli's heart went to her throat. She knew what her aunt was going to say next.

"Are you sure?" said Jay. "Even though it's not common for Hawaiian homes to have fireplaces, they do make an impressive addition to a room, even if they're never used."

Aunt Jessie glanced over at Kayli, as if to say, *I'm sorry we have to get into this.*

Kayli spoke up. "What my aunt is trying to say is that I don't want any fireplaces in our home, whether they're ever used or not. And all the appliances must be electric, not gas."

"We'll be glad to accommodate you," said Leo. "No fireplaces, if that's what you want."

Kayli saw the bewilderment in their faces. She didn't want to explain, but she had no choice. "My parents died in a house fire." There! She had blurted it out, and now the two men stared back at her with even more questions in their eyes. "I was only five," she said miserably. "I survived, but I don't know how or why. Now fire petrifies me—even the flicker of a candle or a match or the cozy flames in a fireplace. They're not cozy to me. They're terrifying."

She hadn't intended to confess so much, but the words had just tumbled out unbidden. She felt mortified, humiliated.

Aunt Jessie reached over and patted her hand. "Tell us what else you have planned for our dream house, Leo. I'm eager to hear."

Jay spoke up, his voice a bit too bright, his gaze focused on Kayli. "We haven't forgotten your art studio, Kayli. It will have skylights and lots of windows to let in the sun. We can even build wall-to-wall shelves for your art supplies and racks to store your canvases."

Kayli flashed an appreciative smile. Jay was trying so hard to make her feel at ease. "You sound like you know exactly what an artist needs."

His eyes crinkled as he gave her a self-effacing smile. "I've dabbled in painting a few times, but I was never satisfied with my work. These days I express myself creatively by drawing beautiful homes for deserving clients such as yourself."

"Then it's our gain, isn't it?" said Aunt Jessie. "We'll look forward to seeing your creativity at work in our home."

Leo sat back and tented his fingers. "Whenever you wish we can get together with our real estate people and show you several sites along the ocean that offer excellent views."

"I'm ready now," said Jessie.

Jay handed her some official-looking papers. "Here's our contract. Take it home, read it over, and let us know if you have any questions. Once you've signed the contract and selected your lot, we'll prepare the blueprints and tailor the floor plan to fit the lot elevation and size."

"Thank you. We'll look these over," said Aunt Jessie. "Meanwhile, you start looking for that perfect oceanfront lot for us."

Chapter 4

"Tell me about my father."

Kayli and Aunt Jessie were having dinner on the lanai—baked salmon, steamed rice, and a fresh fruit salad. The sun hung in the west like a heavy, ripe cantaloupe over a cerulean ocean. A cool breeze stirred, easing the heat of the day.

"Your father had island fever. The islands became too small for him. He got stir-crazy. He wanted more. He wanted to stretch out without touching walls and hitting boundaries. He wanted a different way of life from your grandfather's."

"Is that what drove him to go to the mainland when he was eighteen?"

Jessie nodded. "He saw himself walking in our father's footsteps. He didn't want that. Your grandfather worked all his life in a pineapple cannery. His father before him worked on a plantation harvesting pineapples. He lived in a little tin-roofed bungalow and worked long hours in the fields. Those were the days when Hawaii supplied pineapples to most of the world. Then land became too precious and labor too expensive, so most of the canneries closed. To my knowledge only one or two remain, and they supply pineapples mainly for Hawaii."

"That's sad." Kayli sipped her iced tea. "That must have put a lot of people out of work."

"It did. Many of them went to work for the big hotels when the tourist industry took over."

"What about Daddy? I know he was creative. He built sets for the movie studios."

"Yes, he had a fascinating job. When he first arrived in California, he got odd jobs as a carpenter. After a few years he became a cabinetmaker. But he was so fascinated by the movies he went to work as a prop-maker. Those were the days before computer animation and reality shows. The studios even sent him out on location. He loved his work and he was good at it. In his own way he was an artist."

"Yes, I think so, too." Kayli helped herself to more fruit. "And then you followed my father to California a few years later."

"Yes. Your dad kept writing me about all the opportunities, so I moved there, too. That was several years before you were born. It was hard leaving my parents, but they encouraged me to go. I remember I was so homesick at first. But your mom and dad were wonderful to me. They had such good, pure hearts, and oh, how they loved the Lord. They let me stay with them while I earned my degree in accounting. They never asked for a thing in return. They just wanted me to be happy. And I was happy."

Kayli nodded. She had heard the story before, but she always loved hearing it again, especially the part about her parents being so wonderful. The only way she would ever know her mom and dad was through Aunt Jessie's stories.

"I got a great job and worked my way up to account executive for a big investment firm. You know the rest, honey. I invested in several Southern California properties that rose sky-high in value. Fortunately I sold them before the market took a downturn, and now I have a nice little nest egg for us to live on."

"That's *your* nest egg, Aunt Jessie. Now that I have a job, I'm going to pay my own way, starting with my share of our house payments. You've paid my way long enough."

Her aunt's eyes misted. "I don't think of it that way, Kayli. Even though I never bore children of my own, you've been my daughter since you were five years old. I can't imagine my life without you."

Kayli squeezed her aunt's hand. "I feel the same way. I love you, Aunt Jessie."

"I love you, too, child."

"Did you take your medicine?"

Her aunt held up her pill case. "Every last tablet."

"And your insulin?"

She laughed. "Yes, Dr. Akimo."

"How was your blood sugar today?"

"Close to normal."

"How close?"

"Close enough."

"I just want to make sure you stay healthy, Aunt Jessie."

"I know you do. I love you for that. But you worry too much."

"I know. I've always been a worrier. I guess it's just my nature."

"It's understandable—losing your parents so young."

Kayli gazed out at the darkening sky. "I guess that's it. Most people go around feeling insulated from bad things. They don't think anything could ever happen to them. I guess when you start your life off with a tragedy, your emotions don't have that protective covering. You've lost your innocence. You know bad things can happen because they've already happened to you."

"That's where the Lord comes in," said Jessie. "He holds us in the palm of His hand, and even when bad things happen, He's there for us, never letting go. Everything we have is just lent to us for a season, but He's there forever, loving us, comforting us, giving us hope."

Kayli's eyes were misting now. "I wish I had faith like yours, Aunt Jessie. You make it all sound so easy."

"Not easy at all, honey. It takes a lifetime of days to learn to trust like that, and I'm not there yet. But His mercies are new every morning."

Kayli looked at her watch. "Speaking of morning, I'm going to have to make an early night of it. I have to be at work at the crack of dawn tomorrow."

"Then it's time to clear the table." Her aunt stood up and started gathering the dishes. "How are things going at the gallery? You like it there, don't you?"

"I love it." Kayli got up and helped with the cleanup. "It's so much fun being surrounded by beautiful paintings and people who love art. We're having a reception for a local artist this weekend, and my boss put me in charge. I made and sent out the invitations, selected and hung the works that will be on display, and planned the reception. It's Saturday night. I hope you can come, Aunt Jessie."

"I plan to."

They carried the dishes into the kitchen and set them in the sink. "Kayli, I'll load the dishwasher. You go get your rest. Don't forget that we have an appointment to go looking at lots tomorrow afternoon."

"I remember. That's why I'm going to work early. I'll be home before two."

"Wonderful. That's when Mr. Mahala and the Realtor will be picking us up."

Kayli closed the sliding door to the lanai. "I'm surprised he's coming along. I can't imagine that he has time to go out with every client."

"I'm sure he doesn't. But he's taken a special interest in us. Or should I say your Mr. Jay Mahala has taken a special interest in *you*."

"He's not *my* Mr. Mahala."

"Not yet. But you just wait."

Kayli stifled a chuckle. "What am I going to do with you, Aunt Jessie? You're forever the matchmaker."

"And I won't stop until I see you with Mr. Right."

"Whoever that is."

"It's not important that we know who he is. The Lord knows."

"And the Lord knows I'm not looking for any man right now."

"That doesn't mean Mr. Right isn't looking for you."

Kayli kissed her aunt's cheek. "Maybe you should take your own advice and keep your eye on Mr. *Leo* Mahala. I have a feeling he's a bit smitten with you."

"Be still!" Aunt Jessie playfully swatted her with the dish towel. "I'm not going to get my hopes up at my age."

Kayli grabbed the towel and swished it under her aunt's chin. "Remember, Aunt Jessie, you're never too old to meet Mr. Right."

Jessie snatched back the towel. "Before either of us worries about Mr. Right, we have a house to build."

At seven the next morning Kayli took a taxi to the Queen Street Art Gallery. Usually she arrived a little before nine o'clock, when the gallery opened, but Tara Quan, the owner, had agreed she could come in early today. With a dozen tasks to complete before the artist reception on Saturday night, Kayli's head was spinning. *I'm not a morning person,* Kayli reflected dourly as she entered the quaint gallery sandwiched between a bank and a Chinese restaurant.

She found Tara—a petite, fortyish woman with bundles of energy and exotic good looks—already busy hanging paintings.

"I was going to do that today," Kayli told her boss as she tucked her purse under the reception desk. She gazed around the expansive two-story room at the variety of Hawaiian landscapes and seascapes—mostly oils or acrylics on canvas but also several stunning watercolors and at least a dozen silk-screened serigraphs.

"No problem," said Tara. "There's still plenty to do. Call the artist—Yasuko Tamashiro—and make sure he's coming in this afternoon. I want him to approve our placement of his work. And, for the life of me, I can't get his hanging sculpture to hang right."

Kayli glanced up at the Lucite mixed-media sculpture of birds in flight. The combination of hand-polished clear Lucite and smooth metal castings caught the exquisite grace and delight of soaring birds. But Tara was right. It was hanging too far to one side. The birds looked more like they were nosediving than soaring. "I'll work with it after I call Mr. Tamashiro."

The morning was over and it was lunchtime before Kayli had finished half her tasks. She ran next door to the Chinese restaurant, grabbed some takeout, and ate at her desk while she finished the brochure for the Saturday event.

With a bit of fear and trembling she placed it on Tara's desk for her approval. Tara picked it up, read it over, and handed it back. "Good job. Print a hundred."

Kayli returned to her desk and sat down with a relieved sigh. "Sweet!"

She spent the next hour on the phone with the caterer finalizing the menu for the reception. "No barbecued sausages. I ordered shrimp wontons and egg rolls. And a platter of fresh fruit—nothing too messy. Include papaya and kiwi. They'll add color. And make sure the strawberries are large and bright red."

Had she thought of everything? Probably not. But there was no time left to worry about it today. Right now she had to get home. It would be unseemly to keep Jay Mahala waiting when he was giving them his personal attention.

Kayli grabbed her purse, said good-bye to Tara, grabbed a taxi, and arrived home in time to brush her teeth, put on new lipstick, and slip into slacks and a sleeveless blouse. As she ran a brush through her hair, the doorbell rang. Aunt Jessie got the door and was already greeting Jay and a modish, middle-aged gentleman when Kayli entered the living room. It was exactly two o'clock.

Jay introduced Mr. Yuriko Matsumoto, the real estate specialist, and suggested they sit down at the table to discuss the lots they would be seeing. Aunt Jessie offered them steaming cups of herbal tea, which they graciously accepted. They all sat down around the glass-top table as Mr. Matsumoto opened his portfolio. He handed them several pamphlets with photos and lot descriptions.

"Mr. Mahala told me you do not want to view any properties on the North Shore by Waimea or Sunset Beach. Is that correct?"

"Yes," said Aunt Jessie. "We want to stay closer to downtown Honolulu on the leeward shore. But we do want to be on the ocean. That's important to us."

"Fine. We'll eliminate the Punchbowl area as well. But I trust you'll find the rest of the lots excellent choices. Look them over and we'll visit the two or three you like best."

Aunt Jessie studied one of the flyers. "I like this one in the Diamond Head area—a three-quarter-acre lot with one hundred linear feet of white sandy beach frontage. That sounds perfect."

"Here's another you might like," said Mr. Matsumoto. "An estate-sized beachfront parcel on Kailua Beach, the highly desired south end. It's one-half acre with 125 linear feet of ocean frontage."

"But that's farther from town, isn't it?" said Kayli.

"Yes, but you could take the Pali Highway to downtown Honolulu. And the lot does have several nice coconut palms."

Kayli picked up one of the pamphlets. "What about this one—a large ocean-front lot on the cliffs of Koko Kai in Portlock? Where is that?"

"It's a little farther from Honolulu than Diamond Head," said Jay. "Actually, my dad and I live there. It's a beautiful area with a panoramic view of the ocean."

"Here's another lot on Diamond Head Road," said Aunt Jessie. "It's smaller than the other one, but the flyer says it has a lovely old banyan tree. I love banyan trees. They have so much character and strength. Let's go see that lot first. And then we can see Koko Kai and the other Diamond Head property."

"Fine." Mr. Matsumoto gathered up his papers and stuffed them into his briefcase.

"Shall we go, ladies?" said Jay, standing up. He was smiling at Kayli, his gaze melting her defenses. She felt her face flush as she returned his smile.

As Aunt Jessie requested, they headed first to the lot with the banyan tree. They followed the road around the base of Diamond Head Crater, passed several houses under construction, and finally arrived at a pristine shoreline. Mr. Matsumoto parked his SUV beside the road. The two men escorted Kayli and her aunt across a wide expanse of untended grass to the sandy beach.

Jay walked beside Kayli, his hand touching her back, his presence distracting her from the lush beauty around her. A breeze rose off the ocean and the waves rolled in with a sparkling white froth. She removed her sandals and walked barefoot on the wet sand.

The view was breathtaking, the salty air invigorating, the roar of the surf a reassuring whisper. Fluffy white clouds dipped to the sapphire horizon. The gnarled banyan tree with its twisted trunk stood silhouetted against a luminous azure sky, its outstretched limbs drooping toward the earth like a sentry too old and weary to stand tall.

Kayli looked over at her aunt, who stood with her arms crossed as the wind rippled her hair and dress. "What do you think, Aunt Jessie?"

"It's a little bit of paradise."

"It has a private cove," said Mr. Matsumoto, "and is protected by several reefs. It's not quite as large as the other lots, but it's one of the most serene and undisturbed properties you'll find in Honolulu."

Aunt Jessie offered him her hand. "I'll take it, Mr. Matsumoto."

"What about seeing the other properties?" said Jay.

"I don't need to see them. I like this one."

"Are you sure, Aunt Jessie? This is only the first one we've seen."

"Do you like it, dear?"

"Yes, I love it. But maybe we should look at the others just to be sure."

"All right, Mr. Matsumoto. Show us the other lots. Then we'll go back to your office and sign the papers for this one."

"Whatever you wish, Miss Akimo. Shall we go?"

He walked them to his SUV and they climbed in. He drove them first to the lot just a mile away. It was considerably larger than the lot Jessie liked, but in her words this one lacked the "charm and coziness" of the first property.

Next they drove to the large oceanfront lot in Portlock on the cliffs of Koko Kai. Both Kayli and Jessie admired the rugged cliffs and the panoramic view of the ocean, but the price was steeper than what Aunt Jessie had in mind.

"The truth is," Jessie told Mr. Matsumoto as they walked gingerly over the lava rock terrain, "I like the first lot best. I fell in love with it at first sight. And I fell in love even more with that delightful banyan tree. It's full of character and old weathered beauty."

They had almost reached the car when Kayli stumbled on a sharp, jutting rock. She felt herself falling, as if in slow motion—her hands flying up, the earth rising to meet her. Before her knees hit the ground Jay was there, catching her in his arms. He pulled her against his chest and held her close as she steadied herself. She felt weak and bedazzled in his embrace. When he released her, she didn't want him to let her go.

"Are you okay?" Concern was written in his sea green eyes.

"I'm fine," she said huskily. "Just a little clumsy, I'm afraid."

"It's the uneven ground." He tucked her arm in his. "Don't worry; we'll get you home in one piece."

"Thank you." But it wasn't her physical safety that worried her now. It was the emotional fireworks exploding in her heart over a man she had no intention of pursuing.

Chapter 5

"Which church shall we go to this morning?"

Kayli looked across the table at her aunt. They were enjoying a light breakfast of oatmeal, honeydew melon, and toast. "I don't know. I think we're running out of churches close to our apartment."

Her aunt nodded. "We've visited some very nice churches since we've been here, but none has seemed quite right for us. You liked that little open-air church, but I like a church with walls."

"And I was impressed by that large church with four services on Sunday, but I have a feeling we'd just get lost in the crowd."

"There was that little church on Saratoga Road. The people were so warm and friendly, but it was so small I think I'd feel claustrophobic."

"Same here." Kayli scooped up a spoonful of melon. "I know we're not supposed to focus on what we get out of church—the music or preaching. It's about worshipping God and what we can give back to Him. But we still need to find a place that creates the best atmosphere for worship."

"I don't want to be a church hopper forever—always a visitor, never a member. I want to find a good church home where we can get to know people and start serving the Lord."

"I want that, too. I've prayed about it, but maybe not enough."

"Well, let's pray right now." Aunt Jessie reached across the table for Kayli's hand and began praying earnestly that God would lead them to just the right church. After they both said amen, her aunt flashed a big smile and said, "I think we're going to find it today."

"Maybe so. I looked online and found a church on Pensacola Street—the First Christian Church, a couple miles from here. They preach the Gospel and have lots of programs—Bible studies, potlucks, even a community center. They get people active in ministry. It could be just the place for us."

"Then let's go there today," said Aunt Jessie.

"Okay. I'll call a taxi. But one of these days we've got to shop for a car."

In the taxi on the way to church, Aunt Jessie said, "I enjoyed the reception last night. I thought you did a wonderful job."

"I hope my boss thought so, too."

"I'm sure she did. The artwork was beautifully displayed."

"I was disappointed in the attendance," Kayli admitted. "I expected the place to be packed."

"I thought it was a very nice crowd. And I thought your boss was lovely."

"Tara is remarkable—and a very talented artist herself. She started out by displaying her own paintings in a department store and worked up to her own gallery. She's given many Hawaiian artists a chance to show and sell their work."

"I admire her very much." Aunt Jessie sat at attention. "Kayli, I think we're here. Is that it—the large white stucco building on the corner?"

"Yes, that's it." They got out of the taxi and headed for the entrance. The church was a modern two-story, surrounded by towering palm trees and exotic greenery. A large white cross graced a two-story rotunda.

They entered the crowded vestibule and looked around. Kayli didn't expect to see anyone she knew. Nearly everyone in Hawaii was still a stranger. So it startled her when she spotted a familiar face—a tall, dark-haired man in a classic herringbone suit. She nudged her aunt. "Look, isn't that—?"

"Oh my, yes—our contractor, Jay Mahala."

Kayli's heart started pounding. "I wonder what he's doing here."

"The same thing we're doing. Going to church."

Kayli debated whether to call out to him or just slip into the crowd. Her decision was made for her when he looked her way and waved. As she waved back, he came striding toward her with a smile as big as a Cheshire cat's.

"Kayli. . .Jessica!" He seized Kayli's hand and shook it firmly. "What a pleasant surprise! I didn't know you attended First Christian."

"Attend? No, we don't. I mean, attend church, yes. But not here. This is our first time." *What's wrong with me? Every time I gaze into Jay Mahala's green eyes, I melt and my heart does somersaults. Worse, I can't string two rational sentences together!*

"Is your father here, too?" inquired Aunt Jessie, saving Kayli from further tongue-tied embarrassment.

"No, he's not." Jay's forehead furrowed, his thick brows shading his eyes. "My dad's a believer, but he stopped attending church after my mom died."

"I'm sorry to hear that," said Aunt Jessie. "Your father's a wonderful man and the Lord loves him. Someday he'll come back."

"I hope so. I've been praying he'll realize God still loves him," said Jay.

Aunt Jessie patted his arm. "Now you have reinforcements. Kayli and I will pray for your father every day."

"I appreciate that. Would you ladies like to sit with me in church?"

Somehow Kayli managed to keep her mind on the service even with Jay beside her. She loved the way their voices blended as they sang the hymns and praise songs. And when his arm occasionally touched hers during the message, she felt a little undercurrent of joy.

Just this morning she and Aunt Jessie had prayed that God would lead them to the right church. In her wildest dreams she couldn't have imagined that

He'd send her to a church where she'd be thrown together with the one man she couldn't get out of her heart and mind.

Lord, what are You trying to tell me? Is this a test—or an answer to prayer? Don't let me get sidetracked from Your will. Whatever Your reason for bringing this amazing man into my life, help me to keep my eyes focused on You.

After the service they accompanied Jay out to the courtyard where refreshments were being served. They found a little table while Jay brought them cookies and glasses of lemonade.

Aunt Jessie nibbled a chocolate chip cookie.

"Is that going to be too much sugar?" whispered Kayli.

"Don't worry. I'll only eat half of it."

"I'm sorry," said Jay. "It looks like I'm not being a good influence, bringing you sweets."

"It's okay," said Aunt Jessie. "My niece worries too much about me. I have diabetes, but I took my insulin today. I'll be just fine."

"You probably need something more substantial," said Jay. "Would you two like to join me for lunch?"

"That's very kind of you," said Kayli. "Maybe another time." *Am I turning him down? What's wrong with me? My silly pride? A case of nerves?*

"Did you drive to church?" asked Jay. "As I recall, you don't have a car yet."

"No, we took a taxi," said Aunt Jessie.

"Well, let me take you both out to lunch and then I'd be glad to drive you home."

Aunt Jessie clasped his hand. "That's so generous of you, Mr. Mahala."

"Jay, remember?"

"Yes, of course—Jay. Kayli and I would love to accept your invitation."

"Fine." His eyes twinkled with merriment. "What do you ladies like to eat?"

"Anything. Everything," said Jessie. "What are you hungry for, Kayli?"

At last her heart was quieting and her mind calming down. Whatever was happening here was a good thing. "We don't know the restaurants here in Honolulu, so we'll defer to your wishes. Which one do you like?"

"My favorite spot is Naupaka Terrace. It's a little drive from here. It's in the Ihilani Resort at Ko Olina. How does that sound?"

"Sign me up," said Kayli. The prospect of spending the afternoon with the handsome Jay Mahala was becoming more and more a dream come true.

"Great." Jay removed his cell phone from his shirt pocket. "Tell you what. Let me give my father a call. Maybe he'd like to join us."

"What a good idea," said Aunt Jessie. "It'll be fun making it a foursome."

Kayli could see how pleased her aunt was when Jay's father agreed to join them. He would be ready by the time Jay arrived to pick him up.

As the SUV merged with traffic, Kayli couldn't believe she was sitting in the passenger seat beside Jay on her way to the Mahala estate.

"Didn't you say you live in Portlock?" asked Aunt Jessie.

"Yes," said Jay. "We're almost there. Our house is on the cliffs of Koko Kai, not far from the site we showed you."

As Jay turned onto a winding street that climbed toward the cliffs, Kayli took note of the luxurious estates on each side—exquisite Mediterranean-style houses, sprawling plantations, and cliffside mansions—all nestled among lush tropical plants and trees.

At the top of the hill they stopped at a wrought iron gate. Jay aimed his remote at the fence and the gate opened. He followed the road to a lovely Italian-style villa overlooking the ocean and parked beside the wraparound deck. "My dad built this house for my mother," he said as he helped Kayli and Jessie from the vehicle, "but she didn't have many years to enjoy it."

"I'm sorry," said Kayli. "That has to be very painful for both of you."

He walked them up the porch and unlocked the door. "Actually, my mom's in a far better place. I'm sure the house Jesus prepared for her makes this one look like a shack."

"That's a wonderful way to look at it," said Aunt Jessie.

"I feel the same way about my parents," said Kayli. "As hard as it's been to grow up without them, I always picture them in a glorious home in heaven."

Jay nodded. "Yep. Living in Jesus' neighborhood can't be half bad." He opened the door and led them inside.

White marble floors, two walls of windows, and a massive, handblown glass chandelier made the two-story foyer gleam with light. The marble floor was flanked by fluted columns and extended all the way to the back of the house. Even from the polished entry Kayli could see a wall of windows that allowed a panoramic view of the ocean and sky.

"It's beautiful," she said softly. "You must really enjoy living here."

"Truth is, I don't live here," said Jay.

She looked up at him in bewilderment. "But you just said this is your house."

"I said it's my dad's house. I have a little cottage a stone's throw from here, with a direct path down to the beach. I like to keep my life simple and uncluttered. I've found that having a lot of stuff usually only complicates things."

"You're a wise man, Jay Mahala," said Aunt Jessie. "We could all take a lesson from you."

He chuckled. "That doesn't mean I don't spend a lot of time in this house with my dad. He's alone these days and likes the company. But he's also big on entertaining, so I like having my little cottage to escape to when things get hectic." He crossed the entrance hall to a circular staircase and called up, "Hey, Dad! You ready to go?"

"Be right there, son!"

A minute later Leo Mahala, in a white suit and panama hat, came striding down the stairs with the vigor and panache of a seasoned film star. He greeted them with a firm handclasp and a little embrace. "Good to see you ladies again."

"You do look like the lord of the manor," Aunt Jessie said with a coy little smile.

"Thank you, milady. I'll take that as a compliment."

The drive to the resort at Ko Olina was pleasant and brief. There was no lack of conversation when Leo Mahala was around. Aunt Jessie looked as delighted to be riding beside Leo as Kayli was to be sitting beside Jay.

They arrived at Naupaka Terrace at noon sharp. The hostess led them through a maze of potted plants and exotic greenery to a small, linen-draped table that overlooked the pool. After seating them and handing them menus, she said, "Your waiter will be here in a moment."

Kayli looked around. She liked the place. It had a classy, yet comfortable atmosphere.

Aunt Jessie ordered the Cobb salad, Leo the New York steak, and Jay the sautéed Hawaiian snapper. When it was her turn, Kayli said, "I'll have the sautéed shrimp and sea scallops with the penne pasta."

"A good choice," said the waiter.

"I'm very pleased we have this unexpected chance to be together," said Leo. "I know we have an appointment later in the week to discuss how things are progressing. But this way I can give you an update now."

"Are you saying there's news?" asked Aunt Jessie.

"Yes, there is. The architectural drawings should be ready for your approval by Wednesday. And Mr. Matsumoto tells me the escrow on your lot should proceed without delay. That means we should be able to break ground on your new home in a matter of weeks."

Aunt Jessie looked as if she were about to cry. "It's really happening. If you knew how many years I've dreamed of coming back here and owning a little piece of Hawaii—the land where generations of my family lived and died—well, I can't tell you how happy I am."

Kayli reached over and clasped her aunt's hand. "We're happy for you."

"We sure are," said Jay, visibly touched.

"And I've been thinking a lot about it," said Aunt Jessie, her voice wavering. "I should have said it before, but I didn't know how to express what was on my heart to strangers. But you're not strangers anymore; you're friends."

"Thank you, Jessica," said Leo. "We are friends. And we're listening."

Aunt Jessie took a long drink of water and set the glass down. "Here's the truth. I don't need a big house for Kayli and myself. We could do fine in a little house as long as it had an art studio for her. But I want a big house that God can use. When I was young and struggling, Kayli's parents took me in and treated me like a queen. I'll never forget how kind and generous they were to me."

"Aunt Jessie, I'm sure they were glad to do it. Daddy was your brother."

"I know, honey. But I want to honor their legacy the only way I know how." She turned her water glass between her palms. "I want to create a retreat for people who need a place to get away and be refreshed—for people who are hurting or tired or burned-out on life. That means ministers, missionaries, church people, orphans, poor folk—anybody. I believe God gave me the gift of hospitality. A big house will give me a chance to exercise that gift."

"Jessica, that's a beautiful sentiment," said Jay. "I'll keep that in mind as I work on the design of your house. We'll definitely make it a home God can use."

Kayli studied Jay's profile as he gazed at Aunt Jessie. She loved the empathy and compassion she saw in his face. He was truly a remarkable man. A godly man. She loved being with him, and she sensed that he enjoyed being with her, too. Already her affection for him was growing by leaps and bounds.

But was she on a one-way road to heartbreak? Would the kind and enchanting Jay Mahala ever think of her as more than a client?

Chapter 6

"Well, JJ, will you be seeing your charming Miss Akimo again tonight?" His father sat across from him at the breakfast table nursing a cup of black coffee.

Jay bristled at the pet name. Or was it his father's nosiness? He bit his lower lip and kept silent.

"How many dates this week does that make?" quizzed his father in his usual booming, take-charge voice. "Three, right? Two lunches, one dinner?"

Even more than the pet name, Jay deplored his father's constant matchmaking efforts. If he ever needled his own son like his dad needled him, Jay hoped someone would give him a good swift kick.

"Well, JJ? Are you going to keep your old man in suspense?"

"Stop it, Dad!" Why hadn't he skipped having breakfast together and gone straight to the office? At least there his dad kept the conversation mainly about business.

His father sat back, his black eyes flaring with indignation. "What'd I do wrong now? Can't a father show some interest in his son's personal life?"

Jay sipped his coffee. It was cold now and tasted bitter. Living in the cottage on his father's property still didn't give him enough breathing space. What was it going to take? Moving to another island? Starting his own construction company? That was the trouble. Every aspect of his life was tied incontrovertibly to his father.

"Did you hear me, JJ? Lots of fathers don't care what their kids do. You should be glad you have a father who wants the best for you and knows how to make it happen."

Jay's ire rose. How did his dad always manage to make Jay look like the bad guy? "What's that mean, Dad? Are you saying you've been orchestrating this little romance—or potential romance—between Kayli and me? Are you taking credit for it?"

His father sat forward, his shrewd eyes gleaming. "There! You admit it. A romance is brewing. I knew it."

Jay set his coffee cup down too hard on the saucer. The black liquid sloshed over the rim. It had been easier dealing with his dad when his mother was still alive to act as a buffer between them. Now there was no buffer—just two stubborn personalities that constantly clashed. "You don't have anything to do with it, Dad. Whatever is happening between Kayli and me is purely our business."

"Nonsense! Why do you think I've arranged all these extra little meetings and dinners out with the Akimo ladies? I knew Kayli Akimo was right for you the minute I laid eyes on her."

"And here I thought we were just doing our job—getting to know our clients and building a house that fulfills their dreams."

"We could have done that after the first couple of meetings. Look, son, you're the one who started arranging luncheon dates for the four of us after church on Sundays. You should be happy. You've even got your old man going to church again."

Jay nodded. "Yes, I'm grateful for that. You're not just making me happy, you know; I'm sure you're making Mom happy, too."

His father's eyes misted. He cast a glance skyward; then lowered his gaze, blinking back tears. "Yeah, well, I like to think she's up there in heaven looking down and nodding her approval."

Jay smiled in spite of himself, his own eyes tearing. It amazed him how fast he could go from being angry with his dad to feeling emotions too deep to express. "Yeah, Dad, I'm sure she is."

His father took another swallow of coffee then let out a little sigh. "A guy can't be mad at God forever."

"I'm glad you realize that. God loves you more than you know."

"Yeah, son, I'm remembering that more every day."

Jay pushed back his chair. If he didn't leave now, his tears might get the better of him. "Guess I'd better get going, Dad."

His father raised a hand in protest. "Why? I'm the boss. I'm still sitting here. What's your rush?"

Jay settled back, his hands still on the armrests. "I have a lot to do today, Dad, and I had hoped to finish up early."

"For your date with Kayli?"

"It's not a date. She invited me to a reception at her gallery. It's the second event she's planned, and she's really excited about it."

"You going for the art or the company?"

"Both. I may buy some paintings. I figure our office walls could use a little more class."

"Okay. You got a point. But tell me, are you making any progress?"

"Progress? What do you mean?"

"In your relationship with Kayli. Are you two getting serious?"

Jay's defenses kicked into overdrive. "Dad, the truth is, Kayli and I are just friends. We enjoy each other's company. Neither of us is thinking beyond friendship right now." Even as he said the words he cringed a little. It was the same argument he had been giving himself for days now—*Kayli and I are just friends; there's nothing between us. I'm not falling in love with her.* He hoped he was more convincing with his dad than he was with himself.

His father poured himself another cup of coffee and gestured toward Jay's empty cup, but he waved him away. His dad sampled his brew and smiled. After another swallow, he said, "I see the way you look at her, JJ, and the way she looks at you. You two are in love. What's wrong with you, boy, that you can't admit how you feel? There's nothing wrong with falling in love. It's the most natural thing in the world."

Jay tried going on the attack. "What about you, Dad? You and Jessica seem pretty friendly. What's going on with the two of you?"

"Are you kidding me?" His dad wiped his lips. "I'm too old for that whole dating routine. Sure, I like Jessie. She's a fine lady. We have a good time together. But I'll never forget your mother. No one could take her place."

"True, but you're never too old to make room in your heart for someone else. You're always giving me advice, Dad. Why don't you take some of your own?"

"Now who's playing matchmaker?" His father drained his cup and stood up. "Guess we'd better stow the chitchat and head to the office. You ready?"

Jay stood up and pushed in his chair. "Ready."

"Shall we take two cars or one?"

"I guess we should both drive. I'm going straight to the gallery reception at six."

"Right. Don't forget, son. We break ground tomorrow on Jessica's property. Did you talk to the preacher about coming out and giving the blessing?"

Jay followed his father out to the four-car garage. "I did. Pastor Aiko will be there at ten o'clock."

"Fine. He's a good man, taking time out of his busy schedule. I know Jessica will be pleased."

"So will Kayli. She'd never heard of the Hawaiian custom of asking God to bless a new home or business, so she's really excited about the ceremony."

His father glanced over at him. "I'm looking forward to it myself."

Jay squeezed his father's shoulder. "Me, too, Dad." He opened the door to his SUV while his father headed toward his luxury sedan. "See you there, Dad."

He let his father pull out first and watched until his vehicle passed through the gate. Then he followed. Already the space around him felt empty, void of his father's presence. The silence was unsettling. The whole father-son thing was a mystery to him—a paradox. No matter how frustrated he got with his dad, he couldn't deny the strong emotional connection between them. You couldn't sever a tie like that. No use trying.

Lord, You've got Dad back in church now. Please heal his grieving heart and give him a fresh hunger for a close relationship with You. And don't let my petty feelings get in the way of Your working. Oh, and, Lord, don't let me get in Your way when it comes to Kayli. You know how I feel about her, but don't let me run ahead of Your will. Help me to keep things "just friends" until You show me You want more for us. And, Lord, just so You know, I'm trying to keep my feelings in check, but it's getting harder every day.

At dusk, as Jay headed his SUV toward the Queen Street Art Gallery, he repeated his prayer of that morning. As much as he had denied his feelings for Kayli to his father and even to himself, he was reaching a point where he had to face the truth. He had never felt about any woman the way he felt about Kayli Akimo, and he had no idea what to do about it. After years of squelching his father's matchmaking efforts, he didn't know how to open his heart and simply let love in. What if he proclaimed his feelings for Kayli and then realized God had other plans for the two of them? He'd rather die than hurt her. She had had enough heartache in her life, losing her parents when she was so young. That's why—no matter how difficult it was—he had to keep things light and uncomplicated between them.

After parking by the Chinese restaurant next door, Jay followed several couples making their way inside the gallery. Kayli stood near the entrance greeting people and handing out information about the artists. She looked stunning in a powder blue, formfitting satin gown, her straight ebony hair flowing over her shoulders. When she spotted him, she broke into a smile.

"Jay! I'm so glad you could make it."

"Me, too. You look beautiful."

"Thank you. I'm so nervous."

"You don't look it."

"Good. Make yourself at home. Meet the artists. Take a look at their paintings. Have some refreshments. I'll join you as soon as I can."

"Take your time. I know you have clients to meet and greet."

He wandered around the roomy studio with its two-story ceiling and massive skylight. The decor was spare, leaving guests to focus on the wall-to-wall paintings and small groupings of sculptures and ceramics. After perusing the paintings and meeting Kayli's boss, Tara, and several of the artists, he helped himself to some sparkling cider and hors d'oeuvres.

Kayli joined him after a while. "Tara took over the meet and greet, so I can spend a little time with you."

"Perfect." He offered her an appetizer and she took one.

"I love these little pastry things." As she nibbled it, she looked around at the milling throng. "What do you think, Jay? It's quite a crowd, isn't it? So much better than the last reception."

"Very impressive," he agreed. He set his empty glass and plate on a nearby tray. "The work here is top-notch. I've seen several paintings I wouldn't mind having in my office."

She smiled. "Feel free to make an offer."

"I intend to."

"Have you met Tara yet?"

"Yes. She was very friendly. I like her."

"And the artists? Have you met them?"

"Yes. Several. Quite an eclectic group."

"Our theme is 'Hawaii: The Best of the Old and New.' We were even able to feature some of the work of Madge Tennent."

"Why does that name sound familiar?"

"She's one of Hawaii's most famous artists. For over fifty years she portrayed the women of Hawaii through her stylized sketches and oils. She died in 1972, but she's still very well loved by the Hawaiian people."

"Yes, I remember now. I've seen her work."

Kayli patted his arm and said confidentially, "I just want you to know, Jay, I'm really excited about tomorrow."

He put his hand over hers. "Yes, so am I. We'll finally be breaking ground on your house."

"We'll be there early, now that we finally have our own car. And I can't wait to participate in the blessing ceremony. I've never seen one before."

He nodded. "They're very special. We often have our pastor do one when we start a new project. It's very moving."

"The ceremony will mean so much to Aunt Jessie. It will make her feel even more a part of her Hawaiian ancestors."

"That's the idea. I just think—"

The lights flickered suddenly and the room grew hushed.

Kayli looked around. "Oh no, I hope we're not going to have trouble with the power. Sometimes this old building is—"

The lights flickered several more times.

Someone at the back of the room cried out, "I smell something burning!"

"So do I," said someone else.

The room went dark. Voices rose in alarm.

"The building's on fire!"

"Where's the door?"

"Find the door!"

"Where's the electrical control panel?" Jay asked Kayli. She was gripping his arm so tightly he winced.

Her voice came out shrill with urgency. "It's in—um—the back. Outside. The right side of the building."

Jay could smell the smoke now himself. He pulled out his cell phone, dialed 911, and reported the fire. Then in his most authoritative voice he shouted, "Ladies and gentlemen, the fire department is coming. Go outside. Walk carefully. Follow the light from the skylight."

The next few minutes were a dizzying blur. Several artists grabbed their work and headed for the door. Jay made sure everyone exited the studio with a minimum of confusion. As people milled around outside, he ran around the building and switched off the power box. Then he told the owner of the Chinese restaurant next door that he might want to vacate his premises, as well. Returning to the gallery, he searched for Kayli in the crowd. She wasn't there.

Sirens sounded in the distance. Minutes later two fire trucks pulled up and firemen streamed into the building. Jay pushed through the crowd, found Tara, and gripped her arm. "Have you seen Kayli?"

"No. But she must be here somewhere."

He kept looking. He called her name, but his voice was lost in the din. Finally he spotted a lone figure huddled against a streetlamp on the opposite corner. Breathless, heart pounding, he sprinted across the street. As he approached he could see that it was Kayli. He reached down and pulled her into his arms. She felt so small and fragile. "You're trembling. It's okay, sweetheart. Everything's okay."

He looked into her face. The streetlamp etched her delicate features with contrasting lights and shadows. Her ebony eyes were wide and as glistening as saucers. He had never seen anyone look so terrified. He hugged her against him and kissed her hair. "You're safe, Kayli. Nothing's going to hurt you. I promise, I'll never let anything hurt you."

As he tried to lead her back across the street her body went rigid. "No," she whispered, "I can't."

"It's okay, honey. The fire department is here. It doesn't look like there's any fire. They're just checking to make sure."

Finally he urged her back across the street, but she stood shivering, arms crossed, leaning against him. He kept his arm protectively around her shoulder. He noticed that several firemen had already returned to their trucks. One towering firefighter was speaking to Tara. Jay led Kayli over. He wanted to hear what the man had to say.

As the rugged, russet-haired man glanced their way, Tara said, "This is Captain Moran. Captain, this is Kayli, my assistant, and her friend Jay, the man who called 911."

The captain nodded. "I was just saying that we found the problem. The electrical wiring in the wall shorted out and started the fire. You got us here fast enough, so the only damage is where we had to tear out the wall. All the artwork is safe. You're lucky. This building is old. It could have been a lot worse. You'd better get an electrician out here to redo the wiring."

Kayli grasped the man's arm. "What if it happens again?"

The captain covered her small hand with his large, gloved hand. "I promise you, miss—you get that wiring fixed and you'll be okay. I give you my word. If you ever have another problem, you call the fire department and ask for Captain Rick Moran. I'll come out here myself and make sure everything's okay."

Kayli seemed comforted after that. The captain had reassured her when Jay himself could not. The evening had a gloomy feeling about it now. The reception had been interrupted; everyone was heading home. You couldn't have a party in the dark.

Kayli didn't want to drive home alone, so Jay drove her and agreed to pick her up for the blessing ceremony in the morning. Afterward, he would drive her to the gallery.

Later, as he headed back to his cottage, Jay realized he was more shaken than he had imagined. It had been a disturbing evening. He had never seen anyone so paralyzed by fear. Aloud he murmured, "Kayli, my sweet Kayli, what will it take to make your fears go away?"

Chapter 7

Kayli's anxieties over the fire eased a little the next morning as she took her place at the housing site beside Jay, Leo, and Aunt Jessie for the blessing ceremony. The sun was warm and welcoming and a brisk breeze stirred the leaves and grass, reminding Kayli of the way the invisible Holy Spirit stirred human hearts. Several members of the church congregation, in their historical Hawaiian garb, danced and sang hymns and traditional Hawaiian songs. Their bright red and yellow costumes, orchid leis, and green palm fronds were dazzling against the white cliffs and shimmering cerulean ocean.

Pastor Aiko, in his *Pule Ho'omaka*—opening prayer—entreated God, the *Ke Akua*—Supreme Creator—to bless this piece of His earth and the people who would be stewards over it. He continued that theme in a brief message. "Owning land goes beyond the *palapala*, the paper documents. It is a *kuleana*—a great responsibility. This land was here before we were born and will be here long after we die. May our heavenly Father help us while the land is in our care to protect and nurture it." After his message he sprinkled salt water on Aunt Jessie, Kayli, and the land in a cleansing ceremony he called *huikala*. Then, as he presented them with fragrant maile leis, he offered a *Pule Ho'oku'u*—a closing prayer, asking God to bless them and the new home that would soon be theirs.

As the heat of summer gave way to a balmy Hawaiian autumn, Kayli thought often about the blessing ceremony and what it meant to transform a small patch of God's creation into a home. She and Aunt Jessie watched in pleased fascination as their beachfront lot was changed from an untended field to an actual construction site. At frequent intervals Jay and his father conducted on-site meetings with them—after trenches were dug and plumbing laid for water and sewer; after the foundation was poured; and now, today, after the framework was erected.

At last it all seemed real. No longer just a dream or a promise. There, profiled against a cloudy sky and azure ocean, stood the skeleton of their dream house—the sturdy wood studs, the sills, the rafters—all fit together like a child's Lincoln Logs to create the bare bones of their home.

"It's amazing," said Kayli. "It looks so big."

"It is," said Jay, standing beside her. "Over four thousand square feet."

Kayli gazed around at the piles of cut lumber, pipes, wires, sawdust, nails, and other debris surrounding the structure and at the drywall and roofing materials stacked off to one side. With a droll little smile she said, "The yard's a bit messy, but, otherwise, what do you think of your new home, Aunt Jessie?"

Her aunt, standing a short distance away beside Leo Mahala, caught the humor in her question. "I think it looks a little drafty," she chortled. "But I like the open-air feel."

"The carpenters will be buttoning up the walls over the next few days," said Leo. He offered Jessie his arm. "Would you like to take a walk through your new home while you can still look between the studs into each room?"

"I'd love to."

Kayli and Jay followed them into the framed structure. "I'm not sure which room we're in," said Kayli. "Everything runs together. It's like a maze—with invisible walls."

"We're standing in the great room right now," said Leo. "The far wall will be your glass pocket doors opening onto the beach. We want to connect the inside spaces with the outdoors and keep the design very fluid." He crossed the concrete slab to the opposite side. "Here's your gourmet kitchen. The range will go here, your counters here. You'll have a garden window overlooking the ocean."

"And over here is a separate wing for your houseguests," said Jay, taking a dozen paces to the right. "They'll have their own private living room and kitchenette."

Aunt Jessie clasped her hands together. "It's what I've always dreamed of—lots of room for entertaining. I could fit a whole church congregation in that great room."

"I suppose you could," mused Leo. "A small church, anyway."

Jay reached for Kayli's hand and led her over to another large open space. "And here is your art studio. Your home's U-shaped design allows your studio to open onto the courtyard facing the beach, so it'll be easy to slip outside to paint or sketch."

Kayli stood in the center of the room, gazing around at the sturdy timbers that defined her studio. She tried to imagine how it would look with walls and paint and furniture and easels and canvases. She felt overwhelmed. "Thank You, Lord," she whispered. "This is more than I could have imagined." She turned to Jay and clasped his hands, her gaze meeting his. "Thank you, too. You and your father are making all of this possible. You don't know how much it means to me."

"You don't have to thank me." There was something in his eyes that held her spellbound for a moment—fondness, yearning? She could almost imagine that the two of them were standing here in their own house, planning a future together. Perhaps it was wishful thinking, but she sensed that Jay was feeling the same unexpected emotion. Without warning he drew her into his arms and gently kissed her hair. "I've built a lot of houses," he whispered against her ear, "but none has meant more to me than this one."

She almost said, *And nobody means more to me than you.*

As he held her tight, she sensed that he wanted to say something more, but their breathing remained the only sound between them. It didn't matter. His embrace said more than words could say. She loved the feel of his arms around her, the closeness of his face to hers. In a moment everything had changed between them. Did he sense it, too?

As he released her she caught a glimpse of Leo and Aunt Jessie watching approvingly.

Jay apparently hadn't noticed their watchful, beatific gaze. He was already moving on, clearing his throat, explaining this and that about the house. "We used pre-engineered lumber for the foundation," he was saying, all business again. "And you know we don't sub our work out to other contractors. We do all our own masonry, rough and finish carpentry, roofing, electrical, plumbing, painting—the whole ball of wax."

"I know. Your father explained that the day we signed the contract."

"Oh yeah, I knew that. I just wondered if you remembered."

"Yes, I remember."

Was he trying to erase the unspoken emotions they had shared just moments ago? She was trying her best to follow his train of thought, but the sensation of his arms around her was still uppermost in her mind. He led her around the massive cement slab, rattling on about rebar installation, tongue-and-groove joints, floor joists, and hurricane straps. She didn't have a clue what he was saying, but she feigned interest, nodding and replying at appropriate times, "Yes, I see. . .oh my, how fascinating."

After a while Leo and Aunt Jessie joined them. "You two ready to go?" asked Leo.

"Yes," said Kayli. "Thanks so much for showing us the house. For the first time it's real to me."

"I feel the same way," said Aunt Jessie. "Now I can actually touch the wood and smell the fragrance of the timber and feel the cement under my feet. It's exciting. And best of all, my beautiful banyan tree in the front yard will be the showpiece."

"We'll come out again when the drywall is finished," said Jay as they walked toward Leo's luxury sedan. They were climbing inside when Leo paused and looked to the east. "Hey, JJ, look at that smoke."

They all looked. "Something's burning," said Jay.

As if on cue, sirens sounded in the distance. "Looks like help is coming," said Aunt Jessie, scooting into the passenger seat beside Leo.

"Could be one of our houses." Leo fastened his seat belt and turned the ignition. "We'd better go take a look."

Kayli looked over at Jay beside her in the backseat. "What does he mean?"

"We're going to go see what's burning."

Her heart started hammering. "You're going to the fire?"

"It could be one of our projects. We just want to get close enough to make sure it's not a house we're building."

She gripped his arm in desperation. "I can't go there. Drop me off."

He patted her arm. "It's okay, Kayli. We won't get near the fire."

"No, I can't, please. Turn around."

Aunt Jessie looked around from the front seat. "It'll be okay, honey. Leo wouldn't risk letting us get near the fire."

Kayli looked beseechingly at Jay. "Please, tell your father to turn around. I can't do this."

"Leo, maybe we should turn around," said Aunt Jessie. "Kayli can't be around fire."

"You all stop worrying," said Leo as he drove along the two-lane road that paralleled the beach. "I'll park a block away."

"Please make him stop the car, Jay. I'll get out and walk. I'll call for a taxi."

He slipped his arm around her, his brows furrowed with concern. "I haven't seen that look on your face since the incident at your gallery. It's okay, honey. Just close your eyes. You don't even have to look."

But she had looked. They were on another road now, in a new neighborhood under construction. Less than two blocks away she spotted two fire engines. Firefighters were scrambling around, dragging hoses toward a half-built house. Flames were shooting out from under the roof.

Kayli covered her face with her hands. Her entire body felt numb, paralyzed. She tried to breathe but it felt as if all the air had been sucked out of her lungs. Jay tightened his grip around her shoulders. "Relax, honey. They're putting out the fire."

"It's not one of our houses, and the fire's small," said Leo, sounding relieved. "But something's not right. There's no reason that house should be burning. It's all new construction. No one lives there. There's no sign of workers. The sky's clear. It couldn't have been lightning."

"You think it could be arson?" said Jay.

"It's happened before," said Leo. "There's always some crazy out there who thinks civilization shouldn't be encroaching on nature, especially on the pristine land along the ocean."

"Can we go now?" pleaded Kayli.

"I'm going to stick around and talk to the firemen," said Leo. "I want to know whether we're dealing with an arsonist in the area." He looked around at Jay. "You take the ladies somewhere for a cup of coffee and come back in half an hour."

Jay didn't argue. He switched places with his dad, waited just a moment while his father strode off toward the fire engines, then turned the sedan around and headed back the way they had come. Ten minutes later they pulled up at a

Starbucks drive-through and ordered double lattes. Then he drove them back to their lot and parked. "We'll stay here a few minutes until the smoke has cleared. Then it should be okay to go back." He looked around at Kayli as if to make sure she was okay with the plan.

She nodded. She was feeling better now. The latte was soothing her jangled nerves. The stark panic that had gripped her was dissipating, making her wonder how she could have overreacted so badly. As her fears gave way to feelings of foolishness and shame, she murmured, "I'm sorry, Jay. I didn't mean to act like such a maniac."

Aunt Jessie spoke up. "It's perfectly all right, Kayli. We all understand why you're so terrified of fire. We might feel the same way if we'd been through what you endured as a child."

"That's just it," said Kayli. "I have no memory of the fire that killed my parents. So why do I get so terrified?"

"Whatever it is, it must be buried deep in your subconscious," said Jay. "Have you prayed for God to heal your mind?"

She thought about it. "I don't know if I've ever put it like that. I guess I figured this fear was my cross to bear. But you're right. It is something I should pray about."

"I'll be praying for you, too," said Jay.

He turned on the engine and pulled onto the road. "The smoke is gone. The fire must be out by now."

This time, as they approached the fire engines, Kayli felt only a slight tremor of alarm. The only sign that there had been a fire was a small blackened area under the roof. Leo was talking animatedly with one of the firemen while the others loaded the hoses and equipment back on the trucks.

Jay looked back at Kayli. "Do you want to go hear what they have to say?"

She didn't, but she didn't want to admit it, so she said, "Sure."

"I'm coming, too," said Aunt Jessie.

They all got out of the car and walked the short distance to the trucks. Leo was standing, arms crossed, listening to the firefighter—a tall lumberjack of a man—his helmet pulled low over his eyes, his sturdy face covered with black smudges. "There'll have to be an investigation before we'll know how the fire started."

"If you ask me," said Leo, "and this is just between us—I think it was arson."

"Could be," said the firefighter. "We've had a spate of fires in the area recently. They were just like this one."

"Are you saying someone's targeting new construction?" asked Jay.

"Looks like it." The man removed his fire hat and pushed back shocks of russet hair from his high forehead. His features were strong and sharply sculpted—an aquiline nose, high cheekbones, square jaw. He was likely a handsome man, although Kayli couldn't tell for all the ash and soot. "Some people want Hawaii to stay just the way it was a hundred years ago," he was saying, "wild, untouched, the way God made it. They're afraid every inch of Hawaii's land will end up in cookie-cutter subdivisions."

"It sounds like you may feel that way yourself," noted Kayli. She swallowed hard. Had she actually said that aloud?

As the fireman turned his gaze on her, she chided herself for speaking out of turn. His conversation was with Leo and Jay. He hadn't even realized she was there until now. His dark eyes drilled into hers. Finally he said, "Don't I know you?"

She was so surprised by the question that she couldn't summon an answer for several seconds. Finally she managed, "I don't think so."

He tapped his forehead. "I never forget a face, especially a pretty one like yours. We've met somewhere."

She felt her face flushing with warmth. "I'm sure I would remember. I don't meet many firefighters." *At least not since I was five,* she thought darkly.

"That's it!" he declared, holding out a gloved hand to her. "You're the lady from that art gallery—the one that had the electrical short a month or so ago. You made me promise it wouldn't happen again."

She stared at him in astonishment. "You're *that* fireman?"

"Yeah, your gallery was on—let me see—Queen Street, right?"

"Right. The Queen Street Gallery."

"I was there, too," said Jay. "I remember you now. Captain Morgan?"

"Moran. Rick Moran."

"I wasn't there," lamented Aunt Jessie. "I was home with a headache. I missed all the excitement."

"Oh Aunt Jessie, that was more excitement than any of us wanted."

Jay offered the captain his hand. "Thank you for your good work that night. We appreciated your promptness and quick assessment of the problem."

"Glad I could help." He looked at Kayli. "Did you ever get that wiring replaced, miss?"

She smiled. "Yes, we did. Thank you again. So much could have been lost that night."

He flashed a lopsided grin. "Don't thank me. I was just doing my job."

"Well, I'm very grateful, Captain Moran."

He held his helmet in both hands. "And your name is—?"

"Kayli Akimo."

Leo, Jay, and Aunt Jessie introduced themselves, too.

He politely shook their hands then turned his attention back to Kayli. "Have you always lived here in Honolulu?"

"No. My aunt and I recently moved here from the mainland. The Mahalas are building us a house just over the ridge about a mile from here."

Leo handed the captain a business card. "My son and I own a construction company—Mahala, Mahala, and Associates. I'd appreciate you and your crew keeping an eye on our houses—at least until they catch that arsonist."

"Be glad to, Mr. Mahala." He glanced back at the fire trucks. "Looks like we're ready to go. I'd better get back to my men before they accuse me of slacking off." He gave Kayli one last look. "You have my word, Miss Akimo. If you ever need me, I'll be there, day or night, twenty-four-seven."

She reached out and shook his gloved hand. It felt strong and reassuring. "Thank you, Captain Moran. I'll remember that."

Later that afternoon, as Leo and Jay drove Kayli and Aunt Jessie back to their apartment, their conversation focused on the fire and the hero of the day, Captain Rick Moran.

"I think he was quite taken with you, Kayli," said Jay with a sly little smile.

She couldn't tell whether he sounded jealous or just bemused. "Don't be silly. He was just being nice. That's what firefighters do. They make people feel safe and protected."

Jay gave her a scrutinizing glance. "Is that how he made you feel?"

She cocked her head to one side. "If you must know. . .yes, it is."

"Looks like you have a rival, JJ."

"Yeah, sure, Dad. Guess I'd better get myself a fire hat."

Kayli laughed. "That's not necessary. I'm sure I'll never see Captain Rick Moran again. In fact, I hope and pray I never have to."

"Amen to that," said Aunt Jessie.

Chapter 8

Kayli was framing an oil painting in the gallery's back room when Tara peeked through the doorway and said, "There's a gentleman here to see you."

"A gentleman?" She gently laid the canvas on the table. "Who? You mean Jay Mahala?"

"No, it's not Jay."

"Then who? His father?"

"No, this is a tall, handsome stranger. You'd better come check him out."

Kayli pushed her hair back from her face, licked her lips, and squared her shoulders. Tara had sounded so mysterious. Who would be visiting her here at the gallery?

She adjusted the strap of her lime green sundress as she walked to the reception desk at the front of the gallery. Her gaze swept over the handsome man standing there in a charcoal gray sport coat and black slacks. *Tara's right. He's gorgeous. But why is he asking for me?*

"Hello. I'm Kayli Akimo," she said, offering her hand. "Did we have an appointment to look at some artwork?"

As he accepted her hand his smile spread across his bronzed face. "No, I'm not here for the art." His dark eyes met hers with an unflinching directness. His distinctive features seemed chipped from granite. "I was in the area and just thought I'd drop by and say hello."

She tried unsuccessfully to pull her hand—and her gaze—away. "You have the advantage, I'm afraid. I don't believe we've met."

With a little chuckle he released her hand. "I guess I do look a little different from the last time you saw me."

She was feeling more confused than ever. Surely she would remember if she had met him before. "I'm sorry, I don't remember your name." *Nor do I remember your face. I must be slipping to forget someone as good-looking as you!*

"I'm Rick. Rick Moran—the firefighter who put out the fire here a while back. And the guy you met at that house fire near the beach a few days ago."

Suddenly everything clicked into place. "Forgive me, Captain Moran. I didn't recognize you without the helmet and uniform and smudge marks on your face." Realizing how rude she sounded, she blurted, "But you really clean up well!"

He laughed. "Thanks. My mom always told me that, too."

She decided it was time to change the subject before she dug herself in deeper. “It’s nice of you to stop by. What can I do for you, Captain?”

“Call me Rick, please.” He leaned across the reception desk, his eyes twinkling. “You can go to lunch with me.”

“Lunch?” She hadn’t expected that. “I only have a half hour and—”

“Perfect. We can eat at the Chinese restaurant next door. I assume you can vouch for their food.”

“Oh yes, it’s really good, but—”

“Just tell me when your lunch break begins, and I’ll be back.”

She looked at the clock. “Actually, I could go now.”

“Great. Then let’s go.”

“I’d better let Tara know, so she can come out and be available for customers.” Her mind whirling, she pivoted and walked to the back room. What was she doing going out with a virtual stranger? And yet, he wasn’t really a stranger. He had saved their gallery from serious fire damage.

Tara, working on the unframed painting, looked up and gave Kayli a quizzical smile. “So who’s our mystery man?”

“The firefighter who saved our gallery.”

“Really? Did he come back for his reward?”

Kayli’s face warmed. “He asked me out to lunch.”

“Really? Are you going?”

“I guess so. I don’t see any harm in having lunch together. We’ll just be next door. And it’s not as if I’m seeing anyone seriously.”

“Like Jay?”

“He’s made it pretty clear that we’re just friends for now.”

“Well, then, go and have a great time with Sir Braveheart.”

Kayli grinned. “Thanks, Tara, I will.”

“Take an extra thirty minutes if you like, as long as you make it up tomorrow.”

“If things go well, I just might.” Her pulse was racing as she rejoined Rick.

“All set?” he asked.

She took a deep breath. “All set.”

He walked her next door and the hostess showed them to a little table by the window. As they studied their menus, Kayli wondered what in the world they would talk about.

He looked up from his menu. “What do you like?”

“I love crab Rangoon with cream cheese,” she said, “even though I hear it’s not an authentic Chinese appetizer.”

“I love it, too. We’ll get some. Would you like me to order for both of us?”

“Sure, why not?” It would be fun to see what he selected.

When the waitress came to take their order, he asked for the crab Rangoon, then said, “The lady would like egg drop soup and *Ling Mung Gai*.” He gave

Kayli a reassuring glance. "Don't worry, that means lemon chicken. And I'll have wonton soup and *Kung Pao Chi Ting.*"

"That's chicken with peanuts and chili peppers," he told her after the waitress had left. "And did you know 'wonton' means 'swallowing a cloud'?"

"What a fascinating image." She folded her hands on the table. "You sound like you're well-traveled. Have you been to China?"

He laughed. "Actually, I learned about Chinese food when I was in college. I worked in a Chinese restaurant in Huntington Beach, California."

"Really? You're from California? So am I."

"You're kidding. Where?"

"Seal Beach. I graduated from Cal State Long Beach."

"No way! So did I. When did you graduate?"

"Last year. What about you?"

"It's been six years for me."

"What was your major? Firefighting?"

"No. Criminal justice."

"Then how did you become a firefighter?" She settled back, relaxing.

"I got my training at LBFD—the Long Beach Fire Department Training Center."

Before Kayli could respond, the waitress brought their food. She bowed her head for a moment of prayer then looked up at Rick. He was watching her. She felt a trifle unnerved.

He picked up his fork and speared a morsel of chicken. "Were you praying just now?"

Her face warmed. "Yes. I believe in thanking God for everything He gives us."

"I don't see that very often. I guess that means you go to church, too."

She smiled. "Yes, it does. What about you? Do you attend church?"

"I did when I was a kid, but I don't remember much about it—except that I hated sitting still so long. I always had to be out running around. And I do remember asking Jesus into my heart in Sunday school. It was a long time ago. I must have been all of five."

"Then you're a believer, too. Wonderful! I've found a very nice church here in Honolulu. You might want to try it sometime."

He actually winked at her. "If it means you'll be there, maybe I will."

They both lapsed into silence as they ate. After a while she asked, "How did you end up in Hawaii?"

"I came here about three years ago."

"Just to get away from California?"

"You could say that. My dad died. My mom remarried. A romance went sour. It seemed like a good time for a change of scenery. What about you?"

She gave him a thumbnail sketch of her history—except for the fire—and finished with, "Now my aunt and I are just waiting to move into our new home."

"The one near Diamond Head Road?"

"Yes. How did you know?"

"Your contractor, Leo Mahala, mentioned it the day he gave me his card."

"Really? I don't remember that."

"Yeah, he did."

"Have they found out yet what caused that house fire?"

"They're still investigating, but it looks like arson. Not the first case in that area, either."

Kayli shivered. Why had she been foolish enough to bring up the subject of fire? It was the last thing she wanted to talk about. It was time to change the subject fast. She scoured her mind for another topic. "So does your mom still live in California?"

"No, she moved to Oregon after she got remarried. No family left in California now. How about you—your parents still there?"

She swallowed hard. "Um, yes, they are." It was true to a degree—they were buried there. Why was it so hard to admit they were dead?

"I'm surprised you moved so far away. Did your folks lay the old guilt trip on you?"

"No." She poked at her lemon chicken. "The truth is, Rick, my parents died when I was five. My aunt raised me."

"Oh?" His brows arched with surprise. "I'm sorry."

"Me, too."

"Tell me if I'm prying—was it a car accident?"

"No." The silence grew heavy between them. Finally she said, so softly she wondered if he heard, "A fire." There. She had said it.

Rick sat forward, all his senses seemingly alert. "A fire? Were you there?"

"Yes, but I don't remember it. I don't even have any memory of my parents, except vague feelings and impressions."

"Really? Like what?"

Kayli shifted in her chair. She rarely talked with anyone about this—and here she was confiding in a stranger. "I remember someone holding me and singing to me. She kept calling me 'sweet joy of my life.' She had the most melodic voice I ever heard. It must have been my mother."

"That's a beautiful memory. Much better to carry that with you than memories of the fire."

"I suppose so." She set her fork down. She wasn't hungry anymore. "But it's so hard not knowing what really happened." That was another thing she rarely admitted to anyone.

"You don't know how it started?"

"They say it was a candle. The power had gone out. We had candles burning."

"That's how lots of fires start."

"But I don't know who was holding the candle." She looked down at her hands. She was trembling—on the verge of a panic attack. She had to get out of here—now!

Rick reached across the table and seized her hand. His hand was large and strong and work worn. He had long calloused fingers that were square at the nail. His grip was firm, almost comforting. "You blame yourself, don't you? You think you caused the fire that killed your parents."

Kayli's mouth went dry. For a long moment her heart seemed to pause in midbeat. Clocks stopped ticking. The very air she breathed was sucked out of her.

"You didn't do it, Kayli. It wasn't your fault."

Tears gathered in her eyes and spilled onto her lashes. "But what if it was?"

Rick tightened his grasp. "I promise you it wasn't. You don't know fire like I do. It's treacherous. It has a life and mind of its own. It's an enemy like no other. I've faced it down over and over. I've seen how evil it can be, how ruthless. You were a child. You didn't have a chance against it. And yet you won. You're here. You're alive. You defeated it. That should give you an incredible sense of victory."

She grabbed a tissue from her purse and blotted her eyes. "But my parents didn't make it."

"Then you must live life enough for all three of you."

"I'm trying. I know God has a reason for everything, but I'll never understand why He let my parents die."

Rick's expression hardened. "I don't know why God does a lot of the stuff He does. If He's so loving and powerful, why has He let this world get so messed up?"

"I don't know. I just know He loves us, and when we hurt He's the first to weep."

"You really believe that?"

"I really do. Even when I can't understand Him, I know He's there for me."

"Well, I can't say He's been there for me lately, but then again, maybe I wasn't looking hard enough for Him."

"That could be, Rick. If you trusted Him as a child, He's still there in your heart. Try talking to Him again. You'll be surprised how close He is." She glanced at her watch. "Oh my, Tara gave me an hour, and it's already gone. I've got to get back to work."

Rick signaled for the check. "Listen, I'll get this. You get back to your job."

They stood up and looked at each other. She couldn't find words to describe how he made her feel. He stirred within her a sense of expectation that was both exciting and alarming. How could she possibly feel so many conflicting emotions for a man she had known for only an hour?

He took her hand again between his sturdy palms. "I want to see you again, Kayli."

She lowered her gaze. "I'm sure we'll run into each other again sometime."

His hands tightened around hers. "I'm not leaving it to chance. Go out with me tonight. Dinner—anywhere you wish. Or if not tonight, tomorrow night. This weekend. You say the word."

Her head was spinning. "I really don't even know you."

"Then give us a chance to get acquainted. There's a connection between us, Kayli. Don't you feel it? I sensed it the moment I saw you."

She weighed her options. Her prudent self said, *Be careful*; her adventurous self said, *You've got to see him again!* "How about coming to my church on Sunday?" Surely that was safe enough. "We could sit together and maybe have lunch afterward." *That's when Aunt Jessie and I have lunch with Jay and Leo Mahala, but surely they won't mind this once.*

"I'll be there," said Rick. "What's the address?"

She scribbled it on a napkin, handed it to him, and hurried off with a self-conscious little wave. By the time she got back to the gallery Tara had finished framing the painting.

"So how was lunch?"

"Okay."

"Just okay? You took the full hour. It must have been better than okay."

She wanted to say it was the most surreal hour of her life, that her emotions ran the gamut from pleasure to anguish and that she had confided things to a stranger that she hadn't told another living person. But all she could manage was, "It was. . .nice."

"Are you going to see him again?"

"Yes. On Sunday. He's coming to church and then we're going to lunch afterward."

"Good. You can't go wrong with a church date."

"That's what I figured." But already she was having second thoughts. How was she going to explain to Jay that she couldn't go to lunch with him because she had another date?

Chapter 9

They were running late this morning. Jay had stayed up late Saturday night going over some specs for a new client. This morning he must have turned off the alarm and gone back to sleep. Jay's father sometimes called the cottage and told him to come have breakfast with him. But not this morning. So by the time Jay woke again, he had less than an hour before church started. He quickly showered and dressed and was still running a comb through his hair as he strode from the cottage to the main house.

His father was on the phone—no doubt a business call—and didn't even hear Jay enter the kitchen. Jay rattled the doorknob. His dad looked over from the breakfast table and gave a little wave. That meant, *Help yourself. I'm busy right now.*

Jay poured himself some coffee, glanced in the refrigerator long enough to see there was nothing interesting, then helped himself to half a bagel on the countertop. The cream cheese was sitting out, so he smeared some on the bagel and sat down across from his dad.

Jay sipped his coffee but the room was warm and airless. The coffee only made him warmer. His dad didn't mind the heat. He rarely remembered to turn on the air conditioner or open windows. "We're late for church," Jay mouthed.

His dad nodded and gestured toward the phone as if to say, *I can't get this idiot off the line.* Finally, after another minute or two of conversation, he hung up with a sigh of relief. "I shouldn't have to deal with stuff like this on Sunday morning," he remarked.

Jay bit into his bagel. "Then why don't you let someone else handle it?"

"Because nobody else knows the business better than I do."

Jay nodded. "Enough said."

His father stood up. He was wearing an aloha shirt and khaki trousers. Jay was in a blue shirt, slacks, and tie. "You look comfortable, Dad. Maybe I should take off my tie."

"Do that, son. I thought we'd take the ladies on a picnic today."

Jay loosened his tie. "A picnic? Where?"

"The beach, of course. We'll pick up some takeout somewhere and we're all set. I already put some blankets and lawn chairs in the car."

"Did you tell Kayli and Jessie what you're planning?"

"No, I'll tell them when we see them. You know we don't stand on ceremony with those gals. No formal invitations—just an unspoken arrangement. That's the beauty of it. We all know we're going to spend the afternoon together, so we can make plans on the spur of the moment. It keeps life interesting."

Jay stood up, pulled off his tie, and draped it over the back of the chair. "I think they would like to know you're planning a picnic, Dad. I'm sure they'd like to dress appropriately."

"Hadn't thought of that, son." He scratched his head. "But no problem. We can always stop by their place and let them change."

"I suppose. It's too late to call them now. They'll already be at church."

"Speaking of church, we'd better get going." His father pulled his keys out of his pocket. "I'll drive this time."

Jay grabbed his bagel, swallowed the last of his coffee, and followed his dad outside to his shiny sedan. The morning air was already muggy. The first thing Jay did when he got in the car was turn on the air conditioner.

"Turn it your way," said his dad as he pulled out onto the street. "I don't want that blowing on me."

They were silent for a few minutes. Jay watched the passing scenery, but his thoughts were on Kayli. He hadn't seen her since that day at the housing site. Hadn't called her, either. Why hadn't he? He didn't want her thinking he didn't care. Or maybe he was afraid she'd realize he cared too much. Glancing over at his dad, he asked, "How are things going with Jessie?"

His dad kept his gaze straight ahead, both hands on the steering wheel. "What things?"

"I don't know. Things. Have you thought of asking her on a date, just the two of you?"

"No, why? Don't you like the four of us going out together on Sundays?"

"Sure, I do. I think we all enjoy hanging out together."

"You bet we do. Sundays have become my favorite day of the week."

"That's what I mean, Dad. It doesn't have to be just on Sundays. You could invite Jessie out on a date sometime, just you and her."

His father gave him a sidelong glance. "Now who's matchmaking?"

"I'm not matchmaking. I'm just making a suggestion. I see how Jessie looks at you. She adores you. And she's good company. You could do worse."

His father braked for a stoplight. "What about you, JJ? Your pretty little Kayli would make a perfect wife for you. I haven't seen you making any moves to advance your relationship."

"You know me, Dad. I'm not much for change. I like the status quo just like you do."

"Then why are we having this conversation?" His dad accelerated hard and the car jerked forward. He wasn't a smooth, conscientious driver like Jay. "Our lives are in a good place right now, son. Why rock the boat?"

Jay nodded. "I suppose you're right. But I have been thinking a lot about Kayli lately. I'm thinking maybe you're right about her, Dad. She could be the girl for me."

His father reached over and slapped Jay's knee. "Didn't I tell you? You bet she's for you. You're the one who should be making dates for just the two of you."

"Maybe so." The car felt stuffy and close. Jay turned up the air-conditioning. "I just don't want to tip my hand before I'm sure it's what God wants for us."

"Come on, JJ. I thought you and God were pretty tight. Surely He's given you the go-ahead by now."

"Maybe He has. Maybe I've just been too afraid it was my own voice I was hearing, my own selfish desires."

"There's nothing selfish about wanting the love of a good woman. If God's not in it, He'll put a stop to it fast. Of course, that's advice from someone who hasn't been on a first-name basis lately with the Almighty."

"You could be, Dad. He wants you back. He's waiting with open arms."

"Hey, we were talking about you and Kayli."

"I hear you. I'll give it some thought—what you said about God approving of Kayli and me."

"You love her, JJ?"

He thought a minute. "Yeah, Dad, I do."

"Does she love you?"

Jay suppressed a wry little chuckle. "That's the million-dollar question."

It was funny. He had never consciously asked himself those questions—*Do you love her. . .does she love you?* Why hadn't he? Was he afraid of the answers? Was he afraid of what a commitment to someone would mean for his future?

All of his life he had been well taken care of. An only child, he had never lacked any of the good things life offered. Some would say he was born with a silver spoon in his mouth. He had never had to take responsibility for someone else—the way a husband cared for his wife or a father for his children.

And yet he was a caring, responsible man. At least that's how he saw himself. He worked hard, tirelessly, to make his father's company a success. Strange that he still considered it his father's company when it was just as much his. But he recognized he was also a man who took things for granted—his parents, his job, his home.

It had shaken him to the core when his mother died. It had made him realize that someday he would lose his father, as well. Could he bear investing himself in someone else who might one day leave him, too? It was a selfish, shortsighted question. Of course he wanted a family of his own someday—a wife and children. But it had always been a nebulous idea, a plan for the distant future.

But maybe the future was now. He had never felt about any woman the way he felt about Kayli. Wasn't it time to tell her so?

"It's as cold as Alaska in this car," muttered his father as he pulled into the church parking lot.

Jay snapped off the air conditioner. Within moments oppressive heat invaded the vehicle. A rush of warmth invaded his heart, as well. Shortly he would be seeing Kayli again, sitting beside her, feeling the warmth of her skin against his as they sat elbow to elbow in the straight pew. Yes, God willing, it was time to speak his heart to the woman he loved. *God, give me the words to say. If You want us together, let everything work out for us. Show me this is Your will.*

"Hey, JJ, you just going to sit there? We're already late."

Startled, he swung open the door and nearly sprinted out of the car. As they strode up the church steps, he glanced at his watch. Five minutes late. That wasn't bad. He hoped Kayli and Jessie were waiting in the vestibule. It would be hard to find them if they were already seated.

Sure enough, Jessie was standing just inside the door.

Leo greeted her first. "Thanks for waiting, Jess."

Jay asked, "Is Kayli saving us seats?"

An odd expression crossed Jessie's face. "I'm sorry, it'll just be the three of us today."

Jay masked his disappointment. "What's wrong? Is Kayli sick?"

Jessie lowered her gaze. "No, she's here. But she's sitting with someone else."

"Someone else? Who?"

"Someone she invited to church."

"Oh, okay. That's fine." *Who is it? Tara? Someone else from work?* There was no time for more questions.

They entered the auditorium and slipped into a back pew. Jay scanned the crowd for a glimpse of Kayli. Finally he spotted her. She was sitting near the front between an elderly woman and a broad-shouldered man. *She's probably with the woman. Must be someone from her apartment building. We'll invite her to join us for lunch. Doesn't matter whether it's four or five of us.*

Jay had a hard time concentrating on the sermon. His thoughts kept returning to Kayli as his eyes darted in her direction. He felt slightly miffed. She should have sat with them even if she had brought a guest.

But then again, he and his dad had arrived late. That's why she hadn't waited. He kicked himself for oversleeping. If they had gotten here early they could have made introductions and sat together.

After the service, while Jessie and his father went on to the car, Jay waited in the foyer for Kayli to emerge with her guest. At last the elderly lady ambled by, but Kayli wasn't with her. After several frustrating moments he spotted her in the crowd. His mind did a double take. Kayli was walking in stride with the broad-shouldered stranger.

Jay made his way through the throng and grasped her arm. She stopped and looked at him in surprise.

Now that he was facing her he didn't know what to say. She seemed as speechless as he. His gaze moved to the tall man beside her.

Jay's face flamed. "I'm sorry, Kayli, I just wanted to say—hi." *What a stupid, lame thing to say! What I really want to know is who is this jerk you're with?*

"Hi, Jay." She had finally found her voice, but just barely. "You two have met before. Jay, this is Rick Moran. Rick, this is Jay Mahala."

Jay debated whether to offer his hand. Grudgingly he did. The man pumped it vigorously. "Good to see you again, Mr. Mahala—Jay."

Jay's eyes narrowed. Did he know this man? Not on his life. He wouldn't forget someone who managed to seem larger than life and looked like he'd just stepped out of a movie magazine. "You say we've met before?"

"Rick is the fireman we met the day we saw that house on fire and at the gallery when the wiring shorted out. Captain Moran. Remember?" Kayli's voice sounded breathy, overly enthusiastic. "Your dad gave him his card."

Jay remembered. What he couldn't figure out now was why this guy was standing here with his arm around Kayli. "It's nice to see you. . .Rick." The words tasted sour in his mouth. What he wanted to say was, *Move on, mister. I've got plans with my girl.*

"Rick stopped by the gallery a few days ago," said Kayli, as if that explained everything.

"Interested in art?" inquired Jay dryly.

Rick flashed a triumphant grin. "No. Interested in Kayli. She's quite a girl. But then you know that. You're building her a house."

Jay felt a sinking sensation in his chest. It was as if this Rick character had thrown down the gauntlet and knew instinctively that Jay wouldn't pick it up. But Jay wasn't about to be defeated yet. He turned to Kayli. "Dad planned a picnic for this afternoon. You're coming, aren't you?" When her gaze fled to Rick for his reaction, Jay knew he was in trouble. Through clenched teeth he added, "You're invited, too, Rick, if you'd like to join us."

Rick pulled Kayli a little closer. "Thanks, but we already have plans."

Jay turned back to Kayli. The look that passed between them was crushing. It said, *I'm sorry, it's too late. I've moved on.* He would have felt better if the big guy had punched him square in the nose.

"I'm sorry, Jay. Maybe another time," she murmured, and with that she turned and walked out the door with the big bruiser.

Watching them go, Jay felt like a chastised puppy yelping and running in circles with his tail between his legs. It was stupid and irrational, but he felt abandoned, betrayed. He rubbed his chin as if he could somehow massage away his disappointment. Only now did he realize how much he loved Kayli and how hard it would be to let her go.

Chapter 10

Aunt Jessie was baking cookies—not the store-bought kind that come in a tube or a package, but real homemade ones with bittersweet chocolate chips and walnut pieces. Kayli stood watching her, arms crossed, debating whether to make a fuss about it or just let it go. It was her aunt's life after all; she was an adult; no matter what Kayli said, she'd do just as she pleased.

In spite of her mental arguments to live and let live, Kayli's motherly instincts won out. She went over and put a hand on her aunt's shoulder. "Aunt Jessie, you know you shouldn't be eating cookies. Think of your blood sugar."

Her aunt pivoted and looked her directly in the eye. "My blood sugar's just fine, thank you. And I'm not eating these cookies; I'm *baking* them."

"But then you'll eat them."

"No, I won't, at least not all of them. I'm making a batch for Leo. Besides, I made them with that sugar substitute."

"But you've still been eating too many sweets lately. I worry about you. Diabetes is nothing to fool around with. I just don't want to see you sick again."

"I'm feeling great, honey. You worry about your own life."

Kayli paused to process her aunt's words. "Are you saying I have something to worry about, Aunt Jessie?"

Her aunt opened the oven door and shoved the cookie sheet inside. She set the timer then looked back at Kayli. There was something in her snapping black eyes Kayli hadn't seen before. "Are you going out with that fireman again?"

"Rick? Yes. We're going to dinner. Why?"

"It just baffles me why you're taking up with another man when you have a perfectly good one who's crazy about you."

Kayli swiped the bowl of cookie dough with her index finger and stuck the sugary mound into her mouth. "I'm not taking up with another man."

"Stop that!" Her aunt swatted her hand as she reached for another dab of chocolate-studded batter. "Don't eat it before it's baked. It's not safe. It has raw eggs in it."

"I've seen you sampling raw cookie dough for as long as I can remember," Kayli protested. "And you haven't died yet."

"That's just it. I've been doing it so long I'm immune."

Kayli took another swipe. "Okay, so I inherited my immunity from you."

Aunt Jessie took another look at Kayli, as if sizing her up. "You're all dressed up. Is your fireman taking you somewhere fancy?"

"He's not *my* fireman. His name is Rick, and yes, he did say to dress up. I'm not sure where we're going."

"You really like him?"

Kayli squirmed inwardly. She and Aunt Jessie saw eye to eye on many things, but not on Rick Moran. "I don't know him that well, but he seems nice."

Jessie scooped up spoonfuls of dough and placed them inches apart on the cookie sheet. "You know, Jay was so jealous last Sunday he couldn't see straight."

Now her aunt had her attention. "He was? How do you know?"

"Because I could see he was miserable at lunch with just the three of us."

"What did he say?"

"Nothing. But he was brooding. I could tell. You broke his heart."

"I did no such thing." Kayli was indignant now. "I went to lunch with a friend just as I go to lunch with Jay, who's also a friend. He's never come out and said that he wants to be anything more."

Jessie's dark eyes flashed. "Mark my words. Jay Mahala is head over heels in love with you."

"If he is, he has a strange way of showing it."

"He's a man who's set in his ways. He's been too busy to think about love and romance. Now that he's found you, he doesn't know what to do about it."

"You're making excuses for him, Aunt Jessie. If Jay loves me, then let him speak for himself. So far he seems perfectly happy with friendship."

"That was until your fireman came into your life."

Kayli put her hands on her hips. Her aunt's words weren't making a convincing case for Jay; they were only raising her ire. "If Jay cares so much about me, how come he hasn't called me once since Sunday? If he wants me, why can't he fight for me?"

Jessie nodded. "Maybe he thinks the more gentlemanly thing to do is bow out and let you have your firefighter."

"He's not my firefighter!" Kayli's stress level was heading for the boiling point. "At least Rick asks me out on official dates. Maybe you don't mind Leo taking you for granted and just assuming you'll be available on a moment's notice. But that's not good enough for me." She regretted her words the instant she saw the crestfallen expression on her aunt's face.

"I'm sorry, Aunt Jessie." She went over and gave her a hug. "I shouldn't have said that. I know you're enjoying your relationship with Leo. I wasn't trying to criticize you."

Waving her away, her aunt turned back to her baking. "It's okay. I know you weren't trying to be cruel, honey. I do wish Leo and I could be more than friends, but until I know he's put God first in his life again, I'm content with friendship."

Kayli rubbed her aunt's arm in a conciliatory gesture. "You're a godly, wise, good-looking woman. He's lucky to have you in his life."

Jessie smiled. "I think he appreciates me whether he admits it or not."

"And I appreciate you, too." Kayli kissed her aunt's cheek. "Now, if you'll excuse me, I've got to finish getting ready for my date."

Rick arrived at six o'clock sharp. He took one look at her and said, "Wow! You look gorgeous!"

She did a self-conscious little pirouette in her black cocktail dress and three-inch heels. "Thank you, kind sir. And you look very handsome in your black suit."

"Thank you. I hope the purple shirt and tie aren't too flashy."

"You're asking that of an artist who absolutely loves color?"

"That's what I figured."

He placed his large, square hands on her shoulders. "Have you ever thought of doing a self-portrait?"

"Not really. I prefer seascapes."

"What if I commissioned you to paint one of yourself? Would you do it?"

"I don't know. Where would you hang it—in the fire station?"

"Maybe. Then all the guys would be jealous knowing I'm dating the most beautiful girl in the world."

She wanted to say, *This may be a date, but until I know where you stand spiritually we're still in friendship mode, just getting acquainted.* But she couldn't bring herself to put a damper on their conversation. Rick looked so happy. Why spoil his mood with technicalities?

"I don't live at the firehouse all the time," he was saying as he opened the front door for her. "I have my own little apartment on Kalakaua Avenue near the Ala Wai Canal. I divide my time between that and the station. You'll have to see it sometime."

"The station?"

"And my apartment, too. I'd love to show you some of my clippings."

She gave him a searching glance. "Is that anything like seeing your etchings?"

He laughed. "Not at all. I promise to always be a perfect gentleman. I'm not trying to toot my own horn, but I'd like you to see some of the articles about the fires I've fought and, yeah, even the people I've rescued. I want you to get to know me."

She wasn't sure how to respond to that, so she said nothing. Before stepping out the door she called, "Bye, Aunt Jessie. I won't be late."

Her aunt came bustling out of the kitchen and handed Rick a cellophane-wrapped package. "Here are some cookies for you, Captain Moran. I figure every man loves chocolate chip cookies."

Rick held the parcel up to his nose and inhaled deeply. "I smelled these the moment I came in. I was sure hoping someone would take pity on me and give me one. A whole plateful is more than I could have asked for."

Jessie beamed. "Enjoy them. There's more where they came from."

Rick kissed her hand with a knightly flourish. "Thank you, beautiful lady." Aunt Jessie's face virtually glowed. Rick was doing a good job of winning her over. She even had a little smile on her face when they said good-bye.

"Kayli, I hope you don't mind riding again in my truck," Rick said as he walked her out to his shiny black pickup.

"Not at all. It's actually quite comfortable for a—"

"Truck?"

She chuckled. "Yes. A truck." He helped her inside and she fastened her seat belt. "Where are we going?" she asked when he pulled out and merged with traffic.

"You'll see." He put on a light jazz CD. "If you don't like this, I have easy listening, rock, classics, and country."

"Looks like I won't get bored." As he drove, she glanced over at his sturdy profile. He was a ruggedly handsome man with a sensitive, complex personality—a fascinating study in contrasts. He was fond of good music and art; he could be kind and gentle, charming even Aunt Jessie; he had Kayli confiding her own personal secrets their first time out; and yet he made his living rushing into burning buildings when others were running out. *Was it a man like Rick Moran who risked his life to rescue me when my parents' house was burning? Maybe that's why I'm drawn to him.*

"A penny for your thoughts," he said after a while. "Or considering inflation, how about a dollar?"

She chuckled. "A penny will do. I was just wondering what kind of person willingly puts his life in danger every day to protect others."

Rick drummed his fingers on his leather-wrapped steering wheel. "Someone who loves the thrill of battle, who sees an enemy—even when that enemy is nature itself gone wrong—and wants to conquer it with every fiber of his being."

"That's an amazing answer. I wish I were as brave as you. Fire has been my enemy for as long as I can remember. It's kept me paralyzed with fear. It's the one area of my life I've never had victory over. I admire the fact that you can face it without fear and conquer it."

"I didn't say there was no fear, Kayli. Fear energizes me. It makes me even more determined to take control over one of the most powerful forces on earth."

"Maybe someday I'll stop being afraid," she murmured wistfully.

"Maybe I can help you."

"I don't know how."

"Trust me. I'll figure out something." He turned onto Kalakaua Avenue.

"Are we going to your place?"

"No, we're heading toward the ocean."

"Are we eating on the beach?"

"You might say that." He pulled into the plush Outrigger Waikiki Hotel grounds and entered the lane for valet parking. "At least it'll be easy to spot my truck among all the fancy cars."

After entering the hotel he escorted her arm in arm to Chuck's Steak House, where the view of the ocean and Diamond Head was spectacular. As the hostess showed them to their table overlooking the beach, Kayli flinched. In the center of their table was a glass bowl with a flickering candle. Rick must have noticed, too, for he whispered something to the hostess and she immediately removed the candle.

"Thank you," she told him as he held her chair for her. "Not just for being polite, but for knowing I couldn't sit here with that candle right under my nose."

"No problem. If it's too dark to read the menu I have it practically memorized anyway. I love the steaks here."

"Then I'll let you order for both of us—again."

He ordered as if he were a connoisseur of fine cuisine—shrimp cocktail, warm spinach salad, chateaubriand for two, baked potatoes with the works, fresh asparagus, and cherries jubilee.

"That's enough food for a week," she remarked after the waiter had gone.

"Don't worry. You can take the leftovers home for lunch tomorrow."

"I'm not going to ask for a doggie bag in a place like this."

"Then I will. I'm not trying to impress anyone. . .except maybe you."

She raised her water glass to her lips. "You've done a good job of it so far."

The food was extraordinary. Kayli hadn't realized how hungry she was. Rick was such an eager conversationalist that, once she tossed out an initial question or two about his work, he chatted on and on while she ate.

"The thing about being a fireman," he remarked as he cut his steak into neat little pieces, "is that you have to be a jack-of-all-trades. When we're not fighting fires, we work on the engines, doing repairs and maintenance. They're amazing vehicles—sleek, massive, and powerful. They're all different. You have fire tankers, fire tenders, and fire tanker pumpers. Some have thirty-five-hundred-gallon tanks. One of these days I'd like to take you for a ride with me on a ladder truck. I think you'd like it."

"No thanks. That's one ride I don't want to take."

"I'll convince you. You wait and see."

She laughed. "You'd have to hog-tie me."

"Now that's an interesting challenge."

The more they talked the more she realized his favorite subject was her least favorite—*fire*. Over the next hour he recounted tales of his firefighting exploits, of people he had rescued, awards and honors he had received, and times he had nearly perished in a burning warehouse or hotel.

Kayli tried to listen with polite detachment, but with every frightening detail he shared she felt her body tensing and her anxieties growing. She tried to change the subject, but Rick—his face animated, his hands gesturing expansively—was obviously on a roll. He had a captive audience and was relishing every moment.

"So many new recruits are determined to rush into a burning building without knowing what they're up against. The thing is, the hose team needs to know the potential for a flashover or backdraft. They have to learn how to read the smoke—its volume, density, velocity, and color. You know, it's crazy. So many buildings today are filled with all kinds of plastic and synthetic materials. They generate huge amounts of toxic smoke. I remember one house—when we arrived, thick, black smoke was billowing out of the windows on both the alpha and bravo sides of the structure and—"

"Rick, please, no more. . ."

He paused and looked at her, really looked at her. With a groan he slapped his forehead. "Man, what a jerk I am—I'm scaring the life out of you, aren't I?"

"Getting close, I'm afraid." She lowered her gaze and concentrated on her breathing, willing her body to relax. She must not have a panic attack, not here, not now. "It's not your fault, Rick. It's me. It's my problem."

He took her hand and rubbed her skin with his large, rough hands. "Listen, Kayli, I'm sorry. I shouldn't have been rattling on like this. It's just that I don't often find someone so easy to talk to. Are you okay? Tell me you're okay."

"I'm okay," she said, because that's what he wanted to hear. But in her heart of hearts she wondered if she would ever be okay. On the screen of her mind flashed a familiar image from her dreams—a little girl with a candle in a room full of smoke and flames. *It was me. I know it was. I killed my parents. If it wasn't for me they would still be alive!*

Chapter 11

Kayli sat at her easel spreading an acrylic wash over her canvas—cerulean blue, raw umber, and burnt sienna. Her arm moved with a wide swath, her wrist flexing, her brush emulating the graceful rhythms of an orchestra conductor. She applied several dabs of black pigment, blending them with the blues and browns until jagged rivulets twisted through the blue-brown suffusion. With quick, vigorous strokes she spread streaks of burnt orange and alizarin crimson, like flaming lightning bolts, through the shadowy haze. At last she exchanged her wide brush for a fine-tipped sable brush and sketched the form of a young girl in the midst of the murky, swirling colors. The child was standing alone, holding a candle.

Aunt Jessie entered the room just then and stood watching in silence. Kayli kept working, but her concentration was broken. She felt ill at ease. She knew what her aunt was thinking.

Finally Aunt Jessie sat down on a wicker chair beside the easel. "I thought you were working on a seascape. The sunlight on the water is perfect this time of day."

Kayli set her brush down and swiveled around on her stool, facing her aunt. "I didn't feel like a seascape today."

"But this—!" Her aunt gestured toward the canvas, her voice etched with concern. "Why are you painting this, honey?"

"Because I want to." Kayli scraped bits of dry paint off her knuckles. "How else am I supposed to get my feelings out?"

"You could talk about it."

"About what? The fire? What's the use of talking? I don't have any memories. I just have the dreams. And the feelings and impressions. They're all so elusive. When I try to pin them down, they evaporate. But they always come back."

"Are the dreams getting worse?"

"Not worse exactly. Just more frequent."

"Do you suppose it's because you're dating a firefighter? Isn't that just asking for trouble?"

Kayli dipped her brush in the water container and swished it around. "Most of the time Rick makes me feel safe. In my mind I imagine him being the fireman who carried me from my burning house."

Aunt Jessie sat back and folded her hands on her lap. She looked worried.

"Maybe you should see a professional, honey."

"A psychiatrist? You sent me to a counselor when I was a little girl. It didn't help."

"Maybe it would help now. There has to be an answer. What can I do to help you, sweetheart?"

Kayli shrugged. "You've done more than I could ever ask. You've been a great mother, the only mother I'll ever know."

"But sometimes I feel like a poor substitute. Your mother was such a dear, godly woman."

Kayli squeezed the water from her brush and set it on her palette. "When I first met Rick I told him something I remembered about my mother."

"Really? What?"

"I can't picture her face, but I can sometimes hear her voice in my head. I have the impression of someone holding me and whispering, 'Sweet joy of my life.' Was that my mother?"

Jessie thought a moment. "Yes, I can remember her calling you that. 'Sweet joy of my life.' She doted on you. She loved being a mother."

Kayli blinked back tears. She didn't want to get all weepy now, but she had to get her feelings off her chest. "The other night Rick was talking about his exploits—fires he put out, people he rescued. He even saved a little girl once. But the more he talked about his job, the more terrified I got. I was sure I was going to have a panic attack. When will I ever get over this, Aunt Jessie? When will I stop being afraid?"

"I don't know, honey. I pray for you every day."

"The worst thing is that I'm trying to be a good testimony to Rick because I'm not sure where he stands with the Lord. I think he's a Christian, but he doesn't seem that close to God. How can I convince him he should renew his faith when I have such a hard time trusting Him myself? I feel like such a loser."

Jessie sat forward and placed a comforting hand on Kayli's arm. "Please don't talk that way, honey. You have a beautiful faith in the Lord; don't let anyone tell you otherwise. We all have our struggles."

"That doesn't make me feel any better, Aunt Jessie."

"I know, sweetheart." They were both silent for a minute. Kayli picked up another brush and blended some red and yellow ochre on her palette. She daubed it on the canvas then wiped it off. It was no use; she wasn't in the mood to paint anymore.

Jessie got up and went to the kitchen. She brought back frosty glasses of lemonade and handed one to Kayli. "I've been thinking," she said, sitting back down. "Maybe instead of focusing on your fears, you should simply focus on Jesus and determine to love Him with all your heart, soul, mind, and strength, like the Scripture says."

"I do love Him, Aunt Jessie, but sometimes I still feel like a failure."

Jessie sipped her lemonade. "We all do, Kayli. I think the devil loves to get us sidetracked from loving God and worrying about our own shortcomings, instead. Any time our eyes are on ourselves instead of Him, we're going to feel discouraged."

Kayli hadn't wanted to get off on this subject right now. It was too heavy, too private, and Aunt Jessie could be more direct and hard-hitting than the preacher himself. But now that they were talking, she couldn't hold back the rush of emotions. "I guess that's why sometimes I don't feel very close to God myself," she admitted. "Sometimes it seems like He's not even there."

She was relieved that her aunt didn't flinch at her confession. She simply nodded. "I've been walking with the Lord a whole lot of years, and I still struggle. There have been times when I've felt alone and abandoned—when my parents died, and my brother—your father. You're not alone, honey. I know how you feel. You keep listening and God's voice isn't there. You begin questioning yourself and Him. You ask yourself, what's wrong with me that He's fled away? Why isn't He keeping His promise to never leave or forsake me?"

Kayli picked up her paint rag and wiped her hands. "That's how I feel right now—like things are never going to change and I'm always going to feel like this."

Jessie set her lemonade on a little rattan table beside her chair. She settled back and closed her eyes. "I remember when I first found out I had diabetes. I ended up in the hospital. My blood sugar was sky-high. I felt guilty as sin." She seemed to be talking to herself now as much as to Kayli. "I thought, 'I did this to myself. I'm not worthy. My body's betrayed me. I'll never be a whole, healthy person again.' After a while I had to give all that to God, because I knew it was too much for me to handle. I had to remember it's all about Him, not me." She opened her eyes and looked squarely at Kayli. "I'm always going to be a flawed human being, honey, but if I give Him my weaknesses He'll turn them into His strengths. They won't be wasted. He'll use me, flaws and all."

Kayli reached for her paintbrush again and mindlessly stirred little globs of yellow and purple together on the palette until they became an ugly gray. "You're the best Christian I know, Aunt Jessie. If even you struggle like that, what hope is there for any of us?"

Her aunt gave her a long, hard look. "Honey, don't you hear what I'm saying? The struggles are only half the story. The Bible says, in His presence is fullness of joy. But our emotions get the best of us; they convince us that God isn't with us. God wants us to go by faith that He's always there. Our feelings can change; we can't depend on them. Just as we're saved by faith, so the Bible says we walk by faith. Faith isn't a onetime thing; it's a full-time thing. Every day we go by faith that Jesus is right there walking with us, hearing us, loving us. We know it's true because the scriptures say so, so we accept it by faith, no matter how we feel."

"You're right, Aunt Jessie; our feelings are undependable, especially mine."

"But God is unchanging, always the same." Jessie picked up her lemonade and took a sip. "So when we're feeling bad, we don't wallow in our emotions; we turn our attention to Jesus. We say, 'What can I do for You, Lord? How can I serve You better? How can I love You more?' And the more we tell Him we love Him, the more our perspective changes, and we start seeing things through His eyes, not our own."

Kayli smiled. "You preach it, Aunt Jessie."

A spontaneous grin spread across her aunt's wide lips. "Oh my, I didn't mean to preach a sermon. It's just that my heart aches for you, sweetheart."

"It's okay," said Kayli. "I love hearing you talk about the Lord. You make it all sound so easy."

"Not easy, but possible. All things are possible with Him. We have to get out of ourselves and into His presence before the joy can start. Once we have that joy, then we have His strength, because the Bible says, 'The joy of the Lord is your strength.' That's how we get by in this world."

"The next time I feel afraid I'm going to think of all you've said. I think I'll do better."

"I think so, too." Fine drops of perspiration stood out on Aunt Jessie's face. She pressed her lemonade glass against her cheek. "You talk about how your mama used to call you 'sweet joy of my life.' That's what Jesus is to us, honey. He's our sweet joy. Our life. The sweet joy of our life."

"I love that idea," said Kayli. "That's what I want—for Him to be the 'sweet joy of my life.' "

"Do you feel better, honey? Less down on yourself?"

"I do, Aunt Jessie. You always have a way of making things better. When I was a little girl you kissed my hurts and made them better. Now that I'm grown you know how to reach the invisible hurts and make them better."

"Girl, that's the best thing you could ever say to me." Tears glazed Aunt Jessie's eyes. She got out of her chair and took her lemonade to the kitchen, came back with a cloth, then wiped the water ring off the table.

Picking up her brush again, Kayli mixed white and yellow paint and swept her brush over the deep blues and browns. The canvas looked brighter already. With swift, determined strokes she covered the entire canvas with a light, golden wash. Gone was the solitary girl with her candle and the billowing darkness that surrounded her. *Now if only my fears can be vanquished as easily!*

"They say even Mother Teresa struggled with what they call 'the dark night of the soul,' " she said as she added more white to the canvas.

"That's right," said Jessie. "I hear she felt empty of God's presence for much of her life. I don't know why she felt that way—maybe she focused too much on what she considered her own unworthiness—but I believe it doesn't have to be that way. There's a verse I remember from the old King James: 'Thou wilt keep him in perfect peace, whose mind is stayed on thee.' That's the secret, Kayli. When the doubts and fears come, focus only on Him. And love Him, love Him, love Him!"

Kayli looked toward the lanai. Already the sun was starting to set; the sky was darkening. She put her brush in the water and stood up. "Look what time it is. Rick is picking me up at seven."

"Another date with your firefighter? Didn't you just see him the other night?"

"It's not a date, Aunt Jessie. He's showing me the firehouse. We're just friends, absolutely nothing more."

"Try telling him that. That boy has marriage on his mind."

Kayli put her acrylics away and washed her brushes. "At least someone cares about me that way."

"Sounds to me like you're on the rebound."

"How can I rebound from something that never was? Besides, when I first came here I said I didn't want to get serious about any man. And I mean that."

Jessie got up, stretched, and arched her shoulders. "You mean, until Jay Mahala gives you some encouragement?"

"You win, Aunt Jessie. You know me way too well!" Kayli wrapped her arms around her aunt and kissed her smooth, warm cheek. "Thanks for the pep talk. It was just what I needed."

With a new sense of confidence in the Lord, Kayli accompanied Rick to the firehouse—a gray ranch-style building with red doors. She met his colleagues, took the grand tour of the station, saw his uniforms and gear, and got a close-up view of one of the massive fire trucks—what Rick called a "poly tanker," with shiny apple-red paint and bright, polished aluminum trim.

"I wish I could show you HFD's command center truck, but it's out on a call right now."

"Is it another fire truck?"

"No, it's much more—a technological marvel complete with telescopic camera, video cameras, a state-of-the-art communication system, and even a bathroom and onboard galley. It allows commanders to communicate with their men from air-conditioned comfort. It provides the crew a workplace and a break from the harsh elements. Personnel can check the crew's medical status and make sure they have food and water regularly."

"Sounds like quite an innovation."

"It is, especially for us here in Hawaii. On the mainland, if the fire gets out of hand, they can call in firefighters from other states across the nation. Here we're on our own, thousands of miles from help. Oh sure, we can call in backup units from other cities and firefighters from other islands. But if we don't do the job, it doesn't get done."

"You're giving me a whole new appreciation for our fire department."

They went back inside the firehouse and sat down at a table in the kitchenette. He got two cans of soda from the fridge then set two photo albums in front of her. "I figured I'm not going to get you to my apartment, so I brought my scrapbooks here to show you—assuming you're still interested in seeing them."

"Of course I am." She opened the first one. There were several photos of Rick in various outfits—a green jumpsuit, a yellow parka and safety vest, a navy bomber jacket. "I like this one," she said, pointing to a photo of Rick in a black double-breasted Bogart-style trench coat. "You look like you should be in one of those foreign intrigue movies."

"Yeah, well, if firefighting doesn't work out, I may try Hollywood."

He pointed to a black-and-white snapshot. "This was during my EMT training—that's Emergency Medical Technician." He turned the page to another photo. "This is when I got my First Responder certificate."

She smiled. "I like this one of you in the fleece jacket and cute little beanie."

"That was taken in California right after I'd finished boot camp. We were on a practice drill in the San Bernardino Mountains." He flipped over several pages. "If you like the beanie, you'll love my canvas boonie hat and orange navigator jacket with all its fancy reflective tape."

She laughed. "Oh yes, that has to be next year's fashion trend."

"No way. I'll leave the fashion stuff to you." He reached over and squeezed her hand. "You always look hot no matter what you're wearing."

"Thank you." She gently retrieved her hand and turned the page. "What about this one?" She pointed to a photo of Rick in what appeared to be a naval officer's uniform—black trousers; a jacket with two rows of shiny brass buttons, yellow stripes, and epaulets; white gloves; and a captain's hat with gold braid across the front.

"That's when I was working for the Long Beach Fire Department. It's called a Class A uniform. We wear them for special occasions—official programs, government ceremonies, funerals, that sort of thing." He closed the book and opened the second one. It was filled with newspaper clippings about the exploits and accomplishments of fire departments in California and Hawaii. Several articles featured Rick and showed him in the act of fighting brush fires and warehouse fires. Even if they were just photographs, Kayli cringed at the sight of billowing black smoke and dancing flames. She closed her eyes. *Lord, help me. I've got to conquer my fears someday!*

Rick turned to another article. A large color photo showed him climbing down a ladder with a little girl in his arms. Flames shot from the windows of the building and smoke was everywhere. Yet Rick looked calm and composed.

"How do you do it?" she asked. "How do you go into a burning building and save someone and make it look like a walk in the park?"

Rick sat forward, shoulders hunched, elbows on the table. "It's like this," he said in a confidential tone, "it's my mission in life to fight fires. Every fire is a test, a battle, a challenge. Who will win—the fire or me?" He reached across the table and took her hand. "You know what it's like, even if you don't consciously remember it. You were brave. You personally confronted that deadly enemy and won. You didn't let the fire destroy you. Do you have any idea how much I admire you for that?"

She shifted uneasily in her chair. She didn't want his admiration for surviving something as horrific as the fire that claimed her parents' lives. She didn't deserve his praise. "I wasn't brave. I was helpless and terrified." As a sob rose, the words caught in her throat. "I was a child—a child! Don't you understand, Rick? It might have been my fault. How can you admire me when I might have been the one who caused the fire?"

His hand tightened on hers. "It doesn't matter how it started. The important thing was the battle. You faced it and survived. You won, Kayli, not the fire. If you can hold on to that truth, you'll be okay."

Chapter 12

Rick's words seemed almost prophetic. As September gave way to October, Kayli's nightmares stopped and her fears receded. She was practicing Aunt Jessie's advice to focus on Jesus whenever a fear or anxiety entered her mind. It was working. And maybe her fears had lessened because life was so pleasant and her days so full. She spent her weekdays at the gallery—a job she was born for; on Saturday mornings she often set up her easel on the beach and painted sun-washed seascapes; on Sundays she spent mornings in church and afternoons either with Rick or with Jay, Leo, and Aunt Jessie.

As much as it amazed her, she was enjoying the company of two very different but extremely appealing men. Jay took her to fine restaurants, concerts, and art galleries. They heard the Honolulu Symphony Orchestra at the Blaisdell Concert Hall, spent a day at the Bishop Museum and Planetarium, another day at the Foster Botanical Garden, and still another at the Lyon Arboretum. They spent long hours talking about art and music, about Hawaii and its history, about their families and their faith. She felt comfortable with him, at ease, as if she had known him all her life. She couldn't have asked for a better friend.

At sunrise one Saturday morning she and Jay hiked to the summit of Diamond Head Crater. As they followed the steep path through dark tunnels and old war bunkers, she reminded herself that she and Aunt Jessie would soon be living in the shadow of the dormant volcano.

At the top of the crater they climbed the one hundred stair steps to the small lookout, Kayli gripping the rusty iron handrail all the way. For a long while they stood gazing at the panoramic view of the Pacific Ocean, the sparkling white high-rise buildings of downtown Honolulu, and the sweeping surf at Waikiki Beach. The view was stunning—the ocean a blend of turquoise and cerulean near the shore, a deep azure near the horizon.

As they stood arm in arm at the crowded railing, the rising sun warmed them and the wind swept through their hair and clothes with an electrifying energy. The whole world seemed to be stretching out before them like an astonishing gift. Although the climb had been exhausting, it was well worth it. After descending back to the crater's base, they caught their breath and revived themselves with mango smoothies from the waiting lunch truck.

If Kayli had thought sunrise on Diamond Head was magnificent, sunset turned out even better as she and Jay took a dinner cruise along the Kahala coastline. They had greeted the sun that morning and now bade it good night. As the last filaments of shimmering orange light disappeared on the horizon, Jay held her close, his chin resting on her head. More than ever in her life she yearned to be kissed, and yet—to her keen disappointment—he let the moment slip away.

With Rick, on the other hand, every date was exciting and unpredictable—they surfed, snorkeled, and ran the breakers in an outrigger canoe off Waikiki Beach, explored downtown Honolulu on rented bicycles, and went hiking at Round Top Forest Reserve and horseback riding at Kualoa Ranch. Rick was tireless; he always seemed to have more energy than she had. They were so busy doing things that they rarely had time for simple, quiet conversations. Sometimes it seemed that the more time she spent with Rick, the less she knew him. And yet, he, too, had become a good friend.

It seemed to Kayli that she was forever destined to be just friends with the men in her life, although she sensed if she gave Rick the slightest encouragement he would proclaim his love for her to the heavens. Jay remained a mystery—at times giving her an affectionate hug or a lingering glance that seemed to speak of love, but at other times growing silent and withdrawn.

As the days of October slipped by, Kayli found she had less time for dates. The new house was demanding more of her attention. She and Aunt Jessie went to the design center to pick out their appliances, window coverings, carpet, and flooring. They had a field day browsing through all the thick sample books, debating on colors and brands, textures, and styles. They were like kids in a candy store with too many choices. It took days for them to make their decisions.

They spent the rest of October shopping for furniture—a task that made Kayli appreciate Jay's preference for cottage simplicity. Their California furniture, presently in storage, would be well suited for the large guest wing. For the main rooms of the house Aunt Jessie favored something more traditionally Hawaiian while Kayli preferred more modern Asian accents. They compromised and selected Hawaiian decor with tropical accents for most rooms—whitewashed rattan floral-print furniture, koa wood rocking chairs and dining room set, colorful hand-knotted area rugs for the hardwood floors, bamboo bead curtains for the bathrooms, and potted palms and tropical plants for nearly every room. Aunt Jessie created an Asian theme for the living room with a shoji screen room divider and a *kotatsu*—a square, squat coffee table for serving sushi and tea.

By November their dream house was completed. The final walk-through was scheduled for two weeks before Thanksgiving. Their new furniture would be delivered a week before the holiday.

Jessie had already invited Leo and Jay to join them for their first Thanksgiving dinner in the new house. When Rick learned that Kayli would be spending the holiday with the Mahala men, he was quick to express his disappointment. He had hoped she would spend the day with him. Against her better judgment she invited him to join them for Thanksgiving dinner, as well.

As Kayli and Aunt Jessie prepared for the final walk-through, the main topic of conversation was how they were going to be ready to entertain guests on Thanksgiving Day and, even more so, how they were going to keep peace between Kayli's two would-be suitors.

"You know they don't like each other," Aunt Jessie reminded her as they wrapped their china dishes and glasses in newspaper. As soon as the walk-through was finished they could start taking their possessions to the new house, so they were packing their breakables now.

"I know they don't like each other," Kayli conceded, "and that's really a shame because they're both very nice men."

Jessie placed a paper-wrapped glass in the cardboard box on the counter. "Yes, they're very nice. And they're both crazy about you."

"Rick may have a crush on me, but I'm not so sure about Jay."

"Well, I'm sure. That man has love in his eyes."

"It's too bad it can't extend to his lips. All these months he's hardly said a word about how he feels. He's made little hints at times, but nothing substantial. I think he feels the same attraction I feel, but he won't admit it. Rick is just the opposite. It takes all my effort to keep him from proclaiming his love on a billboard or in skywriting. I'm sure he would rush me off to the altar if I gave him the slightest encouragement."

"But you haven't, have you?"

"You know I haven't, Aunt Jessie. I've tried to remain just friends. I care about Rick, but I don't love him. He told me he's a believer. He goes to church with me when he isn't on duty and he says all the right things, but sometimes I have a feeling he's just trying to please me. When I try to talk to him about the Lord, he dodges my questions. I feel such a burden for him. He's rescued and saved so many others, but what if he doesn't really know the Savior of his soul? What if I'm the only one who can reach him?"

"God didn't call us to missionary dating, honey. You'd better find out where he stands, and if he's not ready to walk with the Lord, you'd better let him go."

Kayli nodded. "I just wish I knew for sure."

"I understand. But what about Jay?"

"What about him?"

Aunt Jessie placed several more wrapped glasses in the box. "Maybe he's just waiting for a signal from you. Maybe you need to let him know how you feel."

"You mean, tell him I care about him as more than a friend?" She closed the box and sealed it with tape.

"Why not? What's the worst that can happen?"

"He could reject me." Kayli took a black marker and wrote "FRAGILE—GLASSES" on the side of the box.

"Wouldn't it be better to know once and for all how he feels than to go on not knowing?"

She set the box on the floor by the door. "You may be right, Aunt Jessie, but

I can't risk doing something stupid and losing his friendship."

"Well, it's up to you, of course. But I don't think Jay and Leo would be doing our walk-through themselves if they didn't consider us friends, maybe even more than friends. They'd send the project manager or someone else from the company."

"You're right." Kayli paused a long moment, chewing her lower lip. "What if they disappear from our lives now that the house is done?"

Aunt Jessie gave her a scolding glance. "Do you really think those two men have befriended us for months just because they're building us a house? Do you honestly think they give every client such royal treatment?"

"No, but sometimes I wonder where things are heading. When we first came to Hawaii I said I didn't want a man to complicate my life. Now I have *two* men complicating my life."

"Would you have it any other way?"

"I suppose not. But the one I really want may not want me."

Her aunt nodded. "I'm in the same boat, honey. I've lived for half a century and never had a man in my life. I can't believe at my age I'm getting all moony over someone. Maybe there's something in the water."

"Whatever it is, we've both got a serious case of it." Kayli glanced up at the clock. "Oh my, look at the time. We've got to meet them at the new house in an hour."

"An hour? We've got to get prettied up—now!" Jessie was already scurrying toward her room when she called back, "While we're looking over our new house, we want them looking us over, right?"

Kayli suppressed a laugh. "Oh, Aunt Jessie, what am I going to do with you? I never know what you're going to come up with next."

By the time they pulled away from their apartment, they both felt harried—too much packing, too little time to primp. But still they managed to arrive at the new house a full minute before Jay and Leo.

The two men joined them in the front yard where the sod had recently been laid and the grass was looking lush and green. From the outside, the sprawling, split-level house with its cedar shingle roof looked like a picture from a house and garden magazine. Aunt Jessie's beloved banyan tree stood off to the right like a proud sentry guarding their abode.

"Are you two ladies ready to see your new home?" Leo asked as he placed the keys in Jessie's hand.

She took his arm as they climbed the steps to the covered, wraparound lanai. "We sure are ready. I know this house is going to bless our socks off."

"That shouldn't be hard, since we're wearing sandals," Kayli told Jay as they followed them up the steps.

Aunt Jessie's hand shook slightly as she opened the carved teak door with its stained glass window. They entered the high-ceilinged marble foyer and took in the crown molding and exquisite crystal chandelier. They went from room to room, inspecting the vinyl-framed sliding windows, the beadboard wainscoting on the walls, the plush carpet and open-beam ceiling in the living room, the vintage tile and recessed lighting in the custom kitchen.

"It's freshly painted," said Jay, "so we'll need to open the windows and let in some air."

Over the next half hour both Kayli and Aunt Jessie marveled over their new home, singing its praises with lots of "oohs" and "aahs." They kept asking each other, "Did you see this? Did you see that?" as they inspected the granite countertops or the palm-shaped ceiling fans or the natural redwood and cedar cabinets.

"You notice we trimmed the baseboards, windowsills, and interior doors to match the color of the cabinets," said Leo. "And even with all the windows and glass pocket doors, there are still many walls on which to hang Kayli's paintings."

"It's lovely," said Aunt Jessie. "So much more beautiful than it was even a couple of weeks ago. Every room is a work of art. The house has just what I requested—clean and simple lines with a feeling of openness and light. . .and a gorgeous view of the ocean."

"I'm glad you're pleased," said Leo, beaming.

"It'll look even more perfect when our furniture is delivered," said Jessie. "I don't have words to tell you what this house means to me, Leo."

He squeezed her hand. "I want your home to nurture and renew you. I want you to feel this is exactly where you want to be."

"That is how I feel. You know me so well."

Kayli and Jay headed down the hall as Jessie and Leo shared an embrace.

"Let me show you your studio," he said, taking her hand. Confidentially he added, "You know this house has been a special project for Dad and me. Neither of us has made such a personal connection with our clients before."

She gave him a playful smile. "Are you saying not everyone gets the red carpet treatment like we have?"

He grinned. "Not quite this red. Don't get me wrong. We make our clients happy. But you and Jessie—you've taken us by surprise. We didn't realize how important your friendship would be to us. We really wanted to go all-out for the two of you."

"You have, Jay. Aunt Jessie and I really appreciate all your hard work. But even more, we've appreciated getting to know you both. I hope we can keep on being friends even if we're not meeting to discuss house plans and inspection dates and all that stuff."

He squeezed her arm. "You bet. You're not going to get rid of us that easily." They arrived at a closed door on the far side of the house. "Here we are. This is my favorite room. I hope you like it."

Kayli caught her breath as she entered her spacious studio with its wall-to-wall windows and pocket doors, expansive skylights letting in the sun, and white bamboo walls and custom tile flooring. Tears sprang to her eyes. "Amazing! The last time I saw this room, it was just drywall and cement. This is absolutely stunning."

Jay slipped his arm around her. "What do you think of all the built-in cedar shelves and storage racks?"

"I think I'd better start painting faster so I'll have canvases to store in them."

"You have two full walls for hanging your paintings. And you can open the pocket doors to let in the outside. This room is as close as we could get to giving you an outdoor studio."

Impulsively Kayli gave him a hug. "Thank you, Jay. You've really made my dreams come true."

Her hug of gratitude was suddenly something more. Jay held her tight and buried his face in her hair. "It was my pleasure, Kayli. I'd do anything to make you happy."

She looked up and searched his eyes. "Jay, what are you say—"

With a tender, nimble motion he brought his lips down on hers and kissed her soundly. As shock gave way to pure bliss she relaxed in his embrace and returned the kiss. It was one of the most delightful experiences of her life. When he released her, her knees buckled. He pulled her up and held her against him. "Are you okay?"

"Yes. Just surprised. And a little dazzled."

"I've wanted to kiss you like that so many times." He brushed a strand of hair back from her forehead.

"You have?" She could hardly catch her breath. "Then why didn't you?" *You'll never know how much I wanted you to kiss me!*

His dark brows furrowed. "I felt we needed to develop a deep friendship before we let ourselves be distracted by the seductiveness of romance. I suppose it's my practical, cautious nature, but I didn't want to run ahead of God. Or maybe I was afraid once I kissed you I could never let you go."

"I wish you had told me how you felt."

"And then, of course, things got complicated when you started seeing Rick Moran."

"You know we're just friends. That's all."

"That's not the impression I get. The way he behaves, he considers you his girl."

"But I'm not." Kayli touched her lips. She could still feel the pressure of his mouth on hers. The spicy fragrance of his aftershave still hung in the air. "Is that why you act so distant sometimes—you think I'm Rick's girlfriend?"

Jay scratched his head. "I suppose. I knew I was already hooked. Like I said, I couldn't imagine letting you go, and yet I didn't want to move in on another man's territory."

She shook her head. "I'm no one's territory."

"You know what I mean. You spend a lot of time with the guy."

"I spend a lot of time with you, too. What do you think that is—chopped liver?"

They both laughed at her off-the-wall analogy. Jay's green eyes formed their familiar smiling half-moons. "So you're really not in love with this Rick Moran guy?"

She clasped his arms impetuously, nearly shaking him. He looked startled, disarmed. "No, no, no!" she cried, the words erupting with the force of a red-hot lava flow. "Can't you see? It's you I love, Jay, not Rick!"

For a split second she couldn't believe she had actually said the words aloud. *Now I've done it! I've poured out my heart like a lovesick fool. What if he rejects me?*

Her fears were silenced as he gathered her into his arms and swung her around so vigorously her feet left the floor. "I love you, too, Kayli," he declared. "I've been waiting for God to confirm that we're meant to be together. With Rick in the picture I was afraid God was telling me no. But it's a yes! You love me. I love you. If that isn't the proof I need, I don't know what is!"

Chapter 13

Dad, isn't it amazing that we're enjoying the company of two awesome ladies from the same family?" Jay was splashing on aftershave, perhaps a little too much, but he wanted to smell good for Kayli. His dad had stopped by the cottage to see if he was ready for the Thanksgiving dinner.

"It's convenient, if you ask me," said Leo, "although I never thought I'd be doing so much double-dating with my son—if that's what you call it these days."

"I don't know, Dad. What do you call it?" Jay reached into his closet and selected an aloha shirt and khaki pants. "Are you dating Jessie or just having dinners out with a friend?"

"Why do we have to put a label on it, son? I enjoy her company. She enjoys mine. Why does it have to be anything else?"

"It doesn't, Dad, unless your feelings go a little deeper."

"I don't analyze my feelings. That makes things too complicated. Keep things simple, that's my motto."

Jay put his wallet and car keys in his pants pocket. "So the way you see it, you and Jessie will just go on this way indefinitely?"

"Why not? What are you trying to say, JJ?"

"Nothing, Dad. Just talking."

They headed outside to Jay's SUV. "Sounds to me like you've got something on your mind, son. Maybe what we're really talking about here is you and Kayli."

Jay got in on the driver's side; his dad slipped into the passenger seat. Jay started the engine and followed the winding driveway out to the road. "I guess you hit the nail on the head, Dad."

"So what gives? Tell me."

"It's just that things have changed between Kayli and me."

"Changed. How? Stop beating around the bush, boy."

"We told each other how we feel."

"How you feel? How you feel about what?"

"Each other."

"Do I have to drag it out of you, son? Spit it out."

Jay accelerated into traffic. "We love each other, Dad."

"That's not news. I told you that a long time ago."

"I know. And now it's official. We've told each other. I feel a real peace about it, Dad. Now everything's out in the open, and that means—"

"Are you getting married?"

"I believe marriage is in our future, but we've got to take it one step at a time."

"Don't waste time, JJ. You get her to the altar fast. She's a gem. I told you that the first time I saw her."

"I know, Dad." Jay drove for a while without speaking. At last he said briskly, "There is one little complication."

His father raised his hand in protest. "No, no, no. You don't accept any complications, you hear me?"

"It's Rick Moran. She's been seeing him for some time, too. I thought maybe she was falling for him, but she assures me they're just friends. But he has feelings for her, so she wants some time to tell him about us before we make any public announcements."

"I hope she doesn't take too long. You should be shopping now for an engagement ring."

"All in good time, Dad." Jay turned onto Diamond Head Road. "Meanwhile, when we go to dinner today, don't say anything about this, okay? Rick Moran will be there, too, so mum's the word."

"If you say so. But this would have been a good time to announce your love to the world—a big Thanksgiving Day celebration."

"Don't worry, Dad. There'll be plenty of time to celebrate."

Minutes later Jay pulled his SUV into the driveway of the new house. He always felt a little flicker of pride when he saw one of the houses his company—more accurately, his dad's company—had built. He felt a special warmth for this house, maybe because he was so captivated by the young lady inside.

Kayli answered the door and welcomed them into the foyer. She looked stunning in a red silk kimono dress, her ebony hair combed back from her face and cascading to the middle of her back. Jay embraced her—she felt so small and warm and good in his arms—and gave her a light kiss on the cheek. The moment felt a little awkward. He wanted to give her a real kiss, but he wasn't sure who was watching. His father gave her a hug and winked, as if to say, *You have my blessing.*

"Come join the festivities," she said, her cheeks rosy, her dark eyes dancing. "Everybody's in the great room." Jay followed her, inhaling the delicious aroma of roasted turkey and chestnut stuffing. He noticed that she had already hung many of her paintings on the walls. The place looked fantastic—comfortable, elegant, and inviting.

Jessie came striding from the kitchen, wiping her hands on a dish towel, and gave Jay and his father a vigorous hug. Her face was flushed and her smile as wide as the ocean. She was in her element—the consummate entertainer, her energy boundless. "Good to see you both. Jay, I love your aloha shirt. Leo, you look mighty handsome today. Come meet our guests."

One by one she introduced everybody. "This is Yuki Yamagata from our church. She and her children are staying with us for a few days until she starts her new job. And this is Toshiro Tani and his wife, Miko, and their three children. They're missionaries in Japan. They're on furlough and visiting some of the churches here in Honolulu over the next week or two. And, of course, you already know Rick Moran, our brave firefighter." With a little titter of laughter, she flicked the dish towel and said, "Now you all get acquainted while I get the food on the table. Oh, and the youngsters will be eating in the great room and the adults in the dining room."

While everyone mingled, Jay went to the kitchen and helped Kayli and Jessie set out the food. He didn't want to get stuck making small talk with Rick Moran. As it turned out, Rick somehow managed to claim the seat beside Kayli while Jay found himself across from her. The linen-draped table looked distinctly Hawaiian with a leafy runner of banana leaves and ferns and a centerpiece of white and lavender orchids. Hawaiian music wafted from the CD player on the buffet. The ambiance would have been perfect except that Rick was obviously seizing the moment with Kayli, not to mention seizing her hand, as well. He had to remind himself that it was just a matter of time before Rick Moran would be out of her life for good.

Jay had been so focused on Kayli and Rick, he didn't realize that Jessie was standing at the head of the table holding a book in her hands.

"Before we say grace, I wanted to share a little about Hawaii's Thanksgiving tradition," she said in a strong, lyrical voice. "Thanksgiving Day coincides with a four-month season of giving thanks that we native Hawaiians call *Makahiki*. We not only say 'Happy Thanksgiving,' but also, '*Lono-i ku-makahiki*.' "

She glanced down at the open book. "No one knows when the first Thanksgiving feast was held in the Hawaiian Islands, but the first recorded one was likely here in Honolulu. The families of American missionaries from New England celebrated on December 6, 1838, and again on January 1, 1841. Their Thanksgiving festivities are documented in old journals by Lowell Smith and Laura Fish Judd. So expressing our gratitude to God is as much a Hawaiian legacy as it is of every other American."

Everyone around the table applauded.

Jessie set down the book and lifted her hands in a gesture of petition. "So, my friends, let's hold hands and thank God for all He has given us today."

Jay felt a stab of guilt for feeling irritated that Rick was the one holding Kayli's hand, not he. *Sorry, Lord. This day is about You, not me.*

Jessie was already praying. "Thank You, heavenly Father, for all these dear friends here today and for this home You've provided and the food on this table. Help us remember that the greatest gift is Your precious Son, Jesus, who died to save us from our sins. May we always remember that the cross is embedded in the very heart of God, and it is there because of us. Amen."

Jessie sat down. "Dig in, everybody, before the food gets cold!"

Dinner was a combination of traditional roast turkey, mashed potatoes, cranberry sauce, and island delicacies—yellow passion fruit, sweet potato salad with edible begonias, wild rice salad, and Hawaiian sweet bread rolls.

As everyone ate, conversation around the table was punctuated with several exclamations of praise and approval. "This meal rivals my grandmother's cooking," said the missionary Toshiro Tani.

His wife agreed. "I must have your recipe for the sweet potato salad."

"I think the secret's in the begonias," said Jessie with a pleased smile.

"What did you baste the turkey with?" asked the girl named Yuki. "It gives the turkey such an exotic taste."

"That's a special mango glaze. It was my mother's recipe."

"It's delicious."

When everyone had eaten, Jessie and Kayli cleared the table. Jay was about to offer his help, but Rick jumped up first and insisted on carrying the heavy china plates to the kitchen. Minutes later Jessie returned with a pumpkin pie and cheesecake.

"I cannot tell a lie," she said as she set them on the table, "I baked the pie but I bought the cheesecake."

"Well, then I'll sample a little of both," said Leo, gripping his fork.

"An excellent idea," said Aunt Jessie. "So will I."

Others agreed that was the way to go—they would try a small piece of each one.

"Be careful, Aunt Jessie," whispered Kayli. "Remember your blood sugar."

"Oh honey, it's a holiday, and I'll eat only a little sliver of each. Now who wants the first piece?"

After they had finished dessert, Rick pushed back his chair and stood up.

"Aren't you going to eat all your pie, Rick?" asked Jessie.

He gripped the back of his chair. "No, Jessie, I have something better than dessert."

"Better than this pie?" said Leo. "What could be better than this?"

Kayli looked up questioningly. "What are you doing, Rick?"

Jay's breath caught in his throat as Rick Moran pulled a jewelry box from his pocket, got down on one knee, and said, "Kayli, will you marry me?"

She stared at him as he opened the box, withdrew a sparkling diamond ring, and slipped it on her finger. It took all of Jay's willpower to keep from jumping up, darting around the table, and—and what? That was the problem. What was he going to do? Punch the guy's lights out? Proclaim his own love for Kayli? Tell everyone this was a terrible mistake—that this guy was deluded if he thought Kayli would marry him?

Jay ended up sitting right where he was, saying nothing. Not a word. But his heart was hammering in his chest as Kayli looked down at the ring and then up at Rick. Worst of all, everyone around the table except Leo and Jessie started applauding and saying congratulations.

Rick sat back down, looking pleased as punch. "Thank you, everyone. I know this comes as a shock to Kayli—giving her an engagement ring when I haven't even told her I love her." He swiveled in his chair, looked directly in her eyes, and said, "I do love you, Kayli. You're the girl of my dreams. Please say you'll be my wife."

That was it. Jay had had enough. He sprang to his feet and the words erupted from his lips like gunfire. "You can't marry her! She's in love with me!"

Chapter 14

Pandemonium broke out around the dinner table. Everyone was speaking at once. Kayli couldn't get a word in edgewise.

"Jay thinks you're in love with him?" Rick protested. "Where'd he get that nonsense?"

"Son, you set this smug lug with a fire hat straight," insisted Leo.

Jay declared, "Tell him, Kayli. Your future is with me, not him."

"Please, everyone, it's Thanksgiving!" cried Aunt Jessie, raising her hands.

Kayli finally found her voice. "Listen to me—all of you! I'm not marrying anyone!"

The room suddenly grew quiet. All eyes were on her. "It's true," she said, her voice wobbly. "I have no plans to marry anyone right now."

Aunt Jessie stood up and started clearing the dessert dishes. "That settles the matter for now. Let's concentrate on our reason for being here today—our gratitude to God and our friendship with one another."

Kayli reached over and touched her aunt's hand. "Sit down, Aunt Jessie. You look tired. You've been working too hard. I'll take care of the dishes."

"No, I'm fine, dear. I just feel a little breathless. I'm going to. . ." Jessie set the dishes down with a little clatter and leaned against the table with both hands. "I am feeling. . .rather dizzy."

Kayli pushed back her chair and stood up. Before she could reach her aunt, Jessie swooned and crumpled to the floor. Shock and panic exploded in Kayli's chest. "Aunt Jessie!" Weak-kneed, she knelt down and cradled her aunt's head in her lap. "Aunt Jessie! Please, someone get help!"

Jay and Rick were already on their feet. "Call 9-1-1!" Rick told Jay.

Leo darted around the table and stared down, slack-jawed, at Jessie. "Somebody do something! You hear me? Help her!"

"Everyone pray," said Jay as he punched in the numbers.

Rick stooped down and felt along Jessie's neck for a pulse. He checked her eyes and wrists. "She's alive and breathing on her own. We'll keep her comfortable until the ambulance arrives."

Leo bent down on one knee and caressed Jessie's face. "Come on, girl, don't you leave me now. I love you, baby. Stay with us, you hear?"

Kayli was sobbing now. "What's wrong with her? She was fine just a minute ago."

"She has diabetes, right?" said Rick.

"Yes."

"She's on insulin?"

"Yes."

"Did she take it today?"

"I don't know. We were so busy fixing dinner, she may have forgotten."

"High blood sugar can cause a loss of consciousness. Where's her meter? I want to test her glucose level."

Yuki brought over a sofa pillow for Jessie's head while Kayli ran to her room to get her meter. Rick tested Jessie's blood. "It's well over six hundred. She could be experiencing severe hyperglycemia."

"Should we give her an insulin shot now?" asked Kayli.

"Not yet." Rick pulled out his cell phone and dialed a number. "We'll need a list of her medications. I'm getting patched in to the rescue unit that's on its way here. I'll let them know what we're dealing with."

While Rick spoke on his phone, Jay came over and gave Kayli a comforting embrace. "She's going to be all right, sweetheart. She's a strong woman."

Kayli buried her face against Jay's chest. "I know, but right now she looks so sick and helpless. She can't die. Please, God, don't let her die."

Rick pocketed his cell phone. "They said to administer her insulin."

"I'll get it," said Kayli.

Within minutes she heard a siren. Usually that sound stirred fear and anxiety within her, but today she felt overwhelming relief. Jay opened the door for the paramedics. They wheeled in a gurney and nearly pushed Kayli and Leo out of the way as they swarmed around Aunt Jessie.

"She has diabetes mellitus, type two," Rick told them. "She's dehydrated. Blood glucose over six hundred. My guess is extreme hyperglycemia."

"We don't know if she took her insulin today," said Kayli, "but Rick just gave her an injection."

One of the rescuers told another, "Start an IV with potassium and sodium." Rick filled them in on what he knew of Jessie's history. "Her niece is here. She can tell you more."

With trembling fingers Kayli handed them a folded paper she had retrieved from Aunt Jessie's bureau. "Here's a list of her medications. Tell me—will she be okay?"

Two men lifted Jessie onto the gurney. "We can't rule out diabetic coma," said one. "The doctors will know more when they've run some tests."

"Diabetic coma?" Kayli repeated in disbelief. "That's serious, isn't it?" She could hardly bring herself to say the words. "Is she going to die?"

"Not if we can help it," said another rescuer as he strapped Jessie down.

Kayli clasped his arm. "Can I ride with her?"

"Sorry, miss. We'll be working on her. Follow in your car. And be sure to bring all of your aunt's medications. The doctor will want to see them."

Kayli watched numbly as they rolled the gurney out of the house and placed it in the back of the rescue vehicle. *That's precious cargo. Take care of her, please!* She wrapped her arms around herself as if to ward off the horror and pain already engulfing her mind. "I can't lose her," she whispered between sobs. "She's all I have."

She watched as the rescue truck roared away, its siren screaming again. Jay drew her into his arms and whispered, "You still have her, honey. You have the Lord. And me."

Kayli pulled away. She couldn't think about anything but Aunt Jessie right now. "I've got to get her medicine." She ran to the kitchen and looked in the cupboard where her aunt kept all her prescription bottles. Fortunately they were all there in a plastic bag. She grabbed it and returned to the dining room.

"Who's going with me to the hospital?" asked Leo, his voice husky with emotion. He was already standing at the front door.

"We're with you, Dad," said Jay, falling into step beside Kayli as she crossed the room to the foyer.

"I'm going, too," said Rick.

Kayli glanced back at her houseguests. "Will you all be okay?"

Miko stepped forward. "Of course we will. We'll take care of things here. You go and be with your aunt."

"Tell her we're praying for her," said Toshiro.

"I'll call the church and put her on the prayer chain," said Yuki.

They piled into Jay's SUV—Jay driving, Kayli beside him. He followed the ambulance all the way to the hospital. Kayli's mind was spinning like the pinwheels she played with as a child, her thoughts running helter-skelter. *How could this happen? I shouldn't have let her eat those rich desserts. Why didn't I remind her to take her insulin? She exhausted herself working on our new house. She's not that young anymore. Why didn't I make her rest? Dear Lord, what if she never gets to enjoy her dream house? Father, You say You won't give us more than we can bear. Please don't take Aunt Jessie from me!*

At the emergency entrance Jay said, "I'll let you all off and go park the car."

Kayli jumped out and ran to the parked ambulance. Leo and Rick were close behind. She stood and waited as the paramedics removed the gurney and wheeled it through the emergency doors. She craned her neck for a glimpse of Aunt Jessie, but the medics were moving too fast. She followed them into the emergency room, hoping to see her aunt, but they had already pushed the gurney into another room and shut the door.

Leo squeezed her arm. "Go to the desk over there. You'll need to fill out papers."

Kayli did as Leo suggested. She waited nervously at the admitting desk as the nurse helped another patient. When it was finally her turn, her mouth went dry and she couldn't think of what to say.

"They just brought her aunt in," said Leo. "She didn't look good. We need to see her."

"Do you have her medical card?"

Kayli hadn't thought to bring it. She hadn't even brought Aunt Jessie's purse. "I have her medicine." She held up the plastic bag.

The nurse took it. "These will have her medical record number. The rest of her information will be on the computer." She handed Kayli a packet of papers. "Just fill these out and bring them back to the desk."

"When can I see her?"

"It'll be a while. She'll be examined. The doctors will determine her condition, what treatment she needs, and what tests need to be run."

Kayli could see she wasn't making any progress with the nurse, so she took the papers to the waiting room, sat down, and began filling them out. Leo sat down beside her and proceeded to crack his knuckles, first one hand, then the other. Rick paced the floor and finally said he was going to go find Jay. It seemed odd that he would be seeking Jay when only an hour ago the two had nearly come to blows.

When she finished filling out the papers she returned to the admitting desk. "I left some spaces blank. I didn't know what to put down."

"That's fine. We've called her doctor, and we have her records on file."

"Is there any news yet?"

"Not yet. You might as well relax, have some coffee, read a magazine. It could be an hour or more before the doctor has any news."

Kayli's heart sank. That wasn't what she wanted to hear. She returned to Leo and repeated what the nurse had said.

"Then we'll wait," he said. Tears loomed in his eyes. "I never told her how I felt about her," he said brokenly. "I never told her I loved her. And now I'm going to lose her, just like I lost my wife."

Kayli put her hand over his. "Don't say that, Leo. We've got to trust God that she'll be okay."

"That's just it." He wiped his eyes with his handkerchief. "She wanted me to trust God again, like I did in the old days. She told me how she prayed for me every day. I've prayed in my heart for God to forgive me for turning my back on Him, but I don't know if He has. She has this faith that's bigger than all of us, and I didn't know how to even come close to that."

Kayli slipped her arm around Leo's shoulder. "God loves and forgives you, Leo. He's here with us right now."

Jay and Rick came striding in. Immediately the room sparked with their energy. They both bombarded her with questions to which she had no answers. Realizing that, they both sat down, Jay beside her, Rick beside him.

"You all don't have to stay," said Kayli. "We might be here all night."

"So be it," said Jay. "I'm not going until I know Jessie's okay."

"Same here," said Leo. "That woman means the world to me. I just pray I get a chance to tell her so."

Kayli nodded. "She means the world to me, too. I was so young when I lost my parents. Aunt Jessie has been my life. I can't lose her."

"You won't lose her," said Rick. "We did everything right. We gave her her insulin. We got her here in time. She'll make it."

Sometime around midnight Kayli drifted off to sleep, her head lolling over on Jay's shoulder. Sometime later—was it minutes or hours?—she was startled awake by a man's voice. "Miss Akimo?"

She sat bolt upright. "Yes?"

A wiry, bespectacled man in a white coat offered his hand. "I'm Dr. Lee."

She gripped his hand as if holding on for dear life. "How's Aunt Jessie?"

"She's resting. She's been taken to her room."

"Will she be okay?"

Dr. Lee sat down across from Kayli. "Your aunt had a close call. She developed a condition called 'diabetic hyperosmolar syndrome.' Her blood sugar level was so high the blood became thick and syrupy and dehydrated her body. Left untreated, it could lead to shock, coma, and death. Prompt action on your part probably saved her life."

Kayli closed her eyes. "Thank God!" Looking back at Dr. Lee, she said, "But it wasn't just me. Rick here—and Jay—and the paramedics—everyone helped."

"When can we take her home?" asked Leo.

Dr. Lee tented his fingers, apparently weighing his words. "We'll keep her here for observation for a few days. Her vital functions—heart rate, blood pressure, and body temperature—have been stabilized. But she's not entirely out of the woods yet. We're giving her intravenous fluids to restore water to her tissues and insulin to bring her glucose levels down. We ran a number of tests—a hematocrit, electrolyte blood tests, and glucose tests. I'd like to run some more tests tomorrow—a CAT scan, MRI, and EEG, to rule out any damage to the brain. I'd also like to check her kidneys."

"Can we see her now?" asked Kayli.

"Yes, just one or two at a time. She's still lethargic and may not respond." Dr. Lee stood up and made a little bow. "Miss Akimo, it's very important that your aunt take her insulin as prescribed and avoid sugary foods. Next time she may not be so lucky."

"There won't be a next time," said Leo, standing up and offering the doctor his hand. "I'll see to that."

After Dr. Lee left, Jay helped Kayli to her feet. "Honey, I'll find out Jessie's room number and we'll go see her. Are you feeling okay?"

"Yes, just a little groggy and stiff from sitting in that hard chair so long."

"I'd like to see her, too," said Rick.

"We'll all go and take turns seeing her," said Leo. "After the day we've had we're all in this together."

As they headed down the hall to Aunt Jessie's room, Kayli glanced down at her left hand. She was still wearing the engagement ring that Rick had put on her finger. In all the commotion she hadn't given it back to him. She waited until they were alone outside Jessie's room then removed the ring and placed it in Rick's hand. "I'm sorry. I can't accept this."

He tried to press it back into her palm. "At least take some time and think about it."

She held up her hands, palms open. "You've been a wonderful friend to me, Rick, and I wouldn't hurt you for the world. But my heart belongs with Jay. I hope you can understand."

His expression hardened, his dark eyes smoldering. "I understand that you're making a terrible mistake. You belong with me, Kayli. Someday you're going to realize that."

A chill traveled along her spine. "I'm sorry you feel that way. I never led you to expect more than friendship from me."

"Are you going to marry him?"

"We haven't talked about it yet, but—"

"Don't do it, Kayli. He's wrong for you. Can't you feel the connection between the two of us?"

"I can't talk about this now, Rick." A knot of tension tightened along the back of her neck. "All I can think about is Aunt Jessie and getting her well again. You saved her life today, and I'll always be grateful."

"I don't want your gratitude; I want your love. Mark my words. Someday you'll be mine."

Before she could say a word of protest, Rick turned on his heel and strode down the hall without a backward glance.

Kayli watched him go, her own emotions raw and unsettled. If she hadn't known it before, she knew it now. It was time to put Rick Moran out of her life for good. From now on she would concentrate only on nursing Aunt Jessie back to health and planning her future with the man she loved, Jay Mahala.

Chapter 15

Christmastime in Hawaii wasn't much different from Christmas in Southern California. There were palm trees, sunshine, and heat, with a little extra humidity thrown in. There were Santas ringing bells on street corners, fake snow on green lawns, and "White Christmas" playing in the beachfront shops and restaurants. But this Christmas was going to be the best one of Kayli's life. Aunt Jessie was home from the hospital and feeling better than she had in weeks. Leo had become Jessie's devoted suitor and was showering her with gifts, cards, and cute little love notes.

To Kayli's relief she hadn't heard from Rick Moran since that traumatic Thanksgiving Day. Surely that meant he was forgetting her and moving on with his life, maybe even looking for someone else to love.

And Jay—what could she say about Jay?—except that over the past few weeks he had truly become the love of her life. They had spent countless hours taking long walks on the beach, talking over romantic dinners, and praying together about their future. The more she experienced his gentle, loving, tender side, the more she adored him.

And now, on Christmas Eve, she and Jay and Leo and Aunt Jessie were about to celebrate the holiday with a cozy dinner at Jessie's marvelous new home. Since the guys were bringing dinner—takeout from their favorite Chinese restaurant—Kayli and Jessie didn't even have to cook.

While they waited for the Mahala men to arrive, they busied themselves with a few decorations—a wreath for the door, garlands for the dining room walls, and sprigs of mistletoe which Kayli hung from the chandelier in the foyer. They set out bowls of popcorn in the great room to string for their fresh seven-foot Norfolk Island pine tree.

"I love the scent of real pine," said Kayli. She felt Christmasy in her forest green jersey dress and red pendant necklace and hoop earrings. "It will be fun decorating the tree with Jay and Leo."

"Oh my, yes!" Jessie sat down on the rattan sofa, her gaze still fixed on the tree. "Isn't it amazing how far we've come since last Christmas?"

"It sure is." Kayli sat down beside her aunt. "Last Christmas we were still trying to decide whether to move to Hawaii. I was finishing up my classes and getting ready to graduate."

"And I was wondering if I dared whisk you away to my little island homeland across the ocean."

Kayli nestled against her aunt's shoulder. "I'm glad you did. If we hadn't come here, we never would have met Jay and Leo."

Jessie laughed. "Who would believe the two of us would be dating two charming men who happen to be father and son? Only in the movies!"

Kayli twirled her pendant necklace. "Leo really is devoted to you, Aunt Jessie. I love the way he looks at you. He's definitely a man in love."

"And I love him, too. Oh, do I love that man! So I guess something good came out of my medical emergency. It made Leo realize we were meant to be together."

"That's a good thing, but I pray it never happens again. You scared us half to death. I'm just so thankful the Lord brought you back to us."

"It was scary," Jessie admitted. "I finally feel like my old self—better than my old self. I've learned my lesson. The only Christmas cookies I'll be eating are sugar free."

"Some of your diet recipes aren't half bad—even the veggie dishes."

Aunt Jessie stifled a chuckle. "Except the brussels sprouts casserole—you weren't too fond of that one."

"And the carrot soufflé. That was gross. But the asparagus crepes and green bean salad were delicious. And the bacon and spinach quiche—that's my favorite."

"You're making me hungry." Jessie looked at her watch. "Where are those men with our dinner?"

Aunt Jessie had hardly got out the words when the doorbell rang. They both jumped up at once. "Kayli, you go get the door. I'll put on a pot of tea."

Halfway to the foyer Kayli called back, "Turn on the CD with the Christmas music."

At the door she paused, smoothed back her hair, and took a deep breath. Would Jay notice the mistletoe above her head? The bell rang again. She turned the knob and opened the door wide. Jay and Leo were standing with their arms loaded with brightly wrapped packages and a large white sack labeled CHAN'S CHINESE CUISINE.

Jay laughed. "Don't just stand there. Help us!"

She took the bag of Chinese food and two of the smaller gifts. "Looks like Santa has come," she teased. "Or, since you're wearing aloha shirts instead of red suits and white beards, maybe you're Santa's helpers."

"Santa's helpers, my foot! Just tell me where you want these," said Leo, juggling the foil-wrapped boxes in his arms.

"Under the tree in the great room."

They deposited their packages under the tree while Kayli crossed the expansive room and set the food on the kitchen counter. Leo went and gave Jessie a hug while Jay took Kayli's hand and led her back to the foyer.

"Is there more stuff in the car?" she asked.

"No, we got everything."

"Then where are we going?"

He positioned her in front of the door. Pointing up at the mistletoe he said, "I noticed that on the way in. I wanted to be sure to collect my kiss."

Before she could reply, he drew her into his arms and brought his lips down firmly on hers. The kiss lasted so long she felt breathless. When he released her she held on to his arm to steady herself. "Wow," she murmured, "that mistletoe is powerful stuff."

"Maybe we need a replay." He embraced her again, and this kiss was even better. "I love you, Kayli," he whispered against her hair. "I count the hours until I can hold you in my arms like this."

"Me, too."

He traced the line of her lips with his index finger. "We've got to find more places to hang that mistletoe. It's quite addicting."

"Yes," she agreed. "Even better than caffeine and chocolate chip cookies."

He cupped her head between his palms and studied her intently. "Let's see. We could put a halo on your head and hang some mistletoe on it. Then I could kiss you anytime, wherever you went."

She grinned. "But so could everyone else."

He frowned. "We can't have that. Your kisses have to be for me alone."

"Guess we'd better forget the mistletoe then."

He winked. "Don't worry, I'll think of something else."

Arm in arm they strolled back to the great room where, in the open kitchen area, Jessie was setting out the little cardboard containers on the table. "We'll skip the formal dining room tonight. The kitchen nook is more cozy."

Leo rubbed his hands together. "Sounds good to me. Shall we sit down?"

"Yes, please do." Jessie set the teapot on the table. "Everything is ready."

For the next half hour they feasted on egg drop soup, garlic spareribs, sweet and sour pork, beef with broccoli, cashew chicken, and steamed rice.

When they had finished, Leo pushed back his plate. "Chan's never disappoints."

"This was a nice change," said Kayli. "Usually on Christmas Eve we have a traditional ham dinner."

"Which we have to cook," Jessie added. "This was a wonderful treat. Thank you, gentlemen."

"It's not over yet," said Jay, reaching into the plastic bag. He brought out two fortune cookies and handed one to Kayli and one to Jessie.

Jessie waved him away. "No dessert for me—unless they're making sugar-free fortune cookies now."

"Same here." Kayli handed her cookie back to Jay. "I'm stuffed. You guys go ahead."

Jay placed the cookie back into her palm and folded her fingers over it. "This is a very special cookie. I think you'll like it."

She shrugged. "Okay, if it means so much to you."

"You, too, Jessie." Leo closed her hand around her cookie.

"You two are acting very mysterious," said Jessie. "What's this all about?"

"Just open the cookie," said Leo.

"Open them at the same time," said Jay.

Kayli and Jessie exchanged baffled glances then each cracked open her fortune cookie. Kayli did a double take. Something glinted amid the broken pieces. She reached inside and removed a sparkling diamond ring. She looked in astonishment at Jay. "What is this?"

His smile spread across the width of his face. "What does it look like?"

"A ring."

He nodded. "Very perceptive."

Kayli looked over at Aunt Jessie. She was holding up a ring, too.

Kayli could hardly find her voice. "Is this what I think it is?"

Jay pointed to the little slip of paper in the broken cookie. "Read your fortune and find out."

With trembling fingers she picked up the paper and read, " 'Will you marry me?' "

Aunt Jessie read hers. "Mine says the same thing!"

"Well? What do you say?" Jay cupped his hand over Kayli's just as Leo clasped Jessie's. Kayli had never been at a loss for words—until now.

Leo's voice broke slightly. "So, Jessie, what's your answer? Will you marry me?"

Jessie sprang from her chair and wrapped her arms around Leo's neck with such ardor that his chair nearly tipped over. "Yes, Leo. Yes, yes, yes!"

Jay stood up, took Kayli's hands in his, and pulled her to her feet. "One yes, one to go. I love you, sweetheart. I never expected to feel this way—so happy, so in love, so excited about our future together. I can't imagine living without you. Will you spend the rest of your life with me?"

She melted in his embrace. "Yes, Jay, that's just what I want. It'll be the three of us together—you, me, and the Lord."

"We'll start with three. But one of these days it may be more—maybe four, five, or six. I'd love a big family."

She laughed. "Let's not count too high. We haven't even set a wedding date yet."

"All in good time. What do you think of spring—April or May?"

"We could make it a double wedding," Leo told Jessie. "That is, if the kid doesn't mind sharing the spotlight with his old man."

"What I want to know," said Jessie with a twinkle in her eyes, "is how you got these rings into the fortune cookies."

"Dad knows Mr. Chan," said Jay. "He made them up special for us."

Kayli laughed. "Think what would have happened if someone else had accidentally gotten these cookies."

"No chance," said Jay. "We had everything planned to the letter." He took Kayli's ring and slipped it on her finger. "Do you really like it?"

She held up her hand for all to see. "I love it. But not as much as I love you."

Leo took Jessie's hand and slid her ring on her finger. "Does it fit okay, Jess?"

She twirled the ring. "Perfect."

"Good. That's done. Now I can relax." Leo took her hand, led her over to the wicker sofa in the great room, and they sat down. Kayli and Jay took the love seat.

Gazing at her ring, Kayli snuggled up to Jay. "After all this excitement, I'm not sure what we should do for an encore. Hanging ornaments or stringing popcorn for the tree may be a letdown."

"Not for us." Jay's arm circled her shoulder. "Dad and I haven't had a real old-fashioned Christmas since Mom died. We haven't had a tree in three years. I always went to church, but otherwise we pretty much ignored the holiday."

"Not anymore," said Jessie. "We're all going to the midnight service at church. And we're going to decorate this tree until there's not an empty branch left. And then we're going to drink eggnog and eat frosted sugar cookies shaped like Santas and sleighs and candy canes. Don't give me that look, Leo—mine will be sugar free. No more surprise trips to the hospital, I promise."

"That's a relief," said Leo, taking Jessie's hand.

They spent the next few hours enjoying what Kayli could only describe as a perfect Hallmark Christmas. They strung popcorn and draped lights and garlands on the tree; hung ornaments; ate cookies and fudge and popcorn they hadn't strung; and adorned the tree with tinsel—although they ended up laughing and throwing most of the popcorn at one another. When the tree was done, they sipped eggnog and listened to Bing Crosby sing "I'll Be Home for Christmas."

Later, while Leo and Aunt Jessie sat at the kitchen table playing a game of Chinese checkers, Kayli and Jay went outside and walked down by the beach. They sat on a small outcropping of rock several feet from where the waves washed ashore. She scooted over close to him; he wrapped her in his arms and kissed her. The rhythmic roar of the surf was like gentle background music.

"I've waited all evening to hold you like this," he whispered.

She nuzzled his neck. "Me, too."

"This sure beats being 'just friends.' "

She smiled. "I didn't think you'd ever realize I wanted to be more than friends."

"And here I thought I was playing it cool."

"Too cool. When I think of all the times I lamented to Aunt Jessie. . ."

"But you made it pretty clear you weren't looking for a man."

"I wasn't—until I met you."

He stroked her cheek. "My dad knew the minute he laid eyes on you that you were the one for me."

"Perceptive man."

"At first I wanted to prove him wrong. Then I realized how right he was."

She looked up at him. "When we're married, will your dad be my father-in-law or my uncle?"

"Both."

"I like that."

Jay ran his fingers lightly through her hair. "What's amazing is how well I've gotten along with my dad since we started seeing you and Jessie. I think she's mellowed him. It's weird. Maybe I've mellowed, too. I don't even mind him calling me JJ anymore."

"I think it's sweet. Maybe I'll call you that, too," she teased.

He laughed. "I suppose anything from your lips should be music to my ears. But let's just keep it Jay, okay?"

They fell silent. Kayli savored the moment—relaxing in Jay's arms under a starry sky with the taste of salt spray on her lips and a balmy breeze cooling her face and ruffling her hair.

But when Jay spoke again, his tone was guarded. "I was just wondering—"

"Wondering what?"

"Have you seen Rick Moran lately?"

"No. Not since Thanksgiving night when I gave him back his ring. Why?"

"I don't know. I just wonder if we've heard the last of him."

"I imagine he's pretty busy these days. The newspaper said there've been more arson fires in the area. The whole department is on alert. He's probably been putting in extra hours."

"I hate to hear about the fires, but I'm glad he's too busy to pursue you."

"I told him we'll always be friends. He saved Aunt Jessie. That makes him a hero of sorts."

"Just make sure that's all he is."

"Are you jealous?" She walked her fingers over his arm. "You're the only one I love, Jay, the one I want to grow old with."

He cleared his throat. "That reminds me."

"What? You're already thinking about us growing old?"

"No. I'm thinking about what our life will be like after we're married."

She assumed a bantering tone. "Won't it be 'happily ever after'? That's what all the fairy tales say."

He chuckled. "I'll do my best to give you 'happily ever after,' but if you're expecting the luxury lifestyle my dad has, I'm not sure I can promise that."

"Are you saying we're going to live in your little cottage by the sea? I really don't mind."

"It's not the money, Kayli. I've got money. It's more than that."

"If you're concerned about our living arrangements, Aunt Jessie will probably move in with your dad, so maybe we could live here. Or if you prefer the cottage, maybe Aunt Jessie could make this house a retreat for visiting ministers and missionaries. Or maybe—"

"I'm not talking about houses, sweetheart. I've been doing a lot of thinking and praying about my life. I feel a real peace about the two of us. . ."

"I'm glad. So do I."

"But. . ."

She inhaled sharply. "This sounds serious."

"It is. The truth is, I'm not sure I can keep working for my father."

She looked up at him. The moonlight silhouetted his finely chiseled features. She couldn't see his eyes though, couldn't quite read his expression. "Are you planning to leave the company?"

"I don't know. It's just that my dad has always thrived on building luxury estates for people. In college I learned how to design and build good quality houses. Now, with all the experience I've had, I'd like to start my own business designing and building homes for low-income people."

"Really? I think that's awesome."

"You do?"

"Of course. You'll be giving back to the community. I think God will honor that."

"That's how I feel, too. In fact. . ." He shifted, his shoulders tensing.

"What else, Jay? I can tell you have more on your mind."

"It's probably not realistic. It's not even fair of me to expect you to—"

"Just tell me."

He pressed his cheek against the top of her head. She could feel the tightness in his jaw. "I've always dreamed of going to the mission field someday, Kayli, not as a preacher or anything like that. I don't think I'd be good at preaching. I'm not outgoing like my dad. But I'd love to go to third world countries and teach the people economic ways to build houses and churches for their families and communities. My regular job building affordable houses could support the mission trips. We could take two or three a year, going wherever the Lord leads us. Just talking about it makes my heart start racing. I've never even told my dad this, because I know what he'd say. He'd tell me to stop being so foolish and get back to work as usual. The truth is, I'm scared to death you'll tell me the same thing."

She reached up and caressed his cheek. "Do you really think I'd say that?"

"I hope not. I hope I know you better than that."

"You do, Jay. I love the idea. Just hearing you talk this way, hearing the passion and excitement in your voice makes me excited. I knew you hadn't found your passion the way I have with my art. I knew you derived a certain amount of satisfaction working for your dad, but it wasn't passion. Now I understand why."

He turned her shoulders to face him. "So you're saying you're with me in this? You're willing to see where this whole new thing takes us?"

She clasped his face in her hands. The moonlight reflected in his green eyes, illuminating unshed tears. He had never looked more attractive to her. "I'm more than willing. I'd love to be a part of it."

He held her close and kissed her with a passion born of a oneness of spirit and a new level of closeness and understanding. She yearned for this moment to last forever.

A familiar feminine voice broke through the tranquil night. "Kayli, Jay, are you out there? It's getting late. We're leaving for the Christmas Eve service."

Kayli looked at Jay as if to ask, *Should we pretend we're not here?*

With a sigh he got to his feet and pulled her up beside him. "We'll continue this conversation later. We have a lifetime to talk. Right now I think God has a blessing waiting for us at church."

Holding hands, they swung their arms between them as they walked back to the house. Silently Kayli mused, *If I didn't know it before, I know it now. This is the man of my dreams—a man after God's own heart.*

Chapter 16

Kayli, what are you doing New Year's Eve?" It was Rick Moran on the phone. She hadn't heard his voice in weeks, and now, coming out of the blue, it caught her off guard.

"There's a service at church," she replied, hoping she didn't sound too evasive. "A potluck, movie, and midnight communion."

"Really? I haven't been to church lately with all the extra fire duty. I was going to suggest dinner and a concert, but the church service would be a good alternative. How about it? Will you spend New Year's Eve with me—for old time's sake?"

Kayli's mouth went dry. Rick sounded like his old self, as if nothing had changed between them. Surely he knew better than to think she would go out with him.

"Kayli? Are you still there?"

"Yes, Rick, I'm here."

"Good. Thought we got cut off. I've missed you. It's been over a month since you gave me back the ring. I've tried to give you some breathing room. I called a few times but always got hold of people I didn't know. What's your aunt Jessie doing—taking in half of Honolulu?"

"No, just some nice people from church and a missionary family who needed a helping hand for a few weeks. They're gone now."

"Oh, well, I didn't even leave my name. I figured you were busy enough with all the company. Anyway, I hope you had a nice Christmas."

"Yes, it was very nice." She glanced down at her engagement ring. *The best Christmas of my life.*

"Great. I spent mine putting out fires—literally. But I have the next few days off and was hoping we could go out. You didn't answer me yet about New Year's Eve. I know you're seeing Jay Mahala, but he can't begrudge us a little time together, can he? What do you say?"

Somehow she found her voice. "I'm sorry, Rick. I can't."

"Let me guess—you're all tied up with Jay?"

Kayli struggled for the right words. There was no easy way to say it. "We're—engaged."

The line was silent for a long moment. Just when she thought they had been disconnected, Rick's voice broke across the wire. "You're engaged? I was under the impression you weren't sure where things were heading with you two."

"It happened just last week. Christmas Eve. We haven't set a date or anything."

Rick made a guttural sound low in his throat. "So you're sure this is what you want?"

"Yes, Rick. I feel God wants me with Jay."

"What if I told you I'm convinced God wants the two of us together?"

"I'd have to say He hasn't shown me that."

"You never gave us a chance, Kayli." His voice was heavy. "Just so you know. I'm not giving up on you."

Kayli's voice quavered. "I'm sorry. I don't know what else to say, Rick."

She could hear him inhaling sharply. "Listen, babe, I didn't fight you when you gave back my ring because I figured I'd bide my time until you came to your senses. You're making a big mistake. I hope you realize it in time."

"I never meant to hurt you, Rick. I'm sorry. Rick? Are you there?"

The line was dead. *He hung up on me.* She returned the phone to its cradle and collapsed in a nearby chair, shaken. As much as she loved Jay, a part of her still cared about Rick. She had never intended to hurt him. What if he turned against God because of her?

On New Year's Eve she was still struggling with mixed feelings over Rick Moran. As she slipped into a sleeveless white dress and rhinestone sandals and fastened a gold locket around her neck, she wondered what she could have done differently. Had she led Rick on? Had she said or done anything to make him think they were more than just good friends?

A knock sounded on Kayli's door followed by Aunt Jessie's voice. "Are you ready, honey? The guys will be picking us up soon. The potluck starts in half an hour."

Kayli opened the door, grabbed her clutch bag off the bureau, and followed Aunt Jessie down the hall. "What about the green bean casserole? Is it done?"

"I'll check." The doorbell rang. "Oh, they're here, Kayli. You get the casserole; I'll get the door."

Kayli went to the kitchen, put on oven mitts, and removed the steaming casserole. It looked perfect—crispy onions blending with green beans and creamy mushroom soup. She looked up just as Jay entered the kitchen. Beaming from ear to ear, he strode over and gave her a hearty embrace. "Happy New Year, sweetheart."

She returned the smile. "We still have a few more hours."

"I know, but I wanted to be the first to say it." He hugged her again. "Boy, I missed you. It gets harder and harder to be apart."

"I was thinking the same thing." She set the casserole in a large cardboard box. "I hope this won't spill in your car."

"I'll put it in the back. It'll be fine." He leaned close. "I have some news."

"Really? Good news, I hope."

"I think so. I had a long talk with my dad."

"What about?"

"I told him I either need to get out on my own or take more leadership in his company. I said I'd like to head up a division geared to low-income housing. Not the usual boxy, tacky stuff that no one wants to live in, but nice, classy homes that anyone would be proud to own."

"Oh Jay, I'm so glad you finally told him how you feel. What did he say?"

"At first he scoffed at the idea, but the more I talked, the more I could see he was listening. Finally he said he'd think about it. And he admitted that it's time I bring my own vision to the company. He even said he and Jessie might travel a little, so I'll need to take on more responsibility."

"That's what you want."

"Right—although I told him you and I would be doing some traveling, too."

"We will? Where?"

"We have to take a honeymoon."

She laughed. "I know that. I thought you were talking about something else."

"Actually I was. I plan to do some of that mission work I talked about—taking some time off two or three times a year to help design and build homes for needy communities. I was thinking the first one might not be a third world country after all."

"Then where?"

"Right in our own United States. The mainland."

She frowned. "Now I'm confused. Where would you go?"

"New Orleans. I know it's been years since the hurricane nearly destroyed the city, but there are still a lot of displaced people there. Many still don't have homes to go to."

"I hadn't thought of that."

Jay picked up the casserole and they headed for the door. "How would you feel about going there for a few months next summer?"

"It would be exciting. I'll be right beside you helping out."

They stepped out on the lanai where Jessie and Leo stood talking. "It'll mean taking time off from your job at the gallery."

Kayli nodded. "I think Tara would allow that."

"Allow what?" inquired Aunt Jessie.

"It's a long story," said Kayli. "I'll tell you all about it later."

"Now you've piqued my curiosity."

Jay put the casserole in the car. "You gals ready to go?"

Kayli was about to climb in on the passenger side of Jay's SUV when she glanced up at the sky. What she saw stopped her in her tracks. "Look! Smoke!"

They all looked up. "A fire north of here, near the crater," said Leo.

"Could be a brush fire," said Jay. "Or another house fire."

Kayli's heart hammered. "The newspaper said there have been several arson fires in this area."

"This one's not far away," said Leo. "It's moving pretty fast."

Jay pulled out his cell phone and punched in a number. After a moment he said in a solemn voice, "I want to report a fire near Diamond Head Road. Yes, along the base of the crater. Okay, thank you." He closed his phone and looked at Kayli. "Someone's already reported it."

"Thank God!" She hugged her arms and rocked slightly as sirens screamed in the distance. "The fire's coming this way. It's already bigger than when we first noticed it. We've got to get out of here."

"I smell it now, too," said Jessie. "The wind's blowing it this way."

Kayli gripped Jessie's arm. "I can't stay here, Aunt Jessie. I can't!"

"I know, dear. But we can't leave until we know what we're up against."

Kayli fished in her bag for her cell phone. "I've got to call Rick. He'll know what to do." With shaking fingers she punched in his number. Would he even talk to her after their conversation the other day? She was relieved when he answered on the second ring. He seemed sympathetic as she told him about the fire.

"Don't panic," he told her. "I'll check it out and get back to you, okay? Meanwhile, relax and stay close to home."

"We can't go to the service," she told Jay after hanging up with Rick. "We have to be ready in case the fire gets too close." Even as she managed to say the words, terror was spiking inside her.

"You're right," Jay agreed. "The smoke was light at first. Now it's getting heavier and blacker."

"Do you think we're in any danger?" asked Jessie.

"I don't think so," said Jay. "Your property is cleared off pretty well. But there is some heavy brush north of you, in the path of the fire. I'm concerned about embers drifting onto your roof."

"We'd better water it down," said Leo. He was already rolling up his sleeves.

"You girls go inside." Jay nudged them back toward the house. "We'll take care of things out here."

They went inside, but Kayli was too on edge to stay there. She felt skittish, as if she were about to jump out of her skin. She went out the back pocket doors leading to the beach, putting the house between them and the fire. Jessie followed her. From the backyard the fire appeared even more menacing. The northern sky was a mass of black, billowing clouds. Panic tightened in Kayli's chest. "What are we going to do, Aunt Jessie? We're in its path. It could burn our house down."

Jessie steered her back into the house. "We're not going to look at it, Kayli. God is watching over us, and He'll help the firefighters put it out. Meanwhile, we'd better look around and see what to take in case they evacuate us."

Kayli gazed around the room. "I can't imagine what to take."

"Our important papers."

"They're in the safe in your room."

"And your paintings."

"My artwork—I couldn't possibly save it all. How could I decide which paintings to take? They're like my children."

"And what about our clothes and jewelry?" said Jessie.

"And our photographs and videos." Kayli pressed her fingertips against her temples. Her head was pounding, the pain searing.

A muffled drone sounded overhead like the whine of bees. Help was coming. She gingerly stepped outside to the front lanai and looked up. A helicopter roared by like a red metallic wasp. It hovered over the ocean drawing up water, then set off toward the fire.

She could see the flames now like frantic orange fingers clawing the blackened sky. As the helicopter released its tank of water the fire abated for a minute. But soon it was back as fierce as before. The relentless flames advanced in a ravaging dance, as if they had a life and mind of their own.

All of her old fears assailed her. She had to escape. If she didn't run now, she would lose her mind, if not her life, to the devouring, windswept blaze.

Chapter 17

To her amazement, Kayli didn't bolt and run, even though the fire was growing worse and coal-black smoke shrouded the azure sky. Sheer willpower or the very hand of God kept her from fleeing. Or maybe it was the timely arrival of Rick Moran. A frenzy of writhing flames was already ascending the grassy ridge just beyond Jessie's house when Rick pulled up in his black pickup. He jumped out and came striding over in his yellow parka and safety vest. Kayli ran to him. "The fire's getting closer by the minute. Should we evacuate?"

Jay and Leo put down their garden hoses and walked over. "We're watering down the roof but we're not sure it'll do much good."

"Every little bit helps," said Rick. "Large chunks of ash could be falling soon."

"When will they put it out?" Kayli's voice was shrill with urgency.

"Here's what I know." Rick put a firm hand on her shoulder. "I drove over as close as I could to check things out. While I was there I got a call to report for duty, so I can't stay long. I'll be manning the command center truck on location near the blaze, so I'll try to feed you updates as often as I can."

"How bad is it?" asked Leo.

"There's a ring of fire making its way across the ridgeline near the base of the crater. We all know Diamond Head's climate is much drier and hotter than other parts of the island, but we still don't usually see fires like this." Rick gestured with his hands. "It looked containable at first. But after it burned through the light grass it hit the heavier fuels—the thick brush at the base just north of here."

Kayli shivered, even though the heat of the day meshing with the smoke made the air oppressive. "The wind is blowing the fire toward us."

"Actually, the winds are fluctuating," said Rick. "It's a terrain-driven fire, not wind-driven, if that's any comfort."

"Do we need to leave?" asked Jay.

Rick grimaced. "Better gather your valuables and be ready in the event we do call for an evacuation."

Kayli covered her mouth with her hand. "I think I'm going to be sick."

Jay came over and slipped his arm around her. "It's going to be okay, honey. Just stay calm."

She licked the dryness from her lips. "I've been terrified of fire all my life. It keeps tormenting me. Why doesn't it stop?"

Rick pummeled his large fist against his palm. "It's not going to hurt you, Kayli. I don't care if I have to battle it with my bare hands."

She clasped his arm. "No, Rick, I can't be responsible for you risking your life like that."

He turned his face toward the conflagration, his brows furrowed, his jaw set, as if staring the blaze down. "I promise you it won't win. Right now the helitankers are dropping water from the ocean to knock down the flames. We've got a bulldozer cutting a firebreak through the brush upslope on the crater. That'll impede the inferno. As long as the flames don't jump the fire line or the road and hit the overgrowth near the beach, we should be okay. Just pray our crews on the ground get a stop on it."

"I am praying," said Kayli. "I haven't stopped since I saw the first plumes of smoke."

Rick knuckled her chin. "Don't worry. If we need to, the ground commander will call in more units. We will get control of the fire. But as a precaution, go inside and gather your things. If they call for an evacuation you'll be the first to know."

As Rick's truck pulled out of the driveway, Jay put his hand at Kayli's back and led her across the lanai to the door. "I'll help you pack your things, honey."

"Me, too," Leo told Jessie as they went inside. "Let's get busy. You two can come over to our place tonight. You can have the house to yourselves. I'll stay in the cottage with Jay."

Jessie gave him a quick hug. "That's so kind of you, Leo."

Kayli stood in the middle of the room. "I don't know where to begin."

"Start with personal items like pictures, diaries, videos, jewelry, and official papers," said Jay.

They spent the next half hour stacking boxes, bags, Jessie's old photo albums, and Kayli's paintings in the foyer beside the door. Jay checked closets and cupboards for anything that looked important. Kayli threw a few clothes in a tote bag. She was collecting her laptop and paint box when the phone rang.

Rick's voice crackled over the line. The connection wasn't good, but when she heard the words, "The fire's seventy percent contained—no evacuation," her heart leaped for joy.

She ran out to the living room exclaiming, "The fire's contained!"

The others rushed outside and stared at the northern sky while Kayli lingered in the doorway, her nerves still jittery. Gray-white plumes had replaced the voluminous black smoke. A burnt, acrid smell drifted on the breeze and a fine ash fell like confetti, but, yes, the fire was nearly extinguished.

"That was way too close a call for my sensibilities," said Jessie.

Leo looked at his watch. "It's too late for the potluck, but we could still make the rest of the service."

"Not me," said Kayli. "I'm a basket case. And as long as there's even a smoldering ember out there, I'm taking you up on your offer of a place to stay, Leo."

"Me, too," said Jessie. "You never know about these things. We'll both feel safer at your house tonight."

"Well, first we'll need something to eat," said Jay. "Do you want me to go get some fast food? I'm afraid it won't be a fancy New Year's Eve dinner."

"We have a green bean casserole in your car," said Kayli. "We could start with that. And, if my hands stop shaking, I could throw a salad together."

"We have some leftover roast beef in the fridge," Jessie chimed in.

"Sounds like a feast to me," said Leo. "It's more than you'll find at my house."

The meal turned out better than Kayli expected, and except for her jangled nerves, she actually enjoyed herself.

While she cleared the table, Aunt Jessie browsed through her old photo albums with Jay and Leo.

"Where did you find those?" asked Kayli, looking over Jessie's shoulder. "I haven't seen those albums since I was a child."

"They were in an old trunk, honey. I haven't looked at them in years myself. I forgot they were there until we went looking for our valuables today."

Thumbing through a dog-eared, blue velvet album, Jessie came across several faded pictures of long-dead relatives in her Hawaiian lineage. "There's no one from my family alive today except Kayli and me," she noted with a wisp of nostalgia. "So I guess if anyone's going to carry on the Akimo name, it'll have to be Kayli."

Jay looked over at her and winked. "Looks like we've got our work cut out for us, sweetheart."

They all laughed.

Their laughter faded when the doorbell rang. "Who could that be?" Jessie wondered.

Kayli headed for the foyer. "I don't know, but I'll get it."

When she opened the door, she was taken aback by the imposing figure of a firefighter in helmet and jumpsuit. "Rick?" His face was smudged with black streaks and his helmet shadowed his eyes.

"Just wanted to stop by and see how you're doing." He removed his helmet and smoothed back his matted hair. He smelled heavily of smoke.

"I'm fine," she murmured, wondering whether to invite him inside. "Is the fire out?"

"Ninety-nine percent."

"Wonderful!" She surveyed his grimy clothes. "It looks like you did it single-handedly."

"Not quite. I had a lot of help." His voice took on an unsettling excitement. "Our crew confronted a massive wall of flames. But not one man flinched. We forged ahead like warriors in a battle between good and evil. We won against the elements, Kayli, against nature herself—nature gone haywire, out of control. We subdued it, defeated it. You have no idea how exhilarating that can be."

She gave a nervous little toss of her head. "It looks like you've saved the day once again."

He managed an uneven grin. "I'm not here for words of gratitude. I just wanted to make sure you're okay. I know how you feel about fires."

She smiled ruefully. "I think my pulse has finally returned to normal. I'll survive."

"Yes, that's what I love about you. You're a survivor." He took a step back on the lanai. "I guess I'd better let you get back to your party."

"Oh, it's not a party," she said quickly. "It's just—"

"I know. It's you—and your fiancé." He rubbed his chin with the back of his hand and put his helmet back on. "I'd better get back to the firehouse and change out of these clothes."

With a little twinge of guilt and relief she stepped back into the foyer, her hand on the doorknob. "Thanks for stopping by, Rick. And thanks for—well, you know—putting out the fire and all that. I know there's no way to repay you."

He paused. "There is one thing."

"Really?" She was caught by surprise. "What's that?"

"Have lunch with me sometime next week."

Her mind raced, searching for an acceptable way to say no.

"If you don't want to go out alone with me—if it seems too much like a date—then let me bring lunch to you and your aunt. That's harmless enough, isn't it? Even your Mr. Mahala shouldn't mind your breaking bread with a weary firefighter."

"You're right. Call me next week—or I should say next year—it's not long 'til midnight."

He saluted her. "Good night, beautiful lady. I'll call you. . .next year."

"Good night, Rick." As she closed the door, a chill raced through her. More and more she felt uncomfortable in Rick's presence. How could he take such delight in something as horrific and terrifying as a fire? And now that he had saved her once more, she felt obligated to see him again. It seemed uncanny that he was forever her rescuer and she always the lady in distress. She was tired of always being the victim; for too many years that dreadful label had shaped her personality and defined her entire life.

Lord, will it ever change? Will I ever have a brave bone in my body? You are my strength. Help me to face life head-on and be the victor, the overcomer, the courageous woman Jay deserves.

Chapter 18

Two nights later the dream returned. Kayli was a little girl again. As in all the dreams before, she was a solitary child in a satin and lace nightgown carrying a candle, walking through the darkness, calling for her mother. In her dream a scream reverberated through the shadowed rooms—perhaps her mother's voice, perhaps her own. And then the blackness of night gave way to the eerie orange glow of flames devouring curtains, racing up walls and across the carpet, consuming everything in its path.

Kayli woke with a start and sat up in bed, perspiration beading her forehead, her heart pounding like a jackhammer. The brush fire had unearthed long dormant emotions and fears she still hadn't dealt with. "Will it never end?" she moaned, lying back down. "Will I always be a prisoner of the past, of that night I can't even remember except in my dreams?"

She gazed up into the darkness of her bedroom, willing her racing heart to be still. She was a grown woman; she was here in Aunt Jessie's house. She and Jay were looking forward to an amazing future together. Why then did her emotions always get stuck in the past, locked into that one fateful night?

"Lord, either help me remember or help me forget. I can't bear living in this limbo forever. How can I start a new life with Jay if I'm still an emotional wreck? He deserves a woman who's got it together, not a broken, hurting person who's constantly scared of her own shadow. How can I say I'm a woman of faith if my faith doesn't help me get over this fear?"

She looked at the alarm clock on her nightstand. Five o'clock in the morning. She rolled over and fluffed her pillow. "Father, please unlock the door of my mind. Give me back my past so I can face it and deal with it once and for all."

She stretched out and allowed herself to slip back to the edge of slumber. There, in that fragile symmetry between wakefulness and sleep, images began tumbling into her consciousness, one after another. A scene unraveled on the screen of her mind. Kayli saw herself, a mere child, in her bedroom under the covers with her stuffed Pooh Bear and Tinker Bell doll.

It's dark. Even her Cinderella night-light isn't on. It's quiet, too quiet. Usually music drifted from her parents' room down the hall. Tonight the only sounds are rain on the roof and thunder rumbling in the distance. Beyond the sheer curtains lightning splits the sky in bright, jagged bolts. She covers her head so she won't see the eerie flashes.

She wants her parents. She gets out of bed and pads down the hall to their room.

As she opens the door she sees the rosy glow of candles—one on the dressing table in an antique lamp and another on the highboy beside her parents' bed, not far from the curtains.

Her mother bends down and picks her up in her arms. "Are you frightened, honey?" she asks. "The electricity is out. There's nothing to be afraid of."

She takes Kayli over to the bed and the child sits between her father and mother. She tells her daddy she's scared of the dark. Can she sleep with them? He kisses the top of her head and tells little Kayli she'll rest better in her own bed. Her mother hands Kayli a candle of her own in a milk-glass holder and walks her back to her room. She waits while Kayli carefully places the candle on the dresser and slips into bed. Kayli smells the perfume on her mother's neck as she sits down on the bed and embraces the child. Tucking Pooh Bear and Tinker Bell under the covers with Kayli, she whispers in her daughter's ear, "I love you, sweet joy of my life." Kayli falls asleep watching the candle flicker and dance in the darkness.

A crackling noise jars little Kayli awake. She'd never heard a sound like that before. The room is dark except for flashes of lightning through the window and slivers of moonlight peeking through the clouds. She gets out of bed and clasps her hands around the milk-jar glass, but the candle has gone out. With her free hand feeling the way, she treads down the hallway toward her parents' room, her nightgown swishing around her ankles. Smoke. It makes her cough. Her eyes water. It's hard to breathe.

She pounds on her parents' door. She cries out, "Mama! Daddy!" She touches the doorknob, but it's too hot to turn. She tries to push open the door, but it won't budge. She hears a popping sound on the other side of the door. The smoke gets worse, so Kayli runs back to her bedroom, still carrying the darkened candle. She sets it back on the dresser and climbs back into bed. She hears sirens far away but coming closer. She pulls the covers over her head and sobs as darkness and smoke engulf her.

As the child gasps for air, strange noises other than the rain and thunder invade her senses. Doors bang, wood splinters, glass breaks. Through the smoke someone sweeps into the room—a huge, shadowed figure. The stranger hoists the terrified child into his arms. He tucks her under his heavy raincoat and carries her through a pathway of flames into fresh air and pelting rain. The flames terrify her, but she feels safe and protected in the stranger's strong arms.

Kayli opened her eyes wide and stared up at the ceiling. Dawn was breaking. The images in her mind were already fading away, losing their stark reality. She got out of bed, went to the bathroom, and splashed water on her face.

Was it real? Is that what really happened? Or was it just my imagination playing tricks on me? I asked God to show me the truth. Was this His answer to my prayer?

She went to the kitchen and fixed herself a cup of coffee. Trembling , she held the cup in both hands and sipped slowly. *I've got to get hold of myself. I've got to process this.*

She glanced over at the telephone on the counter. It was too early to call Jay, but she had never needed him more than at this moment. At last she relented and phoned him. She could tell by his groggy response that she had awakened him.

"I know this sounds crazy, Jay, but can you come over now? I need to talk."

"Be there as soon as I can throw on some clothes."

He was at the door a half hour later. "What's up, honey? Are you okay?"

"I'm not sure."

She showed him into the kitchen and poured him a cup of coffee. Sitting down across from him she said, "Aunt Jessie is still asleep. I don't want to have this conversation with her. I think it would be too upsetting."

Jay's green eyes fastened on hers. "What is it? Tell me."

Haltingly she told him about the dream. "It was so real. All my life I've had nightmares about the fire. But this was like an altered state, like I had tapped into something in my subconscious I'd never come close to before. I can still see my bedroom before the fire and hear my mother's voice saying, 'I love you, sweet joy of my life.' I felt as if she were right there with me. Every detail was heightened, vivid. What do you think it was?"

"They say all our memories are stored somewhere in our minds. Maybe you just happened to open the right file."

"You make it sound so cut-and-dry." She sipped her coffee. "I need to know if my memory is true. If it is then I know I didn't start the fire. That's a secret burden I've carried all my life—the fear that I was the one who started the fire that killed my parents."

"Wasn't there a report pinpointing where the fire started?"

"I know it started in my parents' bedroom, but in my dreams I was always the one holding the candle."

"What do the newspaper clippings say?"

"What newspaper clippings?"

"The ones in your aunt's photo album. I saw them the other day when we thought we were going to have to evacuate. They fell out of the album. When I put them back I noticed they were about the fire. I almost mentioned it to you, then decided against it. You were already upset enough."

Kayli set her coffee cup down hard on the saucer. "I don't remember ever seeing them, Jay. I might have sometime when I was little, but I don't know whether Aunt Jessie would have shown them to a child."

"She probably put them there years ago and forgot them. She said it had been ages since she'd seen those albums."

Kayli pushed back her chair and stood up. "I want to read them."

Jay stood up, too. "We put the albums in the bookcase in the living room. It was the blue velvet one. I'll go get it."

He was back moments later with the album. He quickly found the articles and handed them to her.

Kayli's heart pounded as she gently unfolded the yellowed paper. Silently she read the first article, but her eyes filled with tears so quickly she couldn't keep reading. She handed them to Jay. "Will you read them?"

Solemnly he read each one. She sat and listened, hot tears running down her cheeks. When he had finished he got up and drew her into his arms and held her close as she sobbed. When she had no more tears to shed, he led her over to the sofa. She sat wrapped in his arms for a long while, saying nothing, too overwhelmed with emotion to utter a word.

Finally he said, "At least you know it wasn't your fault. Your candle wasn't even lit. Your mother probably put it out after you fell asleep. The accounts match your memory. The fire started in your parents' room. The fireman found you in your bedroom overcome with smoke."

"It must have been started by the candle I saw on the highboy near the curtains."

"Whatever happened, there is nothing you could have done to change it. If you had slept with your parents that night you would have died, too."

She shivered as the burden of guilt fell away. "God let me survive for a reason. I don't want to squander my life by living in fear."

"Not a chance, sweetheart." He kissed her forehead. "God gave you this memory to help you exorcise the ghosts of the past. He wants you to get on with your life and live it with purpose and joy."

"And that's just what I'm going to do." Kayli's smile broke like a sunburst. She suddenly felt giddy, as if her emotions had done a somersault. She had never felt so happy and free. She clasped Jay's hand against her cheek. It felt strong and sturdy and reassuring. "I'm starting a brand-new life, Jay. Best of all, you'll be with me all the way."

He nuzzled her hair. "You bet I will, sweetheart. Think what God can accomplish with the two of us putting our heads together."

"I can't wait. Where do we begin?"

"Let's start by calling my dad over and fixing him and Aunt Jessie a breakfast befitting the New Year—bacon and eggs or pancakes with strawberries and whipped cream. Or fruit and granola, if that's all you have. Then the four of us will sit down together and start planning a fantastic double wedding—unless, of course, you'd prefer separate weddings."

"No, I like being unconventional for a change. I say, the more the merrier. Instead of just the two of us, we'll be standing at the altar with the people we love most in the world."

Chapter 19

Hey, JJ, do you think the girls will be ready for an April wedding?"

"I think so, Dad." They were sitting in his father's luxury office, his dad at his wide mahogany desk, Jay ensconced on a tidy corner of the desk. They were supposed to be discussing the specs for a Waikiki high-rise, but as usual these days the subject drifted to their upcoming double wedding. "The girls agreed on the date. They have three months to prepare. That should be long enough."

"They're not going to make it some big Hollywood production, are they?"

"Are we talking about Kayli and Jessie? They're the model of discretion and good taste."

"I know." His father spread out the specs but kept his gaze on Jay. "Frankly, I don't mind if it is a big production. How often does a man get married to the woman of his dreams?"

"You can say that again, Dad. If I know our gals, the wedding will be fun, exciting, and well planned."

"They'll probably invite half of Honolulu."

"And I'm sure it will be a traditional Hawaiian wedding." Jay stood up and straightened his shoulders. He enjoyed talking about the wedding, but he had something else on his mind right now. "By the way, Dad, guess what our girls are doing this afternoon. They're having a guest for lunch—Rick Moran."

"He's like a bad penny—just keeps showing up."

"You know I don't like the guy."

"Well, yeah, he almost took your girl."

"But it's more than that. I can't put my finger on it. But I guess I can't complain about a harmless lunch. It's not like Kayli's going to be alone with him. And the guy does put his life on the line every time he fights a fire."

"You've got to admire him for that. But he doesn't take no for an answer. He knows you're engaged to Kayli. So why is he still coming around?"

"That's what I'd like to know. When she first told me about their lunch date I asked a few questions about his background. He came to Honolulu a few years ago. Before that he was with the Long Beach Fire Department in California."

Leo shrugged. "That doesn't mean anything, does it?"

"Probably not. But I put in a call to Dave Barrett, a detective friend of mine in Los Angeles. Asked him to do a little sleuthing for me on the side—see if he could come up with any information about Rick. He's supposed to call me back anytime now."

"So you're actually checking up on the guy?"

"Crazy, huh? I've just got a nagging feeling that something's not right. He comes on too strong. I want to make sure there's nothing in his past to worry about."

Leo sat back in his chair. "Hey, son, you doing anything for lunch?"

"Not a thing. How about you?"

"Nope. What say we grab a bite after finishing these specs?"

Jay nodded. "Sounds like a plan to me."

Kayli adjusted the straps of her goldenrod-yellow sundress and glanced down, as she often did, at the sparkling diamond on her finger. If only she were getting ready for a lunch date with Jay instead of Rick Moran. But she had promised Rick this one last lunch together. Of course, she hadn't expected Aunt Jessie to be called away at the last minute. Now it would be just the two of them—a fact that left her feeling a little ill at ease.

The doorbell rang. You might know—Rick was early. She inhaled sharply, glanced toward the kitchen where the table was set with Jessie's best china, silver, and linen napkins, then strode to the door and opened it.

Rick stood on the lanai in a pinstriped suit, his russet hair slicked back, a bouquet of red roses in his hand. "These are for you." He swooped in with the grace of a bird in flight and kissed her cheek.

She took the flowers, holding them like a shield between them. "Thank you, Rick. You shouldn't have. Flowers and a fancy suit for just a simple little lunch?"

"You wouldn't let me bring the food, so I brought flowers instead." He followed her into the kitchen. "Besides, this is an important date for me. I've been looking forward to it all week." He glanced around. "Where's Aunt Jessie?"

Kayli found a glass vase in the cupboard and put the roses in it. "She got a call from someone at the hospital. One of the families who stayed with us brought in an injured child and wanted Jessie to come watch their other children for a few hours. She just left, so it'll just be the two of us."

He smiled. "I think we can manage without Aunt Jessie."

Kayli removed a steaming dish from the oven and set it on the table in the nook. "I hope you like broccoli and cheese quiche. They say real men don't eat quiche, but I hope that's not true in your case."

Rick sat down at the table. "I'll eat anything you fix. The company is more important than the food."

She took a fruit salad and a pitcher of iced tea from the refrigerator and set them on the table. "I guess we're all set." She sat down and put her napkin in her lap. "Would you like to ask the blessing?"

His brows furrowed. "No, you go ahead."

She prayed, but the words felt forced. She couldn't help thinking how special grace always was with Jay. She felt no spiritual connection with Rick. Even making light conversation seemed an effort today. "Did they find out if the brush fire was an accident?"

"Looks like arson." Rick helped himself to the quiche and salad. "If the fires continue at this rate we may have to bring in more men."

"They have no idea who's starting the fires?"

"Not a clue. So far he's been too smart for any of us."

"He has to make a mistake sometime."

"You would think so. But so far. . .nothing."

They ate in silence for a while. Rick seemed a little on edge, not his usual talkative self. "Is anything wrong?" she asked.

His jaw tightened as he gazed at her. There was a smoldering glint in his dark eyes. His voice was low, almost sullen. "I suppose this will be our last time together."

They had finished eating, so she picked up their empty plates and carried them over to the sink. "I think that's best, Rick. I'm going to be a married woman soon. That doesn't mean we can't still be friends."

He cracked his knuckles. "Yeah. Friends. Whatever that means."

She cleared the rest of the dishes from the table. If only she had never agreed to this lunch. If only Jay were here. Her growing anxieties were already doing a number on her stomach.

As she set the plates and glasses in the sink, she sensed Rick coming up behind her. Before she could react, he wrapped his muscular arms around her waist and held her tight. She could smell his strong aftershave and feel his clenched jaw against her cheek. Her stomach churned. She froze as he swept her long hair aside and kissed the back of her neck.

"I love you, baby. You feel so good in my arms. I'm the man you should be marrying."

Panic rose in her throat. She thought she might be sick. She worked herself free and pivoted sharply, facing him, her heart thundering. Something told her to stay calm. *Reason with him.* Breathless, she managed to get out the words, "What do you think you're doing, Rick?"

He ran his rough fingers over her lips. "What does it look like? I'm showing you how I feel about you. I love you, Kayli. I've always loved you."

Her mouth went dry. Reason wasn't going to do it. She pushed his hand away. "Stop it. You know there's nothing between us."

"That's where you're wrong. There's everything between us." He gripped her bare arms until she winced. "You feel the connection, I know you do. Admit it."

"Get out of here," she demanded, "before I call the police!"

Rick looked almost amused. "You're a fighter, babe. That's how you triumphed over the fire. That makes me love you all the more." In one swift gesture he seized her in his arms and crushed her against his chest. His mouth came down hard on hers, bruising her lips. "Let me show you how I feel, Kayli. I'll make you forget Jay Mahala ever existed."

Jay and his father were just preparing to leave for lunch when their office manager stepped inside the door. "Jay, there's a call for you on line one."

"Thanks, Liana." He picked up the phone and said hello.

"Jay, this is Dave."

"What did you find out?"

"Plenty. You want the condensed version?"

"Sure."

"Moran is obviously a bold, ambitious man. Made it to fire captain. Lots of exploits. Even made the newspapers quite a few times with his heroics. After a spate of fires in the Long Beach area, things turned sour. Rumors circulated that he had started the fires. No one was ever able to prove arson, and Moran was never officially charged. He agreed to leave the department when he learned the police investigation might implicate him. The fires stopped after he left."

Jay tensed. This was the last thing he wanted to hear. *Father in heaven, what am I supposed to do now?* "Thanks, Dave. I think you've answered my questions."

He hung up the phone and turned to his father. Leo was just hanging up his cell phone. "It's bad news, Dad. It's possible Rick Moran is our arsonist."

The color drained from Leo's face. "The news is worse than that, son. That was Jessie on the phone. Someone summoned her to the hospital on a false alarm. She tried phoning Kayli and no one answers."

Alarm shot like a bullet through Jay's chest. "That means Kayli's alone with Rick." His pulse racing, he took long strides toward the door. "Call her. Warn her, Dad. Keep trying until she answers. But call the police first. And the fire department, too."

"Where are you going?"

"To rescue my bride! Pray that I'm not too late!"

Chapter 20

The phone was ringing.

"I've got to get it this time." Kayli struggled to break away from Rick's fierce embrace. "Jay knows I'm here. He'll think something's wrong if I don't answer."

Rick grudgingly released her. "Go ahead. Get it. Watch what you say."

She grabbed the phone and said hello. Her voice came out raspy, hardly there.

"Kayli, is that you? This is Leo. Are you okay?"

Somehow she managed to say yes.

"Are you alone there with Rick?"

Yes again.

"Can he hear me?"

"No."

"Listen, Kayli, I don't want to frighten you, but he's a dangerous man. He got Jessie out of the house so he could be alone with you. Get away from him as quickly as you can. Make an excuse. Just get him out of there."

Her mouth felt like sandpaper. "I—I can't."

"Are you okay? Has he hurt you?"

She couldn't catch her breath, couldn't make her temples stop throbbing. "I can't talk now."

Leo's voice grew shrill. "Listen to me. He may be the arsonist. He might have started all the fires."

Kayli swayed. She gripped the edge of the counter. Shock spiked through her, electrifying every nerve ending. *It can't be!* "Thanks for calling," she rasped. *Please, Lord, don't let me faint.*

She hung up the phone and looked back at Rick. Why hadn't she noticed before how cold and menacing his eyes could be?

"Who was it?"

"Leo."

"What'd he say?"

"He said you might have set the fires."

"He's crazy."

"Did you?"

Rick walked over and took her face in his hands, almost like a parent would a child. She wanted to run but couldn't move.

His expression softened as he searched her eyes. "Okay. I set the fires. I admit it. But I never hurt anyone. I swear it. I was careful about that. I always picked isolated brushlands or unoccupied structures. And I always made sure we could get to them in time to put them out. Don't you see, Kayli? I needed to prove that I could conquer them and survive—like you did with the fire that killed your parents."

"Don't you dare compare your actions to mine." She spit out the words. "I didn't start that fire."

"Maybe you didn't." His large, calloused hands still cupped her face. "I told you once it doesn't matter how a fire starts. It's how you defeat it that counts. It's a living, breathing thing, Kayli—a demon straight from hades. Conquering it is like subduing the devil himself."

Tears gathered behind her eyes. "How could you, Rick? You could have killed people. I thought you were a hero. You're nothing but a sadistic monster!"

He dropped his hands to his side. "I'm sorry you feel that way. I thought you'd understand. You've hated fire all your life because it killed your parents. I hate it, too. But I respect its power, its energy, its ruthlessness. I was born to subdue and dominate it."

He walked a few paces away from her, removed his pinstriped jacket, and tossed it over the sofa. Turning back to her he said, "Sometimes in Long Beach I paced the firehouse for weeks waiting to do battle. The fires were few and far between. I couldn't stand the monotony. I was ready to attack, but there was no adversary. Then one day I decided to help things out a little. The crew needed the practice anyway. So I started a small fire in an abandoned warehouse. Our crew attacked that fire and vanquished it. Afterward, I felt this incredible exhilaration. The whole firehouse was filled with an excitement that comes only from defeating a worthy opponent."

"But they didn't know you set the fire yourself."

"It doesn't matter. The result was the same."

Kayli hugged her arms to keep from trembling. "Rick, turn yourself in. You're sick. There are doctors who can help you."

He hit the granite countertop hard with his fist. "I'm not sick! What does it take to convince you?"

"Please go," she urged, tears rimming her eyes.

"I'll show you." He grabbed up his jacket and stalked out of the great room toward the foyer.

Kayli sank down on the sofa, buried her face in her hands, and released great, racking sobs. All her fears and pent-up emotions surged over her, unleashed like floodwaters breaking through a dam. She felt as if she had just sidestepped a moving train.

After a moment she stopped weeping and listened. Peculiar popping sounds were coming from the living room. She looked toward the foyer, every cell in her body alert. She had assumed that Rick left the house. But had he? She sniffed the air. Faint tendrils of smoke filled her nostrils.

She jumped up and raced to the living room, her heart exploding in her chest. "No, no, no!"

With a sweeping glance she took in the macabre scene. Rick was setting fire to the drapes, the furniture, the potted palms, Aunt Jessie's shoji screen, even her own paintings!

With an adrenaline surge that shocked her, she rushed at him, shrieking for him to stop. She hit him full force with her body, knocking the cigarette lighter from his hand. He stumbled, caught himself, then lunged toward her, gripping her wrists. She twisted and turned but couldn't break free.

All around her hungry flames were devouring the curtains, leaping across the shoji screen, and turning the potted palms into glittering, spangled light shows. With a vise grip on her wrists Rick pushed her down into a wicker rocking chair, almost toppling both her and the chair. He placed his hands squarely on her shoulders and leaned in so close she felt the heat of his breath.

"It's just the two of us now, sweetheart. I want you to see the flames—see their power, their beauty. See how the blaze hypnotizes you, transforms you. Look at it. You haven't seen a sight like this since you were five years old. Only this time we'll let the fire win!"

She closed her eyes as long-suppressed memories engulfed her. *God help me—I'm going to die!*

"No!" The stark force of her own voice shook her out of her reverie. In one swift motion she raised her legs and kicked Rick hard in the midsection. He stumbled backward, fell over the kotatsu table, and crashed through the flaming shoji screen. He was lying dazed, his torso twisted amid the burning wreckage.

Kayli sprang from the rocker and darted past the rattan furniture and exotic plants festooned with flames to reach him. Toxic smoke rolled through the room sucking the air from her lungs and parching her throat. Choking, her eyes watering as she dodged falling fireballs, she knelt down, grabbed him around the shoulders, and tried to hoist him to his feet. He was too heavy—and too disoriented to cooperate. She couldn't budge him.

Help me, Lord!

As the scorching heat crackled around them, she summoned all her strength and dragged him inch by painful inch toward the foyer. The lethal smoke was already enveloping them, sapping her energy, clouding her mind. She released Rick's deadweight and collapsed on the tile floor beside him. She had gone as far as she could—almost to the door. But not close enough. The fire had won after all.

❧

The instant Jay pulled up beside Kayli's house he knew there was trouble. Through the front windows he saw flames climbing the sheer curtains and smoke pouring out from under the door. *Too late,* he thought. *It can't be! Kayli, my beautiful Kayli.* He jumped out of his SUV and ran across the wide expanse of lawn to the lanai. He took the steps two at a time. Covering his face with his forearm, he kicked the door wide open, ducked under the blanket of smoke, and went inside.

"Kayli! Where are you?"

He had taken only a few steps when he stumbled upon Kayli's motionless form. Rick Moran lay beside her, sprawled on his stomach. *Dear God, please let them be alive.* He swept Kayli's limp body up into his arms and carried her outside. He felt her neck for a pulse and put his ear near her lips. Yes, thank God, she was alive and breathing. Gently he laid her down on the grass and went back for Rick. Gripping Rick's wrists, he dragged him out of the smoke-filled house, across the lanai, and onto the grass beside Kayli. As he stooped down to search for a pulse, he heard sirens in the distance.

When Kayli awoke, the first thing she saw was Jay sitting beside her bed, watching her intently. She blinked several times and looked around. "Where am I?"

"The hospital."

"My throat hurts."

"I know, honey." He pressed her hand against his cheek. His hair was mussed and he had soot on his forehead. "You got some smoke in your lungs, but the doctor says you're going to be fine."

"What happened?"

"What do you remember?"

"I don't know." Her mind felt sluggish, her thoughts jumbled. But as everything fell into place, she groaned. "Wait. I remember."

"It's over, honey. Everything's going to be okay."

"Rick—is he—"

"He's alive. He's in the jail infirmary."

"He's crazy. He needs psychiatric treatment."

"The court will decide what to do with him. He's not your concern anymore."

Kayli covered her face with her hands. "I don't know how I could have been so wrong about him. He's a—a pyromaniac. He set fires because he wanted the glory of being a hero."

"He's no hero. Real firefighters are heroes. They risk their lives every day. Rick Moran doesn't deserve to even polish their boots. I hope they put him away for a long time."

"He's a sick man. When I think of how I trusted him, I shudder."

Jay gently massaged her shoulder. "Do you feel like talking about what happened?"

"Yes, I want you to know the whole story." Haltingly she told him everything she remembered, finishing with, "Somehow I dragged Rick to the foyer. That's the last thing I remember. How did we get out of the house?"

"I pulled you both out."

She looked at him in surprise. "But how did you know?"

"I was getting suspicious of Rick, so I had a detective friend check him out. Although nothing was ever proved, the police suspected him of starting several fires in Long Beach. Then, when I found out he had tricked Jessie into leaving the house, I knew you were in trouble. So I made a beeline for your house."

She managed a smile. "You saved my life."

"And it looks like you saved Rick's. That's pretty amazing for a girl who's afraid of fire."

"It's weird, isn't it? When I saw him lying there nearly unconscious amid the flames, there was no question. I wasn't that helpless little girl anymore. I knew what I had to do. And even though I was afraid, I also felt empowered." She let out a little sigh. "Of course, if you hadn't rescued us. . ."

Jay nodded. "Let's just say we were both heroes."

"Or let's say God was the hero; He saved us all."

"Amen to that." He smoothed back her hair. "Jessie is waiting to see you. She was really worried."

"What about the house? How bad is the damage?"

"It'll take some work to get it back into shape, but Dad and I have already agreed you girls can stay at our house until it's repaired. Dad will bunk with me in the cottage."

"You don't have to do that, Jay."

"We want to." He leaned over and kissed her lips. "Remember, the four of us have a wedding to plan."

"Our wedding—oh, what beautiful words!" She went into his arms. "Just think—in three months we'll be husband and wife. I can't wait!"

"Me neither. I'm counting the days. I can't tell you how scared I was when I thought I might lose you." He held her close. "What was it your mother used to call you? You mentioned it the other day."

"Sweet joy of my life."

"Yes, that's it. That's what you are to me—the sweet joy of my life. Forever."

Epilogue

Kayli Akimo and Jayden Joseph Mahala
and
Jessica Akimo and Leolani Mahala
cordially invite you to share their joy
as they enter the holy state of matrimony
in a double wedding at sunset
on the second Saturday of April
on the Beach at Kahala Hotel & Resort
Honolulu, Hawaii
Reception following

At sunset, with a dazzling backdrop of sparkling waterfalls, a dolphin lagoon, and the Pacific Ocean, the double wedding began with the sound of the conch shell—an ancient ritual that summoned the witnesses of earth, air, water, and fire. In her heart Kayli was inviting God—the infinite Creator of earth, air, water, and fire—to infuse her life and marriage with His presence.

A harpist and two guitarists strummed Hawaiian melodies as the grooms—in white tuxedos, with leafy green maile leis draped around their necks—took their places under a trellis wrapped with a thousand orchids and waited for their brides. Jay looked as handsome as Kayli had ever seen him—tall, broad-shouldered, his head high, his mahogany-brown hair ruffled by the breeze. He was truly her hero, her soul mate, the love of her life. Leo, standing beside him, looked handsome and distinguished, too; there was no denying the adoration in his eyes for Jessie.

Kayli glanced over at her aunt, who looked magnificent in a white satin empire dress with beaded lace. "Ready, Aunt Jessie?"

Jessie's smile lit up her entire face. "I've been ready for this day all my life!"

"Me, too!" Kayli swiveled, shifting the chapel-length train of her white lace Hawaiian *holoku* gown. She fluffed her long ebony hair and made one final adjustment of the orchid *haku* lei that wreathed her head.

She knew as she looked across the white sand beach at her waiting groom that this would be the wedding of her dreams. While childhood fears had once scarred her life, this day marked the beginning of new hopes and dreams that only God could have orchestrated.

When the "Hawaiian Wedding Song" began, Kayli and Aunt Jessie—holding bouquets of white roses—strolled down the petal-strewn path to their grooms. Who could have imagined they would be sharing such a breathtaking day as this?

When they reached the trellis, their grooms stepped forward and took their arms. Jay gave Kayli a beaming smile, his green eyes crinkling in their familiar half-moons. "Love you," he whispered.

Pastor Aiko stepped forward and greeted the guests with his usual warm smile. "We welcome our *ohana*—our circle of family and friends. What a beautiful evening in Honolulu for a *male 'ana*—a wedding. Two weddings in one! Oahu is the perfect 'gathering place'—a little bit of paradise. To me, heaven seems a little closer in Hawaii than any other place on earth."

After offering a blessing, he led them in the exchange of leis. "A lei is like a wedding ring—a circle that never ends, like God's love for us. Saint Augustine said, 'The measure of love is to love without measure.' *He punawai kahe wale ke aloha*. . .love is a spring that flows freely. It flows from the very heart of God. Jay and Kayli, Leo and Jessica, that is the kind of love God wants you to have for each other."

Kayli's heart sang as she and Jay exchanged leis and kisses and then vows and rings. Their eyes stayed fastened on each other as Pastor Aiko read 1 Corinthians 13, the "Love Chapter." Minutes later, after he pronounced them husband and wife and told the grooms to kiss their brides, Jay gathered Kayli into his arms and kissed her with such ardor and tenderness, she wanted to laugh and cry at once.

As he released her, she caught a glimpse of Leo kissing Jessie. With a gallant flourish he tipped her back and gave her an amazing kiss, the way they did in the movies. Jessie laughed and murmured something about being swept off her feet. Leo winked and gave Jay a thumbs-up. Jay crowed, "Way to go, Dad!"

Kayli's joy crescendoed as she saw the joy and delight in Aunt Jessie's face.

Thank You, heavenly Father, for giving us our hearts' desires. And thank You for being greater than my fears! We love You and praise You, Lord!

At the end of the ceremony, as one of the musicians played "Over the Rainbow" on his ukulele, Pastor Aiko gave each of them a heart-shaped wicker basket covered with lace. Together they opened their baskets and released pure white doves into the orange sunset sky. The doves—graceful as angels—flew heavenward, their regal wings spreading wide as palm fronds.

Nestling her head against Jay's chest, Kayli watched spellbound as the doves ascended and circled in a symphony of white against the lowering sun. As her eyes met his, she knew they were thinking the same thing. The doves were a symbol of the Holy Spirit soaring freely in their hearts, filling them with joy and blessing their marriage with eternal love.

A Letter to Our Readers

Dear Readers:

In order that we might better contribute to your reading enjoyment, we would appreciate you taking a few minutes to respond to the following questions. When completed, please return to the following: Fiction Editor, Barbour Publishing, Inc., P.O. Box 719, Uhrichsville, OH 44683.

1. Did you enjoy reading *Hawaiian Dreams* by Carole Gift Page?
   ❑ Very much. I would like to see more books like this.
   ❑ Moderately—I would have enjoyed it more if ______________

____

____

2. What influenced your decision to purchase this book? (Check those that apply.)
   ❑ Cover ❑ Back cover copy ❑ Title ❑ Price
   ❑ Friends ❑ Publicity ❑ Other

3. Which story was your favorite?
   ❑ *By the Beckoning Sea* ❑ *Sweet Joy of My Life*
   ❑ *To Love a Gentle Stranger*

4. Please check your age range:
   ❑ Under 18 ❑ 18–24 ❑ 25–34
   ❑ 35–45 ❑ 46–55 ❑ Over 55

5. How many hours per week do you read? ______________

Name ______________________________

Occupation ______________________________

Address ______________________________

City______________ State__________ Zip__________

E-mail ______________________________